Steampunk

Extraordinary Tales of Victorian Futurism

EDITED BY

MIKE ASHLEY

FALL
RIVER
PRESS
New York

FALL RIVER PRESS

New York

An Imprint of Sterling Publishing
387 Park Avenue South
New York, NY 10016

Illustrated edition © 2012 by Fall River Press
Originally published in 2010 by Nonstop Press

This 2012 edition published by Fall River Press
by arrangement with Nonstop Press.

Book design by Scott Russo

ISBN 978-1-4351-4193-3

Distributed in Canada by Sterling Publishing c/o Canadian Manda
Group, 165 Dufferin Street Toronto, Ontario, Canada M6K 3H6

Distributed in the United Kingdom by GMC Distribution Services
Castle Place, 166 High Street, Lewes,
East Sussex, England BN7 1XU

Distributed in Australia by Capricorn Link (Australia) Pty. Ltd.
P.O. Box 704, Windsor, NSW 2756, Australia

For information about custom editions, special sales,
and premium and corporate purchases, please contact
Sterling Special Sales at 800-805-5489 or
specialsales@sterlingpublishing.com.

Manufactured in China

2 4 6 8 10 9 7 5 3 1

CONTENTS

FOREWORD:

BRIT BOFFIN DELIVERS STEAMPUNK'S PURE QUILL! OR AFTER SUCH KNOWLEDGE, WHAT THRILLS?

"IT'S NEVER TOO LATE to have a happy childhood."

This bumper-sticker-quality slogan, often interpreted as a slightly disreputable excuse for intransigent Peter-Pan-style misbehavior and shirking of adult responsibilities, seems to me somehow admirable and endorsable on a higher plane, and also to be a sentiment particularly tied up with the science-fiction weltanschauung.

We all know another expression that is a kissing cousin to the one above: "The Golden Age of science fiction is thirteen."

Put the two maxims together, and you get something that may be more tediously and laboriously expressed thus:

"A youthful sense of wonder invoked by apprehension of the true dimensions of the cosmos and the depiction of the mysteries of creation in the literature of the fantastic—a frisson frequently experienced most intensely in early adolescence—may, with some effort and imagination, be recaptured even by jaded and stale adults via a deliberate and forceful revirginization of the intellect and emotions, in the presence of appropriate eidolons."

Whew! I warned you it was going to be a laborious and tedious restatement, didn't I?

In any case, I believe you now grasp how these twinned sentiments define the core ethos of the true science fiction fan. Even in our most cynical moments, appalled by the flood of stale, mercenary literary trash masquerading as novelty, coarsened by our own addiction to mindless repetitive kicks, beset by the quotidian hardships of mature existence, teased and betrayed by the empty eye-candy of Hollywood, we somehow maintain an undying spark of idealism that may be fanned back into a flame with the proper attitude and objects of worship.

When I ponder along these lines, I am always reminded of a self-observation made by legendary SF editor David Hartwell, who—not bragging, and with all due humility and gratitude—was once heard to say, "I became the adult I envisioned myself being as a child." Lucky Hartwell! For most of us, invoking—and living out!—that youthful, idealistic self-concept requires the painful stripping away of layers of hardened indifference and disappointment, guilt and fear of betrayal.

One method of summoning up such potent ghosts of our heart's dawn is to return to our roots, whether literally or literarily.

The SF reader today is lucky enough to have easy and unimpeded access to the entire corpus of our genre's history. True, much of the canon remains lamentably and in a technical quibble "out of print," in the sense that no major or minor publisher lists a certain title on their official backlist. And yet, as critic Barry Malzberg has observed, when sixty seconds of internet activity is sufficient to secure either a digital or hard copy of practically any book you can name, then "out of print" has very little practical meaning any longer.

But of course, having curated old-school texts available in handsome new editions is the gold standard for enjoyment and revivification of the reader's spirits. Presses such as NESFA, Wesleyan, Haffner and Baen have introduced new generations of readers to the classics of the genre, and allowed old-timers to freshen up their memories. And in fact, the opportunity, for instance, to read thirteen volumes of *The Complete Short Stories of Theodore Sturgeon* (North Atlantic Books) is not merely an exercise in nostalgia but an unprecedented chance to totally reassess an author's career and perform new feats of scholarship made possible only by this unique presentation.

All of this prelude about being "born again" into Our Lord Science Fiction, and the necessity of proper psychoactive sacraments, brings us of course to the volume you hold in your hands. But before I begin extolling the worth of these stories and their editor, allow me to offer a small new insight into the allure of steampunk, an a-ha moment that occurred to me only as I framed my thoughts here.

By now, I and hundreds of others, both within and without the field, have written ourselves hoarse on the peculiar virtues and traits of this fascinating subgenre, so I won't rehash all the learned analyses again. But since the phenomenon of steampunk shows no sign of—well, losing steam—and in fact seems to be still accelerating, there must exist some hidden engine at the heart of the mode which we have not yet identified.

I believe it is this:

Steampunk is science fiction's age thirteen.

Steampunk is the adolescent SF genre dreaming of the adult it hopes to grow up to become.

Steampunk is science fiction's subconscious attempt to have—or re-have—

a happy childhood, shorn of all the fossilized crap encrusting the medium.

Mike Ashley makes much the same point in the opening paragraphs of his witty and learned introduction, but in a more scholarly way, compared to my perhaps overly poetic metaphors. But this only marks a minor difference in style and angle of attack between us, not in shared vision.

Having had the privilege of cohabiting with Mike Ashley in a certain online forum of savants for over a decade, and of enjoying his patronage as expert commissioning editor of several of my stories, I can say with all proper objectivity that this man is not only one of the most erudite and insightful historians and critics of our field, but also an admirable fellow who, like David Hartwell, has succeeded in maintaining unbesmirched his wide-eyed, passionate love affair with science fiction. His generous embrace of the field in all its manifestations and all its ages is heartening and inspiring.

Ashley is one of only a very few editors learned enough to have assembled this treasure trove of truly enjoyable and eye-opening Ur-steampunk. His Indiana-Jones-style expeditions through the bowels of the British Library, his safaris through jungles of moldering pulp, have acquainted him with exotic tribes and species unknown to lesser explorers.

But the real brilliance of this volume lies in the very stroke of its conception: to forsake the secondary texts of modern authors—which, however entertaining and relevant, are, after all, knockoffs and pastiches and xeroxes, to greater or lesser extent—and to return to the pure quill, the Victorian roots of the genre, as codified entertainingly and at first-hand by our ancestors.

The assemblage of these unjustly forgotten stories—each with its perceptive Ashley introduction, in which he offers biographical, cultural and critical insights galore—provides us with a chance to divest ourselves of a century of preconceptions, misconceptions and misprisions, and to return to the dawn of a literature, when the future—our present—still shone with a numinous radiance.

Get young again! You have nothing to lose but your sour old puss!

—PAUL DI FILIPPO

INTRODUCTION:
WHEN STEAMPUNK WAS REAL

THERE'S SOMETHING so gloriously reassuring about steampunk fiction. The idea that perhaps the Victorians got it right and that we do live in a world of airships and vast calculating machines and automatons, all visible from the safety of our luxurious deep leather chairs, perhaps in the smoking room of the Explorers' Club.

And who's to say they didn't get it right. It was the Victorians who more or less invented science fiction. Oh yes, sure, there were plenty of earlier stories about trips to the Moon or about island utopias or lost races, but they were simply getting the seating arranged for the big feature. Mary Shelley really got things going by showing what the wonders of electricity might bring with the possibility of recreating man in *Frankenstein* in 1818 and then things really began gathering pace. As new scientific and technological marvels came along, so writers pounced on them to see what else the future might bring.

It is perhaps a bit bizarre, then, that the genre should be called "steampunk" and not "electricpunk" but there is no doubt that it was the opening up of the world through steam trains and the opportunities that steampower introduced that ushered in the Industrial Revolution and began the true scientific revolution that allowed science fiction to prosper. It doesn't really matter that electricity superseded steam as the main power source, because by then the legacy of steampower was so great that it personified the marvels of technology.

If steampowered science fiction started anywhere it was probably in the dime novels, and in particular with *The Steam Man of the Prairies* by Edward S. Ellis, first published in 1868. I decided to spare readers the full text of this story which is perhaps a little unsophisticated for modern tastes, but as it is the true progenitor of all steampunk, I thought it might be interesting to reproduce here the original description of the Steam Man which was built like a steam engine to pull carriages across the plains. It was created by the deformed teenage genius inventor Jack Brainerd.

It was about ten feet in hight, measuring to the top of the 'stove-pipe hat,' which was fashioned after the common order of felt coverings, with a broad brim, all painted a shiny black. The face was made of iron, painted a black color, with a pair of fearful eyes, and a tremendous grinning mouth. A whistle-like contrivance was made to answer for the nose. The steam chest proper and boiler were where the chest in a human being is generally supposed to be, extending also into a large knapsack arrangement over the shoulders and back. A pair of arms, like projections, held the shafts, and the broad flat feet were covered with sharp spikes, as though he were the monarch of base-ball players. The legs were quite long, and the step was natural, except when running, at which time, the bolt uprightness in the figure showed different from a human being.

In the knapsack were the valves, by which the steam or water was examined. In front was a painted imitation of a vest, in which a door opened to receive the fuel, which, together with the water, was carried in the wagon, a pipe running along the shaft and connecting with the boiler.

The legs of this extraordinary mechanism were fully a yard apart, so as to avoid the danger of its upsetting, and at the same time, there was given more room for the play of the delicate machinery within. Long, sharp, spike-like projections adorned those toes of the immense feet, so that there was little danger of its slipping, while the length of the legs showed that, under favorable circumstances, the steam man must be capable of very great speed.

The door being opened in front, showed a mass of glowing coals lying in the capacious abdomen of the giant; the hissing valves in the knapsack made themselves apparent, and the top of the hat or smoke-stack had a sieve-like arrangement, such as is frequently seen on the locomotive.

The steam man was a frightful looking object, being painted of a glossy black, with a pair of white stripes down its legs, and with a face which was intended to be of a flesh color, but, which was really a fearful red.

With that "steampunk" was born. The dime novels were full of steam creatures after that, and even Jules Verne created one—a steam elephant, no less—in *The Steam House* (1880). The British writer, Anthony Trollope, known for his Barchester Chronicles, incorporated a steam bowler in a game of cricket in *The Fixed Period* (1882).

So I would argue that steampunk was well under way by the 1880s but came into its own in the 1890s. This decade saw so much technological development that writers were struggling to keep up with it. At the same time the emergence of cheaply priced popular illustrated magazines full of short stories allowed a huge market to develop for science fiction, mysteries and strange tales. *The Strand* led the way because of the popularity of Arthur Conan Doyle's Sherlock Holmes stories. These magazines, in Britain and the United States, hungered for unusual fiction that would capture the public imagination and the writers would respond. There were the likes of George Griffith, Cutcliffe Hyne, M. P. Shiel, George C. Wallis, George Allan England and, of course, towering above them as the adopted Father of

Science Fiction, H. G. Wells. His novels, especially *The Time Machine*, *The War of the Worlds*, *The First Men in the Moon* and *When the Sleeper Wakes* contain all the imagery that would later be plundered by the masters of steampunk. Wells's work is too easily available to be reprinted here, but his imaginative power pervades the book.

But that should not diminish the abilities of the writers collected here. You will find, for instance, that some, like George Parsons Lathrop, utilised ideas ahead of H. G. Wells. Others, like Owen Oliver may have followed in Wells's wake, but with original and unusual ideas of his own. What I have done is selected stories that on the whole are lesser known but which, between them, create many of the concepts and images that have become associated with steampunk—airships, automatons, secret societies, vast engineering projects, anti-gravity, moving walkways and so on. This was how the Victorians and Edwardians in Britain and their American counterparts saw the future—our present.

Science fiction continued to grow and prosper, of course, but it mutated. The wonderful visions and hopes of the Victorians became overtaken by the real world, especially by the First World War. So we might argue that the great era of steampunk ran from around 1880 to 1914 and those are the years covered in this book. Or at least, the years when the stories were written. Their ideas and visions go way beyond, ultimately to 13 million years in the future.

Here then are the days when the future was young and everything was possible. The days of steampunk prime!

—MIKE ASHLEY

Mr. Broadbent's Information

HENRY A. HERING

THE IDEA OF the mechanical man or automaton is as old as myth. Jason, in his quest for the Golden Fleece, encountered Talos, a bronze giant made by the god Hephaestus to protect the island of Crete. It walked around the island three times each day making itself red hot and embracing any strangers it encountered. Mechanical toys, usually of clockwork, were made throughout the Middle Ages though the first genuine life-like bio-mechanical toy was that of a flute player made by the French inventor Jacques de Vaucanson in 1737. These toys became very popular and were also represented in fiction, one of the earliest being the Talking Turk in "Automata" by E. T. A. Hoffmann, published in 1814.

It was the idea of creating man that really launched science fiction with the creature in Mary Shelley's *Frankenstein* (1818), and it was the "steam man" featured in the popular dime-novel adventures, starting with *The Steam Man of the Prairies* by Edward F. Ellis that brought the dawn of steampunk.

We should not call these steam men or automata by the name robots. That word did not pass into the English language until the translation of Karel Capek's 1920 play *Rossum's Universal Robots* in 1923 and it soon caught on. For the steampunk period they were automata and, as the essence of steampunk, they feature in our first two stories.

Henry A. Hering (1864–1945) wrote quite a few stories that qualify as science fiction for the popular magazines of his day. Most fell into the crazy invention category that was popular at that time, several featuring his eccentric American inventor Silas P. Cornu. The most intriguing is "Silas P. Cornu's Dry Calculator" (*Windsor Magazine*, January 1898) which includes an interesting description of a proto-computer. Although born in Yorkshire, Hering was of Prussian descent which may explain why in "The O.P.Q. Rays" (*Windsor Magazine,* March 1908) the German army finds it easy to invade and defeat the British. Hering is probably best remembered for his collection *The Burglars Club* (1906) but in later life he collected together his early stories as *Adventures and Fantasy* (1930), which includes the following story, first published in 1909. —**M.A.**

"By specializing it may be possible for science to create a type of animal capable of doing the heavy work of the world—creatures of vast physical strength, coupled with a higher form of intelligence than has been evolved as yet in any animal, excepting man."

—PROFESSOR OSTWALD, Leipzig University

AM JAMES BROADBENT, the author. I hold the record for fiction production—forty-eight novels in twelve years, each one turned out with clockwork regularity in three months, and each one consisting of precisely one hundred thousand words. I don't write masterpieces, but I have a reputation for good, solid, sensational stuff, and I keep my contracts to the letter. What with serial, volume, American, and occasional continental rights, my books bring me in an average of £200 apiece. In other words, my income is £800 a year. It is my ambition to make it a thousand. For this purpose I agreed to produce five novels this year, but I could not do it in London. I was good for four books a year there; and not a chapter more. An extra stimulus was necessary for the production of a fifth, and I thought I should get it in Devonshire from the moors, the sea air, and the sunshine. There, at any rate, I should have perfect quietude.

In this I was mistaken. The month after I took possession of my cottage a dangerous criminal escaped from Dartmoor. He had plenty of choice of habitations in which to seek a temporary refuge; and it was distinctly annoying that he should make a bee-line for mine. You no doubt read the account in the papers, and may remember that he was captured in my study by the police after a desperate struggle, in which I, an interested onlooker, was injured. I had to wear my right arm in a sling for a month, and for a literary man this is a drawback.

However, by daily practice, I found I could attain considerable dexterity on the typewriter with my left hand. I compose direct on to the machine, rarely altering what I type; and last Monday I was working against time in order to make up for the hours I had lost, when a figure walked through the open French window. I finished my sentence and swung round on my chair.

A less reassuring object I have never seen. It was apparently a very short man, dressed in an ill-fitting coat which reached nearly to the floor, and a cap brought down low over his face. His chin was buried in his collar, and I only saw an ugly nose and a swarthy cheek.

I stared at him in surprise and annoyance. "Well?" I asked.

"Forgive me for not taking off my cap," he said. "There are reasons."

He spoke in a high falsetto, stopping once in the middle of a word, then

giving a curious catch, and continuing. There was a singular artificiality about his voice. It reminded me of a gramophone. He added: "I throw myself upon your mercy. I am an outcast."

He spoke these words without feeling, mentioned his position in the universe as a mere matter of fact, and again there was the curious catch in his voice.

"I suppose you're another escaped from Dartmoor?" I said, mentally resolving to leave the neighborhood forthwith.

"Oh, no," he replied. "I come from Baxter's. I'm one of his creations."

"The deuce you are!" I exclaimed, and I have no doubt my voice expressed the annoyance I felt. Bad as it was to be saddled with an occasional visitor from Dartmoor, it was worse to be within the reach of Baxter's abortions.

Baxter, as all the world knows, has created life artificially, and he is now developing the process. I remember his speech at the last Academy dinner, when he responded for Science. "What I aim at producing," he said, "is an automaton endowed with strong vitality, great muscular strength, and a rudimentary brain, an automaton capable of doing the work of an unskilled laborer or artisan. I will anticipate the criticism that such a production will have a profound influence on the labor market by stating that I shall never rest content until I have placed it within reach of the pocket of every working man, who will then have a mechanism in his house capable of doing his work for him at a minimum of cost, and enabling its owner to walk into the country, take part in his favorite sport, or spend his time in the public library—whichever course he may deem to be the best for advancing his immortal destiny. That is how I intend to employ my discovery for the benefit of the human race."

Of course his speech was received with applause, but some thought he was going a bit too far. I think it was the *Herald* that said he ought to be content with having created life artificially before a committee of international scientists. It was certainly impious, and ought to be illegal, to create entities possessing rudimentary brains; and only a President of the Royal Society, an ex-president of the British Association, a man with a dozen high university degrees and an international reputation, who, moreover, had the Order of Merit, and was a peer of the realm, would have been allowed so much latitude. Lord Baxter was no doubt the master-mind and the superman of the twentieth century, but there was no reason that he should be put on the same level as the Law of Gravitation.

I thought of these words as I watched the little object in its ill-fitting clothes as it wandered casually about my room. I had no objection to Baxter making his brainy automata so long as he kept them to himself; but when they became a nuisance to others it was certainly time to stop him.

Still I will admit I was curious to see what sort of a thing my visitor was. "Won't you take off your coat?" I said.

"I'll take it off, if you'll give me shelter till to-night," it replied.

"All right," I answered. "You can stay till to-night." It was sheer curiosity that impelled me to say this. I could never make use of the incident in my work. I deal with the universal, and not the abnormal.

With a little giggle it threw off its coat and cap, and stood revealed. A feeling of repulsion came over me when I saw the build of the thing. It was about five feet high, and had the body of an animal, with human legs and arms, an animal head with a prodigious cranium, on the sides of which two animal ears stuck grotesquely upward. It was a species of Faun.

"Then you're one of Baxter's automata," I said after a pause.

"I'm not," it replied indignantly. "I'm one of his special experiments. He's keen on animals with human brains just now, and I'm the biggest success he's had so far." It spoke with ridiculous complacency.

"Well," I replied, "if you're satisfied with Baxter, and he's satisfied with you, what the blazes are you bothering me for? What are you doing in this direction at all? Baxter lives fifty miles away, doesn't he?"

"I wish you wouldn't speak so crossly," said the Faun. "A very little makes me cry. I've run away from Baxter's to see the world. I knew perfectly well he'd resolve me into my elements when he'd done with me, and I determined to run away some day. But it's a big thing to do, for Baxter's a difficult man to circumvent. I don't think I should ever have got away but for Billiter."

"Who's Billiter?" I asked.

"His assistant. He has a shocking record—was knocked off the medical register, and has all sorts of things against him. I'm sure he tortures—I've heard yells from his room. But Baxter doesn't interfere. He generally has his frog singing to him at the time, and Billiter reckons on it."

"Frog singing!" I exclaimed. "Croaking, you mean."

"I don't. He's made a frog with a voice like Tetrazzini's. You don't know what Baxter does. He can graft brains or voice on anything. He's got a ferret with an intellect bigger than Kant's. The frog sings to him by the hour—never tires—and the ferret is always working out problems in mentality that neither Baxter nor any other man could do. I don't know where Baxter will stop. He doesn't know himself. He was very pleased when he made me from my nucleus, and developed me in the oxilater. Did the whole thing in a fortnight, and grafted my brain on afterwards. I'm the biggest all-round success he's had so far. The ferret has a larger brain for problems, but no common-sense."

"And what about the automatons? He said he was going to make an automaton that could—"

"Oh, I know what he promised," interrupted the Faun. "He rehearsed his speech to me in the lab till he knew it. He doesn't care a hang for the human race, and he was laughing at you all the time. He's made a couple of automata—great lumbering things as ugly as sin, with a lot of muscle and a pin's head worth of brains. He's stuck 'em up in corners, and doses 'em with phosphates when they're hungry. He's got 'em ready if anyone calls to see what he's doing, but they're no good for work—their mentality is too low. That's why the ferret is working out problems for him. Baxter can't hit on a medium brain. Gosh! What a business it is. He never knows what his spawn will hatch into till he opens the oxilater. I've known him cultivate a thousand nuclei with only two per cent of moderate successes. He freezes the others and destroys them, or lets Billiter do it, who always keeps a few for himself. Billiter cultivates dwarf freaks—bulls with six legs, more or less, and men's heads—satyrs, you know—dwarf elephants with fins, flying camels, and sports like that. He has an amazing collection. Baxter says he oughtn't to keep such things, but he lets him all the same. He has to. He daren't go against Billiter for fear of his laying information with the authorities. He'd never be allowed to do what he does if the nation knew it. Oh, I've sized them up."

"How old are you?" I asked.

"Nine or ten months, I reckon," it replied.

"You know a lot for your age," I remarked.

"I know I do. My brain is the smartest ever made." Here the Faun smirked with its irritating complacency. "Baxter has just crammed me with knowledge ever since I was made, to see how much my head will carry, and he can't fill it. In addition to all the scientific stuff I have to read for him, I always go through the daily paper," it said proudly.

"What about neighbors and visitors?" I asked. "Isn't Baxter afraid of anything leaking out?"

"We don't have many visitors. If anyone comes Baxter shows them round the laboratory, and trots out his automata under promise of secrecy. I and the frog and the ferret are shoved into Billiter's museum till they're gone. And as for neighbors, our nearest lives five miles away. We get on all right as a rule while Baxter is there, but he has to go to London sometimes, and then there's trouble. We've had a sickening time just now. That's why I am here. Billiter got drunk, fixed up the automata like prize-fighters, and made 'em pound away at each other. They were hitting out like mad when I saw 'em last, and they'll be hopelessly damaged by this time. The frog had been singing to him for twenty-four hours on end; and he'd given the ferret the deuce of a calculation to work out. It was phosphate time for both of 'em, but Billiter wouldn't give it. It made me cry to hear the frog sing so imploringly about her food; She was singing flat, too, and the ferret had gone wrong with his additions, all for want of food; but Billiter only raved at them. I told him he ought to be ashamed of himself, but he only swore he'd do for me, and tell Baxter it was suicide. He'd have kept his word if he'd got me; but I tripped him up, ran out of the room, and locked him in."

Here the Faun stopped to snigger at the recollection of its smartness. "If those automata had the slightest sense they'd have started pounding away at Billiter," he continued. "As it is they'll only do for themselves, and I don't expect either the ferret or the frog will be alive when Baxter gets home. Anyway, I've got clear of the place, and I shan't go back in a hurry. I found a coat and a cap of Baxter's and these boots, and slunk out in the evening. I walked all last night, and I've been mostly hiding since daybreak. I saw your door open, and came in. Now you know all, and you've promised to give me shelter for the day."

It was uncanny in the extreme to hear these words proceed from the great mouth of the Faun. They came glibly enough, but in every sentence there was the little "click" which betokened a fault in the machinery, and the voice itself was hard and metallic. It was no doubt amazingly clever of Baxter to have got so far in his creations, but it was obvious that he would have to go a good deal further before the general public would be disposed to welcome his progeny into their households. I resolved to get rid of my visitor as soon as ever possible.

"What time do you propose to move on?" I asked.

"At dusk. I think I'd better continue to travel by night. If people saw me it might get into the papers, and then Baxter would read it. I'll go at sunset."

"Where to?"

"I don't know," said the Faun. "I want to see the world immensely. I've quite taken to it from what I have read in the Encyclopaedia and the newspapers. An awfully active place, I believe—rather different from Baxter's, although, of course, he's busy in his way. And so are you, no doubt," it added politely; "but I want to hear the roar and rumble of the never-ceasing traffic of our great metropolis, as the *Daily Tinkler* puts it. I want to see a play, I want to see the aristocracy in the Park on Sunday morning, and I should like to go to a boy and girl dance."

"Yes, that's all very well," I said; "but you've got to earn your living, you know. How do you propose to do it?"

"Oh, I shan't require much," said the Faun. "I judge from what I've read that food costs a great deal. I only want a little phosphate now and again.

Tuppence a month will feed me. Then I notice from the advertisements that beds cost a great deal. I never go to bed, so that's another item off."

"Well, anyway, you'll want a shakedown," I remarked—"a bit of straw in a corner somewhere."

"Please don't confound me with the lower animals," said the Faun stiffly. "I do not want either straw or linen. I do not sleep at all."

"What!" I exclaimed. "You never sleep!"

"None of Baxter's creations sleep. That's one of his great points. He's got ahead of nature in that. No, we just go straight along with a bit of phosphate now and again for a pick-me-up. That's where we have our pull over regular folk. I can work twenty-four hours a day if you like. Think what a lot I could do in that time. Couldn't you employ me temporarily—just till things are a bit settled, and I've got accustomed to the world?" It pleaded.

"In what capacity could I employ you?" I asked.

"As secretary; if you like. You don't know how invaluable I should be. I remember everything I see, hear, or read. I've gone halfway through the *Encyclopaedia Britannica*, and I remember every word of it. Shall I recite you the first page? 'A. The first symbol of every Indo-European alphabet, denotes also the primary vowel sound. This coincidence is probably only accidental. The alphabet . . .'"

"Thank you, thank you, that will do," I interrupted. "I will take the rest for granted."

"Or, if you wanted poetry, I could recite the two Paradises of Mr. Milton," persisted the Faun. "They are long, but very interesting.

" 'Of man's first disobedience, and the fruit, of that forbidden tree . . . ' " It began. I let it go for ten minutes or so and it never stumbled, or was at a loss for a word.

"Thank you, that's enough," I said at last. "It is highly creditable to your memory; but I don't see how it would be of any use to me. I am a writer myself, and I prefer my own composition to anything in the *Encyclopaedia Britannica* or in Milton. That sort of stodge would be no good at all to me."

"But I can be of use to you in a dozen other ways," said the Faun. "I typed for Baxter, and I could do the same for you. Yours is a different instrument; but I could work it for you. Watch me."

It pulled my machine forward, and commenced to tap the keyboard—at first slowly, but every second with "increasing" quickness and confidence. Once learnt it never forgot the position of a letter. The last line was typed as quickly as I could have done it myself.

"There," it said coaxingly, handing me the sheet, "I'm sure I can be of use to you. Take me on trial, please."

I took the Faun on trial. I dressed it up in some old clothes of my own, which fitted absurdly; but as I walked about the room dictating my novel, I was almost persuaded that my indefatigable and highly intelligent amanuensis behind the typewriter was a human being. Certainly no human being ever was half as useful to me.

Two days later a great idea occurred to me. It had always been my ambition to do a sound historical novel of the Stuart period, but this would necessitate research and reading, for which I had neither time nor inclination. But now I had as my assistant a being capable of working twenty-four hours a day, a being, moreover, that never forgot a word it read! The opportunity was unique, and I must take advantage of it. As soon as I had finished the novel on which I was engaged I must start my historical romance. I wired at once to town for Clarendon's *History of the Rebellion*, on which the Faun could browse from eleven at night until eight o'clock in the morning, and so be able to give me the setting for my tale.

It was, as I have said, a great idea, and I think it would have been the country's gain as well as my own if the plan could have been carried out, for archaeologically and historically, at any rate, my novel would have been perfect. But it was not to be. The following day—yesterday, that is—I was taking my regulation two turns round my garden preparatory to starting the afternoon's work. In a few minutes I should be describing the death-struggle in the roof-garden of a New York restaurant between Raymond Kneller, the multi-millionaire, and the man he had so cruelly wronged. I was arranging the situation in my mind, when suddenly a man came round the corner of the house—a big man in a fur-lined overcoat. I knew him in an instant. There was only one man in England with that leonine head, those deep-set eyes, that cruel mouth, that arrogant nose and chin.

It was Lord Baxter.

"Mr. Broadbent," he said, "I believe you have one of my automata on your premises, and will thank you for its return."

So it had come at last. There was to be a fight for the possession of the Faun. I was not going to lose it without a struggle. It had already made itself invaluable to me, and without its aid I could not possibly tackle the Stuarts.

"I have no automaton in the house," I replied firmly.

"Um," he said quietly. "Perhaps we differ as to terms: I think you have in your possession a being resembling a Faun, with a mental capacity above its station in life. You surely do not deny that?"

"I neither affirm nor deny," I answered. "I would simply point out to you that my house is beyond your authority. If I have such a being on my premises, there it stops."

"Tut, tut, sir," replied Baxter. "I have every authority over the creature. His whole mechanism is mine. I created him. If he doesn't belong to me, pray who is his owner?"

"He belongs to himself."

"I am afraid we shall not agree on that point."

"Possibly not, Lord Baxter, and upon very few others, I believe. Your wretched progeny has taken refuge here as you surmise, and I request you to leave it here where it is pursuing an industrious life in the peace and comfort which was wanting in your laboratory."

"And if I do not, sir?" Inquired Lord Baxter acidly.

"If you do not, I shall place the whole matter before the world. I am a writer by profession, and have some influence with the public. I think the result will be that your scientific liberty will be considerably curtailed."

"Pooh," said Lord Baxter contemptuously. "I'm afraid you overrate your influence. I've just glanced at one of your books in the village inn, and it seems to me that it is you who ought to have your liberty curtailed. A man who pours out such balderdash at the rate I understand you do is either a public nuisance or a public danger. I have a notion you are both. But I have no time to waste with triflers. My train goes in half-an-hour. Permit me." Without waiting for permission, he strode through the open window of my work-room.

I followed. The Faun had evidently heard his voice. It now stood there behind the typewriter, quivering from head to foot, its long ears twitching with fright.

"Ah, here is our little friend," said Baxter sarcastically—"prettily dressed, too, and ready for travel. Get your coat and cap—my coat and cap, I believe, and come along. Billiter has a nice dish of phosphates waiting for you."

"I'm not coming," clicked the Faun shrilly. "I'm going to stay with Mr. Broadbent. You won't let him take me away," it pleaded piteously to me.

"Certainly not," I replied. "I ask you to leave my premises instantly, Lord Baxter."

"I am going—with my automaton," he answered.

"It's not an automaton," I said. "It is a sentient being, and as such—"

"He's simply an experiment," interrupted Baxter, "and not a particular success at that. I ought to punish him for running away, but if he comes back with me we shall continue to live in harmony as before."

"I'm not coming back," said the Faun sullenly.

"In that case," said Baxter, thrusting his hand into his pocket, and producing a box, "I'm afraid I shall have to put an end to your existence. I'm experimenting for the good of mankind, and have no time to argue with one of my failures."

He opened the box, showing an electric battery, and projecting wires with antennae.

"This may interest you, Broadbent," he said. "You could introduce it into your absurd tales, and make them up-to-date for once. This is a little electric arrangement on the principle of the Marconi apparatus. It sends messages to bodies in harmony with it, and in this case, I regret to say, the message is going to be a little unfriendly. Each living organism has its own peculiar rate of vibration, and I can regulate my instrument into exact correspondence. I happen to know the particular rate of vibration of our friend with the snout and ears, and can make him dance to any tune I like. I press the button here, and you observe that our friend does the rest."

As he spoke the Faun gave a hideous shriek, and doubled up in agony.

"A neat contrivance, isn't it?" Continued Baxter in his bantering voice. "Your own rate of vibration, Broadbent, is slightly higher. If you have any curiosity to feel the same symptoms I can easily arrange the experiment. I presume your affairs are in order. If you have any messages to leave behind you might write them down while I am finishing off our friend here. Shall I press the next button?" He said to the Faun. "It would mean a somewhat painful death."

The wretched animal had fallen to the floor. Tears were streaming from its eyes.

"No" it now sobbed. "I'll go with you."

"I thought so," said Baxter. "I should have been disappointed with that brain of yours if you'd said anything else. Get your topcoat."

He turned to me and produced a cigarette case, which he offered me. "No? Well, permit me, please. I must have my smoke after an interesting experiment," he remarked as he struck a match.

The man's callousness was as appalling as was his power. But I could at any rate impress upon him that his proceedings were no longer unknown to the outer world.

"Lord Baxter," I said, "we may as well understand one another. You are carrying on experiments that would not be sanctioned by the Government of the country."

"On the contrary," he replied, "I am working at my automata expressly for the benefit of the country."

"And what about your Tetrazzini frog and your calculating ferret? What about Billiter and his sports?"

"Ah!" He said with an ugly smile. "So our little friend has been talking? I expected as much. As you say, it is just as well we should understand one another, Broadbent. Now between you and I and this thing," He went on, pointing to the Faun, who now stood at our side in topcoat and cap, "I should forget everything you have heard or seen, if I were you. You know my power, and it may interest you to learn that distance does not count with me. I know your approximate rate of vibration on the cosmic plane, and can act accordingly. It would be just as easy for me to double you up from my laboratory by pressing the first button in my little box as it was to operate on our friend just now, and nothing would be easier than to make an end of you by pressing the second button between the songs of my accomplished frog. Verb sap. All things considered, I should strongly advise you to forget this little interlude in your existence. Now I have only just time to catch the train. Come along," he added to the Faun.

Tears were still raining from its eyes. "Good-bye, Mr. Broadbent," it clicked hoarsely, "Don't forget me." Then it pulled its cap down over its face, and followed Baxter out of the window. That is the last I saw of them. I turned to my work, and tried to continue it; but try as I would the picture of the unhappy Faun and its captor came back, to me. What would happen to it on its return to the laboratory? In the best case Baxter would make an end to it when it suited his purpose, and what might not Billiter do in the meantime?

These thoughts effectually prevented my working all yesterday. I am now five chapters behind in my novel—an unprecedented position for me—and whilst I have this matter on my mind I feel I can do no writing. I have therefore decided to let the public know what is happening in Lord Baxter's laboratory, urging that immediate steps shall be taken to protect his hapless creations. I have no use either for a Tetrazzini frog or a calculating ferret, if these are found to be still alive, but I am prepared to offer permanent asylum to the Faun. Indeed, Lord Clarendon's *History of the Rebellion* is now waiting for it on my table.

I am aware that I run considerable personal risk in making this exposure. Baxter knows my approximate rate of vibration on the cosmic plane, whatever that may mean, and probably can operate upon me from any distance; but if I should come to an untimely end the authorities know on whom to fix the crime.

And now with a clear conscience, I am going to describe the terrible struggle in the roof-garden of the New York restaurant in the "The Multi-Millionaires."

The Automaton

REGINALD BACCHUS
AND
RANGER GULL

THE IDEA OF A chess-playing automaton goes back to the time of Wolfgang von Kempelen (1734–1804) who created such a contraption in 1770. It was known as The Turk and was exhibited throughout the courts of Europe. The automaton chess player became iconic and appeared in several stories. Probably the best known is "Moxon's Master" by Ambrose Bierce (1899). The following story appeared soon after in the January 1900 issue of *The Ludgate*.

The two authors would both acquire notoriety. At the time they wrote this and several similar stories they were sharing accommodation in central London which became a regular meeting place for the literati. Both were journalists who were also editing a weekly society paper. Bacchus (1873–1945), or George Reginald Bacchus ["Reggie"], to give him his full name, came from a military family and had inherited money. He became a theatre critic and in the spring of 1899 married the actress Isa Bowman who, as a child, had been one of Lewis Carroll's photographic models. The marriage did not last long and Bacchus led a rather desultory life writing a notorious erotic work, *The Confessions of Nemesis Hunt*, based to some degree on Isa Bowman.

Ranger Gull (1875–1923) was born Arthur Ranger Gull, the son of a country vicar. He later adopted the first name Cyril, and later still took on the pseudonym Guy Thorne by which he became best known. Under that alias he wrote *When it was Dark* (1903) which looks at the social and religious chaos that follows the revelation that archaeological evidence has been discovered to prove that Christ was never resurrected. The book was an international bestseller and established Gull's reputation. Alas it gave him even more opportunity to drink—he once claimed he was never more than a few hundred yards from a bottle. He settled in Cornwall and produced a mass of novels, many of them science fiction, including *The Greater Power* (1915), *The Air Pirate* (1919), *The City in the Clouds* (1921) and *When the World Reeled* (1924). Over time his plots became repetitive—he often rewrote earlier stories—but at his best he was a very creative writer and deserves to be better remembered. In his later years he became diabetic and died in London aged only 47. —**M.A.**

BOUT THE MIDDLE OF THIS CENTURY public interest in the game of chess received a remarkable impetus from the arrival in London of it man named Greet, a Jew from Poland, who brought with him an automatic chess-playing figure. This figure had been first exhibited at Prague some six months before, and its subsequent tour of the great cities on the continent of Europe had excited an extraordinary interest. Most of the best-known masters of the game had taken up its challenge in St. Petersburg, Paris and Vienna, but one and all had suffered a defeat, inexplicable in its suddenness and completeness.

Mr. Greet now announced that his figure was ready to play against, and beat, anyone in England who should care to oppose it. The Automaton (for this was the name that the public had given to the figure) was exhibited a number of times in London, and on each occasion a crowded and mystified audience witnessed the uncomfortable spectacle of an image made of wood and iron, defeating in an easy and masterful manner several well-known exponents of the most difficult game in the world.

The machine consisted of a large figure of wood, roughly hewn and painted to resemble a man. It was about twice the size of a full-grown human being, and when playing was seated in a chair made on a very open design. It was quite motionless, except for the jerky movements of its arm and of the two long steel pincers that served it for fingers. It made no sound save the one word "check," that rasped out from its wooden throat, and the final "checkmate," pitched in a higher and more triumphal key.

This soulless machine was a master of all the known gambits, and seemed to play them with a supreme inspiration not granted to any living professor of the game. Public excitement about the matter was acute, and speculation ran high as to the probable methods employed to bring about so marvelous a result. Every facility was afforded to the public for inspection. Before and after each game the figure was opened in full view of those among the audience who might care to come upon the stage, and the closest scrutiny revealed nothing but a mass of cogs and wheels, among which it was quite impossible for a man to be concealed. Moreover, Mr. Greet was quite willing to allow the Automaton to be moved about on the stage at the direction of its opponent, so that the theory of electrical communication with a player concealed beneath the platform, had to be abandoned by those who had conceived such an opinion. During the games, Mr. Greet sat or walked about on the stage, but two members of the audience were always accommodated with chairs by the chess table, and it was obvious that there could be no communication between the figure and its proprietor. In this way the public mind became unpleasantly harassed, and Mr. Greet's purse grew to a comfortable fullness with the entrance money of the hundreds who blocked the door at each performance. The uncanny nature of the whole affair attracted numbers to the spectacle who did not even know the moves of the game, and many a man set steadfastly to the learning of chess, and the baffling of the problems proposed in the weekly papers, that he might better comprehend the nature of the mystery that was puzzling London.

So with a clientele composed of professors and amateurs of the game, engineers and scientists, and the great General Public that loves a mystery, Mr. Greet might have remained in London for a long period of great

pecuniary satisfaction. Then, without any warning, it was announced in the papers that the Automaton had made its last move, for the present at any rate, in the metropolis, and would shortly set out on a tour through the principal towns of the provinces.

Birmingham, Manchester and all the great centers of the North and Midlands were visited with the usual triumphs, and one morning the public were startled at their breakfast tables with the brief announcement that Mr. Greet would back his Automaton against any chess player in the world for £2,000 a side, the match to take place in the Theatre Royal at Bristol within three weeks' time.

No one had been more completely mystified or more intensely amazed at the triumphal progress of the Automaton than Mr. Stuart Dryden, considered by most people to be the leading chess player in England. He had himself refrained from hazarding his reputation in a contest with the thing, for, after carefully watching the easy defeat of those noted professors who had been bold enough to put its skill to the test, he had been forced to confess that in this machine, by some unfathomable means or other, had been placed an understanding of the game that he could not hope to compete with. He felt, however, that a time must come when he would be obliged to court the defeat that he knew to be certain, and the growing nearness of the contingency embittered every day of his life. He worked ceaselessly at problems of the game, and studied with the greatest care the records of the matches that had been played against the Automaton, but he found it quite impossible to coax himself into the least degree of self-confidence.

Professor Dryden was a bachelor, possessed of a small regular income, which he had always supplemented largely with his earnings at chess by way of stake-money and bets. He was a man of solitary habit and lived much alone in a small house in the northwestern quarter of London. An old woman attended to all his wants; he was surrounded by a large and complete library, and between his little house and the St. George's Chess Club he spent almost the entire portion of his life. It was his custom to rise early every morning, and after a long walk in the Regent's Park to arrive at the Chess Club about noon. There, as a rule, he stayed till about ten o'clock of the evening, when he would return to a quiet supper and several hours with his books.

On the morning that Mr. Greet's announcement had been made public to the world, he left the house very early indeed, before the arrival of the daily papers.

On this morning he was in an exceptionally bad temper. He was by nature a sullen man, and the continued triumphs of this Automaton, which pointed to a probable reduction in his income, had been gradually making him more and more sour. Then, to complete his misery, he found last night, on his return from the club, that by the failure of a company, considered sound by the most skeptical, his small private means had been reduced almost to a vanishing point. All night long he had lain sleepless with anxiety, and as he tramped the Regent's Park this morning his head burnt feverishly and his heart was very bitter against the world. The glorious freshness of the morning kindled no spark of happiness in his morose mind, and the children who met him stalking along the paths ran nervously from his dour expression. He examined the future with care, but could see nothing but ruin before him, as what now remained of his private income would be quite insufficient for his support. Moreover, in confident expectation of a successful season at the chess-table, he had of late allowed himself many extravagancies, and his creditors were beginning to put unpleasant pressure upon him. Several tournaments, from which he was confident of gain, had been put off, since all interest was centered in the Automaton, and a mere contest between man and man fell tame after the almost supernatural strife with Mr. Greet's image. Poor Mr. Dryden was unable to compose his ruffled temper or to suggest to himself any plan for the future, and wearying of the monotonous greenness of the park he turned his steps towards the club, though it was much earlier than he was wont to go there.

The St. George's Chess Club was a temple sacred to the upper circles of chess-players. The social or financial position of a member mattered little, but it was essential that he should be a real expert in the practice of the game. In this way a very motley and cosmopolitan gathering was usually to be found in the comfortable clubhouse situated in an inexpensive street near Hanover Square.

Mr. Dryden walked straight upstairs to the smoking-room, and was astounded to find it, usually so empty in the morning, quite crowded with an excited throng of members. All of those present had attained or passed the middle age of life. Every face carried some strongly marked personality, and a rapid conversation was being carried on in different languages.

Mr. Dryden was inexpressibly annoyed. He had promised himself peace and had found chaos, and his ugly face assumed a still more repulsive expression. He looked the very embodiment of friendless old age; a sour, tired old man whose death would conjure a tear from no single eye.

A little Frenchman was the first to notice Dryden's entrance. He leapt to his feet and waved his hand towards him. "*Tiens, Dryden!*" He exclaimed; "*voila notre sauveur.*" The babble of the room stopped at the words, and all, faces turned to the door. The old man stood there, slowly furling his umbrella and looked enquiringly round. Then he spoke slowly.

"You will pardon me, gentlemen, if I do not quite understand. Why saviour, and of what?"

"Why, our saviour! We're going to try for Greet's dollars," drawled a voice from the corner. "You're the only man for us. We'll put up the chips."

"Once more I am at a loss," said Mr. Dryden; "Mr. Laroche and Mr. Sutherland, you have puzzled me. I presume you are talking about the only Greet that interests us. What new thing has he or his Automaton done?"

Twenty members shouted the explanation, and, half smothered in news-papers, Mr. Dryden was forced into a chair, and formally asked if he would act as representative of the club and take up Mr. Greet's challenge.

"It has beaten all the rest of us," said the President sadly, "but surely in the first chess association in Europe there must be one player who can get the better of that infernal machine. There shall be one, and you shall be that one, Dryden. You can take a line through this. I know by exactly how much you are my master, and that thing showed about the same superiority over me. So you'll start about square. This is the scheme we've arranged. The club finds all the money if you lose. If you win, you take half and we pocket the rest. That's fair enough, is it not?"

Mr. Dryden did not take long to decide. However sure he felt that he was no match for the mysterious intelligence that guided the hand of the Auto-maton, the temptation of the money, and his own straitened condition left only one course possible to him.

"I accept," he said; "make all arrangements in my name, and let me know time and place and anything else that may be necessary. For these three weeks I will shut myself up. If there is anything about the game that I do not already know, perhaps in this absolute seclusion I may wring it from my brain. I suppose that I shall see you all, or most of you, on the appointed day. *Au revoir*, gentlemen. I thank you very much for the honor you have done me."

The members rose in a body, a motley crowd of all nations, each one greatly excited, and congratulations in every tongue smote on the back of Mr. Dryden's head, as, shielded by the President, he walked sedately down the staircase.

Left to himself, he set out in the direction of Charing Cross, for he entertained the notion of paying a visit to an old friend in the country. This gentleman, the Rev. Henry Druce, was incumbent of a village cure in Kent, and though his name was unknown to the public, he enjoyed among the professors of chess a high reputation as a master of the game. In the seclusion of Mr. Druce's peaceful vicarage Mr. Dryden felt sure that he would find rest for his worried brain, and valuable suggestions for the work that he was to do.

The train wandered happily out of the suburbs into the pretty county of

Kent, and after many tiresome waits drew up at last at a tiny wayside station, all white in a gorgeous setting of many-colored flowers. The glare of the sun's rays that beat back from the glowing platform into Mr. Dryden's tired eyes staggered him for a moment, as he stepped out of the gloom of the carriage. The hot quivering atmosphere was very distinct to the eye, like the hot-air waves that one sees above a shaded lamp. The country was full of dull, murmuring noises, and among them the voices of the porters and the rumble of the train seemed indefinite and unreal.

Mr. Dryden was unable at once to assimilate himself to the new surroundings, and long after the train had banged over the points and glided away into the haze he still stood looking vaguely over the broad fields, scattered with lazy cattle, that lay against the railway on the other side. He was startled into consciousness by a voice asking if he wished to travel on the omnibus that was about to start for the village. Following the man to where, in the dusty road, a boy in a big straw hat was lazily flicking the flies from the two sleepy horses that stood dejectedly in front of the little yellow omnibus, he was presently jolting into view of the scattered houses of the hamlet. The vicarage was an old-world house in an old-world garden, and as Mr. Dryden walked up the white-flagged path to the porch, he was afforded a view of Mr. Druce, comfortably disposed for his afternoon nap in a long chair by the window. The vicar was, however, delighted at the intrusion, and very excited by Mr. Dryden's tale of Greet's challenge and his own acceptance. They talked for a while about the mysterious figure and its inexplicable victories, till suddenly Mr. Druce, who throughout the conversation had been somewhat hesitating and shy of manner, turned to his visitor and said:

"It appears to me that in London you have ceased in a measure to enquire into the reason for these wonders. You are beginning to accept the victories of the Automaton as inevitable, and to believe, I am amazed to find, that the thing is in reality an almost supernatural triumph of science. Now surely, Dryden, you cannot think that that steel hand is guided by any other than a human intelligence. It is absurd; you might just as well believe in magic and the black arts. I have not seen it, but I read, and am told, that facility is given to the audience for examination; that it is opened, and is apparently empty of aught save machinery; that it is detached from the stage or its chair; in fact, that its secret is so clever that every one has been baffled. Now it is quite plain to me that somewhere, either inside it, or close at hand, is a man, possibly unknown to us all, but obviously a chess player of extraordinary brilliance, who by some means or other plays the Automaton's game. That is quite certain. The problem is, therefore, who is the man? The names and the movements of all the great players are known to us through the papers. I can tell you in a minute where is Iflinski, or Le Jeune, or Moore. Besides, there are not half-a-dozen men in the world who could have played the games so far recorded. Now I have a theory. I am a good Christian, I believe, both by profession and practice, and I have hesitated long in my mind before I was compelled to believe in this theory of mine. It brings me to think evil of a man who has been my friend and were I not so certain, Dryden, I would never breathe it to a soul. You are the first to hear. Listen. Of course, I long ago gave up the supposition of a wonderful scientific discovery, or anything of that sort. Since then I have simply been trying to find out the man. I have compared the games played by Mr. Greet's figure with those played by most at the greater living masters, and I have found in one case a striking similarity. Even then I should not have spoken had not coincidence aided me still further; had not, in fact, my friendship for the man I suspect enabled me to follow his movements and be privy of his disappearances. It is—and I am grieved that he should have lent himself to such a deception—Murray."

Mr. Dryden gave a gasp of astonishment.

"Murray!" He said, "Philip Murray of the Queen's Library, the biblio-phile, the old white-haired gentleman who comes sometimes to the club and plays a game or two; I can hardly believe it, Druce."

"It was hard for me to believe it myself," said Mr. Druce, "and I have only told you half of what I know. In my mind the truth of the thing admits of no doubt. I will tell you more of my proofs."

"But the man couldn't have done it." Broke in Mr. Dryden. "He couldn't have beaten these men, he couldn't have played the games. I've seen him playing in the club, he is no extraordinary player. No, Druce, find some one else for the spirit of the Automaton."

"Don't be so impatient, and don't be led astray by the idea of Murray's incapacity," said Mr. Druce. "You don't know him properly, neither you nor anyone else at the club; but I do. He cares nothing for notoriety. Chess is his recreation, not his business; but I can tell you, Dryden—and many hundreds of games have Murray and I played together—that he is the first master of the game in England. Enough for his ability. Listen to these facts. How long ago is it that the Automaton was first exhibited in Prague? Eight months exactly. At that time Murray disappeared from England and was absent for six months, precisely the length of time that Greet was taking his figure through the big cities of Europe. The fact alone of his disappearance may be only a coincidence, but look at this, my sister Lizzie's husband is at the Embassy in Vienna. She saw Murray three times in the streets during the time that the Automaton was there. She mentioned the fact in a letter to me, because, she said, he seemed to avoid her in so strange a manner. Tom Rollit, writing from Antwerp, told me how he met Murray in a cafe, and how constrained he seemed. The day was the second day after Greet and his figure had begun their matches in that city. I didn't pay much attention to this at the time, but after the Automaton had come to London, and I had repeatedly called on Murray to have a chat about the thing, and been as often told that he was away, I became suspicious. He is a man who has all his life been most reluctant to leave his home, and after the first time that in my study of the games I had noticed a resemblance between Murray's play and that of the Automaton, my suspicion; became very strong. It was then that I remembered his several journeys to Europe just before his long absence. He has always professed an extra distaste for continental travel. I remember too, how I had met Edouard Roulain, the man who has had such an extraordinary success in Berlin as a prestidigitateur, in the hall of Murray's house on the occasion of one of my visits. When I asked him about the man—for I should like to have met him—he changed the subject at once and somewhat rudely. Again—it is really wonderful how so much circumstantial evidence has come my way—he was in Manchester when the Automaton was there. I was calling, and I could not help noticing that the maid who showed me to the drawing room carried a letter addressed in his handwriting, that bore the postmark of that town. Mrs. Murray put the letter quickly in her pocket, and when I asked her where her husband was, she told me that he had gone to Edinburgh about a book. You must agree with me, Dryden, that that is enough. Well, I've got one last proof, the most conclusive of all. When they went to Birmingham, I followed and took a room that commanded a view of the stage door of the hall. All day long I sat in that window, concealed by the curtains, and every day, sometimes only just before the show, sometimes two or three times during the day, I saw a man, heavily bearded and with spectacles, walk into the hall, with Murray's walk. Once I saw him with Greet, but generally he was alone. That man was Murray I have no doubt at all. He is the brain of the Automaton. Philip Murray has worked one of the biggest deceptions on the world that has ever been conceived, and I doubt not he has nicely feathered his own nest in the working of it. What do you think of my story?"

"I own that I am fairly astounded," said Mr. Dryden, "and I cannot think how it is done. I tell you I have looked inside the thing, from both sides, and it's full of wheels. I've pushed it about the stage; and I've sat there during the play and never taken my eyes off it."

"Did Greet let you put your hand inside and touch the machinery," said Mr. Druce.

"Well, I never thought of doing that, nor, when I come to think of it, did anyone else; but I saw wheels, and cogs and springs, as distinctly as I see you."

"That can be arranged by an elaborate system of mirrors, some improvement on the Pepper's Ghost idea. Edouard Roulain is quite clever enough to fool anyone by a trick of that sort. It's my belief that Murray gets inside it; I don't think it could be worked by any other means. I expect that the plot was conceived somewhat after this fashion. Edouard Roulain, in the course of his investigations, stumbled on a really exceptionally brilliant idea for an optical delusion. It then occurred to him that this idea might be put to more profitable use than mere exhibition. How he hit on the notion of the chess-playing Automaton, I can't think. He has been a friend of Murray's for some time, I found that out; and very likely he told Murray of his find and asked for suggestions. Murray may have got it from some old book, or perhaps thought it out himself. Wait a minute though; I never told you how I proved Roulain's connection with the affair. When the Automaton was in London, I met him repeatedly about the town; but that was before I was so sure about Murray, and didn't think much of it. He had grown a moustache, but I recognized him easily. I daresay he's gone now, he wasn't in Birmingham."

"What about Greet?" Said Mr. Dryden.

"Oh, he is only a figurehead; perhaps he doesn't even know the secret. He has been an operatic manager all over Europe and the States; he took Roulain to New York when he made his first great success there. He is about the best business manager they could have."

"Well, I suppose I must grant you that Murray does work it—exactly how he does it doesn't matter much. What I want to think out is how does this knowledge help me? Suppose that you or I give the thing away, what do we gain? Have you thought of doing it yourself?"

"No, I have not. To tell you the truth, I have rather been enjoying the joke, and were it not for my orders, I should have in time thrown down the gauntlet myself. If there is one man in England who knows Murray's play, it is myself, and I think I might have got the better of him. The feeling of mystery that has surrounded the Automaton has helped him immensely; he would not have had so complete and easy a success if his opponents had not been frightened out of their best game. I could see that by studying the records of the play. As it is, I shall do nothing; but if this knowledge will be any help to you in your game, you are most heartily welcome to it. Believe me, that I shall so far escape from my seclusion as to be a most interested spectator of the match at Bristol."

"I am immensely obliged to you, old friend," said Dryden, "I will make it no secret from you that I am in a very bad way for money. A totally unlooked for misfortune has deprived me of the greater part of my regular income, and the interest that has followed this Automaton has caused several of the important tournaments, that I should have made money out of, to be abandoned. If I can win this match, I get £1,000, which will set me straight, and from my victory I shall gain a reputation that will put me in the way of much future gain. If I were to write a book on chess; it would enormously enhance its sale."

"I am sorry to hear of your distress," said Mr. Druce, "which I had never suspected, and I am the more glad that I may be of a little use to you. You will stop to dinner, of course, and before you go I will give you the records of a great many of Murray's games. He has had enough of his mysterious triumph, and it is quite time the joke came to an end."

Dinner was quiet and pleasant, and though the presence of Charles Cunliffe, the curate, who was fresh from Magdalen, and cared for nothing except stamped leather bindings and the fine embroidery of a cope, excluded chess from the conversation, the three men found the subject of continental travel a convenient exchange for opinions. Mr. Cunliffe had in undergraduate days paid several visits to Boulogne, and held elaborate ideas on the subject of racial distinctions.

Mr. Dryden bade farewell to the two clergymen in the little station, now cool and pleasant in the moonlight, and during the seventy minutes of his journey to Charing Cross, examined feverishly the bundle of papers that Mr. Druce had given him. For the next week he kept himself strictly from the world and held unceasingly to his task of investigating Mr. Murray's methods. At the end of that time there came to him the conviction that he had met his master. As before he had known that the uncanny spirit of the Automaton would surely beat him, so now he realized with a pain—all the worse because it swept away the hopes that Mr. Druce's story had inspired—that in the brain of the little old Scotch librarian was the same power, none the less real now that it had lost its odor of mystery.

Meanwhile his creditors had become more instant in their demands, and poor Mr. Dryden, crushed with despondency and overwhelmed with debt, conceived a hatred towards the automatic figure and its inmate that increased in bitterness as each day brought him nearer to the contest that he felt certain would prove his Waterloo.

For the three weeks he kept entirely to his own house and held no communication with the outside world, except for a short correspondence with the President of the club on the matter of the challenge, and the arrangements for day and hour. He received one short letter from Mr. Druce, wishing him good fortune and assuring him that he would be among the audience to watch the downfall of the Automaton.

Whatever mistrust of his powers he might entertain, it was not his own money that he would sacrifice by abandoning the match, and in the interests of the club he was bound to go through with the affair.

Four days before the match he came to Bristol and took apartments in a house in the Hot-wells that faced the river. The coming match had aroused extreme interest in the town, and crowds were continually assembled about the station at Temple Mead, in hope of a prior view of the Automaton.

On the day after his arrival he sat for many hours at the window, watching the tall spars of the ships show stark against the cliffs as the vessels were towed to and from the city. The chatter of the riverside loafers that reached his ears treated always of the Automaton, and the improbable speculations that were hazarded brought a weary smile to his face. About sunset he left the house, and, following a winding path, climbed the edge of the gorge, coming out upon the Clifton Down. For a little while he sat there, watching the silent beauty of the scene. The dying sun had lent a greater glory to the city that sloped from the sides of its seven hills to the hollow beneath him, and the Avon traced a line of rosy flame through the gorge, till it lost itself at last in a forest of masts and the dull smoke-cloud of the furnaces. Then the sun seemed to grow in size and rush quicker to its bed. For a moment it hung over the Somersetshire woods, firing every tree into a glory of a moment. Then it was suddenly gone, and the white coolness of evening came directly over the country and the town. The majesty of hill, champaign and valley, lent an infinite composure to the trouble of Mr. Dryden's thoughts, and presently he began to take the road to the city, purposing a cheerful dinner at some inn. A merry party of travellers filled the coffee-room at the "Greyhound" in Broad Mead, and their amusing conversation about the Automaton induced Mr. Dryden to disclose his identity. He became the center and hero of the party, and two hours passed with a pleasant speed.

About nine o'clock, a little rosy with wine, he set out on his way homewards. The mischance of a random turning led him from his proper road, and presently he came out upon the open space of the Queen's Square. The comfortable freshness of the air invited him to stay, and he sat for some time upon a convenient seat. He had come into a pleasant reverie, in which the Automaton played more the part of a comedian than of the villain, when a rumbling noise lifted his eyes to the roadway. A large cart of the strangest conceivable shape, somewhat like the body of a grand piano set upon its edge, was being driven past. It swung round the corner that led to the theatre, which was close at hand, and he heard it clatter for a little over the cobbles before it came to a sudden stop. He had a strong idea that this must be the arrival of the Automaton, and without quite knowing why he did so, got up and followed. On reaching the theatre he saw the cart drawn up a little beyond it. He hesitated to go nearer; and then noticed that the gallery door stood a little upon the jar. In a pure spirit of adventure he pushed it back and made a difficult progress down the long dim-lit passage and up the dark rickety staircase. When a plump of cold air upon his face told him that he had won the entrance into the body of the house, he made his way delicately to a seat and sat awaiting possibilities. He was not long in suspense before he heard distant voices and a considerable noise of a heavy body being advanced over rollers. Then a light came out from the wings and went across the stage. It seemed a tiny speck of flame in the great blackness of the theatre, lighting little save the face of the man who carried it. Mr. Dryden made out a heavy moustache and concluded at once that this must be Edouard Roulain. The man stooped and lit a few of the centre footlights, which turned a square patch of light on the stage. A hand lamp was burning in one of the wings, but through the rest of the house the darkness thickened, backwards till it wrapped the gallery, in which Mr. Dryden sat, with an impenetrable gloom. Presently the noise of rollers began again, and two men came into the patch of light, pushing the great painted figure of the Automaton. One, a person of ostentatious figure, he recognized immediately as Greet, and with a thrill of excitement he realized that the other, a little bearded man of a peculiar gait, could be none other than Murray himself. The language of the three men was deadened by the distance, but he saw that the one whom he supposed to be Roulain was busied about the mechanism of the figure. When the clicking of the wheels stopped, Mr. Murray walked up to the figure and spoke a few words to Greet and Roulain. Mr. Dryden could not hear distinctly, but a loud laugh came from the two men on the stage. Then Mr. Murray took off his coat, opened the Automaton and stepped inside it. Presently its arm began to move and the steel pincers of its fingers to shift about on the table.

He was only inside for a few minutes, and as soon as he reappeared, Mr. Dryden, in the fear that they might make it a business to see to the closing of all doors, began to fumble his way out of the theatre. Providentially the door of the gallery entrance was still open, and when he had gained the street, he hid in a doorway a few yards distant from the stage entrance. The men were talking as they came out, and he recognized Murray's voice at once. "That will be all right, Greet," it was saying; "you had better come and see me in the morning. I am staying in Bedminster—42, Leigh Road; it's across the river, you must take the ferry."

They passed down the road, and when they had gone out of sight, Mr. Dryden began his journey back to the rooms in the Hot-wells. Though nothing had been revealed to him that he had not been already cognizant of, the fact of having been with his own eyes privy to the secret of the trickery, made him greatly excited. He was conscious of a distinct hatred for Mr. Murray that he had not before experienced. There was something of jealousy in his anger. He bitterly grudged the old librarian his invention of the Automaton and the money that was coming to him from its exhibition. If he could only beat it, he thought, and then the dreadful feeling of hopelessness, that had left him during the varied excitements of the last few hours, came back and beset him with redoubled force. The much-needed repose of sleep was denied him, for all through that night the nightmare figure of the Automaton was with him in his dreams, and when, late next morning, he left his bed, his face was drawn and haggard and his mind a maelstrom of hatred and despair.

The day was very wild for the season, and continual thunderstorms gathered and broke their fury about the crags of the Avon Gorge. Mr. Dryden did not leave the house, but watched from his window the thunderclouds drive through the funnel made by the cliffs, and scatter over the houses and fields beyond. He felt a companionship in the ill humor of the elements, and the shrieking of the wind played a fantastic accompaniment to the bitter theme of his thoughts. Hatred of Murray was echoed in every scream of the gale, in every splash of the driven rain against the windowpanes, while the roaring menace of the thunder fashioned his anger into an ever-growing self-confidence. All through the afternoon, as the rage of the storm grew stronger his spirits rose higher, and at dinner a brilliant idea came to him. He would surprise Mr. Murray in some quiet place on his way to the theatre, and make known to him his discovery of the trick. The knowledge that the secret was out, coming to him at so critical a moment in the career of the Automaton must, he felt sure, have a deterrent effect on Mr. Murray's play, while his own knowledge that within the painted figure his invisible rival was uneasily fearful, would lend a confident strength to himself.

The prospect of meeting the spirit of the Automaton in the flesh awoke other possibilities in his mind, and at first he cursed himself for not having conceived a plot for the kidnapping of his antagonist. However, it was now too late, and he dismissed the idea with the reflection that even had he thought of it before he could have with difficulty found trustworthy accomplices. About half-past seven he set out for the meeting that he promised himself. The gloom of the day had in no way abated and it was already quite dark. What he had overheard of Mr. Murray's conversation with Greet suggested the river ferry to him as an advisable place, and there, about eight o'clock, he commenced to wait. The match was to be played at 9:30, and the doors were not open to the public till half-an-hour before that time, so he judged it quite certain that Mr. Murray would start for the theatre some time between eight and nine. The loneliness of the place lent horror to the storm, but Mr. Dryden cared little for the drenching rain or the flaming lightning as he staggered against the wind to keep his post by the ferry. Some twenty minutes had gone when a vivid flash lit the surrounding scene into half-a-minute's uncanny radiance, and he saw the figure of a man detach itself from the black shadow of the houses and come to the top of the river bank. Then all was dark again. The wind blew him the sound of a familiar voice shouting for the ferryman, and through the noise of the gale he seemed to recognize the rasping intonation of the Automaton's "Check." A lighted doorway gave up another figure carrying a lantern, and he could just see the two grope their way down the greasy flags that led to the boat. The tide was nearly at its lowest, and long oily rolls of mud sloped from the roadway on either side to where the last of the ebb hurried on its race to the sea. The power of the current made the crossing a long one, and he could only see the intermittent twinkle of the lantern through the rain. For a long way it moved slowly up the stream and then edged gradually back towards the opposite landing place. There was a grating noise, the chink of a coin, and Mr. Dryden saw the figure of a man that limped a little come laboriously up the difficult path. He waited in the shadow, and when Mr. Murray came full into the light of the lamp that marked the ferry-place, stepped forward and laid a hand on his shoulder.

"Ah, Murray," he said, "we are well met; for though this evening brings us another meeting, I had rather I found you here. I have a matter to discuss with you."

"I beg your pardon, sir," said the other, in a voice that shook with ill-repressed astonishment. "You have made a mistake. I do not know you, nor is my name Murray. I beg you will excuse me, I am about a business that presses."

"Don't be foolish, Murray," said Mr. Dryden. "I tell you I recognize you; you've as much time as I have for a talk."

"Again, sir, I repeat that you are wrong," said the other. "I am not Murray, and your interference is impertinent. Good night."

"Oh, you aren't Murray, aren't you; you think to face it out!" Said Mr. Dryden; "but I know you, you fraud. "What about these?" And, making a rapid step forward, he caught at his companion's beard with both hands. It came away at once, jerking the spectacles with it. They fell and shattered on the pavement.

"Now are you Murray?" Shouted Mr. Dryden in a voice of passion. "Damn you, you shall own it! I've found out all about you and the Automaton trick, and I've come here for a little business talk. If you'll only be sensible, we can soon come to terms."

"You have discovered my identity and you have me at a disadvantage," said Mr. Murray. "What do you want of me? Tell me quickly, for the time presses."

"There can be no match till I come, so you needn't hurry," said Mr. Dryden. "Listen. I must have that money, and it's just possible that you may beat me. I didn't come here to threaten, only to frighten you out of your play by discovering my knowledge. It was your refusal to acknowledge yourself that gave me the idea. Now here is my proposal. You let me win, and I say nothing; beat me, and I expose you. An exposure would cost you a lot more than the £2,000 you lose to me."

"I shall do nothing of the sort," said Mr. Murray; "you make a great mistake if you think you can bully me. I had known you, Mr. Dryden, as a gentleman of good manners and repute. I am sorry to find out my mistake. You may do your worst, prove the trick if you can. Now let me pass."

"You refuse then; well, you shan't go. Curse you Murray, I must have the money. Don't struggle or I shall hurt you. Oh, you will, will you? Take that, then."

Swinging his heavily mounted stick, he struck the old librarian a crushing blow behind the ear. The old man fell headlong, and, rolling over, came upon the mud slope. Down this he began to slide, gathering force as he went, till Mr. Dryden, who was watching, aghast at his action, saw the stream catch the feet and swing the whole body round into the river. For a second the face showed white above the black water. Then it was gone into the darkness.

For a short time Mr. Dryden stood thinking. He found to his astonishment that he knew no remorse. One thought alone possessed him; that now he must win the match and the money. The conditions of the game distinctly stated that, should the figure make no move, the victory went to its opponent.

He gathered up his victim's hat, and the false beard, from where they lay on the ground, and stuffing the dripping hair into the hat, flung it out over the river. Then he turned and walked quickly towards the theatre.

Mr. Greet and Monsieur Roulain arrived at the theatre a few minutes only before the time appointed for the match. Roulain unlocked the door of the Green Room, which had been reserved for their private use, and they went in to find the Automaton ready seated in its chair. They both concluded at once that Mr. Murray; as was his habit, had arrived earlier and was already concealed within the figure. Roulain contented himself with opening the outer panels, in order to make sure that his invention of mirrors revealed nothing to the public but the accustomed mass of machinery. When he was satisfied he rapped twice upon the back of the figure, and after a few seconds an answering knock came back to him. It was the signal he had arranged with Mr. Murray. Then, summoning two attendants he had the Automaton wheeled on to the stage. Directly afterwards the curtain was raised, discovering to the audience, that thronged every corner of the house, the solitary figure of the Automaton in its chair. Mr. Greet stepped forward to its side, his comfortable figure resplendent in an evening suit that glittered with jewels, and after bowing unctuously in response to the plaudits that rang out, made a little speech in which he recapitulated briefly the conditions of the match. He finished with the usual invitation to the audience to come on the stage and examine the figure. This ceremony was quickly disposed of. People throughout the country had come to accept the mystery of the Automaton, and flocked to the performances merely as amateurs of a new sensation, without seeking to further probe the secret. Some score of folks, chiefly of the lower middle class, sought the nearer view that the stage afforded, and after Mr. Greet had courteously delayed the over-inquisitive fingers of a countryman from Clevedon, he retired, to appear again with Mr. Dryden.

Mr. Dryden, whom the action of the storm had reduced to a condition of unhealthy dampness, appeared in a spare suit of Mr. Greet's, which hung upon his angular figure in a succession of unexpected creases and folds. The audience, unprepared for this element of the grotesque, mingled their applause with a ripple of merriment; but Mr. Dryden, in whom the conflicting emotions of triumph and fear waged an incessant battle, was entirely unconscious of any influence outside his own brain. He bowed to the house and cast a look of surveyal across the floor and round the tiers. In a box that overlapped by some feet on to the stage, sat Mr. Druce, a little hidden by a fold of curtain, the ample contour of his face creased into a twinkle of expectant merriment. Mr. Dryden paid him a mechanical salute and then became conscious of Mr. Greet's voice proffering an introduction to two gentlemen of the press who were to occupy seats upon the stage. He shook hands with the politeness of habit and sat down amid a silence of attention, so great, that the concerted breathing of the audience came upon his ear with a distinct and regular ebb and flow of sound.

The mood of simple curiosity with which former spectators had watched the Automaton's triumphs was on this occasion changed to an intense fervor of interest that threatened in many cases to lapse into hysteria. When on former occasions competitors had climbed the platform, like yokels at a village fair sheepishly certain of defeat from the professional wrestler, the public had speculated pleasantly on the probable duration of the contest, and been content to laugh and wonder at the unusual spectacle. But this was no matter of a lightly-accepted challenge, or of an end that admitted of no serious contemplation. Here were two thousand pounds a side at issue, and the picked chess player of England set down to do battle for fame and fortune against the all-conquering intelligence of the wooden sphinx.

Mr. Dryden sat, his wrists resting lightly upon the edge of the table, gazing intently into the calm features of his lifeless *vis-à-vis*.

The thing was immeasurably unpleasant.

Little attempt had been made to conceive more than the roughest image of man. The forehead sloped backwards, and the long crooked nose that rose above thin tight-set lips and a hard chin had a flavor of the American Indian, while the whole aspect of the morose, seated figure, one arm clasped to the body and one poised forwards with half bent elbow, conveyed a haunting suggestion of some hawk-faced god of Babylon. A cold sweat came over Mr. Dryden's brow as his nervous fingers stretched over the chessmen, for he was to make the first move. The full disaster of his affairs was unpleasantly real in his mind, and something burning seemed to press on the back of his eyes. Then the scene on the picture-sheet of his brain shifted to the ferryside, and as he saw again the tide catch the body of Mr. Murray and whirl it out to sea, self-recovery came to him at once. He straightened his arm and advanced a pawn upon the board. As he did so the familiar click of the released mechanism of the stop-watch, brought an aspect of custom, and he sat back in his chair in the tranquil knowledge that the end of the time limit would find the Automaton still motionless, and the wager his. Behind it, at a little distance, sat Greet, in a like comfortable confidence, while the two pressmen, their bodies bent forward, their hands clasped between their knees, brought near to Mr. Dryden the air of intense excitement that hushed the silent hundreds at his side.

The stopwatch had marked four-minutes when there was a creaking noise in the Automaton. First the shoulder and then the elbow began to move, and to Mr. Dryden's unspeakable horror the pincers of the hand unclasped, and, poising for a moment, clipped the Queen's Pawn and rapidly moved it forwards. The murderer's face grew ashen grey with fear, his eyes blinked rapidly and his heart stood still.

His first thought was that Murray was not, after all, the guiding spirit of the Automaton, that he had killed an inoffensive man for no reason. He heard again the dull sound of breaking bone, and the sucking noise of the rolling body on the mud. He could think of nothing else, till the far-away voice of the umpire, announcing that four minutes had gone, pricked his brain into a little consciousness. He hastily stretched out his hand and made a rapid, unconsidered move. As he did so his fingers came for a brief moment in contact with the iron paw of the Automaton, and at the moment of touching he knew who his adversary was. He felt so strange and terrible a message flash to his brain that his whole body became cold and rigid in a moment.

He could not keep his eyes from the lens-like eyes of his adversary, and he felt rather than saw the intelligence that looked out at him, for he knew he was playing with no earthly opponent.

He made another disastrous and hurried move. Then the head of the Automaton trembled, the lips parted, and it said, "Check" loudly and distinctly. The voice was Mr. Murray's voice.

At the end of the five minutes Mr. Greet noticed something strange in Mr. Dryden's attitude. Going hastily up to him, he saw his eyes were wide open but without sight, and when he touched his hand it was cold and stiff. Mr. Dryden was quite dead. The curtain fell, and they carried the body to the green room, while in a terror-stricken silence the vast crowd left the theatre. Their last footsteps were still echoing on the other side of the curtain when Greet and Roulain came back to the stage. The doctors and attendants were trying to restore the body of Mr. Dryden in the little room at the back. Greet opened the panel of the figure and called in hoarse, agitated tones to Mr. Murray to come out. There was no answer, and Roulain fetched a candle and they looked into the hollow in surprise. There was no one there!

The Abduction of Alexandra Seine

FRED C. SMALE

MANY OF THE science-fiction stories that were written at the end of the nineteenth century looked forward with optimism toward the wonders that technology might bring. Top of the list, ahead of such benefits as an endless supply of food, moving walkways, television and longevity was the personal aircar. This was at a time when everyone was still aglow with the freedom provided by the bicycle. The motor-car had yet to establish itself but it was the aircar or other form of personalised air transport that everyone desired.

We all think of Wilbur and Orville Wright as the first to fly a heavier-than-air machine, but others had achieved it before them, though not in such a controlled manner. Clément Ader managed to get his beautiful bat-winged Avion off the ground in 1890 and it is supposed to have flown about 50 metres. Later attempts were only marginally better. There were several others who made valiant attempts during the 1890s, including Hiram Maxim, inventor of the machine gun, so the idea of powered flight was very topical. Earlier, in 1852, Henri Giffard had created a steam-powered airship, and for decades many believed the airship would be the transport of the future. Like the automaton, it is another iconic steampunk image. The airship remained fashionable throughout the 1920s and until the Hindenberg disaster in 1937, but there are those who believe its day may yet return.

Little is known about Fred C. Smale. He may be the 35-year-old nurseryman from Torquay in Devon who lists himself as a florist and author on the 1901 census. He contributed occasional stories to the popular magazines and wrote a humorous fantasy *The Mayor of Littlejoy* (1899) about a man who discovers he is descended from fairies. —**M.A.**

**EIGHO! THIS IS GRUESOME WORK,"** exclaimed Bowden Snell, as he leaned back in his old Victorian chair and placed a cocaine lozenge in his mouth.

A particularly atrocious crime had been committed that morning in the suburb of Slough, and Snell, in his capacity of graphist to the *Hourly Flash*, had been sent to procure a record of it, by means of the Antegraph, then coming into general use with the news offices.

He had the advantage of possessing a good instrument, and five or six minutes had been sufficient in which to obtain good retrospective views of the crime, from the first frown of the murderer to the last dying throe of the victim.

Bowden Snell was now developing the film in his room at the *Flash* office, and the aerocar that had brought him was still outside the large bay window swinging gently to and fro at its moorings in the summer breeze.

It was now sixteen o'clock, and the pictures were needed for the seventeen o'clock edition. The murderer had been caught of course; a constable, equipped with the new collapsible wings, had swooped down on the guilty ruffian ere he had reached Windsor, whither he was making, doubtless with the intention of taking an aerocar from the rank on Castle Hill.

Bowden Snell was not young, being over fifty, and the more rapid methods of the times made it difficult for him to compete with younger men; but the *Flash* people retained him chiefly because of his extensive knowledge of the great province of London.

His films completed and dispatched by tube to the lower offices, Bowden Snell mechanically pressed a button in the wall beside him, and commenced to apply himself voraciously to the resulting salmon cutlets. The apartment and its conveniences were placed entirely at his disposal by the proprietors of the *Flash*, and being a lonely man—a widower in fact—Bowden Snell made it almost his home.

He had scarcely eaten a mouthful when the room was suddenly darkened by the apparition of a second aerocar of strange old-fashioned construction, which bumped clumsily against Snell's own machine, and ultimately drew up at the window.

Immediately a young man, clad in white from head to foot, leaped into the room. His face was brown with exposure to the sun, and he looked anxious and travel-worn.

"Arbuthnot!" Exclaimed Bowden Snell, "You here? What on earth—?"

"Ah, how familiar it sounds to hear one of your dear old-fashioned sayings, Mr. Snell," said the newcomer. "On earth indeed! When I haven't touched earth for sixteen hours. Do give me a bite of something, for Heaven's sake; I'm famishing," and the young man looked longingly at the salmon cutlets.

Still bewildered, the other turned to the wall and hurriedly pressed a number of buttons.

"Steady, I say; steady," said the young man, with a faint smile. "Roast turkey, cold salad, mushrooms, fried soles, Burgundy—a bit of a mixture, eh?"

Somewhat confused, the elder man checked himself and turned from the buttons.

"But how is it you are here?" He asked. "I thought you were in Japan, helping to develop that part of the empire."

"I must talk and eat at the same time," replied Arbuthnot. "Potatoes, stuffing, and green peas, if you don't mind—thanks. Mr. Snell, I am in great trouble."

"Hum, it hasn't affected your appetite, at any rate," said the other.

"Perhaps not; but I can tell you the air of the Ghauts is pretty keen, at least I found it so this morning as I came through."

"Well, don't hurry yourself; I'll go on with my own luncheon," said Snell, reseating himself.

"All right," replied Arbuthnot, with his mouth full, "I won't waste more time than I can help. Listen: I took to Japan with me two telepathic instruments."

"Ah, a lady's whim, eh?" Suggested Bowden Snell.

"Something of my own idea as well," replied the young man, a slight flush overspreading his handsome face. "You see, one couldn't be running home here to England every few weeks, and Ally and I thought it would be nice to sit and talk to each other sometimes, even though thousands of miles of clouds floated between us."

Bowden Snell nodded indulgently; and Arbuthnot, leaning back with a sigh, lit a cigarette—he was a steady young man, and abstained from drugs.

"Now this morning a strange thing happened," he continued. "You must understand I have one instrument upstairs and the other down in my sitting-room; it isn't always so easy to hit the mark in Japan, you know, owing to the earthquakes, so that when Ally missed one with a message the chances were that she would hit the other."

"I see."

"Well, I was sitting down having a smoke after the day's work—of course it was evening there—when the signal of the instrument clicked, and I instantly placed my ear to it. Then I heard my dar—Ally's voice, I mean, seemingly in great distress, calling me, saying, 'Help, help, Jack! I am being carried away,' and then there was a dead silence."

The young man paused, and passed a trembling hand across his damp

brow. He went on—

"I rushed upstairs to the other instrument, thinking that possibly it might be catching what the other missed, but I heard nothing more, though I shouted continually."

"Shouting's never any good; only rattles the mechanism," said Bowden Snell. "Of course you took the direction?"

"Yes, I thought of that," replied Arbuthnot. "It was due west, and two degrees from normal."

"Two degrees from normal, eh!" Repeated the other, musingly. Then he took a scrap of paper from his pocket and made a few rapid calculations, at the end of which he exclaimed

"Hullo, she must have been in the air then."

"Of course," answered the young man, "that is how I worked it out; three hundred feet from the ground, and fifty miles south of Greenwich."

"About that," concurred Bowden Snell. "Well, what are you going to do, and what do you want of me?"

"I thought of you immediately," said Arbuthnot, "and, placing a few food-pellets in my pocket, I jumped on my machine and came away just as I was. Luckily my aerocar, which is, as you see, one of the old-fashioned ones—I can't afford a new one—was charged, and I can tell you I made her rattle coming along over Thibet, Russia, and Germany. Once I caught up the daylight, yet it took me sixteen hours to do the journey," he concluded, apologetically.

Bowden Snell smiled grimly. He thought of the old days of his boyhood, when a voyage from Japan was considered a very serious undertaking, occupying weeks of wearisome crawling over land and water.

"And now," cried the young man, jumping up from his chair," I have come to you, my father's old friend, to ask you to help me. You know this great province of London as well as any man, and, moreover, your particular occupation gives you immense facilities for discovering what I want to know."

"And that is?"

"I want to find Ally," said Arbuthnot. "I am to blame for wasting time as I have, but I was really famishing."

"What is she like, to begin with?" Asked Bowden Snell

"Oh, I forgot; you have never seen her, have you?" Replied the young man. "Look," and taking a small case from his breast-pocket he handed it to Snell, who said as he took it—

"I was in Canada the afternoon you brought her to my house remember, so that, as you say, I never have seen her." He then applied his eye to an aperture in the case, and pressed a knob. Instantly a faint ticking sound was heard, and the holder started violently. "Young man, who is this girl? What is her name?" He asked agitatedly as he returned the case.

"Do you know her?" Said Arbuthnot in surprise at the effect the vitograph had produced on his companion. "Her name is Seine; at least—" and the young man hesitated a moment—"that is the name she goes by—Alexandra Seine. To tell you the truth, her real name is not known. She was discovered in Paris when we entered the city in '30. Of course, she was only a tiny child then, and as no clue to her identity could be found, they christened her Alexandra, after the then Dowager Empress, and Seine after the river on the banks of which she was found. An English lady adopted her, and that's all her history."

Bowden Snell had been sitting with his face buried in his hands whilst the young man had been speaking.

"Paris!—1930!—My little Violet—can it be?" He cried disjointly. "The very same smile—her very movements!"

"Your daughter!" Exclaimed Arbuthnot in amazement, momentarily forgetting the urgency of his errand.

"Yes, yes. Come here a moment," and the elder man led him to the far end of the apartment, which was curtained off and there, facing a blank white wall stood on a pedestal, a box-shaped machine somewhat resembling the old magic-lanterns pictured in the books of our boyhood. It was evidently fixed there for film-testing purposes.

Snell drew the curtains after them, and they stood almost in darkness. Carefully taking a small square sheet of gelatinous substance from his pocket-book, he inserted it in the instrument and pressed a knob at the side. Instantly a bluish flame kindled within, and on the blank wall appeared the life-sized figure of a pretty woman dressed in the late Victorian style—large sleeves, curled hair, skirts reaching to the ankles and all. She smiled bewitchingly, yet with a slight touch of sadness, and held out her arms towards the mute observers, her lips moving at the same time; then she seemed to step forward, and the vision faded.

"My Ally to the life!" Exclaimed Arbuthnot. "But how did you get her graphilm? And in that queer costume! Was it a masquerade?"

"That was not 'Ally,' as you call her," replied Bowden Snell; "it was her mother and my dear dead wife. If I could have inserted her voice-record at the same time, I have no doubt it would have been a further proof, but the cylinder is at home."

"Your wife!" Cried Arbuthnot. "Can it be?"

"I served with the City Imperial Volunteers at the Siege of Paris in '30," replied Bowden Snell as he carefully replaced the film in his book. "My wife and child were in Paris when the war broke out. My wife was killed by a chance shell; our babe, it seems, escaped." Then, subduing his emotion with an effort, he seized Arbuthnot by the arm and exclaimed, "Come, come, let us find her; don't ask questions now, let us away!"

"Yes." Said Arbuthnot. "But whither? We have no clue."

"Let me think, let me think." Said Snell, passing his hand over his forehead; then, stepping quickly across the room, he pressed a knob in the wall, causing a little shutter to fall.

"What place?" Asked a faint voice.

"Give me the whole of East London, from Greenwich to St. Paul's," replied Bowden Snell, "In sections of square miles."

"It's rather dark," said the voice, grumblingly, "but I'll try."

"Come, Arbuthnot, you had better look as well," said Snell, motioning the young man to his side.

The two men applied their eyes to circular orifices in the wall, and waited.

"Do you see anything?" Asked Arbuthnot, presently.

"Nothing," replied the other, "only the usual crowd of aerocars above and athletes walking in the streets below. It is almost too dark to discern faces. I can see no car that is suspicious. Stay! Ah, no!—Only some air-sailors drinking absinthe."

"What is to be done?" Exclaimed Arbuthnot, despairingly.

"You there?" Called Snell.

"Yes," came the voice in reply.

"Give me a line due east of Greenwich straight away to the sea."

"Apparatus only reaches Swanley; line broken down." Came the reply.

"What a nuisance! When will they perfect these things?" Said Arbuthnot, impatiently.

"Give me as far as you can then," cried Snell.

"Right."

"Now then, keep your eyes open." Warned the elder man.

"Look!" Arbuthnot cried suddenly. "There she is!" And then Snell clicked a switch on his left.

"I've checked it." He said, in tones of suppressed excitement. "You are sure it is she?"

"Quite," said Arbuthnot, agitatedly; "but who is the man with her? I cannot see."

"Great Heavens! 'Eagle Malvowley, I might have guessed it, the fiend!" Cried Bowden Snell.

"Malvowley! What, he that owns the secret castle in the Balkans?" Queried Arbuthnot, breathlessly.

"The same." Answered Bowden Snell; "He is bearing her thither, the villain. But where are they? We must follow at once."

"I cannot understand." Said Arbuthnot, straining his eyes at the aperture. "There is open sea beneath, and yet the operator said—"

"You there?" Came the voice.

"Well?" Said Snell, quickly.

"The instrument is a little out of order. By mistake I started you from the French end; you have checked it in mid-channel."

"That is all right, thank you," said Snell. "That explains it." He said, turning to his companion. "But let us watch. How is this—they seem stationary?"

"They are stationary," cried Arbuthnot, after a moment. "Come, let us away."

Bowden Snell turned off the knob and followed the younger man to the window.

"My machine," he said briefly, "it is the swifter."

Arbuthnot leaped in, and Bowden Snell followed him.

With a whiz and a flutter they rose through the cool evening air and, after soaring undecidedly over the ancient dome of St. Paul's, sped away in an easterly direction.

The air was fairly full of business cars, which rose in shoals from the heart of the province and dropped in various suburbs about Essex, Suffolk, and Kent.

Once away from the great centre, however, our travelers were able to put on full speed, and in a few minutes the silvery gleam of the Channel appeared in sight.

They searched the air with strained eyes as they sped along; but, beyond the usual Continental and Far East cars, they saw nothing of consequence.

As they neared the sea they decided to descend, and dropped lightly at the very water's edge, on a secluded beach between Dover and Folkestone. They stepped out on the yielding sand, and stood by the rippling waves.

A huge full moon was just appearing above the horizon, and its pale beauty was reflected in touches of silver on the darkening sea. Far above them a few aerocars wafted their way towards their various destinations, and the alert customs officers in their crimson-painted machines flitted restlessly hither and thither.

The two men stood silent for a few moments, awed by the beauty and solitude of the scene.

"We are beaten." Bitterly exclaimed Arbuthnot at last.

"Wait," said Bowden Snell as he narrowly scanned an approaching car; "if I am not greatly mistaken that is Jim Travers of the *Minute Gun*. It looks like his machine; yes, it is. Above there, Travers!" He shouted lustily.

"Hello, Snell!" Came the reply, "what's amiss?" And the car swooped

gracefully to within a few yards of their heads, Travers looking over the side at his fellow graphist.

"Have you seen 'Eagle Malvowley in your travels?" Asked Snell.

"Just passed him about half way across," was the welcome answer. "He had a breakdown—jammed lever, I fancy—and is fluttering about like a wounded gull."

"Anyone with him?" Shouted Arbuthnot, as with Snell he stepped hastily aboard their machine.

"Couldn't see; too dark," replied Travers, as he resumed his progress Londonwards. "Anything special on?" He called back. "If so, telepath us at the office, there's a good fellow."

But, with a shout of thanks, Bowden Snell and Arbuthnot were already soaring over the sea.

"He's just back from Baden Races—lucky I saw him," muttered the former, as he pulled out all the speed-bars.

Arbuthnot was in a state of fierce excitement; he peered anxiously forward, and at length his bloodshot eyes detected a fluttering object between himself and the full-orbed moon.

Mutely he grasped Snell's arm and pointed.

"I see," said the other, laconically; and with a skillfully executed upward swoop he guided the machine to within a dozen yards of the apparently uncontrollable fugitive car, in which a tall, slight man with a dark, saturnine countenance was uttering vicious oaths, and spitefully hammering at some part of the machinery. Arbuthnot jumped recklessly on to the high platform of their car, and with a gasp of mingled fear and relief beheld the beloved object of his search lying on the bottom of the other machine—to all appearance lifeless.

Malvowley was so engrossed in his task that he had not noticed the approach of his pursuers, but a fierce hail from Arbuthnot caused him to leap up.

With an execration he picked up some ball-shaped object and hurled it at his interrupters, but in his sudden surprise he missed his aim.

Bowden Snell hastily seized a lever and drew it back with a jerk. The car rose vertically some fifty feet above Malvowley's.

"Rippite bomb," said Snell, with a white face, as the missile struck the water below and burst with the soft seductive whir of that deadly explosive.

"You are helpless, Malvowley." Cried Arbuthnot. "Hand over Miss Seine at once."

"Come and take her," yelled Malvowley, defiantly; "I won't miss you a second time," and he seemed to apply himself again to the task of repairing his gear.

"We must board him," said Snell; "it is our only chance. If he once gets his machine in hand again he will be the other side of Europe in five minutes.

She's a racer, built for the America Cup Race of last year. I will swoop close to him, and you must leap for it."

"I'll try it," said Arbuthnot, desperately. "If I miss, you must descend on the chance of picking me up."

"Now, then!" Cried Snell, as they swept down.

With a fast-beating heart Arbuthnot hurled himself into the car, knocking the surprised Malvowley into a corner, where he lay momentarily stunned.

With lightning movements the young man seized the unconscious girl in his arms and passed her over to Bowden Snell, who, pale as death, stood ready to receive her. Arbuthnot had scarcely time to leap back after when Malvowley recovered himself, and, with horrible oaths, rushed to the side of his car.

"Curse you!" He shrieked, "I'll wreck you; I'll send you all to eternity!"

"Up-up-quick!" Shouted Arbuthnot. "Another bomb!"

They rose with sickening speed, and Malvowley, foaming with demoniacal rage, hurled another deadly missile up after them, putting all his strength into the attempt.

They were too quick, however, and the bomb fell back again on Malvowley's own car, exploding on the contact, and scattering the machine and its unhappy occupant into a million fragments.

Some of the wreckage struck the victors as they still soared upwards, but they were rising too rapidly to suffer any injury. When at last, pale and trembling, they found courage to look down, only a few pieces of floating wood and aluminum far below remained as witnesses of Eagle Malvowley's fearful end. To their great joy, Snell and Arbuthnot discovered that the rescued girl had merely fainted, and in a short time the keen upper air revived her.

It appeared that Malvowley had swooped unexpectedly down upon her as she was walking on a lonely road near Reading, and despite her cries had carried her off. She had retained presence of mind enough to note the sun's position and rapidly make the mental calculation necessary in order to obtain her lover's exact direction; she then telepathed, but ere many thoughts had left her brain, her captor had suspected something, and brutally flung her into the bottom of the car.

Having telepathed to allay the natural anxiety of her guardian at Reading, they sped back to Snell's private house at Bexley. The happy girl smilingly caressed her lover's hand, and leaning her head against her newly-found father's shoulder, said brightly—

"Rescued maiden; long-lost daughter. It seems like one of the old-fashioned novels, doesn't it?"

"Romance is never old-fashioned, my dear; it is for all time." Said Bowden Snell.

The Gibraltar Tunnel

JEAN JAUBERT

THE VICTORIANS were great at enormous construction and civil engineering projects. The first underground railway in the world, the Metropolitan Railway in London, was opened in 1863. It ran from Paddington to Farringdon and was the start of the London underground system. These original tunnels were built by the cut-and-cover method. The first deep tunnelling with tunnel shields, which became known as the "Tube", happened on what is now the Northern Line and was opened in 1890 and it was throughout this decade and the early 1900s that most of the London Underground, as we know it, was completed.

Thoughts of a Channel Tunnel linking England and France had been around since the early 1800s though exploratory work was not started until 1881. Two man-size bores were dug for over a mile on both sides of the Channel before the idea was shelved. There was always a fear that the Tunnel would compromise Britain's security and usually when the Tunnel was depicted in fiction it was under threat of invasion, such as in *How John Bull Lost London* (1882) by Edgar Welch or *Pro Patria* (1900) by Max Pemberton. The present rail tunnel, the second longest in the world, was started in 1988 and opened in 1994.

The idea of a tunnel across the Straits of Gibraltar, linking Europe with Africa, is far less common in fiction. In fact I'm not aware of one earlier than this story by the French engineer Jean Jaubert, published in 1914. In recent years Spain and Morocco have confirmed their plans to construct such a tunnel, and it remains to be seen how prophetic Jaubert was. —**M.A.**

**ALLOA! HALLOA!** Are you there? Mr. Glencoe? Halloa! I am sorry to have to inform you sir, that it is absolutely impossible to run the train. Yes, I mean the train cannot start. Why? Well, sir, to put it frankly, the tunnel's not safe. The roof seems to shake at the passing of even the light cars, and at about the tenth mile the roof is dripping water like a rain-storm. My confidential reports of yesterday and the day before warned you as to the state of the tunnel. But, indeed, it is not merely natural moisture. Down there, just now, it was like a thunderstorm. Indeed, sir, I realize perfectly that the opening of the tunnel has already been put off a week. Circumstances have been too strong for us. The reports that have got about are certainly regrettable. But surely we can't risk a catastrophe to put a stop to them! Yes, yes, yes; I am absolutely convinced there is danger, sir, and very grave danger. What! Afraid? I? Of course, you're joking. But remember I have warned you!"

Hanging up the receiver with a vicious snap, the engineer of the Gibraltar Tunnel Railway Company, Mr. James Harward, very young, very intelligent, with a great air of decision about him, left the telephone in disgust, "The shares are falling on Change," he muttered, with a slight shrug, "and so at all costs the run must be made. Well, we shall see what we shall see!"

Banging the door after him, he left his office.

This was at Ceuta in the days when the great Gibraltar Tunnel was only just finished.

After the proved success of the tunnel under the English Channel, this new project of linking up Europe with Africa had been received with enthusiasm. With the trans-Saharan railways and the great English line from Cairo to the Cape already completed, this tunnel would supply the last link in the great chain of railways, and henceforth a journey could be made on dry land from the South of England to the Cape of Good Hope.

On every side the enterprise found supporters; the Gibraltar Tunnel Railway Company was formed, and the work of constructing the under-sea tunnel commenced. Unfortunately, the conditions here proved less favorable than in the Dover–Calais Tunnel; the ground—friable and unstable—lent itself but ill to the work of the excavators and masons. Innumerable and unforeseen difficulties had to be met and overcome, and the work was in consequence delayed, the opening of the tunnel put off, and by the time the day of its sensational inauguration dawned all sorts of sinister rumors were afloat as to the solidity of the foundations.

James Harward withdrew, his mind full of a lovely vision. With her slim figure, her exquisite, dark face, her merry smile and deep yet roguish eyes, Blanche Glencoe was not at all of the Anglo-Saxon type. Rather did she remind one of the lovely women of the South. Her mother, indeed, was Italian.

In this moment of enchantment all his anxieties, his doubts, his fears, returned to the young engineer with redoubled force. He took his seat beside the motor-man.

If only the journey were accomplished without mishap! A few hours earlier he had looked the risk in the face calmly, even with a certain professional indifference. Now that he knew Miss Glencoe to be on board his whole being revolted at the thought of a possible accident. His heart throbbed heavily; he loved this girl Blanche! He had never realized it fully till that moment when she flitted across the platform to enter the train; then his powerful emotion had flashed the searchlight of truth to the very depths of his soul.

At their first meeting Blanche Glencoe had made a deep impression on him, but he told himself it was only the artist in him which worshipped at the shrine of her tender beauty; this, he thought, was admiration—respectful admiration, not love. And so, little by little, all unconsciously, he had become love's bondsman. Always her image had been before his eyes and in his heart. And Blanche? Was it folly, he asked himself, to imagine she might reciprocate his affection? He tried to call to mind every little detail of her demeanor towards him that was indicative that she was not indifferent to him. Would she—

A gesture from the mechanician woke the young man out of his love dream.

The incline was now almost imperceptible. The under-sea level had been reached; the motors were running again, and under their impulsion the train rushed on swiftly and smoothly. In the walls of the tunnel the engineer caught a passing glimpse of one of the isolating-switches which were installed at certain intervals along the line, and which enabled any section of the live rail to be isolated, thus cutting off the power from any faulty section, if necessity arose.

The shrill ringing of a telephone-bell suddenly made itself heard above the thrumming of the wheels. A wire was installed above the train the whole length of the route, and a special transmitter with roller contact maintained uninterrupted communication with the telephone in the car.

"Halloa! Yes, everything's all right so far, sir. I know; I only hope you may be right all through, sir. Oh, they are enjoying themselves—very gay indeed. Why, of course, sir, you can rely on my absolute discretion. Very good sir. Good-bye."

Harward hung up the receiver and again set himself to scrutinizing the route ahead. Already the walls were no longer dry—a little water filtered through the surface. Several isolating-switches had already been passed and in a few minutes the lowest point in the under-sea tunnel would be reached. Here two tremendous culverts, carrying off the water that had percolated into the tunnel descended at a steady gradient to the solid bottom strata. At the works above-ground powerful pumps, erected at the mouth of the shafts that connected with these draining galleries, pumped the water up to the surface.

The nearer the train got to the middle of the tunnel the wetter the walls became; they streamed with water, and, as the engineer had said, a veritable rain fell from the roof and flooded the permanent-way. Under the passing of the heavy train the whole tunnel vibrated in an alarming way. The rumbling of the wheels became a hollow roar. One could well understand Harward's apprehensions; this abnormal state of things was surely the precursor of some dreadful catastrophe?

James Harward put the question to himself as he anxiously followed the flight of the miles on the indicator. Then the gradient changed; the critical point was passed. Harward breathed more freely. Soon now the European shore would be reached and the danger passed. The rain from the roof ceased and at each revolution of the wheels the damp grew less and less. All peril seemed passed, and the engineer, overjoyed, began to reproach himself for his foolish fears and to feel rather sheepish at having voiced them to Mr. Glencoe. Oh well, everything was going all right, so what did it matter?

Then suddenly the electric lights flickered for a moment and went out. The humming of the motors ceased and the speed slackened. In a black obscurity, which was only emphasized by the feeble flicker of the hastily-lighted emergency lamps, two hundred yards below the level of the sea, and nearly eight miles from the tunnel's mouth, the Gibraltar Tunnel Express came to a standstill.

In the power-house at Algeciras the chief electrical engineer, with a curious look on his face, stood at the ammeter and noted the registration of the current absorbed by the train. A foreman approached him.

"Well, what is it?" Asked the engineer.

"The delivery of water from the pumps has increased tremendously since this morning, sir. We must put on more pressure at once."

"I'll come and see."

The two men went towards the shaft. A special gauge registered the level of the water at the bottom. At the moment it registered two hundred and fifteen yards below the level of the sea.

"Hardly fifteen yards below the floor of the tunnel," said the engineer. "We must reduce that at once."

The motor of the pump thrummed a little more, but still, slowly, the level rose instead of decreasing; the engineer knitted his brows.

"Get the emergency pump running," he ordered, "and put her at full pressure."

A second thrumming joined itself to the first, and the delivery of water was doubled; the level ebbed little by little, and the engineer went back to the power indicator.

What was this that met his gaze? It was impossible! The electric consumption had suddenly increased tenfold! No, he was making no mistake; overloaded, the machines behind him were slackening. The engineer flung himself towards the tunnel telephone. Mr. Glencoe already had the receiver in his hand.

"Halloa! Halloa! What's wrong? How do you mean nothing? No damage? You are in darkness? But there is no interruption of the current here with us; the machines are delivering six thousand amperes. You have no current on the train? But how can that be when we're sending you plenty?"

At this moment the foreman ran in, his face expressive of dismay.

"Sir! The level!"

"What now?"

"It is one hundred and ninety-eight yards."

"What! It was at two hundred and fifteen a moment ago!"

"It has suddenly risen. In less than a quarter of an hour! The pumps are flooded."

"But—then—the line is flooded, too!" Cried the director, overwhelmed.

"And the third rail is short-circuited by the sea-water," added the engineer, curtly.

The silence of tragedy descended on the three men.

"At all costs we must send them some current," said the managing director, after a moment. "Start the stand-by machines, and at full pressure."

The engineer went off to carry out the order, the while Mr. Glencoe and the foreman hurried towards the pumps. Arrived there a cry of horror broke from their lips; the level was at one hundred and seventy-five yards; twenty-five yards higher than the floor of the tunnel at its lowest point.

JAMES HARWARD HAD NO NEED to telephone in order to follow the march of events; his fears had been realized. Under the weight of the train fissures had been produced in the tunnel, and through the unstable ground enclosing it the sea was now inexorably making its way—in little trickles at first—but every moment the volume increased and the danger grew. First the draining-gallery was swamped, then the water crept up to the rails; and now the sea-water connected the third rail with the other two and a short circuit was the result; the current supplied from the generating-station to the third rail came back to the works through the sea-water, without coming into contact with the now silent motors of the train.

The water was rising now at a terrifying rate. There was no time for the passengers to save themselves on foot.

Fortunately Harward did not lose his head. He had been nervous and fidgety under the apprehension of a possible accident, but now that a tangible catastrophe had to be faced he was calm, cool, and collected. To save the train and restore the current, the short circuit had to be rectified; the only way to obtain this result was by isolating the submerged portion of the rails from the rest of the line. Just before the train had come to a standstill they had passed one of the section isolating-switches; he must go back to it and by breaking the contact cut off the current's escape to the water, and thus re-establish the normal circuit with the motors of the train.

The engineer jumped on to the line, and immediately the frightened passengers began to imitate him.

"Keep your seats! Keep your seats!" Harward cried.

But as the guests, huddled together in the uncertain light, seemed little inclined to listen to him he had to stop and parley with them, wasting precious moments—moments that seemed to him centuries, knowing as he did that down there in the dip of the line the sea continued its resistless invasion.

"There is not the slightest danger," he told them in a firm, pleasant voice. "No danger at all. We shall be off again in a minute or two. Get back to the carriages, please."

In the shadows a figure glided to his side. Harward quivered from head to foot as he felt rather than saw that it was Blanche Glencoe.

"Tell me the truth," she whispered, in a gentle voice. "For my mother's sake," she added, lifting clasped hands imploringly to Harward.

"Tell Mrs. Glencoe there is no danger," said the engineer, firmly. "And remember, stay in the saloon, whatever happens; your safety may depend on it," he added, almost in a whisper.

The girl lifted her eyes to his, and for a long second they seemed to look deep into each other's souls. Deeply moved, the man bent his head and with a gesture urged her to reenter the train; and Miss Glencoe, lightly resting her fingers on his arm, mounted the step. This slight contact with the woman he loved unmanned him more than the terrifying emergency he had to contend with.

The fears of the passengers had been calmed and they went quietly back into the saloons and shut the doors, all of them quite unaware of their terrible danger, and quite satisfied with the engineer's assurances that all was well. Now they made jokes at the expense of the company. All fear of a panic was over, and Harward was at last free to race back into the blackness of the tunnel to the isolating-switch, which he knew was a hundred yards or so in the rear.

The farther he got from the train the more clearly came to his ears a humming sound, hollow and indistinct. By the time he reached the isolating-switch the humming had become a roar—deep, rumbling, menacing. The engineer understood; it was the roar of the sea, still a long way off, but advancing steadily, always advancing to claim its prey. And now an acrid smell, still almost imperceptible, tainted the heavy atmosphere of the tunnel; it made Harward cough. What could it be? A stronger whiff dissipated his doubt. It was the unmistakable odor of chlorine! But then—how? Yes! That was it of course; the electric current running through the sea-water decomposed it and chlorine was thus liberated, and this terrible asphyxiating gas was diffusing itself through the tunnel.

Feverishly Harward manipulated the apparatus. Immediately the lights reappeared on the train; the current, now cut off from the sea, was restored. Running as fast as he could the engineer regained the train, and in a moment they were going full-speed ahead.

Was this salvation? Earnestly James hoped so. Behind the train the sea was steadily creeping up; before long the section on which the train was running, would be immersed, there would be another short circuit, the sea would again absorb the current. "We must manage to get off this section and then isolate it before the fatal moment when the sea reaches it," thought Harward. But the next isolating-switch was at the sixteenth mile, over three miles distant, and the sea even now was gaining, gaining, gaining! It was almost on them. They could never do it! Even at full speed they could never do it! And there was nothing to be done nothing! The motor-man had the lever in the last notch; the speed now depended on the power-house above. Ah, perhaps there was a ray of hope there! Harward unhooked the receiver.

"Yes, we are running. We managed to cutoff the damaged section, but we are not making enough speed. Can you raise the voltage? Yes, every ounce of power you can manage. If the sea reaches us we're done for. That's it. Not a moment to lose. What's that? No, the passengers don't guess anything's wrong. For a moment, yes, there was the beginning of a panic. I was able to reassure them. Halloa! Mr. Glencoe is there, you say? Yes? Well, tell him that Mrs. Glencoe and his daughter are on the train. Good-bye."

Harward hung up the receiver. Almost at once the lamps burned more brilliantly, the humming of the motors increased; the works were sending more power. The train, like a sentient thing, seemed to make a last effort to escape its implacable pursuer, hurling itself forward on its mad race to safety.

Overjoyed, Harward noted the flight of the miles—thirteen, fourteen, fifteen; a few more moments and the menaced section would be left behind; a few more revolutions of the wheels—

Then his blood seemed to freeze and a cold sweat broke out on his forehead. The lights were going down!

For the second time the lamps went out and the train was plunged in darkness. For a second time the motors were silenced.

One glimmer of hope remained to James and the mechanician; perhaps their own momentum would carry them off this cursed section. Very slowly they glided towards the sixteenth mile-mark, and then the two men had to renounce this last hope. The wheels, with a grinding noise, ceased to revolve. Again the sea had vanquished the man, again the train was in dire peril.

What was to be done? There were no means here of isolating the rail behind the train; the tremendous current which the power-house was supplying flowed into the treacherous water, while the train, immobile for want of that wasted current, seemed to wait the coming of the sea—the coming of death.

Dismayed, the engineer and the motor-man looked at each other help-lessly. A sudden clamor roused them from their speechless contemplation of the calamity. The passengers, now thoroughly alarmed were demanding explanations. Some of them, wild with fear, wanted to escape along the tunnel on foot.

"It is four miles from here to the tunnel-end," said the engineer.

"Well; what of it? That's only a short walk. One can easily do that."

"You won't have time to do it," replied Harward.

"What do you mean? Not time? What threatens us?"

"Is it fire?" Cried one.

"Is the roof giving way?" Gasped another.

"What is it? What's the danger? What do you fear? Tell us! Speak—speak!"

Harward remained silent. Rage at his impotence was shaking him as with an ague. The circle of faces closed in on him, pressing closer. The carriages were almost emptied; panic-stricken, the passengers crowded on to the line. Their cries filled the tunnel, echoing and re-echoing strangely along the dark roof.

"Will you say what the danger is?" Some one shouted.

"The sea," Harward said, grimly, at last.

"The sea!"

For a moment silence fell on the crowd. Then the frightened questions recommenced, and the engineer explained the situation to them. The guests grew pale. Harward, himself pallid from the strain, clenched his fists in an agonized effort to think out a way of escape. There was none! None! There was absolutely nothing to be done. Must they die here like rats in a sewer? Alas! What miracle could give power to the motors lying there inert?

Then suddenly the too-well-known odor floated again to his nostrils. Denser, thicker than at the first stop, the fumes of chlorine swept up, poisoning the air, tickling the throats of the victims it would soon suffocate. The cup of horror was full and running over.

Instinctively obeying James Harward's order, the terrified passengers returned to the carriages and the doors and windows were tightly shut. Alas! Was it not merely putting off the final catastrophe?

At this moment Blanche Glencoe touched Harward's arm.

"Mr. Harward," she murmured, in a low, firm voice, "is there no chance for us? Is there no hope?"

Harward gently shook his head. He could not speak just then. The girl understood the hopelessness of the gesture.

"It is the end, then?" Went on the girl, as she drew nearer to him. "We must wait here for death." And, as the man still made no reply, Blanche tenderly took his hands in hers. "James," she whispered, creeping still closer to him, "I can tell you, as we are going to die. James, I have always loved you."

Harward bent his head. Blushingly the girl leant her forehead against his shoulder.

"I love you, James. It is a consolation that we can at least die together."

The sense of inevitable doom had filled the engineer with rage and shame; rage with fate, shame at his own impotence. Now the girl's words added revolt to his other feelings.

"No!" He cried, with kindling eyes. "No, you shall not die, my darling. I have an idea. We'll get out of this yet." And almost roughly he hurried the girl into the last car.

Springing into the observation-car, he bent over the tool-box and drew out a heavy hammer; then, running like one possessed, he disappeared down the line, and was swallowed up in the darkness of that suffocating atmosphere.

The third rail ran along the line at the side. By the light of a torch the engineer searched out a joint between two lengths of rail; having found one, he placed his torch on the ground. Then, though hardly able to breathe in the awful atmosphere, he raised the sledgehammer and dealt the joint a mighty blow. Panting for breath, again and again he swung the hammer in both hands, striking the rail with herculean strength; he was pitting himself against the elements for the girl he loved.

The joint resisted. Another mighty blow, and something gave way; a splinter flew; another—and the massive piece of steel was dislocated from its support. One more prodigious, superhuman effort, and a large rent appeared in the rail. But the electric current, thus rudely broken, flared into a roaring arc of flame whose crashing noise echoed terrifyingly down the gallery.

Confused and blinded, Harward fell back. Denser than ever the invading gas swept up, extinguishing the torch James Harward's body disappeared in unfathomable darkness.

Algeciras awaited the coming of the train. This was a great day for the town. The front of every house was decorated; on stately public buildings and humble private houses flags flew and rustled gaily in the wind. In the bay, gay awnings flaunted on slender yachts and spread themselves gaily over the decks of the more bulky steamers. A great crowd; all got up in their Sunday best, strolled leisurely about the streets. But the greatest interest centered round the magnificently-decorated Tunnel Station and the works and offices of the Gibraltar Tunnel Railway. Here the crowd was thickest; here it was excited and impatient. Within, the high officials of the company entertained the haute monde of the town. The crown of completion and success was to be placed on this immense undertaking; the first train from Africa, running through the Gibraltar Tunnel, was about to arrive!

At first the official bulletins of the train's progress created tremendous enthusiasm and kept the people amused. But now there had been no news for some time. The managing director had disappeared. The chief engineer of works, but lately so assiduous in his attentions to the ladies, was not to be found. Only the small fry of officialdom were left, and all they could say was that the train would arrive to time.

"No news is good news," said a youthful electrician, swaggeringly conscious of his brand-new cap of office, addressing a journalist.

"But why have they stopped telephoning?"

"They have nothing to say: I suppose."

"Lopez," interrupted the chief electrician, "get to the power-house quick!" The journalist's ears were pricked and he addressed himself to the chief. "Any fresh news, sir?" He asked; with an amiable air of innocent interest. "No—oh no—none," was the reply. "All the engines must be got to work, that's all."

He moved off.

"That's all!" Murmured the reporter. "I think this is worth looking into."

He went towards the power-house. No employees lounged about the door now. A glance inside discovered to the reporter an abnormal activity. Something was evidently wrong. In one corner the high officials of the company were discussing something excitedly. On tip-toe the reporter approached them.

"Train at a standstill—lost!—Level rising—unheard of!—Engines over-loaded—delay—catastrophe!"

The journalist withdrew and made for the telegraph office. On reading his message the telegraphist looked scared. A few moments later all Algeciras knew that the Gibraltar Tunnel Express was for ever entombed at the bottom of the tunnel!

Then a clamor broke out—the ferocious and yet lugubrious howling of a Southern crowd in face of death. They charged the works; the barriers went down, the gates flew into a thousand pieces. The crowd hurled itself against the walls of the power-house, excited, despairing, mad, wildly demanding details.

''News! News! Give us news!"

Mr. Glencoe, pale and anxious, appeared at a window. Silence fell—a deathly silence.

"The train has started again," he announced. "The delay was only momentary and of no grave importance. The train will be in the station in a quarter of an hour."

And now mad joy took the place of rage and despair; joyful cries, hurrahs, replaced the cries of woe. The surging crowd gave themselves up to wild exultation, mad rejoicing; they surged backwards and forwards, yelling, laughing, shrieking, even sobbing out their relief.

But all too soon apprehension returned, bruising hope and darkening the world. Sinister rumors spread among the people. Again arose the cry for news, news!

The managing director did not appear again.

A wave of despair surged over the crowd. The train had again come to a standstill in the bowels of the earth. Why?

"News! News! Give us news!"

The cry became insistent, menacing.

A man appeared and tried to make himself heard.

"The telephone is no longer working!"

The last link connecting the doomed train with the world above-ground was broken!

Then madness seized the people. Some wave of impulse turned them away from the now useless works and flung them in a headlong stampede towards the mouth of the tunnel. Gathered there they regarded the yawning aperture with haggard, resentful eyes, as if waiting for it to reveal the drama that was being enacted below, as if the despair of the living might succor the unfortunate victims of disaster.

At this moment the air in front of the tunnel became a little foggy and a slight smoke issued from the mouth, rolling slowly out on a level with the ground. Then the volume increased and grew thicker, and it was seen to be of a greenish hue. The first ranks of the crowd fell back, choking, on their fellows. Terror overwhelmed their bodies; agony of mind gripped their souls.

"Sulphur!" Whispered the people, with a shiver of superstition. "Sulphur!"

It was chlorine!

The shrill cries of women, the sobs of bereaved mothers, sounded for an instant above the hoarse clamor of the mob. And above the sun shone brilliantly from an unclouded vault of deepest, loveliest blue. A soft sea-breeze gently swayed the flags and flowers, the great steamers and graceful yachts swung peacefully at their moorings, while little boats skimmed lightly over the sparkling wavelets under the burden of their snowy sails, symbols of peace, of calm, and of prosperity.

In the works anxiety was extreme; the very air was tense with the strivings of men and machinery. Mr. Morton, the chief electrician, was engrossed in his dynamos, which were running at full pressure, overloaded in the endeavor to supply the torrents of electricity demanded by the train below. Apprehensions as to his precious plant diverted his mind somewhat from the possibly imminent catastrophe. The chief engineer of works, Mr. Harlow, in a fury of rage at his own impotence, stormed up and down, cursing the elements, the treacherous soil, and the invading sea, which he had thought to hold in leash.

Mr. Glencoe had completely broken down. It had become second nature to him to give orders and have them blindly obeyed, to impose his will on everyone, to insist that he knew best on every subject, technical as well as financial. All must bend before his will. A latent antagonism, a secret resentment, had divided him from his staff, and more especially from James Harward, who would not always admit the director-manager's omniscience. Now, in the hour of danger, Mr. Glencoe's authority seemed to fall from him; he had no suggestions to make, no orders to impose today.

Returned from the telegraph office, the prying reporter set himself to fathom the tragic problem, to find out the exact circumstances of the catastrophe. He prowled about, waiting on chance and scanning the faces of the officials.

At this moment the news was brought that the tunnel was vomiting forth torrents of chlorine.

"The current has electrified the sea-water," said the electrician: "Those poor people below will be asphyxiated."

"Hadn't we better stop the dynamos?" Put Mr. Harlow.

The managing director was silent. The journalist addressed him sharply.

"Are you going to do nothing? Are you not even going to attempt anything? Surely something—something can be done! Are you made of stone? Or don't you care? Think—think of those unfortunate people! Ah, it is easy to see you are not one of them!"

"My wife and daughter are in the doomed train," Mr. Glencoe replied, in a strangled voice.

The reporter bowed his head.

"Forgive me, sir," he said, after a moment, speaking now in a gentler voice. "But can nothing be done? Can't someone go down into the tunnel?"

"The shaft indicator shows the water to be less than four miles from the mouth," replied Mr. Morton. "It would take an hour and a half to walk it; and in a quarter of an hour all will be over. Besides, even if there was time, the chlorine would not allow of our reaching them."

"Is it the electricity that produces the chlorine?"

"Yes."

"Well, switch off the current."

"How is one to decide!" Burst out the managing director, in agonized tones. "If we don't switch out, every soul will be asphyxiated; if we do, we destroy the train's last chance of salvation."

A heavy silence fell upon the little knot of men. There was nothing to be done. The situation was beyond their control. Unable to bear the tension one by one they rose and silently left the power-house, making a melancholy little procession in the direction of the tunnel-mouth.

THE CHLORINE WAS NOW BELCHING out in huge greenish volumes, driving back the mob. Surely no one could exist down there in such an atmosphere!

"Suppose the passengers have left the train?" Said someone.

"Perhaps they may yet escape on foot," suggested the reporter.

"Do you believe that possible?" Asked the engineer.

"Anyway, I think the current ought to be switched out."

"Yes, cut the current! Stop the current!" Some voices in the crowd took up the cry.

"Switch it off! Switch it off!"

"Perhaps—yes," acquiesced the managing director. He turned to go towards the works. At this moment enormous waves of chlorine burst from the tunnel, as if driven out by some hidden force, and a dull, rumbling sound could be heard; louder, louder it grew, till the earth shook with its reverberating clamor, and at a hundred miles an hour the menaced train crashed out of the tunnel!

At that moment the current was switched off.

The train gradually lost its momentum and came to a standstill, revealing this dreadful spectacle. There, on the driving-seat; still gripping the lever back to the last notch, a dead man sat, his face horribly contorted in the last agony of asphyxiation. In death, and after death, the motor-man had done his duty!

Horror was written on every face. Was this, then, a train of death? Had everyone perished?

"Oh, heavens! How horrible!"

A low whimper of terror—then mad cries of joy! Men had leaped upon the footboard while the train was still running and now flung wide the doors. Inside the carriages, hermetically closed by James Harward's orders, the chlorine had failed to penetrate. The passengers were safe.

In the last carriage a man lay bleeding, his face blackened and tortured. It was the engineer whose heroic devotion had saved the train. The explosion caused by the shattering of the live rail had hurled him senseless on the line. But his men were fond of him, and one of them had run back and by the light of the flaming arc had found his chief's body. Nearly suffocated, he had just managed to hoist it into the last carriage when the train started.

Now Harward was stretched on a seat and by his side, sobbing, knelt Blanche Glencoe.

"It was for us," she murmured, in a broken voice— "for me—that he sacrificed himself, that he died."

A doctor approached and examined the engineer. With a sad gesture he replied to the girl's mute question. All was over.

With streaming eyes Blanche bent over the body of her lover and imprinted on his brow a long, long kiss—the kiss of betrothal—and adieu.

Oh, God! What was that?

Under the girl's passionate kiss a quiver seemed to run through the lifeless body. A tinge of color crept into the white cheeks! Harward seemed to make an effort to move; his lips trembled, his lids fluttered open! Then consciousness crept into his eyes, and with it a look of ineffable happiness. He tried to raise himself, smiled at Blanche, and fell back exhausted.

"He will live," said the doctor, after another and more careful examination. And Blanche, overcome by so many emotions, fell sobbing into her father's arms.

Some months later the London-Africa Express came out of the Gibraltar Tunnel at great speed, bearing on his honeymoon trip to South Africa the new managing director of the Gibraltar Tunnel Railway Company and his charming bride, Blanche Glencoe.

From Pole to Pole

GEORGE GRIFFITH

A TUNNEL from Europe to Africa may be a feat, but why stop there? Why not tunnel right through the Earth? In fact, you may not even need to do that. In the following story Professor Haffkin proposes that when the Earth cooled a hollow tube remained right through the Earth along the axis of rotation, making the Earth like a giant doughnut. Access to the tunnel is via the North or South Pole neither of which, at the time this story was written (1904) had been reached. This idea had been around for nearly a century. It was first proposed in 1818 by John Cleves Symmes (1779–1829), a retired Army captain, who even calculated its position and dimensions. He lobbied government to finance an expedition but was unsuccessful. He caused such a fuss that his ideas were lampooned in *Symzonia* (1820), credited to its narrator Adam Seaborn. This novel takes the adventurer into the Earth's interior where he finds another civilization. The idea caught hold and was incorporated by Edgar Allan Poe into *The Narrative of Arthur Gordon Pym of Nantucket* (1838) which was itself given a new lease of life by Jules Verne who wrote a sequel to the book, *The Sphinx of the Icefields* in 1897. The idea was thus prevalent in the 1890s and also appeared in William R. Bradshaw's *The Goddess of Atvatabar* (1892), a classic hollow-Earth romance.

The fascination of these stories wasn't just for the idea of a Hollow Earth. It was also the intrigue of polar exploration. There were many valiant and often tragic attempts to reach both poles throughout the "steampunk" period. News and speculation about polar expeditions filled papers and magazines. It was not until 1909 that Robert Peary claimed to have reached the North Pole, though Frederick Cook claimed he had reached there a year earlier. Roald Amundsen reached the South Pole in 1912.

George Griffith (1857–1906) was the first major regular British writer of science fiction and much of his work could be classified as proto-steampunk. He was particularly fascinated with flying machines and future wars, explored in *The Angel of the Revolution* (1893), *Olga Romanoff* (1894) and *The Outlaws of the Air* (1895) right through to his last books *The World Peril of 1910* (1907) and *The Lord of Labour* (1911). Like Ranger Gull, Griffith fell victim to the demon drink and died of cirrhosis of the liver in 1906, aged only 48. —**M.A.**

**ELL, PROFESSOR**, what is it? Something pretty important, I suppose, from the wording of your note. What is the latest achievement? Have you solved the problem of aerial navigation, or got a glimpse into the realms of the fourth dimension, or what?"

"No, not any of those as yet, my friend, but something that may be quite as wonderful of its sort," replied Professor Haffkin, putting his elbows down on the table and looking keenly across it under his shaggy, iron-grey eyebrows at the young man who was sitting on the opposite side pulling meditatively at a good cigar and sipping a whisky-and-soda.

"Well, if it is something really extraordinary and at the same time practicable—as you know, my ideas of the practicable are fairly wide—I'm there as far as the financial part goes. As regards the scientific end of the business, if you say 'Yes,' it is 'Yes.'"

Mr. Arthur Princeps had very good reasons for thus "going blind" on a project of which he knew nothing save that it probably meant a sort of scientific gamble to the tune of several thousands of pounds. He had had the good fortune to sit under the Professor when he was a student at, the Royal School of Mines, and being possessed of that rarest of all gifts, an intuitive imagination, he had seen vast possibilities through the meshes of the verbal network of the Professor's lectures.

Further, the kindly Fates had blessed him with a twofold dowry. He had a keen and insatiable thirst for that kind of knowledge which is satisfied only by the demonstration of hard facts. He was a student of physical science simply because he couldn't help it; and his grandfather had left him ground-rents in London, Birmingham, and Manchester, and coal and iron mines in half-a-dozen counties, which produced an almost preposterous income.

At the same time, he had inherited from his mother and his grand-mother that kind of intellect which enabled him to look upon all this wealth as merely a means to an end.

Later on, Professor Haffkin had been his examiner in Applied Mathe-matics at London University, and he had done such an astonishing paper that he had come to him after he had taken his D.Sc. degree and asked him in brief but pregnant words for the favour of his personal acquaintance. This had led to an intellectual intimacy which not only proved satisfactory from the social and scientific points of view, but also materialised on many profitable patents.

The Professor was a man rich in ideas, but comparatively poor in money.

Arthur Princeps had both ideas and money, and as a result of this conjunction of personalities the man of science had made thousands out of his inventions, while the scientific man of business had made tens of thousands by exploiting them; and that is how matters stood between them on this particular evening when they were dining *tete-a-tete* in the Professor's house in Russell Square.

When dinner was over, the Professor got up and said—

"Bring your cigar up into the study, Mr. Princeps. I want a pipe, and I can talk more comfortably there than here. Besides, I've something to show you."

"All right, Professor; but if you're going to have a pipe, I'll do the same. One can think better with a pipe than a cigar. It takes too much attention."

He tossed the half of his Muria into the grate and followed the Professor up to his sanctum, which was half study, half laboratory, and withal a very comfortable apartment. There was a bright wood-and-coal fire burning in the old-fashioned grate, and on either side of the hearth there was a nice, deep, cosy armchair.

"Now, Mr. Princeps," said the Professor, when they were seated, "I am going to ask you to believe something which I dare say you will think impossible."

"My dear sir, if you think it possible, that is quite enough for me," replied Princeps. "What is it?"

The Professor took a long pull at his pipe, and then, turning his head so that his eyes met his guest's, he replied—

"It's a journey through the centre of the earth."

Arthur Princeps bit the amber of his pipe clean through, sat bolt upright, caught the pipe in his hand, spat the pieces of amber into the fireplace, and said—

"I beg your pardon, Professor—through the centre of the earth? That's rather a large order, isn't it? I've just been reading an article in one of the scientific papers which goes to show that the centre of the earth—the kernel of the terrestrial nut, as it were—is a rigid, solid body harder and denser than anything we know on the surface."

"Quite so, quite so," replied the Professor. "I have read the article myself, and I admit that the reasoning is sound as far as it goes but I don't think it goes quite far enough—I mean far enough back. However, I think I can show you what I mean in a much shorter time than I can tell you."

As he said this, he got up from his chair and went to a little cupboard in a big bureau which stood in a recess beside the fireplace. He took out a glass vessel about six inches in diameter and twelve in height, and placed it gently on a little table which stood between the easy-chairs.

Princeps glanced at it and saw that it was filled with a fluid which looked like water. Exactly half-way between the surface of the fluid and the bottom of the glass there was a spherical globule of a brownish-yellow colour, and about an inch in diameter. As the Professor set the glass on the table, the globule oscillated a little and then came to a rest. Princeps looked at it with a little lift of his eyelids, but said nothing. His host went back to the cupboard and took out a long, thin, steel needle with a little disc of thin white metal fixed about three inches from the end. He lowered it into the fluid in the glass and passed it through the middle of the globule, which broke as the disc passed into it, and then re-shaped itself again in perfectly spherical form about it.

The Professor looked up and said, just as though he were repeating a portion of one of his lectures—

"This is a globule of coloured oil. It floats in a mixture of alcohol and water which is of exactly the same specific gravity as its own. It thus repre-sents as nearly as possible the earth in its former molten condition, floating in space. The earth had then, as now, a rotary action on its own axis. This needle represents that axis. I give it a rotary motion, and you will see here what happened millions of years ago to the infant planet Terra."

As he said this, he began to twirl the needle swiftly but very steadily between the forefingers of his right and left hand. The globule flattened and spread out laterally until it became a ring, with the needle and the disc in the centre of it. Then the twirling slowed down. The ring became a globule again, but it was flattened at either pole, and there was a clearly defined circular hole through it from pole to pole. The Professor deftly withdrew the needle and disc through the opening, and the globule continued to revolve round the hole through its centre.

"That is what I mean," he said. "Of course, I needn't go into detail with you. There is the earth as I believe it to be today, with certain exceptions which you will readily see.

"The exterior crust has cooled. Inside that there is probably a semi-fluid sphere, and inside that again, possibly, the rigid body, the core of the earth. But I don't believe that that hole has been filled, simply because it must have been there to begin with. Granted also that the pull of gravitation is towards the centre, still, if there is a void from Pole to Pole, as I hold there must be, as a natural consequence of the centrifugal force generated by the earth's revolution, the mass of the earth would pull equally in all directions away from that void."

"I think I see," said Princeps, upon whom the astounding possibilities of this simple demonstration had been slowly breaking. "I see. Granted a passage like that from Pole to Pole—call it a tunnel—a body falling into it at one end would be drawn towards the centre. It would pass it at a tremendous velocity and be carried towards the other end; but as the attraction of the mass of the earth would be equal on all sides of it, it would take a perfectly direct course—I mean, it wouldn't smash itself to bits against the sides of the tunnel.

"The only difficulty that I see is that, suppose that the body were dropped into the tunnel at the North Pole, it wouldn't quite reach the South Pole. It would stop and turn back, and so it would oscillate like a pendulum with an ever-decreasing swing—until it finally came to rest in the middle of the tunnel—or, in other words, the centre of the earth."

"Exactly," said the Professor. "But would it not be possible for means to be taken to propel the projectile beyond the attraction from the centre if those means were employed at the moment when the momentum of the body was being counteracted by the return pull towards the centre?"

"Perfectly feasible," said Princeps, "provided always that there were reasonable beings in the said projectile. Well, Professor, I think I understand you now. You believe that there is this tunnel, as we may call it, running through the earth from Pole to Pole, and you want to get to one of the Poles and make a journey through it.

"It's a gorgeous idea, I must confess. You've only got to tell me that you really think it possible, and I'm with you. If you like to undertake the details, you can draw on me up to a hundred thousand; and when you're ready, I'll go with you. Which Pole do you propose to start from?"

"The North Pole," said the Professor, quietly, as though he were uttering the merest commonplace, "although still undiscovered, is getting a little bit hackneyed. I propose that we shall start from the South Pole. It is very good of you to be so generous in the way of finances. Of course, you understand that you cannot hope for any monetary return, and it is also quite possible that we may both lose our lives."

"People who stick at small things never do great ones," replied Princeps. "As for the money, it doesn't matter. I have too much—more than anyone ought to have. Besides, we might find oceans of half-molten gold inside—who knows? Anyhow, when you're ready to start, I am."

II

NEARLY TWO MONTHS after this conversation had taken place, something else happened. The Professor's niece, the only blood-relation he had in the world, came back from Heidelburg with her degree of Doctor of Philosophy. She was "a daughter of the Gods, divinely tall and most divinely fair," as became one in whose veins ran both the Norse and the Anglo-Saxon blood. Certain former experiences had led Princeps to the opinion that she liked him exceedingly for himself, and disliked him almost as much for his money—a fact which somehow made the possession of millions seem very unprofitable in his eyes.

Brenda Haffkin happened to get back to London the day after everything had been arranged for the most amazing and seemingly impossible expedition that two human beings had ever decided to attempt.

The British Government and the Royal Geographical Society of London were sending out a couple of vessels—one a superannuated whaler, and the other a hopelessly obsolete cruiser, which had narrowly escaped experimental bombardment—to the frozen land of Antarctic. A splendid donation to the funds of the expedition had procured a passage in the cruiser for the adventurers and about ten tons of baggage, the ultimate use of which was little dreamt of by any other member of the expedition.

The great secret was broken to Brenda about a week before the starting of the expedition. Her uncle explained the theory of the project to her, and Arthur Princeps added the footnotes, as it were. Whatever she thought of it, she betrayed no sign either of belief or disbelief; but when the Professor had finished, she turned to Princeps and said very quietly, but with a most eloquent glow in those big, grey eyes into which he had often looked so longingly—

"And you are really going on this expedition, Mr. Princeps? You are going to run the risk of probable starvation and more than probable destruction; and, in addition to that, you must be spending a great deal of money to do it—you who have money enough to buy everything that the world can sell you?"

"What the world can sell, Miss Haffkin—or, in other words, what money can buy—has very little value beyond the necessaries of life. It is what money cannot buy, what the world has not got to sell, that is really precious. I suppose you know what I mean," he said, putting his hands into his pockets and turning to stare in an unmeaning way out of the window. "But I beg your pardon. I didn't mean to get back on to that old subject, I can assure you."

"And you really are going on this expedition?" She said, with a deliciously direct inconsequence which, in a beautiful Doctor of Philosophy, was quite irresistible.

"Of course I will. Why not? If we find that there really is a tunnel through the earth, and jump in at the South Pole and come out at the North, and take a series of electro-cinematograph photographs of the crust and core of the earth, we shall have done something that no one else has ever thought about. There ought to be some millions in it, too, besides the glory."

"And suppose you don't? Suppose this wonderful vessel of uncle's gets launched into this bottomless pit, and doesn't come out properly at the other end? Suppose your explosive just misses fire at the wrong moment, and when you've nearly reached the North Pole you go back again past the centre, and so on, and so on, until, perhaps, two or three centuries hence, your vessel comes to rest at the centre with a couple of skeletons inside it—what then?"

"We should take a medicine-chest with us, and I don't suppose we should wait for starvation."

"And so you seriously propose to stake your life and all your splendid prospects in the world on the bare chance of accomplishing an almost impossibly fantastic achievement?"

"That's about what it comes to, I suppose. I don't really see how a man in my position could spend his money and risk his life much better."

There was a little silence after this, and then Brenda said, in a somewhat altered voice—

"If you really are going, I should like to come, too."

"You could only do that, Miss Haffkin, on one condition."

"And that is—?"

"That you say 'Yes' now to a question you said 'No' to nine months ago. You can call it bribery or corruption, or whatever you like; but there it is. On the other hand, as I have quite made up my mind about this expedition, I might as well tell you that if I don't get back, you will hear of something to your advantage by calling on my lawyers."

"I would rather go and work in a shop than do that!" She said. "Still, if you'll let me come with you, I will."

"Then the 'No' is 'Yes'?" he said, taking a half turn towards her and catching hold of her hand.

"Yes," she said, looking him frankly in the eyes. "You see, I didn't think you were in earnest about these things before; but now I see you are, and that makes you very different, you know, although you have such a horrible lot of money. Of course, it was my fault all the time, but still—"

She was in his arms by this time, and the discussion speedily reached a perfectly satisfactory, if partially inarticulate, conclusion.

THE QUIET WEDDING by special licence at St. Martin's, Gower Street, and the voyage from Southampton to Victoria Land, were very much like other weddings and other voyages; but when the whaler *Australia* and His Majesty's cruiser *Beltona* dropped their anchors under the smoke-shadow of Mount Terror, the mysterious cases were opened, and the officers and crew began to have grave suspicions as to the sanity of their passengers.

The cases were brought up on deck with the aid of the derricks, and then they got unpacked. The ships were lying about a hundred yards off a frozen, sandy beach. Back of this rose a sheer wall of ice about eighteen hundred feet high. On this side lay all that was known of Antarctica. On the other was the Unknown.

The greater part of the luggage was very heavy. Many and wild were the guesses as to what the contents of these cases could possibly be used for at the uttermost ends of the earth.

The Handy Men only saw insanity—or, at least, a hopelessly impracticable kind of method—in the unloading of those strange-looking stores. There were little cylinders of a curiously light metal, with screw-taps on either end of them—about two thousand of them. There were also queer "fitments" which, when they were landed, somehow erected themselves into sledges with cog-wheels alongside them. There were also little balloons, filled out of the taps of the cylinders, which went up attached to big kites of the quadrangular or box form. When the wind was sufficiently strong, and blowing in the right direction towards the Southern Pole, a combination of these kites took up Professor Haffkin and Mr. Arthur Princeps, and then, after a good many protestations, Mrs. Princeps. She, happening to get to the highest elevation, came down and reported that she had seen what no other Northern-born human being had ever seen.

She had looked over the great Ice Wall of the South, and from the summit of it she had seen nothing but an illimitable plain of snow-prairies, here and there broken up by a few masses of ice mountains, but, so far as she could see, intersected by snow-valleys, smooth and hard frozen, stretching away beyond the limit of vision to the South.

"Nothing," she said, "could have been better arranged, even if we had done it ourselves; and there is one thing quite certain—granted that that hole through the earth really exists, there oughtn't to be any difficulty in getting to the edge of it. The wind seems always blowing in the same direction, and with the sledges and the auxiliary balloons we ought to simply race along. It's only a little over twelve hundred miles, isn't it?"

"About that," said the Professor, opening his eyes a little wider than usual. "And now that we have got our stores all landed, and, as far as we can provide, everything that can stand between us and destruction, we may as well say 'Goodbye' to our friends and world. If we ever get back again, it will be via the North Pole, after we have accomplished what the sceptics call the impossible.

"But, Brenda, dear, don't you think you had better go back?" Said her husband, laying his hands on her shoulders. "Why should you risk your life and all its possibilities in such an adventure as this?"

"If you risk it," she said, "I will. If you don't, I won't. You don't seem to have grasped the fact even yet that you and I are to all intents and purposes the same person. If you go, I go—through danger to death, or to glory such as human beings never won before. You asked me to choose, and that is what I have chosen. I will vanish with you into the Unknown, or I will come out with you at the North Pole in a blaze of glory that will make the Aurora Borealis itself look shabby. But whatever happens to you must happen to me as well, and the money in England must just take care of itself until we get back. That is all I have to say at present."

"And I wouldn't like to hear you say one syllable more. You've said just what I wanted you to say, just what I thought you would say, and that's about good enough for me. We go from South to North through the core of the earth, or stop and be smashed up somewhere midway or elsewhere, but we'll do it together. If the inevitable happens, I will kill you first and then myself. If we get through, you will be, in the eyes of all men, just what I think you are now, and—well, that's about enough said, isn't it?"

"Almost," she said, "except—"

And then, reading what was plainly written in her eyes, he caught her closer to him.

Their lips met and finished the sentence more meaningfully than any words could have done.

"I thought you'd say that," he said afterwards.

"I don't think you'd have asked me to marry you if you hadn't thought it," she said.

"No," he said. "I wouldn't. It seems a bit brutal to say so, but really I wouldn't."

"And if you hadn't asked like that," she said, once more looking him straight in the eyes, "I should have said 'No,' just as I did before."

She looked very tempting as she said this. He pulled her towards him; and as she turned her face up to his, he said, "Has it ever struck you that there is infinitely more delight to a man in kissing lips which have once said

'No' to him, and then 'Yes,' than those which have only said 'Yes'?"

"What a very mean advantage to take of an unprotected female."

A kiss ended the uncompleted sentence.

Then she began again—

"And when shall we start?"

"Seven tomorrow morning—that is to say, by our watches, not by the sun. Everything is on shore now, and we shouldn't make it later. I'm going to the Professor to help him up with the fixings, and I suppose you want to go into the tent and see after your domestic business. Good night for the present."

"Good night, dear, for the present."

And so was said the most momentous "Good night" that man and woman had ever said to each other since Adam kissed "Good night" to Eve in Eden.

IV

THE NEXT DAY—that is to say, a period of twelve hours later, measured according to the chronometers of the expedition (for the pale sun was only describing a little arc across the northern horizon, not to sink below it for another three months or so)—the members of the Pole to Pole Expedition said "Goodbye" to the companions with whom they had journeyed across the world.

There was a strong, steady breeze blowing directly from the northward. The great box-kites were sent up, six of them in all, and along the fine piano-wire cables which held them, the lighter portions of the stores were sent on carriers driven by smaller kites.

Princeps and Brenda had gone up first in the carrier-slings. The Professor remained on the beach with the bluejackets from the cruiser, who, with huge delight and no little mystification, were giving a helping hand in the strangest job that even British sailors had ever helped to put through. Their remarks to each other formed a commentary on the expedition as original as it was terse and to the point. It had, however, the disadvantage of being mostly unprintable.

It was twelve hours later when the Professor, having shaken hands all round, a process which came to between three and four hundred hand-shakes, took his seat in the sling of the last kite and went soaring up over the summit of the ice-wall. A hearty cheer from five hundred throats, and a rolling fire of blank cartridge from the cruiser, reverberated round the walls of everlasting ice which guarded the hitherto unpenetrated solitudes of Antarctica as the sling crossed the top of the wall, and a pull on the tilting-

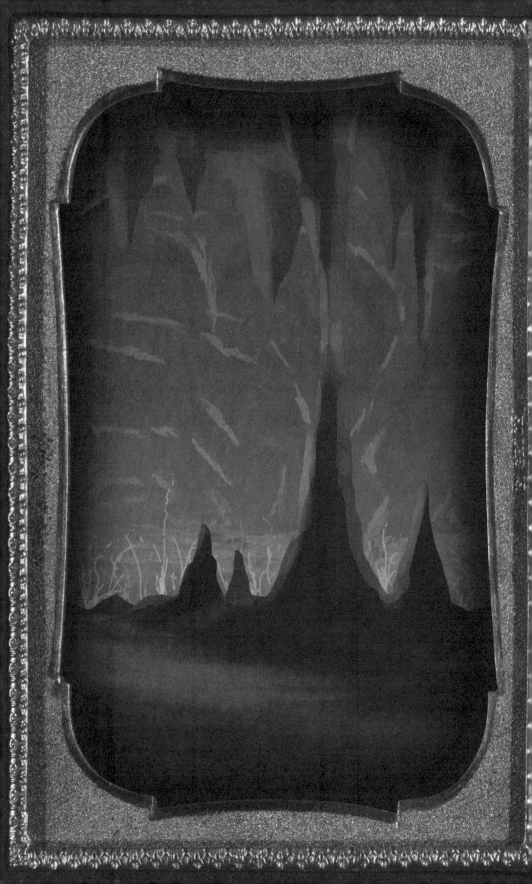

line bought the great kite slowly to the ground.

As the cable slackened, it was released from its moorings on the beach. A little engine, driven by liquid air, hauled it up on a drum. Three tiny figures appeared on the edge of the ice-cliff and waved their last adieus to the ships and the little crowd on the beach. Then they disappeared, and the last link between them and the rest of the world was cut, possibly—and, as every man of the Antarctic Expedition firmly believed, for ever.

The three members of the Pole to Pole Expedition bivouacked that night under a snow-knoll, and after a good twelve hours' sleep they set to work on the preparations for the last stage but one of their marvellous voyage. There were four sledges. One of these formed what might be called the baggage-wagon. It carried the gas-cylinders, the greater part of the provisions, and the vehicle which was to convey the three adventurers from the South Pole to the North through the centre of the earth, provided always that the Professor's theory as to the existence of the transterrestrial tunnel proved to be correct. It was packed in sections, to be put together when the edge of the great hole was reached.

The sledge could be driven by two means. As long as the north-to-south wind held good, it was dragged over the smooth, snow-covered ice and land, which stretched away in an illimitable plain as far as the eye could reach from the top of the ice-wall towards the horizon behind which lay the South Pole and, perhaps, the tunnel. It was also furnished with a liquid-air engine, which actuated four big, spiked wheels, two in front and two behind. These, when the wind failed, would grip the frozen snow or ice and drive the sledge-runners over it at a maximum speed of twenty miles an hour. The engine could, of course, be used in conjunction with the kites when the wind was light.

The other three sledges were smaller, but similar in construction and means of propulsion. Each had its drawing-kites and liquid-air engine. One carried a reserve of provisions, balloons, and basket-cars, with a dozen gas-cylinders. Another was loaded with the tents and cooking-apparatus, and the third carried the three passengers, with their immediate personal belongings, which, among other oddments, included a spiritheater and a pair of curling-tongs and hairwavers.

All the sledges were yoked together, the big one going first. Then came the passenger-car, and then the other two side by side. In case of accidents, there were contrivances which made it possible to cast any of the sledges loose at a moment's notice. The kites, if the wind got too high, could be emptied and brought down by means of tilting-lines.

There was a fine twenty-mile breeze blowing when the kites were sent up after breakfast. The yoked sledges were held by lines attached by pegs driven deeply into the frozen snow. The kites reached an altitude of about a thousand feet, and the sledges began to lift and strain at the mooring-lines as though they were living things. The Professor and Princeps cut all the lines but one before they took their places in the sledge beside Brenda. Then Princeps gave her a knife and said:

"Now start us."

She drew the keen edge backwards and forwards over the tautly stretched line. It parted with a springing jerk, and the next moment the wonderful caravan started forward with a jump which tilted them back into their seats.

The little snow-hills began to slip away behind them. The tracks left by the springrunners tailed swiftly away into the distance, converging as railway-lines seem to do when you look down a long stretch of them. The keen, cold air bit hard on their flesh and soon forced them to protect their faces with the sealskin masks which let down from their helmets; but just before Brenda let hers down, she took a long breath of the icy air and said—

"Ah! That's just like drinking iced champagne. Isn't this glorious?" Then she gasped, dropped her mask over her face, put one arm through her husband's and one through her uncle's, pulled them close to her, and from that moment she became all eyes, looking through the crystal plate in her mask at the strange, swiftly moving landscape and the great box-kites, high up in the air, dull white against the dim blue sky, which were dragging them so swiftly and so easily towards the Unknown and, perhaps, towards the impossible.

V

THE EXPEDITION had been travelling for little more than six days, and so far the journey had been quite uneventful. The pale sun had swung six times round its oblique course without any intervention of darkness to break the seemingly endless polar day. At first they had travelled seventeen hours without halting. None of them could think of sleep amidst such novel surroundings, but the next day they were content with twelve, and this was agreed on as a day's journey.

They soon found that either their good fortune had given them a marvellously easy route, or else that the Antarctic continent was strangely different from the Arctic. Hour after hour their sledges, resting on rubber springs, spun swiftly over the undulating fields of snow-covered ice with scarcely a jog or a jar—in fact, as Brenda said at the end of the journey, it was more like a twelve-hundred mile switchback ride than a polar expedition.

So they travelled and slept and ate. Eight hours for sleep, two hours

evening and morning for pitching and striking tents, supper and breakfast, and the stretching of limbs, and twelve hours' travel.

Lunch was eaten en route, because the lowering of the kites and the mooring of the sledges were a matter of considerable labour, and they naturally wanted to make the most of the wind while it lasted.

Every day, as the sun reached the highest point of its curved course along the horizon, the Professor took his latitude. Longitude, of course, there was practically none to take, since every day's travel took them so many hundred miles along the converging meridians, and east and west, with every mile they made, came nearer and nearer together.

On the seventh morning the kites were all lowered, taken to pieces, and packed up, with the exception of one which drew the big sledge.

They had calculated that they were now within about a hundred miles of the Pole—that is to say, the actual end of the earth's axis—and, according to the Professor's calculations (granted that the Pole to Pole tunnel existed) it would be about a hundred miles in diameter. At the same time, it might be a good deal more, and, therefore, it was not considered advisable to approach what would literally be the end of the earth at a speed of twenty miles an hour, driven by the strong, steady breeze which had remained with them from the top of the ice-wall. So the liquid-air engines were set to work, the spiked wheels bit into the hard-frozen snow, and the sledges, following the big one, and helped to a certain extent by its kite, began to move forward at about eight miles an hour.

The landscape did not alter materially as they approached the polar confines. On all sides was a vast plain of ice crossed in a generally southerly direction by long, broad snow-lanes. Here and there were low hills, mostly rounded domes of snow; but these were few and far between, and presented no obstacles to their progress.

A little before lunch-time the ground began to slope suddenly away to the southward to such an extent that the kite was hauled in, and the spiked wheels had to be used to check the increasing speed of the sledges. On either hand the slope extended in a perfectly uniform fashion, and after a descent of about an hour, they could see a vast curved ridge of snow stretching to right and to left behind them which shut out the almost level rays of the pale sun so that the semi-twilight in which they had been travelling was rapidly deepening into dusk.

What was it? Were they descending into a vast polar depression, to the shores of such an open sea as had often been imagined by geographers and explorers, or were they in truth descending towards the edge of the Arctic tunnel itself?

"I wonder which it is?" Said Brenda, sipping her midday coffee. "Don't you think we'd better stop soon and do a little snowshoeing? I, for one, should object to beginning the journey by falling over the edge. Ugh! Fancy a fall of seven thousand miles into nowhere! And then falling back again another seven thousand miles, and so for ever and ever, until your flesh crumbled off your bones and at last your skeleton came to a standstill exactly at the centre of the earth!"

"Not at all a pleasant prospect, I admit, my dear Brenda," said the Professor; "but, after all, I don't think you would be hurt much. You see, you would be dead in a very few seconds, and then think of the glory of having the whole world for your tomb."

"I don't like the idea," she replied. "A commonplace crematorium and a crystal urn afterwards will satisfy me completely. But don't you think we'd better stop and explore?"

"I certainly think Brenda's right," said Princeps. "If the tunnel is there, and the big sledge dragged us over into it—well, we needn't talk about that. I think we'd better do a little exploring, as she says."

The sledges were stopped, and the tilting-line of the great kite pulled so as to empty it of wind. It came gently to the earth, and then, rather to their surprise, disappeared completely.

"By Jove!" Said Princeps. "I shouldn't be surprised if the tunnel is there, and the kite has fallen in. Brenda, I think it's just as well you spoke when you did. Fancy tobogganing into a hole like that at ten or fifteen miles an hour!"

"If that is the case," said the Professor, quietly ignoring the hideous suggestion, "the Axial Tunnel must be rather larger than I expected. I did not expect to arrive at the edge till late this afternoon."

When the sledges were stopped, they put on their snowshoes and followed the line of the kite-cable for about a mile and a half until they came to the edge of what appeared to be an ice-cliff. The cable hung over this, hanging down into a dusk which quickly deepened into utter darkness. They hauled upon it and found that there were only a few yards over the cliff, and presently they landed the great kite.

"I wonder if it really is the tunnel?" Said Brenda, taking a step forward.

"Whatever it is, it's too deep for you to fall into with any comfort," said her husband, dragging her back almost roughly.

Almost at the same moment a mass of ice and snow on which they had been standing a few minutes before, hauling up the cable of the kite, broke away and disappeared into the void. They listened with all their ears, but no sound came back. The huge block had vanished in silence into nothingness, into a void which apparently had no bottom; for even if it had fallen a thousand feet, an echo would have come back to them up the wall.

"It is the tunnel," said Brenda, after a few moments' silence, during which they looked at each other with something like awe in their eyes. "Thank you, Arthur, I don't think I should have liked to have gone down, too. But, uncle," she went on, "if this is the tunnel, and that thing has gone on before us, won't it stop and come back when it gets near the North Pole? Suppose we were to meet it after we have passed the centre. A collision just there wouldn't be very pleasant, would it?"

"My dear Brenda," he replied, "there is really no fear of anything of that sort. You see, there is atmosphere in the tunnel, and long before it reached the centre, friction will have melted the ice and dissipated the water into vapour."

"Of course. How silly of me not to have thought of that before! I suppose a piece of iron thrown over there would be melted to vapour, just as the meteorites are. Well now, If we've found the tunnel, hadn't we better go back and get ready to go through it?"

"We shall have to wait for the moon, I suppose," said Princeps, as they turned away towards the sledges.

"Yes," said the Professor. "We shall have plenty of moonlight to work by in about fifty-six hours. Meanwhile we can take a rest and do as Brenda says."

It was just fifty hours later when the moon, almost at the full, rose over the eastern edge of the snow-wall, casting a flood of white light over the dim, ghostly land of the World's End. As it rose higher and higher, they saw that the sloping plain ended in a vast semicircle of cliff, beyond which there was nothing. They went down towards it and looked beyond and across, but the curving ice-walls reached away on either hand until they were lost in the distance. They were standing literally on the end of the earth. No sound of water or of volcanic action came up out of the void. They brought down a couple of rockets and fired them from the edge at a downward angle of sixty degrees. The trail of sparks spread out with inconceivable rapidity, and then, when the rockets burst, two tiny blue stars shone out, apparently as far below them as the stars of heaven were above them.

"I don't think there's very much doubt about that," said the Professor. "We have found the Axial Tunnel: but, after all, if it is only a very deep depression, our balloons can take us out of it after we have touched the bottom. Still, personally, I believe it to be the tunnel."

"Oh, it must be!" Said Brenda decisively. And so, in fact, it proved to be.

As the moon grew rounder and brighter, the work of preparation for the last stage of their amazing enterprise grew apace. Everything had, of course, been thought out to the minutest detail, and the transformation which came over their impedimenta was little short of magical.

The sledges dissolved into their component parts, and these came together again in the form of a big, conical, drum-like structure, with walls of thick *papier mache*. It had four long plate-glass windows in the sides and a large round one top and bottom. It was ten feet in diameter and fifteen in height. The interior was plainly but snugly fitted up as a sitting-room by day and, by means of a movable partition, a couple of sleeping berths by night.

The food and water were stowed away in cupboards and tanks underneath the seats, and the gas-cylinders, rockets, etc., were packed under the flooring, which had a round trap-door in the centre over the window.

The liquid air-engines and the driving apparatus of the sledges were strongly secured to the lower end with chains which, in case of emergency, could be easily released by means of slip-hooks operated from inside. There were also two hundred pounds of shot ballast underneath the flooring.

Attached to the upper part of the structure were four balloons, capable at their full capacity of easily lifting it with its whole load on board. These were connected by tubes with the interior, and thus, by means of pumps worked by a small liquid-air engine, the gas from the cylinders could either be driven up into them or drawn down and re-stored. In the centre of the roof was another cable, longer than those which held the balloons, and to this was attached a large parachute which could be opened or shut at will from inside.

VI

WHEN THE MOMENT chosen for departure came, there remained no possible doubt as to the correctness of the Professor's hypothesis. The sun was dipping below the horizon and the long polar night was beginning. The full moon shone down from the zenith through a cloudless, mistless atmosphere. The sloping snow-field and the curved edge of the Axial Tunnel were brilliantly illuminated. They could see for miles along the ice-cliffs, far enough to make certain that they were part of a circle so vast that anything like an exact calculation of its circumference was impossible.

The breeze was still straight to the southward, to the centre of the tunnel. The balloons were inflated until the *Brenda*—as the strange vehicle had been named by a majority of two to one—began to pull at the ropes which held her down. Then, with a last look round at the inhospitable land they were leaving—perchance never to see land of any sort again—they went in through the curved sliding door to windward. Princeps started the engine, the balloons began to fill out, and three of the four mooring-ropes were cast off as the *Brenda* began to rock and swing like the car of a captive balloon.

"Once more," said Princeps, giving his wife the knife with which she had cut the sledges loose.

"And this time for good—or the North Pole—or—well, at any rate, this is the stroke of Fate."

She gave her left hand to her husband, knelt down on the threshold of the door, and made a sideward slash at the slender rope which was fastened just under it. The strands ripped and parted, the *Brenda* rocked twice or thrice and became motionless. The ice-cliffs slipped away from under them, the vast, unfathomed, and fathomless gulf spread out beneath them, and the voyage, either from Pole to Pole or from Time to Eternity, had begun.

The Professor, who was naturally in command, allowed the *Brenda* to drift for two-and-a-half hours at a carefully calculated wind-speed of twenty miles an hour. Then he said to Princeps, "You can deflate the balloons now, I think. We must be near the centre. I will see to the parachute."

They had been thinking and talking of this journey, with all its apparent impossibilities and terrific risks, until they had become almost common-place to them. But for all that, they looked at each other as they had never done before, as the Professor gave the fateful order. Even his lips tightened and his brows came together a little as he turned to cast loose the fine wire cables which held the ribs of the parachute.

The powerful little engine got to work, and the gas from the balloons hissed back into the cylinders. Then the envelopes were hauled in and stowed away. Through the side windows, Brenda saw a dim, far-away horizon rise up all round, and through the top window and the circular hole in the parachute, she saw the full disc of the moon growing smaller and smaller, and so she knew that they had begun their fall of 41,708,711 feet.

Taking this at 7,000 miles, in round numbers, the Professor, reckoning on an average speed of fifty to sixty miles an hour, expected to make the passage from Pole to Pole in about six days, granted always that the tunnel was clear all through. If it wasn't, their fates were on the knees of the Gods, and there was nothing more to say. As events proved, they made it in a good deal less.

For the first thirty-six hours everything went with perfect smoothness. The wind-gauges at each side showed a speed of fifty-one miles an hour, and the *Brenda* continued her fall with perfect steadiness.

Suddenly, just as they were about to say "Good night" for the second time, they heard a sharp snapping and rending sound break through the smooth swish of the air past the outer wall of their vehicle. The next instant it rocked violently from side to side, and the indicators of the gauges began to fly round into invisibility.

"Heavens, uncle! What has happened?" Gasped Brenda, clinging to the seat into which she had been slung.

"It can only be one thing," replied the Professor, steadying himself against the opposite wall. "Some of the stays have given way, and the parachute has split or broken up. God forgive me! Why did I not think of that before?"

"Of what?" Said Princeps, dropping into the seat beside Brenda and putting his arm round her.

"The increasing pull of gravitation as we get nearer to the earth's centre. I calculated for a uniform pull only. They must have been bearing a tremendous strain before they parted."

While he was speaking, the vehicle had become steady again. The wind-gauges whirled till the spindles screeched and smoked in their sockets. The rush of the wind past the outside wall deepened to a roar and then rose to a shrill, whistling scream.

Long, uncounted minutes of sheer speechless, thoughtless terror passed. The inside air grew hot and stifling. Even the uninflammable walls began to crinkle and crack under the fearful heat developed by the friction of the rushing air.

Brenda gasped two or three times for breath, and then, slipping out of her husband's arms, fell fainting in a heap on the floor. Mechanically both he and the Professor stooped to lift her up. To their amazement, the effort they made to do so threw her unconscious form nearly to the top of the conical roof. She floated in mid-air for a moment and then sank gently back into their arms.

"The centre of the Earth!" Gasped the Professor. "The point of equal attraction! If we can breathe for the next hour, we have a chance. Quick, Arthur, give us more air! The evaporation will reduce the temperature."

Even in such an awful moment as this, Professor Haffkin could not quite forget his scientific phraseology.

He laid Brenda, still weighing only a few pounds, on one of the seats and went to the liqueur-case for some brandy. Princeps mean while turned the tap of a spare cylinder lying beside the air-engine which drove the little electric-light installation. The sudden conversion of the liquid atmosphere into the gaseous form brought the temperature down with a rush, and—as they thought afterwards, with a shudder—probably prevented all the cylinders from exploding.

The brandy and the sudden coolness immediately revived Brenda, and after the two men had taken a stiff glass to steady their shaken-up nerves, they sat down and began to consider their position as calmly as might be.

They had passed the centre of the earth at an enormous but unknown velocity, and they were, therefore, endowed with a momentum which would certainly carry them far towards the northern end of the Axial Tunnel; but how far, it was impossible to say, since they did not know their speed.

But, however great the speed, it was diminishing every second, and a time must come when it would be nil—and then the backward fall would begin. If they could not prevent this, they might as well put an end to everything at once.

Hours passed; uncounted, but in hard thinking, mingled with dumb apprehension.

The rush of the wind outside began to slacken at last, and when Princeps at length managed to fit another wind-gauge in place of the one that had been smashed to atoms, it registered a little over two hundred miles an hour.

"Our only chance, as far as I can see," said the Professor at length, looking up from a writing-pad on which he had been making pages of calculations, "is this. We must watch that indicator; and when the speed drops, say, to ten miles an hour, we must inflate our balloons to the utmost, cut loose the engines and other gear, and trust to the gas to pull us out."

There was literally nothing else to be done, and so for the present they sat and watched the indicator, and, by the way of killing the weary hours, counted the possibilities and probabilities of their return to the civilised world should the *Brenda*'s balloons succeed in lifting her out of the northern end of the Axial Tunnel.

Hour by hour the speed dropped. The fatal pull, which, unless the balloons were able to counteract it, would drag them back with a hand resistless as that of Fate itself, had got them in its grip. Somewhere, an unknown number of miles above them, were the solitudes of the Northern Pole, from which they might not get away even if they reached them. Below was the awful gulf through which they had already passed, and to fall back into that meant a fate so terrible that Brenda had already made her husband promise to shoot her, should the balloons fail to do their work.

The Professor passed most of his time in elaborate calculations, the object of which was the ascertaining, as nearly as possible, their distance from the centre of the earth, and, therefore, the number of miles which they would have to rise to reach the outer air again. There were other calculations which had relation to the lifting power of the balloons, the weight of the car and its occupants, and the amount of gas at their disposal, not only for the ascent to the Pole, but also for their flight southward, if happily they found favourable winds to carry then back to the confines of civilisation. These he kept to himself. He had the best of reasons for doing so.

The hours went by, and the speed shown by the indicator dropped steadily. A hundred miles an hour had become fifty, fifty became forty, then thirty, twenty, ten.

"I think you can get your balloons out now, Arthur," said the Professor. "It's a very good thing we housed them in time, or they would have been torn to ribbons by this. If you'll cast them loose, I'll see to the gas apparatus. Meanwhile, Brenda, you may as well get dinner ready."

Within an hour the four balloons were cast loose through their portholes in the roof of the car and attached to their cables and supply pipes. Meanwhile the upward speed of the *Brenda* had dropped from ten to seven miles. The gas-cylinders were connected with the transmitters and apparatus which allowed the gas to return to a normal temperature before passing into the envelopes, and then the balloons began to fill.

For a few moments the indicator stopped and trembled as the cables tightened, then it went forward again. They saw that it was registering six and a half miles an hour. This rose to seven, eight, and nine. Presently it passed ten.

"We shall do it, after all," said Princeps. "You see, we're going faster every minute. I wonder what the reason of that check was?"

"Probably the increased atmospheric friction on the surface of the balloons," replied the Professor quietly, with his eyes fixed on the dial.

The indicator stopped again at ten, and then the little blue, steel hand, which to them was veritably the Hand of Fate, began to creep slowly backwards.

None of them spoke. They all knew what it meant. The upward pull of the balloons was not counteracting the downward pull exerted from the centre of the earth. In a few hours more they would come to a standstill, and then, when the two forces balanced, they would hang motionless in that awful gulf of everlasting night until the gas gave out, and then the backward plunge to perdition would begin.

"I don't like the look of that," said Princeps, keeping his voice as steady as he could. "Hadn't we better let the engines go?"

"I think we ought to throw away everything that we can do without," said Brenda, staring at the fateful dial with fixed, wide-open eyes. "What's the use of anything if we never get to the top of this horrible hole?"

"That's rather a disrespectful way in which to speak of the Axial Tunnel of the earth, Brenda," said the Professor, with the flicker of a smile. "But we won't get rid of the impedimenta just yet," he went on. "You see, as the mathematicians say, velocity is momentum multiplied into mass. Therefore, if we decrease our mass, we shall decrease our momentum. The engines and the other things are really helping us along now, though it doesn't seem so. When the indicator has nearly stopped, it will be time to cut the weight loose."

Then they had dinner, eaten with a mere pretence of appetite, assisted by a bottle of "Pol Roger '89." The speed continued to drop steadily during the night, though Princeps satisfied himself that the balloons were filled to the utmost limit consistent with safety, and at last, towards the middle of the conventional night, it hovered between one and zero.

"I think you may let the engines go now, Arthur," said the Professor, "It's quite evident that we're overweighted. Slip the hooks, and then go up and see if your balloons will stand any more."

He said this in a whisper, because Brenda, utterly worn out, had gone to lie down behind the partition.

The hooks were slipped, and the hand on the dial began to move again as the *Brenda*, released from about six hundred pounds' weight, began to ascend again. But the speed only rose to fifteen miles an hour, and that was eight miles short of the result the Professor had arrived at. The attractive force was evidently being exerted from the sides of the tunnel as well as from the centre of the earth. He looked at the dial and said to Princeps—

"I think you'd better go and lie down now. It's my watch on deck. We're doing nicely now. I want to run through my figures again."

"All right," said Princeps, yawning and shaking hands. "You'll call me in four hours, as usual, won't you?"

Professor Haffkin nodded and said: "Good night. I hope we shall be through our difficulties by the morning. Good night, Arthur."

He got out his papers again and once more went minutely through the maze of figures and formulae with which the sheets were covered. Then, when the sound of slow, deep breathing told him that Princeps was asleep, he opened the trap-door in the floor and counted the unexhausted cylinders of gas. When he had finished, he said to himself in a whisper—

"Barely enough to get them home, even with the best of luck; but still enough to prove that it is possible to make a journey through the centre of the earth from Pole to Pole. At least, that will be done and proved—and Karl Haffkin will live for ever."

There was the light of martyrdom in his eyes as he looked for the last time at the dial. Then he unscrewed the circular window from the bottom of the car, lowered himself through it, hung for a moment to the edge with his hands, and let go.

WHEN PRINCEPS AND BRENDA WOKE after several hours' sleep, they were astonished to find the windows of the car glowing with a strange, brilliant light—the light of the Northern Aurora. Princeps got out, saying: "Hurrah, Professor! We've got there! Daylight at last!"

But there was no Professor, and only the open trap-door and the window hanging on its hinges below told how an almost priceless life had been heroically sacrificed to make the way of life longer for two who had only just begun to tread it together through the golden gates of the Garden of Love.

But Karl Haffkin's martyrdom meant even more than this. Without it, the great experiment must have failed, and three lives would have been lost instead of one; and so he chose to die the lesser death so that his comrades on that marvellous voyage might live out their own lives to Nature's limit, and that he himself might live forever on the roll of honour which is emblazoned with the names of the noblest of all martyrs—those who have given their lives to prove that Truth is true.

In the Deep of Time

GEORGE PARSONS LATHROP

FROM THE CONQUEST of the North Pole to the conquest of space. Space travel has been a fundamental part of science fiction from the very earliest days, but it became particularly prominent in the public consciousness during the 1890s because of the close opposition of Mars. Attention had been drawn to Mars in 1877 when Giovanni Schiaparelli claimed to see canali, or channels. The idea that there may be life on Mars grasped the public imagination and this was encouraged by the American astronomer Percival Lowell. He wrote three books on the subject, *Mars* (1895), *Mars and Its Canals* (1906) and *Mars as the Abode of Life* (1908). Of course H. G. Wells had already taken the public imagination much further in *The War of the Worlds* (1898) which merged the public appetite for the future war novel with the idea of Earth being invaded by the technologically superior but morally merciless Martians.

The following story was written before *War of the Worlds* and, for that matter, before Wells's *When the Sleeper Wakes* (1899), with which it has much in common. It's not impossible that the story gave Wells some ideas because he may well have read it when it ran in the *English Illustrated Magazine* in 1897, to which Wells also contributed. The story includes such ideas as automated factories, synthetic fabrics, suspended animation and the classic science fiction concept of antigravity. George Parsons Lathrop credited Thomas Edison with providing the technical ideas for the story. Lathrop had interviewed Edison a few years earlier, writing "Talks with Edison" for *Harper's Magazine* (February 1890).

George Parsons Lathrop (1851–1898) was an American novelist, editor and scholar. He was also the son-in-law of Nathaniel Hawthorne, having married Hawthorne's daughter Rose in 1871. It was not an entirely happy marriage and they separated in 1895. That was just before this story was written and I wonder whether some of the narrator's romantic anguish may reflect Lathrop's own. Writers should be grateful to Lathrop as he founded the American Copyright League in 1883 which helped secure international copyright law. —**M.A.**

This story is the result of conversations with Thomas A. Edison, the substance of which he afterwards put into the form of notes written for my use. His suggestions as to inventions and changed mechanical, industrial, and social conditions in the future, here embodied, I understand to be simply hints as to what might possibly be accomplished. Mr. Edison assumes no further responsibility for them. For the story itself I alone am responsible. —GEORGE PARSONS LATHROP

BOOK I
"VIVIFICATED"

NEAR THE CLOSE of the nineteenth century the Society of Futurity was formed for scientific experiment on a colossal scale. There was a considerable number of associates, all of whom were bound to secrecy, and these supplied a large endowment fund. To make their obligations of reticence the more sure, the secrets of the society were not told to them, after all, but were preserved by a small head committee known as The Three.

The Three were to be perpetuated in each generation by successors appointed by the first Three. Of the original trio, the famous inventor Gladwin was one, and he found in Gerald Bemis, a young friend of his, a willing subject for a vital test—nothing less than the attempt to suspend his life for two or three centuries and return to consciousness and activity after that interval. It was an old idea, but it had never been carried out except in imagination and in impossible books. Gladwin, however, thought he had now solved the problem, and was anxious to try his solution.

Bemis was a stalwart, handsome fellow, full of life, with a gay smile ever ready to brighten his lips, and with short auburn curls a-dance on his broad, frank forehead. He was highly educated, and an enthusiast in matters of science. But what came still more to the point, he had suffered a reverse in love, and fancied that he could take no further personal interest in the present life. Suicide was alien to his temperament as well as to his strong natural and religious instincts and faith. But "vivification," as Gladwin's new process was called, would relieve him from conscious existence now, and also make him a pioneer of the human race in advancing into another generation beyond, while still retaining membership in his own generation.

"It is done," he exclaimed to Gladwin. "I agree to be vivificated!"

Yet, after the decision had been made, he underwent severe struggles. Now that he was to part from the world for so long a time, the living, moving, human creatures whom he saw upon the streets, in clubs and hotels, at receptions, at fashionable dinners, or at the theatres—so charged with intense interest in their daily affairs, ambitions, and ideas—appealed to him in a new way. "Stay with us!" They all seemed to be saying to him, though their lips moved not. "You are one of us! Don't go! Don't leave us! Take your share of human experience while you are here among us, and can be sure of it!"

The trial was hard indeed. But he persisted; although "Life prolonged without the old companionships," he admitted, "is little different from death."

When the appointed day came, and he went out to Gladwin's high-walled laboratory in a woody solitude near New York, to be sealed up for futurity, contemporaneous life began to dwindle in his view. The crowds he saw in passing, his acquaintance, friends, relatives—even Eva Pryor, whom he had loved so ardently but in vain—all shrank in their proportions until they seemed nothing more than the diminutive and automatic busy reflections of reality in the kinetoscope. With this changed and dreamy mood upon him, there came to him a feeling that he, also, had been reduced to pigmy size, in his own mental vision. Considering the extraordinary ordeal through which he was about to pass, such a sense of his own littleness and insignificance was restful and encouraging. Calmly, therefore, he lay down upon the couch prepared for him in a secret and well-guarded alcove of the laboratory, robed in a simple garment of linen, which was dressed, bleached, sterilized, and scrupulously clean.

Gladwin gave him chloroform until he became unconscious. Then a solution of the lately discovered compound, *Tetrethylcylonammon,* was injected under his skin. This gradually reduced his heart's action and his respiration to zero.

When, under its influence, all movement had ceased and his animation was entirely suspended, he was placed in a large glass cylinder twice the length of his body and lying in a horizontal position.

A powerful antiseptic, *Mortimicrobium*—Gladwin's discovery—was now injected into his veins. It was a liquid that destroyed all organisms not proper to the body or essential to life, and prevented decomposition. The cylinder of glass was then filled with highly antiseptized air—so that no germs could come to life within it—and, by a number of wind-urged gas flames, the end of the tube was fused, drawn to a point and hermetically sealed. Thereupon the whole cylinder, with Bemis reposing in it, was coated several times with collodion, which made a tough, transparent surface and would prevent the ingress of air if the glass happened to crack or break.

So enclosed, as though in a huge cocoon, Bemis was left in the alcove, which was kept heated night and day at an even temperature of ninety-eight degrees Fahrenheit.

There he lay in that fragile case for years, for generations, until three centuries were completed. All the millions of the earth died and disappeared, and new millions took their places. Tempests broke above him, calm weather shone upon his resting-place; the seasons rose, smiled, frowned, went their way amid the roar of winds or blur of snow, and dissolved one into another in unvarying succession; but Bemis never stirred within his chrysalis. Governments changed, wars thundered about him, the race progressed or retrograded. Still Bemis slept on, without breath or motion.

Would he ever awake? Would his soul go abroad again upon the earth conscious, in human form? That was for The Three in office now, at the end of the twenty-second century, to ascertain.

II
HOW THEY TALKED WITH THE PLANET MARS

THE THREE AT THIS TIME were Graemantle, Wraithe, and Stanifex— worthy successors of the first committee. The society had met with almost endless difficulties in conserving even a portion of the old laboratory and Bemis's glassy life-coffin through all the changes of the troubled centuries. But they had triumphed by means of their wealth, shrewdness, tact, and patience. Graemantle, who—owing to the advances made in the saving-up of vitality—had reached the age of one hundred and forty-two, and was regarded as being in the prime of life, was the senior; Wraithe kept the records of the past; and Stanifex was a twenty-second century Conservative, whose function it was to doubt and question everything. The task of awaking Bemis and again inducting him into activity fell to Graemantle, and was performed successfully, notwithstanding the skepticism of Stanifex and the adverse precedents of Wraithe.

But it so happened that at the hour appointed for the rousing of the vivificated man, most important news had come from the north-west, which admitted of no dallying. Communication had been reopened with Mars, and the result was expected to be of vital moment. Graemantle had only time to welcome Bemis to what was practically a new world before starting for Wisconsin.

"But Gladwin—where is he? Where is Eva Pryor?" Demanded Bemis, starting up and rubbing his eyes instinctively, although his sight was clear and he felt amazingly refreshed and awake.

"Gladwin died several lifetimes ago," said Wraithe. "As for Eva Pryor—"

"Come!" Broke in Graemantle. "There is no time to lose over recollections of your infancy. You had better go along with me. It will be a good way to get an idea at once of the new condition of the earth."

So, barely stopping to clothe him in soft silken garments, and to give him a draught of concentrated liquid food that seemed to make up instantly for the missing nourishment of centuries, he led him to an air-cutter. A short flight in this conveyance bore them over the woods from the retirement of the half-ruined laboratory to an electric railway, where they bounded as though by magic on to an electric train moving at a dizzy speed. The rest of the journey Bemis scarcely realized, beyond a sensation of being swept along as though with the whiz of a cyclonic wind. When this ceased they were in Wisconsin, and stepped off into a "walking balloon," which proceeded with long strides of its aluminum legs over a slant of a steep upland.

Here, in Wisconsin, is the Penokee Range of mountains, chiefly remarkable for its belt of iron ore, forty-three miles in length, unbroken and very magnetic. This deposit, averaging 300 feet in width, extends to an unknown, unfathomed depth. It was over the magnetic ridge that they were now stalking. As Graemantle explained: "It contains more iron than all the other deposits of the United States combined; but owing to the large admixture of silicon with the ore, it has never been utilized.

"It occurred to us that we might convert the whole Penokee iron deposit into a gigantic magnet by winding wire around it. The Society of Futurity wanted to talk with other planets; and to do this we must produce on earth magnetic disturbances of great and decided violence. We must produce them periodically too, so that by their force and their definite order of recurrence they would send a shock through vast distances, and compel the attention of dwellers on another sphere. Then they might respond with similar movements, which we could record on *our* magnetometers; and so we could start a conversation.

"Look at that cleft in the range, right under us," He added suddenly. "That's Penokee Gap; and there's our station, with an engine of five thousand horsepower. See those telegraph-poles?"

Bemis looked, and beheld poles stationed like dumb sentries along the mountainsides as far as the eye could reach, carrying a great number of copper wires. "There are five hundred turns of that wire," his new guardian went on; "and each turn is eighty-six miles in length. They encircle this whole mountain mass of iron, which is their core, and make it a colossal magnet, with which we do our planetary telegraphing."

Alighting at the station, they met Professor Glissman, who was in charge—a small, nervous man, with glittering eyes that made him look as though he wore a pair of sparkling spectacles, or would like to do so if his eyes had not been so bright and piercing without them. As he explained the great machine, he punctuated his remarks with a modest and amiable little cough, as though the bigness of the thing needed some apology. "Five thousand horse power may not seem much; but the engine drives this great dynamo here, which has an armature wheel eighty feet in diameter, and the armature consists of very fine iron wire, chemically pure and slightly oxidized, over which is wound copper wire, insulated by semi-vulcanized rubber. That surface is carried round at the rate of 28,000 feet a minute. The current lasts only a second or two, but it is sufficient to bring our 500 eighty-six mile copper wires up to blood-heat. Cast your eye, please"—here Glissman coughed with humility—"on the gigantic switch at your elbow. It is moved by an electrometer, which breaks and closes the current in six hundred places simultaneously, and produces a copper arc seventy feet long."

Then, with a fresh glitter of his peculiar eyes, he pointed out certain leather belts perforated on a definite plan, like a Jacquard loom-card. These belts governed the motor and current controller constantly, with short intervals for return signals. "The engines and dynamo." He said. "If worked continuously, couldn't give more than five thousand horsepower. But we do not take electricity from the machine more than one-hundredth of the time. Hence the enormous potential energy of the fly wheel if; capable of causing a current to be sent out which, during its brief period, is equal to one hundred and eighty thousand horsepower."

The experiments, Bemis was told, had been going on for some eighty-five years. After fifteen years the magnetometer record of the Penokee station suddenly showed—amid the ordinary irregular motions registered on it—a faint periodic motion similar to the waves it was sending into space. Immediately Glissman—who was then a mere child of thirty-one—reduced the period for sending waves from twenty hours to twelve; and thereupon the very same signals came back from the unknown source and were recorded on the magnetometer here.

Thus, by other variations, and by years of toil, an alphabet and a mutual language was worked out. "And at last," Graemantle informed the newcomer, with a glow of triumph, "from the position in space which our invisible correspondents told us they occupied, we learned that we were talking with the inhabitants of the planet Mars!"

At this instant Glissman's whole demeanor changed. "A message!" He shouted exultantly, and rushed toward the magnetometer.

The needle trembled and moved. Bemis heard a faint "Thud! Thud!" on the telegraphic instrument.

It was the voice of Mars talking to earth.

The messages that now began to come slowly from that planet were spelled or thumped out by a dot-and-dash system; but Bemis could not understand them until they were translated for him by Graemantle, since they were in a language unknown to him.

The first sentence ran: "Bronson not arrived. Must be lost."

Bronson, it appeared, was a daring aeronaut, who had made the attempt to fly to Mars in a newly invented "antigravitation machine," known as the Interstellar Express. He was now some ten or twelve hours overdue.

The reply from Penokee was: "Why do you think he is lost?"

Mars answered: "Local meteors frequent in the path of travel. Our telescopes think he collided. Great regret in Kuro."

("What's Kuro?" Bemis asked. "Their own name for their planet," Glissman replied.)

From Penokee: "Shall we send off another man?"

Answer from Mars: "Laughter in Kuro."

(Bemis remarked indignantly, but in an undervoice, as though the Mars people might hear him: "How can they laugh, immediately after Bronson's death in space?" But Graemantle reminded him: "Isn't that the way of the world? It seems to you shocking only because it comes from a distance, abruptly.")

Penokee: "Why laughter?"

Mars: "Because personal communication is so useless compared with that of the abstract intellect or spirit."

Penokee: "But we have told you so often that we want to see you, and bring back a representative of your planet."

Mars: "Well, if you insist—"

So much Graemantle had translated, when Glissman, who was listening to the rest, exclaimed, with a mild approach to a yell, and with eyes simply astounding in their resemblance to sunstroke spectacles: "Hurrah! They're going to send us a missionary from Mars!"

III
BEMIS'S NARRATIVE

IT WILL BE BEST TO CONTINUE this narrative in Gerald Bemis's own words—

This affair of the Mars telegraph and the proposed coming of a representative Kurol, or inhabitant of Mars, was sufficiently startling to make my advent into the twenty-second century, my resuscitation after three centuries of unconsciousness, a mere commonplace. The very strangeness and amazement of the first occurrence with which I thus came into contact made me feel, curiously enough, quite at home in this new period.

There was a slight reaction, however, so soon as I turned in to rest at the spacious but cozy inn attached to the magnetometer station of Penokee. Left to myself for a little, I found that an intense yearning overcame me for some visible token, some living link of connection with the remote past. It was all gone, was hopelessly dissolved into nothingness; of what use could it be to me any more, since I myself was still alive, in full possession of my faculties and with a vast present and future spread out before me? Yet, somehow, that vague, unreasonable longing rose up and enveloped me like a mist or fog, exhaled from some unfathomable gulf, through which I groped vainly for the touch of a familiar hand, or listened in despair for the tones of some human voice that I had known and held dear of old.

I listened. What was that? Close by the couch on which I had thrown myself a voice was sounding at that very moment. "Ah, Gerald, Gerald, I wish I had been kinder to you!"

I could hardly believe the truth; but it surely was the voice of Eva Pryor, echoing after death, through the emptiness of three hundred lost years, and greeting now my sense of hearing as vividly as ever.

"Eva!" I exclaimed, leaping up. But the illusion was soon broken. A phonograph stood by my couch; and the voice, I perceived, was nothing but an audible reminiscence. Still, how came the phonograph there? Who had planned this thing?

Just then Graemantle entered the room.

"So you are not asleep?" He said in a tone that meant more than the words.

"Would you like to see her?"

"Eva? Ah, Graemantle, think of it!" Said I. "To see her would be life!"

He smiled. "The old life, perhaps," he remarked; "not the new. Are you sure the two will agree? However, you shall be gratified."

"No shadows or make-believes!" I cautioned him. "No kinetoscope or vitascope. Give me the reality or nothing. But you cannot give it."

"Wait a moment," he interposed. "Be calm, and realize facts. You, Gerald Bemis, were not the only person vivificated at the end of the nineteenth century."

For a moment my vanity suffered a blow. The distinction on which I prided myself, for which I had risked so much, was snatched away from me. But there came swiftly a more gracious thought. "I see, I see! You saved Eva Pryor from death also—saved her for me. How good of the society! It was nobly thoughtful and sympathetic!"

"No," he answered gently. "Purely scientific. Our former committee did not want to risk everything on one specimen."

"So I was a specimen?" I inquired, almost wishing that I had never entered the glass cylinder.

"Eva Pryor," he went on, "was in such agony at your disappearance—for, of course, no one but the Society of Futurity knew what had become of you—that we were compelled to give her the secret under strict pledges and on condition that she, too, would be vivificated, with several other specimens, or candidates for futurity."

"Then she is alive?" I asked, my pulse bounding.

"She is here!" Graemantle declared, in a resonant voice.

Instantly the room was filled with a soft, diffused electric light from unseen sources; and my mentor disappeared as though he had been a shadow. All my senses and my nerves, my heart, my eyes, seemed to thrill and to be filled with the thought of Eva. It was as though I had been with her only an hour before, gazing into her mysterious grey eyes, admiring the soft, rosy, apricot bloom on her cheeks, and wilting into abject despair at the indifference of her disdainfully smiling lips. And, as this picture of her came before me in thought, there she stood—her actual self—in the doorway, gazing at me wistfully!

We rushed together. I don't know why; for our last conversation, thirty-six hundred months earlier, gave us no excuse for such an action. It was an instinctive rush, I suppose. I loved her, and she seemed to be possessed by a reflex supposition. We embraced, as the surviving members of our once young generation. But, alas! I realized at the critical instant, that for me it meant only this. My old love had gone with the old life and the nineteenth century.

On the other hand, there came upon me, with a tremendous shock, a perception of the fact that Eva, after this long interval, had developed towards me a genuine and ardent affection. Being a woman, she had the right to change her mind; but it had taken her three hundred years of suspended animation to do it; and, unfortunately, I at the same time had changed my mind, just the other way, which a man has no acknowledged right to do.

"Dear, dear Gerald," she sighed, sobbed, laughed, all in one. "Isn't it wonderful? We are united at last."

"Yes, dear friend—dear Eva," said I. She continued— "And I was so cruel, so heartless towards you."

"But that is all over now," I assured her. Then summoning my utmost fortitude, I added, "What does it matter what happened in that old century? We are in a new world. You offered to be a sister to me then. I promise to be a brother to you now—nothing more. So let us dismiss the bygones."

Strangely enough she did not appreciate either the tragedy of the situation or the comedy of it, or the sarcasm of destiny, or the pathos involved—if for two people so far removed from their former lives, who were feeling uncommonly well and rested and comfortable, there could be any such thing as pathos. She simply recoiled from me, and looked angry.

"Dear Eva," I persisted mildly, ignoring these symptoms, "I have done everything I can to satisfy you. When you rejected me, I put myself out of the way. Now that we have both reappeared, I efface myself as your lover. Let us go forward, hand in hand, as members of one family as children of the future, and common sense friends."

Fortunately, at this moment Graemantle came back. "Good friends," he said heartily, "I am delighted to have brought you together again!"

He had touched the right note. Eva's lips curved into a correct expression as of pleasure, and she began at once to play her part of friend and sister, to my role of brother, with great skill and grace.

"I don't know just how the Kurol or Mars missionary is coming," Graemantle went on, "but we shall receive word soon. I sent for my ward, Electra, and my young friend Hammerfleet to assist us in receiving him. They have arrived, and I want to present them to you both."

So saying he touched a lever by the wall; the entire side of the room swung open, and he ushered us into a spacious apartment the assembly-room of the inn where stood, beautifully draped in white with a single diamond of marvelous luster flashing from the rich dark hair above her forehead, a woman of the noblest stature and best proportioned form I had ever seen.

"This is Electra," said our guardian; and turning to her: "You know our friends already, by name and record."

She bowed graciously, and came forward with a smile so absolutely sincere that I could not recall having beheld the like of it before; and she took each of us by the hand in welcome. Then we discovered behind her a tall man, black bearded, almost forbidding in his gravity, but wonderfully handsome, and enveloped in the soft, pliable suit of silk, tinted with prismatic, delicate colors, that everyone, apparently, wore nowadays. "Hammerfleet," said Electra; and we were at once acquainted with him.

I learned afterwards that artificial silk was made in unlimited quantities by squirting nitrocellulose into a continuously worked vacuous space and then reducing it to cellulose by hot sulphydrate of ammonia and pressure, and had taken the place of cotton and woolen goods among the well-to-do.

At the moment, however, the only thought I could grasp was that Electra had impressed me deeply and tenderly. How could anyone help this with her? She was exquisite, serene, commanding, and absolutely without humbug.

It had been a surprise to me to find that I no longer loved Eva Pryor. It was not at all a surprise that I should be captivated by Electra. Charming though Eva was in her way, she had perhaps placed herself at a disadvantage by having insisted on keeping her nineteenth century costume. The angular slope and spread of her skirt, her unnatural wasp waist, the swollen sleeves, and the stiff, ungainly bulging of her corsage had a grotesque and even offensive effect. The extraordinary tangle, also, of artificial flowers, wings, and other rubbish that she carried on her head— for she still wore her hat—was as barbaric or savage as the head-dress, of some early Norse warrior or Red Indian chief.

To all this Electra presented a refreshing contrast of harmony, with grace and dignity and a style of dress modern, yet classic, womanly, yet suggesting the robes of a goddess.

I must have made my impulsive admiration for her very evident, for within a few minutes I was aware that Eva had grown sad and ill at ease, and that Hammerfleet was darting at me half-suppressed glances of anger and jealousy. "So the wind sits in that quarter," I meditated, "and he's in love with Electra!"

But the talk turned at once to the new anti-gravitation machine or Interstellar Express car. "There have been a number of them made," remarked Graemantle; and proceeded to show us one in the house. "A good while ago there was discovered in the Hudson's Bay country great masses of ore containing metal which yielded the spectroscopic line of Helium, a metal unknown before except as observed in the sun. Helium differed in some ways from all other metals, and we could make no use of it until one of our most brilliant scientific men—an African named Mwanga, for Africa is now largely civilized and enlightened—discovered that its molecules under certain treatment could be so arranged as to neutralize gravitation. He came near being carried into space himself while experimenting with a big piece of rearranged Helium that suddenly shot off through the air and was never seen again.

"However, we finally learned to regulate the thing. And now you see this car is furnished with a Helium screen, which, once put into the non-gravitating state, is adjusted and regulated by the voyager, who sits inside this small non-conducting chamber, well provided with stored oxygen for breathing. Of course, many experiments were made before Bronson's last attempt to reach Mars."

"But how," I asked, "can a traveler subsist in so small a space through such a long journey?"

"Oh, it isn't long," was his answer. "It takes about five hours to reach the limit of the earth's atmosphere. When that has been passed, the screen or shield is so adjusted that the car attains to a speed of one hundred thousand miles per second, there being no friction in vacuous spaces to retard its progress. Now, the whole distance to Mars being forty-eight million miles, it should take the stellar car, at the rate of one hundred thousand miles a second, only four hundred and eighty seconds to traverse it. Four hundred and eighty seconds are only eight minutes. But when the car reaches the atmosphere of Mars, the screen must be molecularly rearranged again, so as not to resist too greatly the attraction of that planet. The car must descend through the Mars atmosphere slowly, by ordinary flotation-shutter apparatus."

(The shutter apparatus for sailing in the air and propelling ships was, I found, one of the most useful inventions of the age; and I shall describe it later.)

"To pierce through the Mars atmosphere, then, involves a delay of three hours more, So we have; for earth's atmosphere, five hours; for Mars atmosphere, three hours; and the intermediate distance, eight minutes; that is, in all, eight hours and eight minutes."

"Whew!" I exclaimed in amazement.

Graemantle laughed indulgently.

"And at what rate do your electric trains move?"

"About a hundred and fifty miles an hour."

"Then it takes no longer to go to Mars by the stellar car than it takes to come from New York to Wisconsin?"

"No," said he; "why should it? Time is only an idea. You thought you knew that before; but now you begin to realize it."

"Still," I objected, "the journey to Mars has not yet actually been accomplished."

At this moment a small side door opened and Wraithe and Stanifex, who had just come to Penokee by the electric, and by walking balloon, entered. "Quite right," remarked Stanifex, the doubter, who had heard my last words.

"Wait and see," retorted Graemantle. "I still have confidence."

The floor now opened, and some tables ascended noiselessly through a trap door, delicately set out with pleasing viands, most of which were new to me. Animal food was not present, and the articles of diet laid before us were chiefly vegetable nitrogenous products made by the fixature of nitrogen. Thus we had vegetable steaks, partridges, and so on, which contained all the nutriment of beef and bird without their heaviness, and were exceedingly palatable. Among the liquids we had a new sort of milk somewhat resembling koumiss, but with a daintier taste and a delicious fragrance; also sparkling colored water and a compound called "Life-brew," which was as stimulating as wine, but more sustaining, and nonalcoholic. Alcoholic drinks, I learned, had gone out completely; not by law, but by common-sense, and were used only in medicine or for the punishment of criminals, in rare cases. There was nothing that malefactors dreaded more than a sentence to a month or two of rum, whisky, brandy, or even champagne diet.

I took no note of time, for my three-century sleep had made me almost proof against fatigue. Besides, I was told that the general system of living now, with the night made practically day by subdued and diffused electric "glow-worm" lighting, and with every known means in use of conserving energy and nerve force, had changed the old habit of sleeping and waking. People now rested frequently, nourished themselves scientifically, were able to be up and about at all hours of the night and day; and instead of working a long time at a stretch and then recuperating by exaggerated late night amusements or long periods of sleep, they intermingled brief times of work and play and slumber through the whole twenty-four hours.

Suddenly there came the rapid tinkling of an electric bell—soft and musical, as all sounds were, I noticed, in the new civilization; and Hammerfleet cried, "That's from the Mars telegraph."

We all hurried to the station, and there found this message: "Our missionary, Zorlin, started hours ago. Will be there with you immediately."

It seemed no time at all before there was a rush and a thud outside the station, and Glissman announced that these sounds meant the arrival of a stellar car on the receiving platform. He was right. As we threw open the door, two strange figures came staggering in. One was a sinewy, blonde fellow, limp and tired, as though he had passed through about thirty-five thunderstorms.

"Bronson?" Exclaimed my friends, astounded.

"Yes, I'm here," he affirmed. "And this is Zorlin."

He pointed to his companion, the strangest resemblance of a man I had ever seen; of giant form, and with a face of overpowering intelligence, but at this instant crouching to the floor on hands and knees, half helpless.

"Your atmosphere is so heavy," he said in fairly good English. "I can hardly bear it yet. But I will soon stand up." He shook his vast head of hair and beard; then heaved a mighty breath, struggled to rise, and sank into a chair. This was our missionary.

IV

THE NEW EARTH

WHEN THE TRAVELERS had been refreshed and revived we drew from Bronson an account of his interstellar adventures.

"As I came near Mars," he said, alternately twirling and biting the ends of his long and warlike yellow moustache, "I was aware of strange rubbings alongside the car, and occasional shocks as of hammer-blows. Satan, I suppose, is called 'the Old Boy,' because a boy is the personification of mischief, and second only to Eve in making trouble. My first idea was that the Old Boy was having fun with me, by throwing stones. A rapid survey through my peep-holes showed me I was so far right—I was caught in a meteor-storm. Fortunately, though, the meteors over there do not shoot so recklessly as those that come near earth. They move with a velocity in accord with that of Mars, so that they drop through its atmosphere 'as the gentle rain from heaven.' But they gave me a pretty hard time of it; steering clear of them; and there may have been some magnetic stress accompanying their flight that carried me out of the way. At any rate, it was a long time before I could make a landing. But, with my automatic drag-net lowered from the bottom of the car, I managed to catch two small meteors, which I used as a combined anchor and rudder, in conjunction with the adjusted Helium screen, and finally reached terra-*Martis* long after the observers there had given me up. Once safely aground on the planet, I found Zorlin all ready to embark; and we decided to come right back."

"But they had promised he would come without you," Stanifex interposed. "How could he ever have done that?"

"Ask him," Bronson suggested, pulling his moustache wide at both sides defiantly. "And can we talk English to him?"

"Does he understand?" Electra asked.

"He has the most rapid intelligence I ever met," answered Bronson. "I had to teach him most of the English language on the eight-hours home trip; and he took it all in like water, as fast as I could pour. That is what has fagged me out so." And the stellar aeronaut helped himself to a vegetable chicken-breast, and swallowed a draught of "life-brew" at a gulp.

By this time Zorlin had straightened himself up, and seemed to have grown perceptibly in height and breadth. He was conquering the atmosphere of earth; and after a single sip of sparkling tinted water, he spoke.

"I would have found a way to come," he said easily, yet with a strange accent; somewhat as though his words were snowflake crystals, cold at first but melting as they fell. "We had not thought it worth while; but you have made so much advance lately that it seemed best to help you. We Kurols move by will-power. It is said many of our people have come to you secretly before. We know a great deal about your life. But until just now it was against the law for our people to visit earth; it lowered them, and always did you harm, and caused wars among you, much against our will and desire. Even now, I fear my coming will make disturbance."

He was like a man, but endowed much above a man, and with something weird and incomprehensible about him.

"Will you not tell us something about Kuro?" Asked Graemantle serenely. He was the only one of our group who seemed anywhere near equal to Zorlin. "Or would you prefer to rest?"

"The first duty of a missionary," Zorlin made answer, "is to learn about the country or the world he comes to. After that he can tell things. Not now. I learned much of your speech from our star-talk, the rest from Bronson. But now let us wait."

We waited accordingly, for the hour was near dawn and streaks of morning were faintly hinting at day in the east through the windows, and even Glissman's spectacular eyes looked a trifle dim and weary.

When we rose some three hours later in the glory of a crisp and cool forenoon of autumn it was decided that we should begin a jaunt of observation through the country, back to New York. This was partly for Zorlin's benefit, but it suited me equally well, since I was almost as much a stranger as he. For convenience we took the walking balloon down the mountains, as this was the pleasantest conveyance over rough ground where there were no large air-ships handy.

This vehicle is a shallow car with small hollow sails of silk above it, containing just enough gas to keep it about thirty feet above ground, assisted by a small electric engine in the centre. From the bottom of the car two long rods or mechanical legs, made of aluminum—the lightest metal known—extended down to the ground, where they are reciprocated at regular intervals by an electrometer, which enables them to imitate the motion of walking, and carry the balloon along at the rate of some fifteen miles an hour. They are not meant for high speed, and can travel only, of course, on prepared routes, but are very convenient in certain places.

Air-cutters and the larger air-ships are employed for flying in any direction and with much greater velocity. They are on an entirely different plan from the flying machines which were announced but had not yet come into use when I was last alive. The present air-ships apply the principle shown, for example, in the rapid flutter of the bumblebee's wing. This is the "shutter" principle. The ship itself is built of latticed aluminum strengthened with a small amount of copper, and enclosed with transparent celluloid for protection against weather (celluloid now being generally used in place of glass). Through the centre of the floor are thrust four short aluminum tubes three feet in diameter with three feet of length below, and these are each filled with 2000 very thin celluloid shutters, so arranged that they can be thrown upward, presenting only their thin edges to the air, offering no resistance to it. The instant they are turned down flat they prevent the passage of air from below, and so compress it into great density. "The inertia of the air in the tubes, you see," Hammerfleet remarked, "makes it like a rigid column—more rigid than steel. This forces the car upward when it starts, and it ascends on the top of a continually heightening pillar of air that holds it up buoyantly and firmly. The 2000 shutters in each tube work between balanced springs, and reciprocate at the rate of 15,000 strokes a minute—that is, they open and shut 250 times every second."

The motor by which they worked was, I thought, very ingenious. It is a small electric engine of eleven horsepower, set between the tubes, and has an armature of the finest chemically pure iron wire, wound with silver and insulated with collodion reduced by chemical means to cellulose. The armature, by an automatic device, is balanced to suit all degrees of speed, and has a revolution of 15,000 per minute. The reciprocating parts are of aluminum; the bearings are compressed graphite, lubricated with a volatile oil kept viscous by solid carbonic acid held in a box on the bearings. The motor and mechanism weigh only one hundred and twenty pounds; and the electricity is generated by oxidizing gas-retort carbon infused soda, with oxide of copper as a reducer.

The idea of the ship is radically unlike former machines, which either depended on disturbing and churning up the air or relied on aeroplanes or the rush of air under an upward slant.

This latter and successful contrivance rests on the solid building up of a compressed air foundation beneath it, so that it cannot possibly fall. The direction is controlled in two or three ways; the usual one being by ordinary artificial silk sails, together with a large rudder of stretched silk for tacking and steering, as on the water. By using an aluminum screw, with an auxiliary engine, instead of the silk rudder, one is independent of the wind, and can raise the speed of the air-ship to between sixty and eighty miles an hour.

At the foot of the mountain we changed to one of these equipages, and, as we flew along, we saw many others scudding by in all quarters, far and near. The flotation sail—i.e., the hollow silk sail inflated with gas—I learned, had come into universal use for water-vessels as well, and had added immensely to the speed and excitement of yacht-racing. In fact, as we skirted the great lakes and passed over rivers and ponds, I had a chance to observe craft of all sorts and sizes with these sails, whizzing like arrows before the wind or leaning gracefully away from it and skimming the liquid surface as lightly as water-bugs, but much more beautiful and useful in their movements.

The shutter principle, also, Graemantle told me, had been adapted to steam-ships, or, rather, electric ocean liners and freighters; by using several hundred thin blades at the stern, in lieu of the old propeller, and also on the sides, which—by direct thrust when turned flat against the water—utilized the motion of the waves to condense air, and drove the vessel forward. Sun-engines, which derived electricity directly from sunlight, and another process that extracted it from coal in cloudy weather, supplied the motive power; and electrolysis along the sides of the ship reduced the skin friction of her passage through the deep.

Here and there Eva and I noticed, with curiosity—and Zorlin was with us in this—certain little air packets that were flying around—"all by their lonesome;" as Eva said—always north and south and east or west. They were too small for anyone but a pigmy to hide in, and, in fact, there was no one in them. They went automatically. Zorlin, at last, was unable to maintain his reserve any longer. "What are they?" He asked.

Hammerfleet came to the fore with: "Merely express and mail earners.

We have any quantity of them all over the country and the world. The magnetic lines generally keep them straight on their course; but if they are blown aside, a current is generated by their mechanism that puts them in line again. An automatic aneroid barometer, working a valve, keeps them at the right altitude."

"But where do they go to?" Asked Eva.

"Look now this minute, and you will see. Watch that one. You notice it is driving straight for that tall skeleton wooden tower yonder?"

"Yes."

We fixed our gaze upon the tower. The little express carrier drew near; and, as it touched the top of the tower, was clutched and held firm by an iron frame that caught its sails and stopped it. Then a man in the tower began to unpack the contents of the carrier, and sent them down by chute to an enclosed yard below.

"But I don't see why you need these things, with all your other facilities for transportation," I objected.

"They save an immense amount of bother and of surface traffic," said Hammerfleet, "besides doing away with hand labour. They are also very swift."

"I should think, though, they could easily be robbed by air-thieves."

"No. That almost never happens. There are too many people watching. A thief in the air is much easier to deal with than a thief on the ground. He has no obscure refuge; he is in full view. A limited number of police airboats can give all the protection we need for carriers. They patrol the routes, and carry grappling-hooks with which they can easily arrest any prowling thief-car."

I seemed to win the secret, eye-winking approval of Stanifex, the official skeptic, by asking somewhat peevishly—"What is the use of all this air traffic, anyhow?" I felt a desire to combat Hammerfleet on any subject that came up, because he was jealous of me, or I of him—I hardly knew which—regarding Electra. It also irritated me that he was so well informed as to the details of the twenty-second century, when I felt that I had just as good a right to be in it as he.

"Why, my boy," he replied, with a patronizing emphasis on the word "boy," "don't you see that it is an immense relief to the congestion of surface travel to have all these other means of conveyance? Civilization and the general occupancy of land have spread to such an extent that we must economize ground area. Formerly, human beings, in their degraded desperation, actually burrowed underground like moles, to get from one point to another. *We* rise into the pure air instead. Land, and the right in it, are enormously valuable. Air costs nothing. The race claims a certain right in the air, though; and franchise dues are paid to the people by public vehicles; while private ones are subject to a small tax. Air-ships are not so reliable as other modes of locomotion, but they relieve the railways and highways, and are immensely useful in sailing over mountains, deserts, forests, or impassable rivers, and in times of freshet and flood, besides their ordinary uses. The air-ships have also been of vast service in Polar and African exploration. You ought to realize that our population is large, and is spread out all through the country. So in order to accomplish traffic easily, it is best to divide it between earth and air. We do not live in large cities now, and we have to have plenty of room."

What he said was entirely justified by the landscape beneath us, where we could see the country beautifully laid out in small towns, villages, and hamlets with perfect roads leading from one to another, and large groves or tracts of wild woodland interspersed. Every acre of the open ground, excepting the fields reserved for sports and public meetings, was thoroughly tilled, with electric arrangement for the fixature of nitrogen in the soil, so as to produce vegetables containing sustenance like that of meat, and for raising apples, pears, and peaches a foot in diameter by electric light, and other fruits in proportionate sizes.

Our first stop was at Chicago, which we found was simply a vast trading post, a business fort or stronghold—like all other cities now—where a garrison of clerks and other laborers was stationed in the immense buildings once teeming with superfluous people. This garrison attended to business details with military precision, and was relieved at intervals by other men and women drafted from the population for the same purpose. All around Chicago were the impressive ruins of various World's Fairs, these institutions having now become obsolete. The ruins had been carefully preserved, and drew many thousand sightseers and tourists every year, who paid a small fee in memorial silver for the privilege of viewing them. These fees were afterwards distributed in charity, and caused a good deal of grumbling because their value was so small.

V

THE FOREST OF STEEL

WHEN WE DESCENDED from the air-ship at Chicago I was horrified to notice that Eva retained the hideous old feminine nineteenth century habit of grabbing her skirt violently at the rear with one hand and holding it up, ostensibly to prevent its dragging on the pavement. She did this only on street crossings or wherever, according to her theory, there ought to be dust or dirt or mud or dampness—no matter how dry and clean the crossing might be. Then she would complacently let the skirt fall again and trail at will as a sidewalk sweeper, with the proud consciousness that she had done her whole duty. I wondered whether our vanished sisters of the past had ever realized how objectionable they made themselves appear by this ugly trick, and what would have been thought of men if they had adopted the custom of hoisting their trousers by such a rearward seizure.

There was not much to be seen in Chicago beyond the big garrison buildings, from fifteen to twenty storeys in height, and the deserted streets shaded by these piles of stone. No one lived in the city now unless drafted by Government and compelled to do so. There were even pleasant little borders of grass and flowering weeds along the once tumultuous thoroughfares, which were now covered with noiseless asphalt or gutta-percha pavement; and some of the unnecessary great buildings had been allowed to crumble into mounds or hills, which were planted with trees and shrubs and laid out as pleasure-grounds, giving a variety to the topography and landscape which was sadly lacking in the old times. On the whole, we were much refreshed by the ruralization and the quietness of Chicago; and I enjoyed some delightful strolls with Electra over the crumbled buildings and among the ruins of the ancient World's Fairs.

I could more than fancy that Hammerfleet did not approve of these excursions. He made his distaste for them very clear in his solemn, undemonstrative way. But I took the opportunity to have one or two frank conversations with Electra. Briefly, I made love to her in a strictly honorable, above-board way. That is, I explained that I had been in love with Eva Pryor three hundred years and more ago, that Eva had then rejected me, and that I had since undergone some change of feeling myself.

We were standing on the moldering crest of the old Auditorium, the slope of which went down towards the shore of Lake Michigan in charmingly broken terraces of verdure and blossom and gurgling fountains. Electra had been recalling to me how, when women first entered politics, they had swayed large conventions of intelligent reasoning men by swinging a parasol or a flag and raising some wild shout for a candidate. But this was a so much greater tribute to the blind intelligence of women than it was to that of men that the women decided it would be more convenient to sway a small group of men than to excite a mob of several hundred or a couple of thousand male creatures calling themselves delegates. So the women had reduced the membership of political conventions to a few dozen, every man being carefully selected for his sensitiveness to parasols and feminine influence and outcry. The lessening of the number of delegates had been a great advantage to the women, and it saved them effort, and incidentally it was good for the country. Hence there was no more need for auditoriums, coliseums, or large halls. A convention could now be held anywhere, and quite inexpensively, under the spread of a few Japanese umbrellas held by women and judiciously waved by them at the proper moment.

"Well, Electra," I asked, "Why should *not* women rule the world?"

"Ah! If the world is willing," she said softly, deprecatingly.

"It would be willing," I responded, "since every man is ruled by a woman."

"But how is that?" She inquired.

"By his love for her," said I. "You, Electra, can rule me, and precisely by that means. I love you!"

She smiled, with a clear, pure, genial amazement. Then suddenly she wept; and there was the light of a rainbow on her face, the mingling of sunshiny mirth and of tearful sorrow—such a thing as I never beheld in any other woman, and do not expect ever to see again.

"Why," she exclaimed sweetly, "it gives me great happiness to hear you say so." Then, with a cadence as of a forest rill dropping plaintively into some rocky pool: "You must know that nothing can come of this. Dear Gerald Bemis, it is hopeless. I am pledged; I am bound to someone else. I am what they call a 'Child of the State' and the Government has promised me to another man."

"Who is he?" I asked, thrilled with a sudden fierce defiance of the State and of the man.

As I spoke. Hammerfleet came up behind us, over the crest of Auditorium Hill. Electra moved one hand, indicating him silently.

"You?" I exclaimed, turning savagely to Hammerfleet.

"He is the man," Electra whispered.

"I have heard your conversation unwillingly," Hammerfleet observed to me, unmoved. "But we will not discuss it. I came up here to look for you, and to say that it has been arranged that you and I shall start tonight by train for New York, and make some little side excursions on the way— so that you may see more of the country."

This announcement I recognized as a challenge and a threat, united; but I was resolved to meet whatever it might imply unflinchingly.

"Very well," I answered. "If Graemantle approves I will accept his decision."

We three then went down the hillside, not speaking further, and joined the rest of our party. Whether Graemantle suspected anything sinister in Hammerfleet's plan or not, I could not guess; but I was reassured by his approving it; since it was certain that he could not wish me any ill.

I set out that night with Hammerfleet as a sort of advance guard. Our first stop, early in the morning, was somewhere near Buffalo, when we got out and walked for a while along the highways. Here I noticed the method of getting on and off trains. The cars never stopped. A spring platform bounced passengers from the station on to the end platform of the cars, where they were received on spring cushions. In the case of quick express trains, a parallel train was run at a swifter rate along a neighboring track for a short distance, and the passengers were hurled from this lightly, and upright into the express.

Bicycles, I found, were no longer a fad or a nuisance. Separate paths were provided for them, and, on these, electric bicycles, tricycles, and carriages were run, with power supplied from stations at regular intervals, and at all hotels, by recharging the storage batteries. Horses were but little used for travel, and existed mainly as a form of preserved life, like deer, in parks, or for racing purposes; although, even in racing, their speed was so greatly surpassed by that of flotation sails and rubber-oared boats, and various mechanical four-legged machines for running, that they were now not much more than domestic pets, like cats and dogs. However, although mowing was done chiefly by electric trolley mowers, we saw some draught-horses and carriage-horses in use on farms or on the road

we were traveling afoot. In sandy regions, the wheels of horse-wagons had outward curving flanges, which prevented the sinking of sand into the wheel-ruts, and did away with friction and the loss of power by displacement of the sand. Many wagon wheels also were coated with naphthalene, to counteract the friction and the retarding effect of mud in the roads.

Part of the way we traveled in horseless electric carriages after we grew tired of walking. Then again we took to our feet and after a time halted before a vast expanse of machinery installed under an illimitable shed. It looked like an enormous jungle of metal mechanism.

"What is this?" I asked of Hammerfleet. "It resembles a forest, but a forest of iron and steel."

"That's precisely what it is," he answered. "And we're now going to stroll through it."

We passed in, and were soon lost in the shadows of this wilderness, where the mighty trunks and the waving branches of huge trees were represented by the uprights, beams, levers, cranks, and rods of vast machines.

"All our factory-work is done in this way now," Hammerfleet courteously explained to me. "This tangle of mechanism runs for the most part automatically, and is governed by one man. It covers many acres."

Wheels were spinning round in the most bewildering manner, huge trip-hammers were thudding down, with tons of force, in various places, and, at intervals, some great overwhelming bar of metal weighing thousands of pounds would come swinging down from the roof and almost touch the ground with a heavy swoop that meant death to any man who got in its way.

"Why" I exclaimed, "it is like the maze of life. Anyone who should pass under one of those swinging beams at the wrong moment would be crushed out as though by a blow of doom. They seem to exemplify fate."

"Quite so," he agreed.

"Let us go back," I proposed.

"No," he objected, "that would be cowardly. Besides, you cannot find your way back safely now. The same sort of steel beams are swinging low behind us as in front. If you were to turn back, you would have to run the same risk of being crushed. I am your only guide. You must go forward with me and take your chances."

"Yet," I returned, "you say that this whole forest of moving machinery is regulated by one man? Suppose anything should happen to him; that he should die suddenly; or should be asleep or fainting and incapable at this very moment. The machinery would go on, and we might, perhaps, be destroyed under it."

"This is the situation exactly," answered Hammerfleet. "The engineer *is* asleep. I had him drugged in advance."

"Then you intend to murder me here, in this forest of steel?" I asked defiantly, but with a decided inward shudder.

"Oh, no; I didn't say that," he returned coolly. "But I shall leave you to trace your own course; and if anything fatal happens to you it will be laid entirely to the machinery."

"You villain!" I exclaimed. "So this is your trap for me, is, it? Well, it's a pretty large one for such small game, and I'll see whether I can make my way through."

I started running and dodging ahead, nimbly, but warily through the awful shadows, the bewildering electric lights spotted here and there; and the throbbing, swinging, whirling, or rising and falling masses of metal, all of which appeared to be consciously aiming blows at me.

"Hold on!" Cried my enemy. "You will certainly be killed. Stop! On one condition I will help you out."

"And that?" I shouted back, pausing,

"Is that you never again speak a word of love to Electra or recur to the wild idea of marrying her."

"Death sooner!" I retorted. "I will never consent to such a promise." And once more I started on my perilous advance through the forest of steel.

It was a frightful experience. In all my former life put together I had not suffered so much fearful excitement, anxiety and terror as were crowded into the next few minutes. A numbing chill crept up through me from my feet to my brain, and it seemed to me that I could actually feel my hair growing white.

Suddenly I thought the end had come. Everything seemed to stop. I stopped. Had I really been struck, and was I dead? Or was this merely imagination? Certainly the great moving wilderness of metal had come to a standstill. The next moment I heard an enormous ringing voice sending towards me from the farther border a loud hail: "Bemis, we are here. You are saved!"

It was the voice of Zorlin; and immediately following it came the rich

contralto of Electra; "This way, this way! Come to us, Bemis."

The bright glare of a searchlight swept through the darksome tangle like a ray direct from Heaven, and by it I was enabled to see my path clear. In a few minutes I had joined my rescuers, and Hammerfleet came after me with a deceitful air of solicitude relieved.

BOOK II

VI

IMPROVED CONDITIONS

FROM THE MOMENT of my fortunate escape, Zorlin was my close friend. It was he who, by the extraordinary power of mind reading, and the perception of distant, unseen things, which his people, the Kurols, possess, had divined the plot against me and the peril I was in. He had turned the rest of the party back from their journey to find me, and Electra had caused the machinery to be stopped just in time.

To Zorlin, of course, I told the whole story; and when we reached Graemantle's house, near Ithaca, now one of the suburbs of New York, that wise man was taken into confidence. The result was a reconsideration on his part as to the propriety of letting Hammerfleet marry Electra. They were both "Children of the State," as all persons of unusual physical and mental endowments were permitted to become at the age of forty, after passing through examinations and inspection, and having their internal condition carefully ascertained by X-rays. They were then suitably mated in marriage to someone of equal standard, with a view to perpetuating and increasing the best elements of the race.

All degenerates were kept in asylums, called museums, where they were permitted to have their own literature, music, and amusements under State supervision, with an attempt at gradual reformation; and were not permitted to marry. So, too, criminals were segregated in special districts— the men and the women apart—and were not allowed to marry; in short, were eliminated from the human family and prevented from menacing posterity, all without cruelty or capital punishment.

Now, Hammerfleet had clearly been guilty of an intended crime. He was therefore dismissed from the company of Children of the State, but not yet condemned to imprisonment.

On the other hand, though, I did not come up to the required standard. Besides. I had been only twenty-eight when I was vivificated, and was considered altogether too young to marry Electra, who was forty-five and in the first bloom of womanhood. This made the situation very puzzling. Zorlin, however, recommended that I should not think of marrying anyone.

"In Kuro," he said one day at breakfast, "we do not marry."

"Ah! Then Mars must be something like Heaven," I commented, turning to Eva, who blushed, but did not look unkindly at me. "Suppose we go there," I added.

"Will you?" She said, with an eager readiness that quite touched me. "Oh, I should so like to go—with you!"

"But how do you keep Kuro populated?" I asked Zorlin.

"We are created, in a manner, spontaneously," he replied, "by the exertion of will and unselfish desire, and the fulfillment of many conditions of life and character that you Earth people do not understand. I am sorry to say, too, that you never can, owing to your condition, quite understand or fulfill them. You must live in your way, and can live rightly, but not on so high a plane as ours."

I noticed that he said, "We *are* created," not "We create ourselves." This led to some talk on religion, and he told us a good deal about his home planet. The religion of Kuro is much like Christianity; in fact, it is a clearer, more luminous perception of Christianity than most of us have. God is, for them, the creator; and their belief in the Redemption is the same as ours, except that they take a cosmic view of it in relation to all the inhabitants of all worlds. It is, in their minds, the key of the universe, the solution of the whole problem of life. I shall not go into the matter in this brief memorandum; for, while Zorlin showed that they recognized the sacred history enacted upon Earth as affecting other spheres, he explained that they look upon it as a manifestation of the great central verity which they can also perceive in other manifestations. That which we perceive is perfectly and eternally true; but they think they can see more of this eternal truth, or deeper into it, than we.

I hesitate to dwell on this subject, because—as usual in theological matters his utterances caused much trouble and uproar a little later. That was what he had in mind when he foreboded that his coming would cause disturbance.

It was not long before I learned that there had been a reunion of all Christians on a great and solid basis of harmony; and the advantages of this to the whole earth were very apparent. When I looked back to my old period of the nineteenth century, it seemed incredible that human beings could have extracted and diffused from religion, which is the highest good, so much of misery and hatred.

Mars is smaller than Earth, of course; and Zorlin told us, also, that the number of people is smaller in proportion: so that there are never more than can be developed to the highest pitch of wisdom, health, and efficiency there; and he thought we might learn something valuable from this example. Their average of intelligence is very much above the human; and this accords with the law they claim to have discovered, that the inhabited planets are superior in mind and spirit according as they are farther away from the sun.

"We know more of actual natural science than you; as well as of great spiritual truths. We are in constant mental communication with some of the planets. Besides, we learn a great deal from the meteors that fall gently into our atmosphere. These are usually fissured, and contain in their crevices the germs of plant and animal life, which we carefully cultivate and mature; so that we have large park tracts full of wonderful cosmic flora and fauna. The canals that your telescopes have discovered on our planet are, in part, a system of irrigation for these parks. By virtue of our very general and clear communion with the universe, through this and other means, and by our whole mode of living, we are able to convey a good deal of our intelligence to inanimate substances and what you call 'forces,' so that they act almost as though by a volition of their own. I am glad to see that you to a certain extent are approaching this plane, although you seem to be hampered by the necessity you feel of accomplishing results by physical and mechanical means. No machinery, however ingenious, and no amount of invention, however marvelous, will ever take the place of willpower and character. Those are the things you will have to cultivate. And you will have to cultivate restraint as opposed to expansion, with its ever-increasing laxity, if you hope to have the world wag really well."

It is easy to see how this kind of talk, when often repeated, set people into a ferment wherever Zorlin came.

He was treated as a distinguished guest of the nation and of the entire earth; and I traveled in his wake as a mere incidental satellite. My luster as a survivor of my vanished century was eclipsed by his grandeur of interest.

In spite of what he said, I thought the earth had achieved a vast improvement. New York, like the other large cities, was now a barracks for business and storage, but was plentifully provided with shady trees and open places. Most people lived healthily and simply in the country, and could run down to the former metropolis from a distance of hundreds of miles in a very short time when occasion demanded. Here, as in Chicago, many of the tall buildings, or "skyscrapers," had been made available for landscape gardening, and there were still plenty of them left to house the poor and sick and needy. Afterwards, when I visited London, Paris, Vienna, Berlin, and other European capitals, I found the same state of things, except that their old buildings were lower. Mankind had decided, after long experience and persistent trials, that large cities are unfit to live in; and the human family, when crowded so closely in a limited area, become dirty and nervous, and that its abodes and the very ground on which they stand grow foul and unwholesome. Cities and dwelling-places have been voted down as outposts or annexes of hell.

They were now cleansed, renovated, and made fit for the occupancy of their business garrisons and for laborers and the poor.

Libraries were kept in the cities, and enormous numbers of newly printed duplicate copies of books, ancient and modern, were sent out to subscribers, or sent free to people in the country; or the contents were transmitted to anyone, anywhere, by phonograph and telephone. Similarly, theatrical performances were given publicly in every rural district or in any private house, by kinetoscope or vitascope, with or without words; but this did not at all interfere with the performance of living actors and actresses, who likewise furnished the original performance for vitascope repro-duction, and were able by means of this same invention to give permanent records of gesture and expression for the benefit of pupils in the histrionic art. Collections of paintings and sculpture, instead of being exhibited for a limited time in some one gallery in a city, were carried round to all quarters of the outlying regions in compact and commodious cars built for the purpose, vastly increasing the market for the works of artists.

Everybody, in short, had civilization brought to his front door, wherever he lived, or within easy reach of his home by walking balloon or electric bicycle.

Gas was used almost exclusively for heat and electricity for lighting. Electric lighting had been brought to a point of perfection that made its radiance soft, diffused, and clear, without undue sharpness; and the eyesight of human beings had greatly improved in consequence, near sight and blindness having been much diminished.

Starch, sugar, and protean substances were made in immense quantities by factories on the Amazon, in Indiana, and in Africa, from wood fiber, by chemical transformations—the construction of the molecules of carbohydrates and methods of rearranging this construction having been discovered, so that no energy was absorbed or given out in the transformation. Thus, food of a simple kind was amazingly abundant and cheap. Artificial wood, also, was made from compressed chloro-cellulose and talc, with a solvent, and disintegrated by water under pressure.

Artificial leather was produced by the electrical fixature of nitrogen in carbohydrates. Shoes were molded directly from this material, one machine making three hundred pairs of shoes in an hour. They were afterwards passed through another process to make them flexible, and the porosity of the leather was varied to suit different climates, shoes for damp climates having large pores and those for dry regions having pores that were infinitesimal.

Food and clothing provision, therefore, and wood for building were as abundant as could be. Forest preservation was also carefully attended to, with the best effects on climate and water-supply. Bricks were made six times as large as the old style; and dried in roomy iron chambers with fifty per cent of sand to prevent shrinkage. They were then hoisted into place in large quantities by a machine and laid—several courses at a time—with a cement mixed of lime, clay, and nitre, which produced intense heat and fused the masonry into a solid, permanent mass, so that ordinary house-building was very easy.

Then in respect of health and bodily comfort, a method had been perfected of causing new teeth to grow by means of calcareous, antisepticised bandages.

The wise men of the race had determined that the white corpuscles of the blood are the policemen of organized beings against microbes. By the education of these corpuscles, and inuring then to microbes of every kind, they were made capable of resisting the attacks of the enemy; and even chemical poisons were rendered harmless by the training of the white corpuscles. A compound virus had likewise been discovered and brought into use, consisting of the weakened cultures of rabies, consumption, diphtheria, cholera, splenic fever, erysipelas, typhoid, yellow, scarlet, and malarial fever, and several other diseases of microbic origin. Children received an inoculation with this virus once in seven years, by compulsory law; and the diseases against which it was directed had become rare.

In addition to all this, it had become possible to manufacture pure diamonds by subjecting prepared metal crystals to the action of time, heat, and pressure; while immersed in bisulphide of carbon, in bulbs of pure quartz. By a magnetically deflected arc, the surface was plumbagoed, and pure iron was electroplated over the ball until it increased to twenty times its original diameter. Then the whole was submitted to a gradually rising temperature until the softening-point was reached. Gold and silver were obtained by the reaction between volatilized sulphur and iron, in graphite tubes separated by a porous partition, and raised to 7000 degrees of Fahrenheit by superheated gases, and this had brought about a change in the currency system. Platinum was now the standard of value. Its rate of value was very high, and very little of it was ever seen in circulation; but it made a solid basis. The general currency was based upon the value of permanent taxable property; but this value was scientifically measured, and subject to very little fluctuation. It acted, however, as a balance wheel, controlling expenditure and speculation; and speculation, as it used to be practiced, had almost ceased.

With such advantages and improvements—and I may say that during a brief flight through Europe and the Americas, and the regenerated empires of China and Japan, I found much the same state of things prevailing—it would seem that people ought to be contented. Government, too, is now much more satisfactorily conducted, by small, efficient, and responsible committees, though on a republican plan, instead of by parliaments, congresses, and mobs, as of old. The "federation of the world" has been achieved. The nations of Europe and Asia, with Africa, in their several unions, co-operate with us through a world Committee of Twenty; and the fierce light of honor and responsibility and watchfulness that beats upon these Twenty gives them no chance to fool or prevaricate with the race. Besides, they do not want to do so. It is happier and pleasanter to be honest, and is the highest kind of diplomacy.

The general agreement has brought into play the best, the only true free trade. Every country says frankly what industries it wishes to maintain, according to its condition and needs. Every country is self-reliant and so far as possible, self-sustaining; and the various countries work together for the good of the whole of mankind.

Co-operation has taken the place of hostile competition.

War is at an end. A single old hulk, now, mounted with a telescopic gun, can settle an angry dispute from a distance of two score miles. A telescopic cannon sends forth another smaller cannon that is protected by a secondary all-chamber containing a lesser explosive to counteract the first explosive pressure. This cannon, in turn, generates another one, and the final cannon discharges upon the doomed point or city a bursting projectile that destroys more than could be restored in fifty years.

Still, mankind is not satisfied. There are always people now, as formerly, who drop to the rear of the procession, and there are always passionate and criminal impulses.

VII

THE SUN-TELESCOPE AND DEPARTURE

GRAEMANTLE'S ITHACAN VILLA was a vast establishment, adorned with all the magnificence now so easy—diamonds, emeralds, and rubies set in the walls for decoration; beautiful wall paintings, tapestries—with amusement rooms for theatrical performances, and an Odorifer and Coloriscope. These contrivances were something like church-organs, but filled with clever mechanism that produced new effects. The Coloriscope had innumerable opening and closing shutters that revealed different colors in pleasing succession or in union, like that of musical chords; and the Odorifer was provided with a great number of tubes that sent forth delicious and varying perfumes, either singly or in harmonious combination. But I was still more interested in the sun-telescope not far away from the house—which was a scheme originated by Gladwin. The Society of Futurity had kept it up, but had never got any definite results from it.

It was rigged somewhat like the Mars magnetograph, with poles and wires around a large circle, but had a telephone receiver attached to it.

Through this receiver we could hear strange and awful moanings, but no one had ever been able to get a definite message from it. Zorlin insisted that, according to Kurol philosophy, the sun was the abode of lost souls.

"Do you mean to say," I asked, "that what we regard as the main physical force of light, warmth, life, and heat is Hell?"

"Yes," he affirmed. "Why should there be any question about it? You earthlings debate as to the existence or non-existence of Hell, and there it is, staring you in the face, all the time. Of course it warms and cheers you when it shines moderately. But you cannot look at it with the naked eye without suffering a horrible shock, or even blindness. Are not its effects in summer fiendish and intolerable? And when it shines too intensely, does it not drive people mad and cause epidemics of wrath and suicide? Also it seems quite reasonable that malefactors, lost souls from this earth, should be utilized by being contributed to that immense combustion which gives useful heat and comfort to you here. That would be a sort of compensation for the evil they did while on this planet."

It was a curious notion, not entirely new to some readers and thinkers; yet it caused much dispute among the people he met.

After that, I never could listen to the dreary groanings of the sun-telephone without thinking of what he said. Perhaps this strengthened the desire that was rising in me to get away to some serener clime and *entourage* than this earth's. Then, too, in spite of all obstacles and opposition, I could not give up the idea of winning Electra.

I had talked with Zorlin about it; and while, as a Kurol, he could not quite approve my marrying, he at last consented to accompany me if I could induce Electra to leave the country—in brief, to elope with me.

Going to her, I used all my faculties of persuasion, but she would agree to nothing more than to make a brief tour around the earth with me, on condition that Zorlin should go with us as counselor, companion, and friend. It must be done, however, I told her, without the knowledge of Graemantle, and especially without that of Hammerfleet, who was still at large, although he had been excluded from the house, and was not allowed to see her.

This was how I came to make my trip to Europe and other parts of the globe, and to observe the new state of things everywhere; and a wonderfully interesting and delightful trip it was. But several things prevented it from becoming a genuine elopement.

In the first place, Electra held to her idea that she ought not to marry me. In the next place, Zorlin, being with us, was similarly inclined to prevent my marrying Electra. And finally, just after we had embarked in the commodious air-ship that I had engaged for the journey, I found that Eva Pryor had been smuggled aboard by Electra, and was to be one of our party.

The noble Electra fairly laughed in my face when Eva appeared from the cabin; though she laughed with such good humor and grace that I could not possibly take offence or do anything else but admire her. What impressed me also very favorably was that Eva had abandoned her dreadful nineteenth century costume and was dressed in the peaceful and becoming robes of the new day; for this I took—perhaps conceitedly—as evidence of a gentle and womanly desire to give pleasure to me.

There was soon a very exciting flight and chase; for both Graemantle and Hammerfleet, on learning of our departure, followed us in different airboats.

It was a wild career, indeed, high in air above the whirling globe; but I shall never regret the impulse which led me into it, because we had so many adventures and such charming talks—Electra, Eva, and I, with the missionary from Mars; and because I learned so many things about the temporal advancement of men in this new age.

Ascending from Fire Island at dawn we swept southward along the Atlantic coastline; our ship flying through the atmospheric expanses like a huge bird, without effort. Never shall I forget the exhilaration of that moment and of the next few hours. After the first surprise and disappointment of finding that Eva was with us it was astonishing how soon I reconciled myself to the situation. When you are separated from your own century and all your accustomed surroundings and thrown into the air, even with one of these marvelous boats to float you, there is a sense of desolation in your grandeur which induces an unexpected humility and makes it very comforting to have near you the woman you loved long ago, even if you have decided that you no longer love her. As the days went on and we were held together in this close neighborliness, I became more and mere conscious of something in Eva that soothed me and sustained my cheerfulness. She was so quiet, so resigned, so friendly that I began to like her companionship exceedingly. In some way also which it is hard to define, I could understand her, and she could understand me better than the new woman Electra and the Mars missionary Zorlin. We all, however, seemed to be placed in a new relation, which was much more satisfactory than the relations of people in the old, noisy, restless nineteenth century.

There was no effort among us to keep up conversation, or, as the ancient phrase put it, to "entertain" one another. Each of us occupied and amused himself or herself independently. When conversation became natural or useful we conversed, but there was no occasion for the two women to be silly or vain in order to attract the attention of the two men, Zorlin and myself; and, on the other hand, he and I did not feel called upon to put ourselves into an artificial mood in order to suit some fantastic requirement on their part as to what we ought to do for the purpose of pleasing them.

For the first time in my experience I enjoyed the pleasure of a quiet, healthy, unforced intercourse with other beings of my own kind, and with a guest from Mars who was so nearly like us.

Just as we came over Cape Hatteras we saw, by the aid of a strong field-glass, that Graemantle and Hammerfleet were following in our track; and almost at the same moment a threatening cyclone rose from the south, over the Gulf Stream. Our navigator avoided the cyclone with great skill. As everyone knows, storms of this kind, born of the wild union of cold air currents with tropic heat and moisture rising from the Gulf Stream, pass inward to the United States and follow a long parabolic curve through that country, darting out seaward again at some far north-eastward point. We turned our rudder and flew east over the sea, so as to keep clear of the edge of the enormous tempest as it whirled in over the land.

It was a magnificent and impressive sight, and so absorbed were we in gazing at it, that only at the moment when we were escaping the tail of the cyclone did we observe that Hammerfleet's air-ship had sailed into the main body of it, was spun round like a top in the swirl of mist and wind, and then was broken and thrown down, a wreck, to the ocean below.

Although I was rather exultant over his disaster, I made a prayer for him, for I did not think that he could come out from the ruin alive, and certainly did not wish him any evil, either in this life or beyond it.

It turned out that he did escape whole; but we did not know of this until long afterwards.

At Cuba we stopped to renew our batteries, take in provisions, and rest. We found the island peaceful, happy, and prosperous under a limited Republican Government, and free from all nightmares of tyranny, either white or black. From there—believing that we were now quit of Hammer-fleet, and having decided to convert our journey for a while into a tour of observation—we darted over sea and land down to the Amazon country.

We were received at Para by a branch of the Darwinian Society, and, on their extensive plantations, were attended by apes whom they had developed to an extraordinary degree. These apes had arrived at a fair imitative proficiency in human language, were skilful in agriculture, under proper direction, and made very good servants for the rougher and simpler kind of housework, or for carrying baggage and the like.

One of the most interesting things in the Amazon region was the fact that large tracts of country had been sterilized by saturation with petroleum. This prevented excessive vegetable growth, and enabled the inhabitants, with the aid of great syndicates, to carry on a normal and highly profitable production of rubber trees, and of forests, the wood fiber from which was turned into food and various useful tissues. All sorts of food were manufactured here from wood cellulose with inorganic salts of potash and sulphuric acid, and by the action of bacterial ferments.

Here at Para, also, is made a large part of the world's supply of artificial silk. The disintegrated cellulose of the food-factories, after being thoroughly bleached to dazzling whiteness, is dissolved in one of the chlorinated alcohols, under pressure, to a glossy mass. This is afterwards put into a cylindrical hydraulic press and forced through plates filled with innumerable small discs of sapphire, through every one of which a hole one-thousandth of an inch in diameter is bored by diamond dust. The fiber, when it reaches the hot air of the room in which the press is situated, shrinks immediately by the evaporation of the alcoholic solvent, and is put at once on to reels. The entirely amorphous character of the material and the perfect surface of the sapphire die produce a fabric far more dazzling and beautiful than the silk formerly obtained from the silkworm.

Not knowing what had become of Graemantle, whom we had lost sight of when we were dodging the cyclone, and not wishing to be overtaken and interfered with by him, we had to hurry away from Para and the Amazon. Traveling mostly in the early evening or the early morning, when we were less likely to be observed or followed, we zigzagged through the air over Brazil, crossing the Andes two or three times from east to west and back, and then bearing down to Chile and the Argentine Republic. Everywhere in those regions we found the same system of building in use that had aroused my admiration in the United States. This is the "plastic" system of molding edifices, still more effective than the fusing of bricks into solid masses, which I have mentioned before.

By the plastic method immense palaces are reared for the ordinary dwellings of the rich, with miles of terraces and raised gardens, towers, domes, and long vistas of pillars, surpassing in grandeur even the imaginative conception of ancient Carthage as depicted by the old English painter Turner. State Capitols and all Government or municipal buildings and numerous vast churches filled with gorgeous chapels are built on even a greater scale of magnificence and massive proportions, in designs of exquisite beauty. Large corporations erect their structures by means of iron molds of every variety, all capable of being assembled like parts of a machine, and producing unitedly the total architectural effect desired, These molds are set up in position to form the whole house—the walls, doors, partitions, pillars; ceiling, and, with the aid of iron beams, the roof. The molds are faced with beautiful figures, and also, where appropriate, with sculpture in bas-relief. They are made from models supplied by the very best artists, working in harmony to secure the finest result; and, therefore, the effect of the building, when created, has nothing cheap or mechanical about it.

When the molds are all in place great iron tanks are brought to the spot, containing a stone like semi-fluid mixture, which is pumped through pipes into the molds. In three days this mixture becomes perfectly hard; the molds are taken away, and a complete house or immense palace or cathedral stands revealed. Whole mountains are crushed to powder by gigantic machines, to furnish material for the plastic mixture; and many of the superfluous buildings in the formerly overcrowded cities have been ground up for the same purpose. A palace which would formerly have impoverished the richest of men, or even a prosperous State, is now put up and finished—except for the interior decorations, which must be done by hand—at an expense which among the ancients (of whom I was formerly one) would hardly have paid for the modeling and chiseling of a single great statue.

We extended our journey, with various pauses for rest, and frequent trips by electric trains on land and then by ocean shutter-vessels, to the Antarctic Continent, where the greatest surprise of all awaited me in the large and flourishing community of two or three million beings inhabiting the interior of that ice-girt region and rejoicing in the genial warmth diffused by its central volcanoes? But now I must speak of a thing that had worried us more or less, all along, and eventually brought our curious escape to an end.

VIII
SEA-SIGNALLING—THE FINAL FLIGHT

WE HAD NOTICED AT TIMES when the sky was cloudy, both by day and by night, certain periodic flashes of light appearing on the clouds in quick succession. Electra told me that these were caused by the system of cloud-telegraphy now in use; and to anyone familiar with the Morse alphabet, as I was, it was easy to read the messages so flashed about the heavens, though I could not understand those that were in cipher. Most of them were of a general nature, and had nothing to do with us. But at intervals we observed that telegraphic inquiries were being made on the clouds about our party, and that certain persons whom we were not able to identify—most of them signing these communications with numerals instead of names—were answering those inquiries. I may as well jot down in this place the information I gathered as to the mode of signalling by cloud-flash and by other new methods.

Powerful electric rays are, by means of lenses, brought to thin pencils of intense light. A single one of these is then projected upward against a cloud. A controlling shutter in the path of the beam of light interrupts it at will, so that it may be made to show long or short flashes on the clouds. Words are thus illuminated in the sky, and made to shine in the zenith repeatedly, until an answering reflection is obtained. The chief use of this cloud-telegraphy is, of course, on the sea between ships and "steamers" (as they are still called, notwithstanding that they do not use steam) or for airboats. Conversation may be carried on in this way between vessels many miles apart; and a message received by one can be transmitted to others, so that inquiries and replies fly all around the globe and to remote parts of ocean. The system was found useful in those later voyages to the North Pole, which have not been followed up since a general exploration of the open Arctic Sea was effected. It has also saved many lives, prevented collisions, and caught many fugitive criminals. Sailing vessels are provided with a water-paddle to drive the necessary electric generating mechanism for signaling when the ship is in motion.

In some of the much-traveled sea regions, another method of communication is used for the daytime. A sail-cloth, woven with metallic wire, is hung between the tips of two masts, and is connected to a special electric generating apparatus, producing waves of extreme sharpness and great intensity that follow each other at the rate of seven hundred per second. An electric stress thus propagated to infinite distance is; at moderate distances, strong enough to be collected by the metalized sail of another vessel. One ship, for example, wishes to know whether there is another within the area of signaling, but out of sight. The musical note formed by electric inductive waves is set going, and, by means of a key, is stopped and started again at will. Other vessels in the area have watchers who, at intervals, listen to an exquisitely sensitive telephone made selectively sensitive to waves of exactly seven hundred per second. This is brought about by a tuning-fork attachment to the diaphragm, tuned exactly to respond to waves of that rate; hence, although the part of the waves collected by the sail-cloth is many million times less than could be gathered if it were close to the signaling ship, yet the tuning-fork collects successive waves until the amplexitude of vibration is sufficient to cause audibility. The signaling current is continuous for several seconds. Then the transmitting vessel stops it and connects the sail with its receiving apparatus to listen for a return wave. After the preliminary signals have been exchanged, conversation is carried on in the usual way. It is slow, of course, owing to the time necessary for the successive impulses to rise to the point of audibility; but the method is very accurate and reliable in all but foggy or rainy weather.

For foggy weather signalling there is still another ingenious device. A circular hole, about two feet in diameter, is cut in the vessel below the water-line, and closed by a circular steel plate or diaphragm one-eighth of an inch thick. On the inner side of this there is a thick iron chamber, completely inclosing the space behind the diaphragm; and here is placed a small, shrill, steam whistle, worked by compressed air or steam, and controllable by a valve or key. Alongside of this apparatus is another diaphragm made like the first; but there extends from the centre of it a very short fine steel wire, highly stretched, the other end of which is connected to a sensitive diaphragm, from which tubes lead to both ears of the signalman. By an adjustable attachment this steel wire can be regulated to greater or less tension, as a violin string is, and it is tuned to respond to the note given out by the whistles on other steamers, which are all of precisely the same pitch. In fogs the signalman alternately sounds the whistle and listens for a return, his receiving apparatus not being responsive to any other sound than that to which it is tuned, beyond the rippling or dashing of water on the sides of the vessel and the movement of the propelling shutter machinery, which are continuous and do not interfere with the signalman's hearing a periodic musical sound. The sound-waves of the whistles are communicated to the water by the steel diaphragm in front, and travel through the sea just as in air, but much farther, since the conductivity of water for sound is greater than that of air. One of the most important uses of this machine on large passenger ships is to ascertain the direction of approaching vessels with exactness, and for this purpose they have two sets of diaphragms on opposite sides of the ship, connected telephonically.

Still another contrivance for preventing collisions or giving notice of the nearness of icebergs or derelicts impressed me. This is "the automatic pilot," a small cigar-shaped copper vessel some fifteen feet long and twenty-four inches at its greatest diameter, having within it an electric motor that drives a screw propeller at its end. From the masthead a reel passes two insulated wires, which run from the ship's dynamo electric engine, down to the cigar-shaped "pilot," to which they are joined side by side, about two feet apart. They not only carry electricity to the motor of the pilot, but also cause the pilot to move in harmony with the steamer's course. As soon as the fog appears the "pilot" is launched, and the current passing to it through the wires from the masthead, revolves the motor in the little pilot-craft and sends her shooting ahead of the ship or steamer. If the pilot tends to veer from a straight line one of the wires becomes more taut than the other, and so affecting the steering apparatus as to bring the copper boat back to the right course. I forgot to say that these wires or cables, although having only about the thickness of a knitting-needle, are twisted together from a number of very fine steel wires: and as the speed of the pilot is greater than the ship's and keeps her about half a mile ahead of the latter, the wires always tend to become taut. If the pilot strikes any obstacle the fact becomes known at once to the man at the dynamo, and the engine is stopped and reversed without loss of time. Many serious accidents have been avoided by this precaution. The automatic pilot-boat is taken on board again, of course, when the fog clears.

It will be evident to anyone who reads this little sketch of my first experiences and impressions that, with such means of cloud-flashes and sea-signalling-besides which, it must be mentioned, the construction of ocean cables was now very cheap and great numbers of private cable lines were in use—it would not be possible for our party to escape indefinitely from vigilant and determined pursuers. A good pursuer, by means of the omnipresent telegraph-wires and signal systems, could tap the whole earth, as a woodpecker taps a tree for his prey; and, moreover, the French Submarine Society for mapping the bottom of the sea had its underwater boats and observers in all parts of the world, liable to bob up to the surface of the deep anywhere; so that, if these were to be utilized, one of them might locate our position on or over the ocean at any instant.

However, we led our friends and enemies a pretty good chase, and kept it up many weeks. On our return from the Antarctic Commonwealth to Patagonia (now an important manufacturing country), we ascertained that Hammerfleet had survived his cyclone wreck—having, in fact, been picked up by a submarine geographical boat, and that he was using the wires, the clouds, and metalized sail telegraph to trace us. We therefore concluded to run quickly over to China and Japan, and were well repaid by the evidences of immense progress that we saw there; the same improvements that I have already described having been introduced in those countries. English, now the universal language, has been pretty well domesticated in China, though it still cuts some pigeon-wings in the dance of rustic lips. What interested Eva and me greatly, among other things, was the simple plan of making ice here, as in India and all hot countries, by hoisting balloons which carry water-tanks 20,000 ft. into the air, freeze the water and bring it down again; a constant relay of balloons steadily renewing the supply.

As we passed on through Turkey—a peaceful, flourishing Christian country through strong and rehabilitated Greece and Italy, to Germany, France, and England, we were pleased to observe the wonderful effects obtained by the particular societies, each devoted to a specific fruit or flower, which now produced fruits of a lusciousness beyond belief, and had so changed flowers that the mysterious something in them, called harmonic grouping; gave us an indescribable sensation of beauty totally wanting in the flowers known to the ancients. In art also the Society of Harmonic Curves has brought about great changes. The human form, in this day, is—through wise cultivation—much more beautiful than the average of old times; besides which, painters and sculptors, owing to an improved knowledge of curve harmony, develop from the living model an ideal of loveliness and perfection formerly approached only by the Greeks, and even by them approached but partially. This development of beauty seems to have come from a radically altered, more restful mode of life, a purer application of supernatural religion to existence, and a better realization of the laws of natural science as in accord with religion.

So, too, and from similar causes, the great changes in manufacturing systems have benefited the race. Owing to systems for the electric distribution of power over great areas, the industrial economy of very early times had been restored. Now, among the countless homes of the people, those of the mechanics are each provided with its little workshop, where only one operation in any particular manufacture is carried out. A single part of any machine is passed from house to house until finished, and is then returned to the great assembling shop to be assembled into the complete machine. The profound change in the moral, mental, and social condition of the working people effected by a return once more to occupation in the home, instead of the promiscuous association in large factories, has been one of the most potent agents in improving the state of the population, lessening crime, drunkenness, and other evils; stimulating true education, and restoring to labor its natural poetry and idyllic character. Thanks to the plastic process of building, even the poorest worker has his own home. With the children of mechanics learning their trade at home from the earliest years, highly trained workmen have been developed, who produce mechanisms and fabrics once thought to be impossible, and of a cheapness that is surprising. In those branches of the mechanical arts where labor cannot be so subdivided great factories still hold their place. But they are automatic—like that in which Hammerfleet had tried to entrap me—and need the attendance of only one watcher, so perfected are the science and art of automatic action by the higher type of intellect of the modem mechanic and artisan.

There are many other things of which I would like to speak; but I must bring this memorandum to a close before leaving earth, as I am about to do, for a voyage and an absence which may be permanent.

With all the improvements in machinery, inventions, and modes of life, human nature, also, has somewhat improved; but it has not radically altered. Its passions, good and bad, remain much the same, together with its weakness, fickleness, and treachery. Noting this, and having seen so much of the world even in our rapid journeys, I began to grow a trifle tired of it all and to yearn for something new and for a rest. Moreover, Zorlin had stirred up so much controversy by his private and public talks wherever he went, regarding his large cosmic views in religion, philosophy, and science, that he, also, longed for return to his native planet.

It was when we had arrived at this state of mind that Graemantle suddenly came up with us, just as we alighted from an air-ship, in Norway. After getting us under thorough observation by a number of emissaries, he had obtained from the World Committee of Twenty an order for Electra as an American "Child of the State" to return with him, and he now put her under a mildly paternal sort of arrest. A day or two later Hammerfleet arrived, surprising me while I was taking a walk in a quiet spot outside of Christiania. He looked haggard, vindictive and terrible. I nerved myself to resist whatever attack he might make, but I was not prepared for the particular weapon he produced. He unrolled in front of me a peculiar glittering curtain that uncurled from a rod in his hand, dropping thence to the ground; and in a moment I recognized that it was something I had heard of but had not seen before—nothing less than a hypnotizing machine!

These machines are used medically, for the investigation of nervous disorders and weak organisms; and they are also applied officially to the examination of candidates for the Civil Service and for high office; but the laws of the world and all the nations forbid their use in any other way.

I gazed helplessly at the glittering thing; and it was evident that my enemy was putting it in operation. The next moment I lost all consciousness of myself, as myself. What would have happened I do not know, for I came almost immediately back to myself, and found that Graemantle, Zorlin, and Electra had come to my rescue in the nick of time; having been guided by Zorlin, whose Kurol mind had enabled him to divine from a little distance what was going on.

This episode settled Hammerfleet's fate. He was promptly sent back to the United States in irons, and isolated in one of the penal districts. His merely using the hypnotizing machine was sufficient reason for this; and when he saw the game was up, he confessed that his object had been to hypnotize me back into the nineteenth century, into my glass chrysalis in Gladwin's laboratory, then seclude me personally and keep me permanently hypnotized under this delusion; which would have been practically the same as death for this world.

All through our journeying, I had been more and more impressed with Eva Pryor's gentleness and winning qualities; and, from wondering at first whether I had not made a mistake as to my real feeling towards her, I came to the positive conclusion that I had done so. Now that we had completed our globe voyage, and Zorlin was pining for his home on Kuro or Mars, I had a candid little conversation with her, and wound up by asking her, "How would you like to carry out actually what you once said you would do—go to Mars with me? The Kurols don't marry, and we can act with entire consistency by being brother and sister up there."

"Delightful," she cried, grasping my hand. "Will Zorlin take us?"

A stellar express car was ordered immediately; and I have barely time now to jot down here that we are about to depart. Whether I shall ever come back I do not know, but my mind is quite made up that I will not come back alone.

Postscript by the Editor
A.D. 2201

Bemis has returned to earth and married Eva. "It is worth while," he says, "To have been vivificated for three hundred years and to have gone to Mars in order to find out a woman's mind—and my own."

The Brotherhood of the Seven Kings

L. T. MEADE
AND
ROBERT EUSTACE

THE IDEA THAT THE WORLD is not as it seems but might be controlled behind the scenes by some secret cabal is another of those concepts that took hold in the late Victorian period, particularly through the Sherlock Holmes stories of Arthur Conan Doyle run in *The Strand Magazine*, starting in 1891. Holmes often finds himself pitted against evil masterminds or secret organisations.

The success of the Holmes stories left the publisher and editor of *The Strand*, George Newnes and Greenhough Smith, in a quandary when, in 1893, Conan Doyle killed off Holmes. They turned to other contributors to create similar characters which they could run in regular series. One of those who responded and who became one of the most creative contributors to *The Strand* in the 1890s was L. T. Meade (1844–1914). Born Elizabeth Thomasina Meade in County Cork, Ireland, she was always known as Lillie, and retained her maiden name for all her professional work, even after her marriage in 1879 to the solicitor Alfred Toulmin Smith. She was an immensely prolific writer with around 280 books to her credit, all but one of those written between 1875 and 1914, averaging seven a year. Much of her output was for teenage girls, but responding to *The Strand*'s demands she produced a considerable amount of detective fiction. She usually relied on a collaborator to provide the scientific (often medical) details. One of her collaborators was Eustace Barton (1854–1943), writing as Robert Eustace, with whom she wrote *A Master of Mysteries* (1898), *The Sanctuary Club* (1900) and the series from which the following story comes, *The Brotherhood of the Seven Kings* (1899). In this series the narrator, Norman Head, had once belonged to this eponymous secret organisation which had been founded in Italy by the otherwise seemingly innocent and altruistic Madame Koluchy. He manages to escape her clutches and thereafter devotes his time, along with a lawyer colleague, Colin Dufrayer, to thwarting her evil schemes. Each story hinges upon the use of some new technological or scientific discovery, in this instance X-rays, which had only just been properly studied and identified by William Röngten in 1895. —**M.A.**

THE STAR-SHAPED MARKS

N A CERTAIN SUNDAY in the spring of 1897, as Dufrayer and I were walking in the Park, we came across one of his friends, a man of the name of Loftus Durham. Durham was a rising artist, whose portrait paintings had lately attracted notice. He invited us both to his studio on the following Sunday, where he was to receive a party of friends to see his latest work, an historical picture for the coming Academy.

"The picture is an order from a lady, who has herself sat for the principal figure," said Durham. "I hope you may meet her also on Sunday. My impression is that the picture will do well; but if so, it will be on account of the remarkable beauty of my model. But I must not add more—you will see what I mean for yourselves."

He walked briskly away.

"Poor Durham," said Dufrayer, when he had left us. "I am glad that he is beginning to get over the dreadful catastrophe which threatened to ruin him body and soul a year back."

"What do you mean?" I asked.

"I allude to the tragic death of his young wife," said Dufrayer. "They were only married two years. She was thrown from her horse on the hunting-field; broke her back, and died a few hours afterwards. There was a child, a boy of about four months old at the time of the mother's death. Durham was so frightfully prostrated from the shock that some of his friends feared for his reason; but I now see that he is regaining his usual calibre. I trust his new picture will be a success; but, notwithstanding his remarkable talent, I have my doubts. It takes a man in ten thousand to do a good historical picture."

On the following Sunday, about four o'clock, Dufrayer and I found ourselves at Durham's house in Lanchester Gardens. A number of well-known artists and their wives had already assembled in his studio. We found the visitors all gazing at a life-sized picture in a heavy frame which stood on an easel facing the window.

Dufrayer and I took our places in the background, and looked at the group represented on the canvas in silence. Any doubt of Durham's ultimate success must have immediately vanished from Dufrayer's mind. The picture was a magnificent work of art, and the subject was worthy of an artist's best efforts. It was taken from "The Lady of the Lake," and represented Ellen Douglas in the guard-room of Stirling Castle, surrounded by the rough soldiers of James V. of Scotland. It was named "Soldiers, Attend!"—Ellen's first words as she flung off her plaid and revealed herself in all her dark proud beauty to the wonder of the soldiers. The pose and attitude were superb, and did credit both to Durham and the rare beauty of his model.

I was just turning round to congratulate him warmly on his splendid production, when I saw standing beside him Ellen Douglas herself, not in the rough garb of a Scotch lassie, but in the simple and yet picturesque dress of a well-bred English girl. Her large black velvet hat, with its plume of ostrich feathers, contrasted well with a face of dark and striking beauty, but I noticed even in that first glance a peculiar expression lingering round the curves of her beautiful lips and filling the big brown eyes. A secret care, an anxiety artfully concealed, and yet all too apparent to a real judge of character, spoke to me from her face. All the same, that very look of reserve and sorrow but strengthened her beauty, and gave that final touch of genius to the lovely figure on the canvas.

Just then Durham touched me on the shoulder.

"What do you think of it?" He asked, pointing to the picture.

"I congratulate you most heartily," I responded.

"I owe any success which I may have achieved to this lady," he continued. "She has done me the honour to sit as Ellen Douglas. Mr. Head, may I introduce Lady Faulkner?"

I bowed an acknowledgment, to which Lady Faulkner gravely responded. She stepped a little aside, and seemed to invite me to follow her.

"I am also glad you like the picture," she said eagerly. "For years I have longed to have that special subject painted. I asked Mr. Durham to do it for me on condition that I should be the model for Ellen Douglas. The picture is meant as a present for my husband."

"Has he seen it yet?" I asked.

"No, he is in India; it is to greet him as a surprise on his return. It has always been one of his longings to have a really great picture painted on that magnificent subject, and it was also one of his fancies that I should take the part of Ellen Douglas. Thanks to Mr. Durham's genius, I have succeeded, and am much pleased."

A new arrival came up to speak to her. I turned aside, but her face

continued to attract me, and I glanced at her from time to time. Suddenly, I noticed that she held up her hand as if to arrest attention, and then flew to the door of the studio. Outside was distinctly audible the patter of small feet, and also the sound of a woman's voice raised in expostulation. This was followed by the satisfied half coo, half cry, of a young child, and the next instant Lady Faulkner reappeared, carrying Durham's baby boy in her arms.

He was a splendid little fellow, and handsome enough in himself to evoke unlimited admiration. A mass of thick, golden curls shadowed his brow; his eyes were large, and of a deep and heavenly blue. He had the round limbs and perfect proportions of a happy, healthy baby. The child had clasped his arms round Lady Faulkner's neck. Seeing a great many visitors in the room, he started in some slight trepidation, but, turning again to Lady Faulkner, smiled in her face.

"Ah! There you are, Robin," said Durham, glancing at the child with a lighting-up of his own somewhat sombre face. "But, Lady Faulkner, please don't let the little chap worry you—you are too good to him. The fact is, you spoil him dreadfully."

"That is a libel, for no one could spoil you, could they, Robin?" Said Lady Faulkner, kissing the boy on his brow. She seated herself on the window-sill. I went up and took a place beside her. She was so altogether absorbed by the boy that she did not at first see me. She bent over him and allowed him to clasp and unclasp a heavy gold chain of antique pattern which she wore round her neck. From time to time she kissed him. Suddenly glancing up, her eyes met mine.

"Is he not a splendid little fellow?" She said. "I don't know how I could have lived through the last few months but for this little one. I have been kept in London on necessary business, and consequently away from my own child; but little Robin has comforted me. We are great friends, are we not, Robin?"

"The child certainly seems to take to you," I said.

"Take to me!" She cried. "He adores me; don't you, baby?"

The boy looked up as she addressed him, opened his lips, as if to utter some baby word, then, with a coy, sweet smile, hid his face against her breast.

"You have a child of your own?" I said.

"Yes, Mr. Head, a boy. Now, I am going to confide in you. My boy is the image of this little one. He is the same age as Robin, and Robin and he are so alike in every feature that the resemblance is both uncommon and extraordinary. But, stay, you shall see for yourself."

She produced a locket, touched a spring, and showed me a painted photograph of a young child. It might have been taken from little Robin Durham. The likeness was certainly beyond dispute.

Dufrayer came near, and I pointed it out to him.

"Is it not remarkable?" I said. "This locket contains a picture of Lady Faulkner's own little boy. You would not know it from little Robin Durham, would you?"

Dufrayer glanced from the picture to the child, then to the face of Lady Faulkner. To my surprise she coloured under his gaze, which was so fixed and staring as to seem almost rude.

Remarking that the picture might assuredly be taken from Durham's boy, he gravely handed back the locket to Lady Faulkner, and immediately afterwards, without waiting for me, took his leave.

Lady Faulkner looked after his retreating form and I noticed that a new expression came into her eyes—a defiant, hard, even desperate, look. It came and quickly went. She clasped her arms more tightly round the boy, kissing him again. I took my own leave soon afterwards, but during the days which immediately followed I often thought with some perplexity of Lady Faulkner, and also of Durham's boy.

I had received a card for the private view of the Academy, and remembering Durham's picture, determined to go there on the afternoon of the great day. I strolled through the rooms, which were crowded, so much so indeed that it was almost impossible to get a good view of the pictures; but by-and-by I caught a sight of Durham's masterpiece. It occupied a place of honour on the line. Beyond doubt, therefore, his success was assured. I had taken a fancy to him, and was glad of this, and now pushed my way into the midst of a knot of admirers, who, arrested by the striking scene which the picture portrayed, and the rare grace and beauty of the central figure, were making audible and flattering remarks. Presently, just behind me, two voices, which I could not fail to recognize, fell on my ears. I started, and then remained motionless. The voices belonged to Lady Faulkner and to Mme. Koluchy. They were together, and were talking eagerly. They could not have seen me, for I heard Lady Faulkner's voice, high and eager. The following words fell on my ears:

"I shall do it tomorrow or next day. My husband returns sooner than I thought, and there is no time to lose. You have arranged about the nurse, have you not?"

"Yes; you can confidently leave the matter in my hands," was Madame's reply.

"And I am safe? There is not the slightest danger of—"

They were pushed on by the increasing crowd, and I could not catch the end of the last sentence, but I had heard enough. The pictures no longer attracted me. I made my way hurriedly from the room. As I descended the stairs my heart beat fast. What had Lady Faulkner to do with Mme. Koluchy? Were the words which unwittingly had fallen on my ears full of sinister meaning? Madame seldom attached herself to any one without a strong reason. Beyond doubt, the beautiful young Scotch woman was an acquaintance of more than ordinary standing. She was in trouble, and Madame was helping her. Once more I was certain that in a new and startling manner Madame was about to make a fresh move in her extraordinary game.

I went straight off to Dufrayer's office, found him in, and told him what had occurred.

"Beyond doubt, Lady Faulkner's manner was that of a woman in trouble," I continued. "From her tone she knows Madame well. There was that in her voice which might dare anything, however desperate. What do you think of it, Dufrayer? Is Durham, by any possible chance in danger?"

"That is more than I can tell you," replied Dufrayer. "Mme. Koluchy's machinations are beyond my powers to cope with. But as you ask me, I should say that it is quite possible that there is some new witchery brewing in her cauldron. By the way, Head, I saw that you were attracted by Lady Faulkner when you met her at Durham's studio."

"Were not you?" I asked.

"To a certain extent, yes, but I was also repelled. I did not like her expression as she sat with the child in her arms."

"What do you mean?"

"I can scarcely explain myself, but my belief is, that she has been subjected by Madame to a queer temptation. What, of course, it is impossible to guess. When you noticed the likeness between Durham's child and her own, I saw a look in her eyes which told me that she was capable of almost any crime to achieve her object."

"I hope you are mistaken," I answered, rising as I spoke. "At least, Durham has made a great success with that picture, and he largely owes it to Lady Faulkner. I must call round to see him, in order to congratulate him.

I did so a few days later. I found the artist busy in his studio working at a portrait of a City magnate.

"Here you are, Head. I am delighted to welcome you," he said, when I arrived. "Pray, take that chair. You will forgive me if I go on working? My big picture having sold so well, I am overpowered with orders. It has taken on; you have seen the reviews, have you not?"

"I have, and I also witnessed the crowds who collected round it on the opening day," I replied. "It is a magnificent work of art, Durham. You will be one of our foremost historical painters from this day out."

He smiled, and, brush in hand, continued to paint in rapidly the background of his picture.

"By the way," I said abruptly, "I am much interested in that beautiful Scotch model who sat for your Ellen Douglas. I have seldom seen a more lovely face."

Durham glanced up at me, and then resumed his work.

"It is a curious story altogether," he said. "Lady Faulkner came to see me in the November of last year. She said that she had met my little boy in Regent's Park, was struck by the likeness between her child and mine; on account of this asked the name of the child, discovered that I was his father (it seems that my fame as a portrait painter had already reached her ears), and she ventured to visit me to know if I would care to undertake an historical picture. I had done nothing so ambitious before, and I hesitated. She pressed the matter, volunteered to sit for the central figure, and offered me £2,000 for the picture when completed.

"I am not too well off, and could not afford to refuse such a sum. I begged of her to employ other and better-known men, but she would not hear of it—she wanted my work, and mine alone. She was convinced that the picture would be a great success. In the end her enthusiasm prevailed. I consented to paint the picture, and set to work at once. For such a large canvas the time was short, and Lady Faulkner came to sit to me three or four times a week. She made one proviso—the child was to be allowed to come freely in and out of the room. She attracted little Robin from the first, and was more than good to him. The boy became fond of her, and she never looked better, nor more at her ease, than when she held him in her arms. She has certainly done me a good service, and for her sake alone I cannot be too pleased that the picture is appreciated.

"Is Lady Faulkner still in town?" I asked.

"No, she left for Scotland only this morning. Her husband's place, Bram Castle, in Inverness, is a splendid old historical estate dating from the Middle Ages."

"How is your boy?" I asked. "You keep him in town, I see; but you have good air in this part of London."

"Yes, capital; he spends most of his time in Regent's Park. The little chap is quite well, thank you. By the way, he ought to be in now. He generally joins me at tea. Would it worry you if he came in as usual, Head?"

"Not at all: on the contrary, I should like to see him," I said.

Durham rang the bell. A servant entered.

"You can get tea, Collier," said his master. "By the way, is baby home yet?"

"No, sir," was the reply. "I cannot understand it," added the man; "Jane is generally back long before now."

Durham made no answer. He returned to his interrupted work. The servant withdrew. Tea was brought in, but there was no sign of the child. Durham handed me a cup, then stood abstracted for a moment, looking straight before him. Suddenly he went to the bell and rang it.

"Tell nurse to bring Master Robin in," he said.

"But nurse and baby have not returned home yet, sir."

Durham glanced at the clock.

"It is just six," he exclaimed. "Can anything be wrong? I had better go out and look for them."

"Let me go with you," I said. "If you are going into Regent's Park, it is on my way home."

"Nurse generally takes the child to the Broad Walk," said Durham; "we will go in that direction."

We entered the park. No sign of nurse or child could we see, though we made several inquiries of the park-keepers, who could tell us nothing.

"I have no right to worry you with all this," said Durham suddenly.

I glanced at him. He had expressed no alarm in words, but I saw now that he was troubled and anxious, and his face wore a stern expression. A nameless suspicion suddenly visited my heart. Try as I would, I could not shake it off.

"We had better go back," I said; "in all probability you will find the little fellow safe at home."

I used cheerful words which I did not feel. Durham looked at me again.

"The child is not to me as an ordinary child," he said, dropping his voice. "You know the tragedy through which I have lived?"

"Dufrayer has told me," I replied.

"My whole life is wrapped up in the little fellow," he continued. "Well, I hope we shall find him all right on our return. Are you really coming back with me?"

"Certainly, if you will have me. I shall not rest easy myself until I know that the boy is safe."

We turned in the direction of Durham's house. We ran up the steps.

"Have you seen them, sir?" Asked the butler, as he opened the door.

"No. Are they not back yet?" Asked Durham.

"No, sir; we have heard nor seen nothing of either of them."

"This is quite unprecedented," said the artist. "Jane knows well that I never allow the boy to be out after five o'clock. It is nearly seven now. You are quite certain," he added, turning to the man, "that no message has come to account for the child's delay?"

"No, sir, nothing."

"What do you think of it, Head?" He looked at me inquiringly.

"It is impossible to tell you," I replied; "a thousand things may keep the nurse out. Let us wait for another hour. If the child has not returned by then, we ought certainly to take some action."

I avoided looking at Durham as I spoke, for Lady Faulkner's words to Mme. Koluchy returned unpleasantly to my memory:

"I shall do it tomorrow or next day—you have arranged about the nurse?"

We went into the studio, and Durham offered me a cigarette. As he did so I suddenly heard a commotion in a distant part of the house; there was the sound of hurrying feet and the noise of more than one voice raised in agitation and alarm. Durham's face turned ghastly.

"There has been an accident," he said. "I felt that there was something wrong. God help me!"

He rushed to the door. I followed him. Just as he reached it, it was flung open, and the nurse, a comely-looking woman, of between thirty and forty years of age, ran in and flung herself at Durham's feet.

"You'll never forgive me, sir," she gasped. "I feel fit to kill myself."

"Get up, Jane, at once, and tell me what has happened. Speak! Is anything wrong with the child?"

"Oh, sir, he is gone—he is lost! I don't know where he is. Oh, I know you'll never forgive me. I could scarcely bring myself to come home to tell you."

"That was folly. Speak now. Tell the whole story at once."

Durham's manner had changed. Now that the blow had really fallen, he was himself once again—a man of keen action, resolute, resolved.

The woman stared at him, then she staggered to her feet, a good deal of her own self-control restored by his manner.

"It was this way, sir," she began. "Baby and I went out as usual early this afternoon. You know how fond baby has always been of Lady Faulkner?"

"Lady Faulkner has nothing to do with this matter," interrupted Durham. "Proceed with your story."

"Her ladyship is in Scotland; at least, it is supposed so, sir," continued the woman. "She came here late last night, and bade us all good-bye. I was undressing baby when she entered the nursery. She took him in her arms and kissed him many times. Baby loves her very much. He always called her 'Pitty lady.' He began to cry when she left the room."

"Go on! Go on!" Said Durham.

"Well, sir, baby and I went into the park. You know how active the child is, as merry as a lark, and always anxious to be down on his legs. It was a beautiful day, and I sat on one of the seats and baby ran about. He was very fond of playing hide-and-seek round the shrubs, and I used to humour him. He asked for his usual game. Suddenly I heard him cry out, 'Pitty lady! Pitty lady,' and run as fast as ever he could round to the other side of a big clump of rhododendrons. He was within a few feet of me, and I was just about to follow him—for half the game, sir, was for me to peep round the opposite side of the trees and try to catch him—when a gentleman whose acquaintance I had made during the last two days came up and began to speak to me. He was a Mr. Ivanhoe, and a very gentlemanly person, sir. We talked for a minute or two, and I'll own I forgot baby. The moment I remembered him I ran round the rhododendrons to look for him, but from that hour to now, sir, I have seen nothing of the child. I don't know where he is—I don't know what has happened to him. Some one must have stolen him, but who, the Lord only knows. He must have fancied that he saw a likeness to Lady Faulkner in somebody else in the park, for he did cry out, 'Pitty lady,' just as if his whole heart was going out to some one, and away he trotted as fast as his feet could carry him. That is the whole story, sir. I'd have come back sooner, but I have been searching the place, like one distracted."

"You did very wrong not to return at once. Did you by any chance happen to see the person the child ran to?"

"I saw no one, sir; only the cry of the child still rings in my ears and the delight in his voice. 'Pitty lady,' he said, and off he went like a flash."

"You should have followed him."

"I know it, sir, and I'm fit to kill myself; but the gentleman was that nice and civil, and I'll own I forgot everything else in the pleasure of having a chat with him."

"The man who spoke to you called himself Ivanhoe?"

"Yes, sir."

"I should like you to give me some particulars with regard to this man's appearance," I said, interrupting the conversation for the first time.

The woman stared at me. I doubt if she had ever seen me before.

"He was a dark, handsome man," she said; then, slowly, "but with something peculiar about him, and he spoke like a foreigner."

I glanced at Durham. His eyes met mine in the most hopeless perplexity. I looked away. A thousand wild fears were rushing through my brain.

"There is no good in wasting time over unimportant matters," said the poor father impatiently. "The thing to do is to find baby at once. Control yourself, please, Jane; you do not make matters any better by giving way to undue emotion. Did you mention the child's loss to the police?"

"Yes, sir, two hours back."

"Durham," I said suddenly, "you and I had better go at once to Dufrayer. He will advise us exactly what is to be done."

Durham glanced at me, then without a word went into the hall and put on his hat. We both left the house.

"What do you think of it, Head?" He said presently, as we were bowling away in a hansom to Dufrayer's flat.

"I cannot help telling you that I fear there is grave danger ahead," I replied; "but do not ask me any more until we have consulted Dufrayer."

The lawyer was in, and the whole story of the child's disappearance was told to him. He listened gravely. When Durham had finished speaking, Dufrayer said slowly:

"There is little doubt what has happened."

"What do you mean?" Cried Durham. "Is it possible that you have got a solution already?"

"I have, my poor fellow, and a grave one. I fear that you are one of the many victims of the greatest criminal in London. I allude to Mme. Koluchy."

"Mme. Koluchy!" Said Durham, glancing from one of us to the other. "What can you mean? Are you dreaming? Mme. Koluchy! What can she have to do with my little boy? Is it possible that you allude to the great lady doctor?"

"The same," cried Dufrayer. "The fact is Durham, Head and I have been watching this woman for months past. We have learned some grave things about her. I will not take up your time now relating them, but you must take our word for it that she is not to be trusted—that to know her is to be in danger—to be her friend is to be in touch with some monstrous and terrible crime. For some reason she has made a friend of Lady Faulkner. Head saw them standing together under your picture. Head, will you tell Durham the exact words you overheard Lady Faulkner say?"

I repeated them.

Durham, who had been listening attentively, now shook his head.

"We are only wasting time following a clue of that sort," he said. "Nothing would induce me to doubt Lady Faulkner. What object could she possibly have in stealing my child? She has a child of her own exactly like Robin. Head, you are on a wrong track—you waste time by these conjectures. Some one has stolen the child hoping to reap a large reward. We must go to the police immediately, and have wires sent to every station round London."

"I will accompany you, Durham, if you like, to Scotland Yard," said Dufrayer.

"And I will go back to Regent's Park to find out if the keepers have learned anything," I said.

We went our separate ways.

The next few days were spent in fruitless endeavours to recover the missing child. No stone was left unturned; the police were active in the search—large rewards were freely offered. Durham, accompanied by a private detective; spent his entire time rushing from place to place. His face grew drawn and anxious, his work was altogether neglected. He slept badly, and morning after morning awoke feeling so ill that his friends became alarmed about him.

"If this fearful strain continues much longer I shall fear for his life," said Dufrayer, one evening, to me. This was at the end of the first week.

On the next morning there was a fresh development in the unaccountable mystery. The nurse, Jane Cleaver, who had been unfeignedly grieving for the child ever since his disappearance, had gone out and had not returned. Inquiries were immediately set on foot with regard to what had become of her, but not a clue could be obtained as to her whereabouts.

On the evening of that day I called to see Durham, and found the poor fellow absolutely distracted.

"If this suspense continues much longer, I believe I shall lose my reason," he said. "I cannot think what has come to me. It is not only the absence of the child. I feel as if I were under the weight of some terrible illness. I cannot explain to you what my nights are. I have horrible nightmares. I suffer from a sensation as if I were being scorched by fire. In the morning I awake more dead than alive. During the day I get a little better, but the following night the same thing is repeated. The image of the child is always before my eyes. I see him everywhere. I hear his voice crying to me to come and rescue him."

He turned aside, so overcome by emotion that he could scarcely speak.

"Durham," I said suddenly, "I have come here this evening to tell you that I have made up my mind."

"To do what?" He asked.

"I am going to Scotland tomorrow. I mean to visit Lady Faulkner at Bram Castle. It is quite possible that she knows something of the fate of the child. One thing, at least, is certain, that a person who had a strong likeness to her beguiled the little fellow round the rhododendron clump."

Durham smiled faintly.

"I cannot agree with you," he said. "I would stake my life on the honour of Lady Faulkner."

"At least you must allow me to make inquiries," I replied. "I shall be away for a few days. I may return with tidings. Keep up your heart until you see me again."

On the following evening I found myself in Inverness-shire. I put up at a small village just outside the estate of Bram. The castle towering on its beetling cliffs hung over the rushing waters of the River Bramley. I slept at the little inn, and early on the following morning made my way to the castle. Lady Faulkner was at home, and showed considerable surprise at seeing me. I noticed that her colour changed, and a look of consternation visited her large, beautiful eyes.

"You startled me, Mr. Head," she said; "is anything wrong?"

"Wrong? Yes," I answered. "Is it possible you have not heard the news?"

"What news?" She inquired. She immediately regained her self-control, sat down on the nearest chair, and looked me full in the face.

"I have news which will cause you sorrow, Lady Faulkner. You were fond of Durham's boy, were you not?"

"Mr. Durham's boy—sweet little Robin?" She cried. "Of course. Has anything happened to him?"

"Is it possible that you have not heard? The child is lost."

I then related all that had occurred. Lady Faulkner looked at me gravely, with just the right expression of distress coming and going on her face. When I had finished my narrative there were tears in her eyes.

"This will almost send Mr. Durham to his grave," she cried; "but surely—surely the child will be found?"

"The child *must* be found," I said. As I spoke I looked at her steadily. Immediately my suspicions were strengthened. She gazed at me with that wonderful calm which I do not believe any man could adopt. It occurred to me that she was overdoing it. The slight hardening which I had noticed before round her lovely lips became again perceptible. In spite of all her efforts, an expression the reverse of beautiful filled her eyes.

"Oh, this is terrible!" She said, suddenly springing to her feet. "I can feel for Mr. Durham from my very heart. My own little Keith is so like Robin. You would like to see my boy, would you not, Mr. Head?"

"I shall be glad to see him," I answered. "You have spoken before of the extraordinary likeness between the children."

"It is marvellous," she cried; "you would scarcely know one from the other."

She rang the bell. A servant appeared.

"Tell nurse to bring baby here," said Lady Faulkner.

A moment later the door was opened—the nurse herself did not appear, but a little boy, dressed in white, rushed into the room. He ran up to Lady Faulkner, clasping his arms ecstatically round her knees.

"Mother's own little boy," she said. She lifted him into her arms. Her fingers were loaded with rings, and I noticed as she held the child against her heart that they were trembling. Was all this excessive emotion for Durham's miserable fate?"

"Lady Faulkner," I said, jumping to my feet and speaking sternly, "I will tell you the truth. I have come here in a vain hope. The loss of the child is killing the poor father—can you do anything for his relief?"

"I?" She said. "What do you mean?"

My words were unexpected, and they startled her.

"Can you do anything for his relief?" I repeated. "Let me look at that boy. He is exactly like the child who is lost."

"I always told you there was an extraordinary likeness," she answered. "Look round, baby, look at that gentleman—tell him you are mother's own little boy."

"Mummy's boy," lisped the baby. He looked full up into my face. The blue eyes, the mass of golden hair, the slow, lovely smile—surely I had seen them before.

Lady Faulkner unfastened her locket, opened it and gave it to me.

"Feature for feature," she said. "Feature for feature the same. Mr. Head, this is my child. Is it possible—" She let the child drop from her arms and stood up confronting me. Her attitude reminded me of Ellen Douglas. "Is it possible that you suspect me?" She cried.

"I will be frank with you, Lady Faulkner," I answered. "I do suspect you."

She seated herself with a perceptible effort.

"This is too grave a matter to be merely angry about," she said; "but do you realize what you are saying? You suspect me—me of having stolen Robin Durham from his father?"

"God help me, I do," I answered.

"Your reasons?"

She took the child again on her knee. He turned towards her and caught hold of her heavy gold chain. As he did so I remembered that I had seen Durham's boy playing with that chain in the studio at Lanchester Gardens.

I briefly repeated the reasons for my fears. I told Lady Faulkner what I had overheard at the Academy. I said a few strong words with regard to Mme. Koluchy.

"To be the friend of that woman is to condemn you," I said, at last. "Do you know what she really is?"

Lady Faulkner made no answer. During the entire narrative she had not uttered a syllable.

"When my husband returns home," she said at last, faintly, "he will protect me from this cruel charge."

"Are you prepared to swear that the boy sitting on your knee is your own boy?" I asked.

She hesitated, then said boldly, "I am."

"Will you take an oath on the Bible that he is your child?"

Her face grew white.

"Surely that is not necessary," she said.

"But will you do it?" I repeated.

She looked down again at the boy. The boy looked up at her.

"Pitty lady," he said, all of a sudden.

The moment he uttered the words I noticed a queer change on her face. She got up and rang the bell. A grave-looking, middle-aged woman entered the room.

"Take baby, nurse," said Lady Faulkner.

The woman lifted the boy in her arms and conveyed him from the room.

"I will swear, Mr. Head," said Lady Faulkner. "There is a Bible on that table—I will swear on the Bible."

She took the Book in her hands, repeated the usual words of the oath, and kissed the Book.

"I declare that that boy is my own son, born of my body," she said, slowly and distinctly.

"Thank you," I answered. I laid the Bible down on the table.

"What else do you want me to do?" She said.

"There is one test," I replied, "which, in my opinion, will settle the matter finally. The test is this. If the boy I have just seen is indeed your son, he will not recognize Durham, for he has never seen him. If, on the other hand, he is Durham's boy, he cannot fail to know his father, and to show that he knows him when he is taken into his presence. Will you return with me to town to-morrow, bringing the child with you? If little Robin's father appears as a stranger to the boy, I will believe that you have spoken the truth."

Before Lady Faulkner could reply, a servant entered the room bearing a letter on a salver. She took it eagerly and tore it open, glanced at the contents, and a look of relief crossed her face as her eyes met mine. They were bright now and full of a curious defiance.

"I am willing to stand the test," she said. "I will come with you tomorrow."

"With the boy?"

"Yes, I will bring the boy."

"You must allow him to enter Durham's presence without you."

"He shall do so."

"Good," I answered. "We can leave here by the earliest train in the morning."

I left the castle a few minutes later, and wired to Dufrayer, telling him that Lady Faulkner and I would come up to town early on the following day, bringing Lady Faulkner's supposed boy with us. I asked Dufrayer not to prepare Durham in any way.

Late in the evening I received a reply to my telegram.

"Come by first possible train," were its contents. "Durham is seriously ill."

I thought it best to say nothing of the illness to Lady Faulkner, and at an early hour on the following day we started on our journey. No nurse accompanied the child. He slept a good part of the day—Lady Faulkner herself was almost silent. She scarcely addressed me. Now and then I saw her eyes light upon the child with a curious expression. Once, as I was attending to her comfort, she looked me full in the face.

"You doubt me, Mr. Head," she said. "It is impossible for me to feel friendly towards you until your doubts are removed."

"I am more grieved than I can say," I answered; "but I must, God helping me, at any cost see justice done."

She shivered.

At 7 p.m. we steamed into King's Cross. Dufrayer was on the platform, and at the carriage door in a second. From the grave expression on his face I saw that there was bad news. Was it possible that the worst had happened to Durham, and that now there would never be any means of proving whether the child were Lady Faulkner's child or not?

"Be quick," he exclaimed, when he saw me. "Durham is sinking fast; I am afraid we shall be too late as it is."

"What is the matter with him?" I asked.

"That is what no one can make out. Langley Chaston, the great nerve specialist, has been to see him this afternoon. Chaston is completely nonplussed, but he attributes the illness to the shock and strain caused by the loss of the child."

Dufrayer said these words eagerly, and as he imagined into my ear alone. A hand touched me on the shoulder. I turned and confronted Lady Faulkner.

"What are you saying?" She exclaimed. "Is it possible that Mr. Durham is in danger, in danger of his life?"

"He is dying," said Dufrayer brusquely.

Lady Faulkner stepped back as though some one had shot her. She quivered all over.

"Take the child," she said to me, in a faint voice.

I lifted the boy in my arms. A brougham awaited us; we got in. The child, weary with the journey, lay fast asleep.

In another moment we were rattling along the Marylebone Road towards Lanchester Gardens.

As we entered the house, Dr. Curzon, Durham's own physician, received us in the hall.

"You are too late," he said, "the poor fellow is unconscious. It is the beginning of the end. I doubt if he will live through the night."

The doctor's words were interrupted by a low cry. Looking round, I saw that Lady Faulkner had flung off her cloak, had lifted her veil, and was staring at Dr. Curzon as though she were about to take leave of her senses.

"Say those words again," she cried.

"My dear madam, I am sorry to startle you. Durham is very ill; quite unconscious; sinking fast."

"I must see him," she said eagerly; "which is his room?"

"The bedroom facing you on the first landing," was the doctor's reply.

She rushed upstairs, not waiting for any one. We followed her slowly. As we were about to enter the room, the child being still in my arms, Lady Faulkner came out, and confronted me.

"I have seen him," she said. "One glance at his face was sufficient. Mr. Head, I must speak to you, and alone, at once—at once! Take me where I can see you all alone."

I opened the door of another room on the same landing, and switched on the electric light.

"Put the child down," she said, "or take him away. This is too horrible; it is past bearing. I never meant things to go as far as this."

"Lady Faulkner, do you quite realize what you are saying?"

"I realize everything. Oh, Mr. Head, you were right. Madame is the most terrible woman in all the world. She told me that I might bring the boy to London in safety—that she had arranged matters so that his father should not recognize him—so that he would not recognize his father. I was to bring him straight here, and trust to her to put things right. I never knew she meant this. I have just looked at his face, and he is changed; he is horrible to look at now. Oh, my God this will kill me."

"You must tell me all, Lady Faulkner," I said. "You have committed yourself now—you have as good as confessed the truth. Then the child—this child—is indeed Durham's son?"

"That child is Loftus Durham's son. Yes, I am the most miserable woman in the universe. Do what you will with me. Oh yes, I could bring myself to steal the boy, but not, not to go to this last extreme step. This is murder, Mr. Head. If Mr. Durham dies, I am guilty of murder. Is there no chance of his life?"

"The only chance is for you to tell me everything as quickly as you can," I answered.

"I will," she replied. She pulled herself together, and began to speak hurriedly.

"I will tell you all in as few words as possible; but in order that you should understand why I committed this awful crime, you must know something of my early history.

"My father and mother died from shock after the death of three baby brothers in succession. Each of these children lived to be a year old, and then each succumbed to the same dreadful malady, and sank into an early grave. I was brought up by an aunt, who treated me sternly, suppressing all affection for me, and doing her utmost to get me married off her hands as quickly as possible. Sir John Faulkner fell in love with me when I was eighteen, and asked me to be his wife. I loved him, and eagerly consented. On the day when I gave my consent I met our family doctor. I told him of my engagement and of the unlooked for happiness which had suddenly dawned on my path. To my astonishment old Dr. Macpherson told me that I did wrong to marry.

"'There is a terrible disease in your family,' he said; 'you have no right to marry.'

"He then told me an extraordinary and terrible thing. He said that in my family on the mother's side was a disease which is called pseudo-hypertrophic muscular paralysis. This strange disease is hereditary, but only attacks the male members of a house, all the females absolutely escaping. You have doubtless heard of it?"

I bowed. "It is one of the most terrible hereditary diseases known," I replied.

Her eyes began to dilate.

"Dr. Macpherson told me about it that dreadful day," she continued. "He said that my three brothers had died of it, that they had inherited it on the mother's side—that my mother's brothers had also died of it, and that she, although escaping herself, had communicated it to her male children. He told me that if I married, any boys who were born to me would in all probability die of this disease.

"I listened to him shocked. I went back and told my aunt. She laughed at my fears, told me that the doctor was deceiving me, assured me that I should do very wrong to refuse such an excellent husband as Sir John, and warned me never to repeat a word of what I had heard with regard to my own family to him. In short, she forced on the marriage.

"I cannot altogether blame her, for I also was only too anxious to escape from my miserable life, and but half-believed the doctor's story.

"I married to find, alas, that I had not entered into Paradise. My husband, although he loved me, told me frankly, a week after our marriage, that his chief reason for marrying me was to have a healthy heir to his house. He said that I looked strong, and he believed my children would be healthy. He was quite morbid on this subject. We were married nearly three years before our child was born. My husband was almost beside himself with rejoicing when this took place. It was not until the baby lay in my arms that I suddenly remembered what I had almost forgotten— old Dr. Macpherson's warning. The child however, looked perfectly strong, and I trusted that the dreadful disease would not appear in him.

"When the baby was four months old my husband was suddenly obliged to leave home in order to visit India. He was to be absent about a year. Until little Keith was a year old he remained perfectly healthy, then strange symptoms began. The disease commenced in the muscles of the calves of the legs, which became much enlarged. The child suffered from great weakness—he could only walk by throwing his body from side to side at each step.

"In terror I watched his symptoms. I took him then to see Dr. Macpherson. He told me that I had neglected his warning, and that my punishment had begun. He said there was not the slightest hope for the child—that he might live for a few months, but would in the end die.

"I returned home, mad with misery. I dared not let my husband know the truth. I knew that if I did he would render my life a hell, for the fate which had overtaken my first child would be the fate of every other boy born to me. My misery was beyond any words. Last winter, when baby's illness had just begun, I came up to town. I brought the child with me— he grew worse daily. When in town, I heard of the great fame of Mme. Koluchy and her wonderful cures. I went to see her, and told her my pitiful story. She shook her head when I described the features of the case, said that no medicine had ever yet been discovered for this form of muscular paralysis, but said she would think over the case, and asked me to call upon her again.

"The next day, when in Regent's Park, I saw Loftus Durham's little boy. I was startled at the likeness, and ran forward with a cry, thinking that I was about to embrace my own little Keith. The child had the same eyes, the same build. The child was Keith to all intents and purposes, only he was healthy—a splendid little lad. I made friends with him on the spot. I went straight then to Mme. Koluchy, and told her that I had seen a child the very same as my own child. She then thought out the scheme which has ended so disastrously. She assured me it only needed courage on my part to carry it through. We discovered that the child was the only son of a widower, a rising artist of the name of Durham. Mr. Head, you know the rest. I determined to get acquainted with Mr. Durham, and in order to do so gave him a commission to paint the picture called 'Soldiers, Attend!'

"You can scarcely understand how I lived through the past winter. Madame had persuaded me to send my dying child to her. A month ago I saw my boy breathe his last. I smothered my agony and devoted every energy to the kidnapping of little Robin. I took him away as planned, the nurse's attention being completely engrossed by a confederate of Mme. Koluchy's. It was arranged that in a week's time the nurse was also to be kidnapped, and removed from the country. She is now, I believe, on her way to New Zealand.

Having removed the nurse, the one person we had to dread in the recognizing of the child was the father himself. With great pains I taught the boy to call me 'Mummy,' and I believed he had learned the name and had forgotten his old title of 'Pitty lady.' But he said the words yesterday in your presence, and I have not the slightest doubt by so doing confirmed your suspicions. When I had taken the dreadful oath that the child was my own, and so perjured my soul, a letter from Mme. Koluchy arrived. She had discovered that you had gone to Scotland, and guessed that your suspicions were aroused. She said that you were her most terrible enemy, that more than once you had circumvented her in the moment of victory, but she believed that on this occasion we should win, and she further suggested that the very test which you demanded should be acceded to by me. She said that she had arranged matters in such a way that the father would not recognize the child, nor would the child know him; that I was to trust to her, and boldly go up to London, and bring the boy into his father's presence. The butler, Collier, who of course also knew the child, had, owing to Madame's secret intervention, been sent on a fruitless errand into the country, and so got out of the way. I now see what Madame really meant. She would kill Mr. Durham and so insure his silence for ever; but, oh! Mr. Head, bad as I am, I cannot commit murder. Mr. Head, you must save Mr. Durham's life."

"I will do what I can," I answered. "There is no doubt, from your confession, that Durham is being subjected to some slow poison. What, we have to discover. I must leave you now Lady Faulkner."

I went into the next room, where Dufrayer and Dr. Curzon were waiting for me. It was darkened. At the further end, in a bed against the wall, lay Durham. Bidding the nurse bring the lamp, I went across, and bent over him. I started back at his strange appearance. I scarcely recognized him. He was lying quite still, breathing so lightly that at first I thought he must be already dead. The skin of the face and neck had a very strange appearance. It was inflamed and much reddened. I called the poor fellow by name very gently. He made no sign of recognition.

"What is all this curious inflammation due to?" I asked of Dr. Curzon, who was standing by my side.

"That is the mystery," he replied; "it is unlike anything I have seen before."

I took up my lens and examined it closely. It was certainly curious. Whatever the cause, the inflammation seemed to have started from many different centres of disturbance. I was at once struck by the curious shape of the markings. They were star-shaped, and radiated as if from various centres. As I still examined them, I could not help thinking that I had seen similar markings somewhere else not long ago, but when and connected with what I could not recall. This was, however, a detail of no importance. The terrible truth which confronted me absorbed every other consideration. Durham was dying before my eyes, and from Lady Faulkner's confession, Mme. Koluchy was doubtless killing him by means unknown. It was, indeed, a weird situation.

I beckoned to the doctor, and went out with him on to the landing.

"I have no time to tell you all," I said. "You noticed Lady Faulkner's agitation? She has made a strange and terrible confession. The child who has just been brought back to the house is Durham's own son. He was stolen by Lady Faulkner for reasons of her own. The woman who helped her to kidnap the child was the quack doctor, Mme. Koluchy."

"Mme. Koluchy?" Said Dr. Curzon.

"The same," I answered; "the cleverest and the most wicked woman in London—a past-master in every shade of crime. Beyond doubt, Madame is at the bottom of Durham's illness. She is poisoning him—we have got to discover how. I thought it necessary to tell you as much, Dr. Curzon. Now, will you come back with me again to the sick-room?"

The doctor followed me without a word.

Once more I bent over Durham, and as I did so the memory of where I had seen similar markings returned to me. I had seen them on photographic plates which had been exposed to the induction action of a brush discharge of high electro-motive force from the positive terminal of a Plante Rheostatic machine. An eminent electrician had drawn my attention to these markings at the time, had shown me the plates, and remarked upon the strange effects. Could there be any relationship of cause and effect here?

"Has any kind of electrical treatment been tried?" I asked, turning to Dr. Curzon

"None," he answered. "Why do you ask?"

"Because," I said, "I have seen similar effects produced on the skin by prolonged exposure to powerful X-rays, and the appearance of Durham's face suggests that the skin might have been subjected to a powerful discharge from a focus tube."

"There has been no electricity employed, nor has any stranger been near the patient."

He was about to proceed, when I suddenly raised my hand.

"Hush!" I cried, "stay quiet a moment."

There was immediately a dead silence in the room.

The dying man breathed more and more feebly. His face beneath the dreadful star-like markings looked as if he were already dead. Was I a victim to my own fancies, or did I hear muffled, distant and faint the sound I somehow expected to hear—the sound of a low hum a long way off? An ungovernable excitement seized me.

"Do you hear? Do you hear?" I asked grasping Curzon's arm.

"I hear nothing. What do you expect to hear?" He said, fear dawning in his eyes.

"Who is in the next room through there?" I asked, bending over the sick man and touching the wall behind his head.

"That room belongs to the next house, sir," said the nurse.

"Then, if that is so, we may have got the solution," I said. "Curzon, Dufrayer, come with me at once."

We hurried out of the room.

"We must get into the next house without a moment's delay," I said.

"Into the next house? You must be mad," said the doctor.

"I am not. I have already told you that there is foul play in this extraordinary case, and a fearful explanation of Durham's illness has suddenly occurred to me. I have given a great deal of time lately to the study of the effect of powerful cathode and X-rays. The appearance of the markings on Durham's face are suspicious. Will you send a messenger at once to my house for my fluorescent screen?"

"I will fetch it," said Dufrayer. He hurried off.

"The next thing to be done is to move the bed on which the sick man lies to the opposite side of the room," I said.

Curzon watched me as I spoke, with a queer expression on his face.

"It shall be done," he said briefly. We returned to the sick-room.

In less than an hour my fluorescent screen was in my hand. I held it up to the wall just where Durham's bed had been. It immediately became fluorescent, but we could make nothing out. This fact, however, converted my suspicions into certainties.

"I thought so," I said. "Who owns the next house?"

I rushed downstairs to question the servants. They could only tell me that it had been unoccupied for some time, but that the board "To let" had a month ago been removed. They did not believe that the new occupants had yet taken possession.

Dufrayer and I went into the street and looked at the windows. The house was to all appearance the counterpart of the one in which Durham lived. Dufrayer, who was now as much excited as I was, rushed off to the nearest fire-engine station, and quickly returned with an escape ladder. This was put up to one of the upper windows and we managed to get in. The next instant we were inside the house, and the low hum of a "make and break" fell on our ears. We entered a room answering to the one where Durham's bedroom was situated, and there immediately discovered the key to the diabolical mystery.

Close against the wall, within a few feet of where the sick man's bed had been, was an enormous focus tube, the platinum electrode turned so

as to direct the rays through the wall. The machine was clamped in a holder, and stood on a square deal table, upon which also stood the most enormous induction coil I had ever seen. This was supplied from the main through wires coming from the electric light supplied to the house. This induction coil gave a spark of at least twenty-four inches. Insulated wires from it ran across the room, to a hole in the farther wall into the next room, where the "make and break" was whirring. This had evidently been done in order that the noise of the hum should be as far away as possible.

"Constant powerful discharges of cathode and X-rays, such as must have been playing upon Durham for days and nights continuously, are now proved to be so injurious to life, that he would in all probability have been dead before the morning," I cried. "As it is, we may save him." Then I turned and grasped Dufrayer by the arm.

"I believe that at last we have evidence to convict Mme. Koluchy," I exclaimed. "What with Lady Faulkner's confession, and—"

"Let us go back at once and speak to Lady Faulkner," said Dufrayer.

We returned at once to the next house, but the woman whom we sought had already vanished. How she had gone, and when, no one knew.

The next day we learned that Mme. Koluchy had also left London, and that it was not certain when she would return. Doubtless, Lady Faulkner, having confessed, in a moment of terrible agitation, had then flown to Mme. Koluchy for protection. From that hour to now we have heard nothing more of the unfortunate young woman. Her husband is moving Heaven and earth to find her, but in vain.

Removed from the fatal influence of the rays Durham has recovered, and the joy of having his little son restored to him has doubtless been his best medicine.

The Plague of Lights

OWEN OLIVER

AT THE END of the nineteenth century certain British factions were becoming almost paranoid at how unprepared Britain was for any possible invasion by either the French or the Germans. William Le Queux (1864–1927), one of the pioneers of spy fiction, produced two warning novels, *The Great War in England in 1897* (1894) and *The Invasion of 1910* (1906). The latter was sponsored by and serialised in the *Daily Mail* newspaper and caused a considerable uproar, with questions asked in Parliament.

If Britain was considered ill prepared for an invasion by foreign powers, how less ready was it (or any other country) for an invasion by extraterrestrials? H. G. Wells had shown this memorably in *The War of the Worlds* (1898) and since its publication many authors turned to the thought of alien invasion. One of the most creative was Owen Oliver, the alias used by Joshua Flynn (1863–1933). Flynn was a leading civil servant for over thirty years. He was financial adviser to Lord Kitchener during the Boer War and became Director-General of Finance for the Ministry of Pensions during the First World War. He was knighted in 1920.

As Oliver, Flynn contributed a variety of stories to the popular magazines, and though only a small percentage was science fiction it was still a significant number of stories. There are enough for a small volume but their themes are often repetitive because he enjoyed looking at different ways in which Earth (usually Britain) might be under threat. In "Out of the Deep" (*London Magazine,* July 1904) it was by giant fish who had evolved sufficient intelligence to manufacture artificial flying fish. In "The Long Night" (*Pearson's Magazine*, January 1906), the Earth's rotation unaccountably slows down. In "The Cloud-Men" (*Munsey's Magazine*, August 1911) Earth is invaded by strange vapour-beings. There are plenty more, but perhaps the most original is the following, from *The London Magazine* for October 1904. —**M.A.**

HE OFFICIAL BLUE BOOKS just published, as the result of the Royal Commission on the Plague of Lights, contain the evidence of some two hundred scientists, and an exhaustive report by the two peers, three M.P.'s, and four Fellows of the Royal Society, who formed the Commission, upon the terrible calamity that recently devastated the earth. It may seem presumptuous for me to add to the testimony of such authorities; but I notice that all the learned gentlemen who gave evidence either obtained their facts at second-hand (having themselves escaped the plague by flight or going into hiding), or confessed that during the actual attack their faculties were obscured. As I am one of the very few sufferers who escaped with memory unimpaired, I think it well to set down the events which came under my observation.

It was on the evening of the 12th of June, 1906, that the "lights" first appeared, among a chattering and laughing crowd that was pouring out of the Strand Theatre into Surrey Street. Phyllis Brand was leaning upon my arm. We were newly engaged, and I was looking only at her till I heard cries from the people around us. Then I saw that the air was full of pale yellow lights. Most of them were some distance above, standing out clearly against the dark houses and cloudy sky; but a few were fluttering down among the crowd; round lights of about the bigness of a shilling, and much the same thickness. When they came quite near, it was seen that they went in threes, each at the corner of an equal-sided triangle, some eight or nine inches apart. Someone called "Fire" and the crowd began to sway dangerously.

I put my arms round Phyllis, and forced our way through, with some damage to our clothes and a few bruises, and watched the crowd from a dark doorway a little distance down the street. The excitement increased, and several of the crowd were thrown down and trampled underfoot. Seventeen people were killed, we learnt the next morning. Afterwards they were accounted among the lucky ones.

The treble lights dropped steadily among the fighting mass at the doors, and darted swiftly at some who escaped from the outskirts, always fastening upon their breasts. A white-bearded gentleman beside me declared it was only a meteoric shower, and there was no real harm in the lights. They were luminous, like electric light, he explained, but did not burn. A man with a hoarse voice suggestive of drink remarked that they had sent for a fire-engine, and when it came the crowd would be worse; and anyhow, it wasn't his business, and he was going home. He had taken a few unsteady steps, when a triangle of lights dropped noiselessly upon him. He howled like an injured animal and ran. A woman in evening dress rushed by with the lights upon her cloak. She threw the cloak aside, but the lights had penetrated it, and adhered to her dress. She tore away the flimsy muslin, but they remained on the underwear; and when she plucked this away they were still left—three pale yellow spots upon the flesh. She tore at them with her fingers, till her nails made long red weals, but the fiendish spots remained. A man, hatless and coat-less, with three spots upon his shirt-front around a glittering diamond stud, seized her arm and hurried her away. Phyllis's hold on me relaxed, and I found that she had fainted. I walked stealthily along the pavement, keeping in the shadow as much as I could, carrying her in my arms, and reached the Temple Station safely. The booking-clerk and ticket-collectors had fled, and I carried her down to the platform below.

The people who had the yellow spots upon them were gathered at one end of the platform screaming, and trying to tear them from themselves and from one another. Those who had escaped attack were huddled together at the other end of the platform. A man with the spots upon him tried to join us, and refused to go away. Another man who stood before his children brandishing a big walking-stick felled him. Several women had fainted. A train hustled in, and we crowded wildly into the already crowded carriages, elbowing each other fiercely out of the way. A somber-looking man in a corner woke up and grumbled about the crowding, and asked what was the matter. Somebody told him that hell fire had dropped upon earth. He snorted and offered us some pamphlets upon "The Curse of Alcohol." It is evident that the rest of the passengers also thought that we were all drunk.

I got out at Blackfriars and carried Phyllis, who was still in the faint, into St. Paul's Station. I tried to get some brandy from the buffet, but it was full of wailing people branded with the lights. They did not hurt, they said but they frightened them, because they would not come off: The lights penetrated the clothing and stuck to the skin; but when the clothing was removed they left no mark or rent upon it. In other words, it was the flesh on which they settled, but they showed through the clothing.

I obtained half a pail full of water from the lavatory to bathe Phyllis's hands and face, and she revived. She was very brave, and wished to try to help the sufferers, but I persuaded her that she could do no good. I would have run the risk of contact with them myself, but, of course, I could not let her.

The officials assigned one end of the train to those who were attacked and their friends, and the other to those who were not, and we got back to Dulwich about twenty minutes after time. All the doctors of the locality were at the station, waiting for sufferers who had telegraphed for them. I did not stay to hear what they said, as Phyllis was very weak, and I thought it best to get her home. Also, I confess, I was a little frightened of the light.

Phyllis's father pooh-poohed the matter as an optical delusion, and advised me to go home and get to bed, and I went.

The morning's paper, however, treated the matter very seriously, and gave two whole pages to it. The lights had appeared in most parts of the City and West End at about eleven o'clock; it stated, and had fastened upon people in the way I have described. There had been some hundreds of fatalities through panics in the crowds, and several persons had died of fright. Professor Morden, F.R.S., the great authority upon physical astronomy, considered that a disembodied asteroid, in the form of luminous vapor, had fallen upon the earth; and that, owing to chemical affinity for living tissues, its particles had adhered to the people with whom it came into contact. He could not explain why it, attacked only adult human beings, and not children, dogs or horses; but he was sure that it was too unsubstantial to do any real harm, and that the lights would fade away gradually. Dr Maurice Ray, the specialist for skin diseases, held similar opinions, and pointed out that the perpetual dying out and regeneration of the tissues would in a short time, rid those who had been attacked from the objectionable spots. He gave a prescription for a lotion that would expedite this result.

After calling to inquire about Phyllis, I went up to town by the train that should have started at 9:19. It was late owing to a special having been run to convey those who had been attacked by the lights to the London hospitals. At the Elephant and Castle we came into a swarm of the yellow spots, faintly visible in the light of day. A porter and three passengers had been attacked on the platform, and many people alighted to return by the next train. I went on, as I had an important business engagement. The lights were flitting about most of the streets in the City, but they bore no large proportion to the number of people. An early edition of the evening papers said that there was to be a question in the House, and that Dr. Ray's lotion had been issued to the police, so that they could render first aid to sufferers. A little later placards were stuck up, by order of the Home Office, directing those who were attacked to report themselves immediately to the nearest police-station.

"In view of the uncertainty as to the effects of the plague lights, and their infectiousness or otherwise," the placard said, "it is considered desirable that cases should be isolated and kept under observation. No permanent ill effects are, however, anticipated."

The lights, as I have said, were not very numerous, and they seemed to be flitting about like butterflies in search of something, rather than settling indiscriminately. Some of the newsboys were chivying them with their papers, and throwing their caps at them, and I went about all day without being attacked; but I saw at least a dozen people seized upon in the streets; and a man and woman who were together were branded at the restaurant during luncheon.

The evening papers reported that pairs of the light-triangles appeared to have an affinity for one another, and to endeavor to attack couples, so that infected persons must be carefully avoided. The people who had been first attacked, the report said, were beginning to show signs of mental derangement, talking a strange gibberish, manifesting a marked antipathy to their former associates, unless these were also attacked, and frequently showing demonstrative affection to some one of their fellow sufferers of the opposite sex—"in which case the lights, which differ microscopically from one another in marking, are found to be identical."

"From the manner in which the plague lights select their victims," the report went on, "and work in pairs, and from the forced, and often apparently unwilling attachment between the persons so attacked, it is impossible to avoid the conclusion that the lights are intelligent, but malevolent, beings, seeking to obtain an embodiment in human form; and that those which have been associated in their former sphere seek to associate those upon whom they seize here. It is noticed that, as the afflicted persons grow weaker, the spots grow larger and brighter. Dr. Lurnaker, the great philologist, maintains that the gibberish, which the sufferers frequently talk, manifests the characteristics of rational speech, and conjectures that it is inspired and understood by these evil visitants."

I found Phyllis sitting with her chin on her hand, a newspaper lying on the floor beside her. She was very pale, and she trembled a little in my arms.

"If this evil has come upon the whole world;" she said, "it may come upon us, Frank. It will not matter so much if we are taken together. Promise me that, if you are attacked, you will come to me at once, so that the fellow lights may take me and no one else. I shall not flinch, or worry you with complaints, dear!"

I promised what she asked, but, of course, I had no intention of keeping the promise until I knew how much or how little harm the lights did. I made her promise also that, if she were attacked first, she would come to me, but I fancied that she would not keep her promise either.

I spent the evening at her house. About 10 o'clock her father came in with a late edition of the *Evening Standard*. They called it the "Plague Edition." It stated that the lights had appeared in great force in Paris, Berlin, and New York, and to a less extent at all the great centers of life.

In France the effects of the attack were much more rapid than elsewhere, probably owing to the excitable temperament of the people, and in several cases sufferers had died within a few hours. During the progress of the disease the lights grew in size and upon death detached themselves from the body. In some case the detached lights simply departed; in other instances they seized upon the doctors and nurses.

Sufficient time had not elapsed to record the progress of these secondary attacks. In the primary cases the lights had grown as follows:

Diameter of circles 1/8 inch to 3/8 inch.

Thickness of circles 1/4 inch to 1/2 inch or 5/8 inch.

The distance between the outer edges remained constant, so that the inside edges of the circles approached one another as they grew.

The lights were unaffected by electricity, heat, or the action of any chemical agent which had been tried upon them; but they gave a dark skiagraph, like a solid substance, when photographed by the X-rays, from which it was inferred that they possessed substance, though of a kind unknown to us. The general theory was that they were disembodied spirits trying to reincarnate themselves in human bodies.

In the morning my own newspaper did not appear, but I obtained one at the station, and learnt that the lights had spread all over England, and that many deaths seemed imminent. I started for town, but at Herne Hill I found that the up traffic had been suspended, and that extra down trains were being run to take home the people who had started earlier, many of whom had been attacked. In most cases another set of lights was hovering about the sufferer, doubtless waiting for the second victim. A few who had been seized in pairs were holding one another's hands, and some of these were talking in an unknown tongue, in which a phrase which may be represented in our characters as *La-Lu-Le* constantly recurred.*

The City was swarming with the lights, I heard, and a bright swarm of them was visible hanging over Brixton. People were running from that direction into Herne Hill. A hatless man with the lights on his vest was standing on the top of a cab outside the station praying aloud, and a crowd was kneeling in the street.

As I could not get into a train I walked back to Dulwich, and went to Phyllis. People were leaving their houses, in cabs or on foot, for the country. Probably we should have fled likewise, but her mother was ailing and unable to be moved. I did not ask her. Her father had started for town earlier than I. He did not return, and we never heard of him again. Many people disappeared like that in those days.

Appendix LVI, of the Blue Books gives a few fragments of this speech and conjectural translations. It seems to be established beyond doubt that La-Lu-Le was a profession of affection, but its exact force is thought to have differed according to the syllable accented.

An early evening edition, hastily printed on a small portion of a single half-sheet, related that all the hospitals and public buildings in town were full of sufferers, and that whole streets had been commandeered for those who were crowded out. A local Plague Committee was hastily formed to make arrangements in West Dulwich. I offered my services, and worked all the morning at getting one of the houses in order, and laying in provisions, etc. As I was going back to Phyllis's to lunch, along Thurlow Park Road, Doris Fane rushed out from her house. She had the triangle of lights upon her blouse, and another was fluttering behind her. They were much the same color as her pale yellow hair. She was white and half distracted with fear, and she ran to me and clung to my arm. We had always been friends, and I think, if I hadn't met Phyllis, I should have grown fond of her.

"See!" She cried, pointing to the light following behind her—"See! It is looking for its mate. He will be my lover, when it finds him. I shouldn't be so frightened if it were you. Didn't you know that I cared for you, Frank? I can tell you now, because I am going to die. Take them away—Oh! Take them away!" She tore wildly at the fiendish lights upon her breast.

The other lights hovered around me—brushed my arm. I closed my eyes and shuddered. It was the thought that Phyllis would wait for me, look for me in vain, that frightened me most; but when I opened my eyes again, the lights were fluttering away, up the hill, towards the high school. Doris released her hold upon my arm and followed them slowly, looking backward with her eyes fixed on me.

I went on to Phyllis's house in Croxted Road. A number of the lights were flitting about the road. When they came near me I ran. I did not hope to escape them, but I wanted to get to Phyllis first. When I reached her gate I heard Dr. Hallam's voice through the open window. We had been rivals for Phyllis, and I had won. He was a better man than I, but there is no accounting for a woman's fancy.

"Let them take me too," he cried. "I am willing to die with you. I always loved you Phyllis."

"Hush!" She said gently. "Hush! I love Frank. I always shall while I am myself." Then she saw me and flung out her arms, and I saw the yellow spots on her dress. They looked like golden ornaments; and the others looked like a halo of stars over her dark hair. "Frank! Frank! Run away, dear. It has taken me. It wants you—the other one. You are safe from the rest. I know. Run away from me and you will be saved. God bless you, dear!"

I vaulted in at the window and took her in my arms. I did not notice when the other lights settled on me, or anything but the tears in her eyes. She smiled at me through them. Presently I looked down and found the three yellow spots on my breast. They did not burn, or hurt in any way, but they seemed to be drawing my very soul out of me. After a few moments Hallam came up and touched my arm.

"You must go to the hospital," he said huskily, "both of you. I will come quickly and do what I can. I will arrange with the nurse to look after your mother, Phyllis. I was mad just now, and you must forget. I don't think it's much use, the treatment that they recommend, but I'll try it. I'd save you for one another if I could. Anyhow, you are together. You are lucky."

We went together to the hospital. It was in the high school and the houses adjoining it. A number of fellow-sufferers were there, and others were thronging in. Those who came singly were excited and restless, and some of them called wildly for their stars—meaning, doubtless, the "mates" of the lights that had seized upon them. Those who were in pairs mostly behaved like lovers, as some of them had previously been, we knew. Some, however, were evidently strangers, or unfriendly. These were sullen, or reviled one another.

We found a quiet corner in a garden, and sat there for a time holding hands. We did not feel any pain or illness, only very weak; and I think, perhaps, this was the effect of excitement rather than the stars. At length it occurred to me that we could help those who were more afflicted than we. So we went in again. We found Hallam and Doris Fane sitting together in the hall, looking at one another with set faces—hers flushed and angry, his pale and grave. The twin lights had bound her and him!

We went a little nearer to speak to them, and I felt the lights leap on my breast. At the same moment Phyllis started and seized my hand, and he and Doris suddenly rose.

"Frank!" Phyllis cried. "His stars are calling mine. Don't let them take me from you."

"They shall not take you," I said; and I seemed to hear the lights that held me hiss. Then we walked up to them and shook hands. And a struggle took place that I cannot describe or wholly understand, but I know.

I cannot give any reason for the thing that saved us, but I know. So does Phyllis. So do Hallam and Doris. The twin lights that held us four had been wrongly mated. Mine wanted those of Doris, and hers wanted mine. Hallam's wanted those of Phyllis, and hers wanted his. But they were bound otherwise, and having seized upon us they could not leave us, and struggling to leave us they did not take any great hold upon us or do us any great harm. That is how I have escaped to write these things.

We did not lose our faculties, or talk gibberish like the other sufferers, and we did not fail utterly in body as they did, and die; and for two days and nights we toiled almost without cessation to minister to them; toiled till we were giddy and almost dropped. At first we had the help of a few elder children who had not gone to the homes established for them. The lights did not attack the children, as I have said before.

Few people came into the hospital after the first day, as most of those who were not attacked at the beginning had fled into the country, where I fear those who were attacked perished more miserably, no homes having been established for them. Two or three, however, came in singly, drawn by the triple light to its mate on someone with us. Two of our patients also left, beating their breasts, and saying that they must seek their stars—the "love-lights" some of the poor, demented sufferers called them.

Those who remained with us—some sixty originally—were helplessly inert for long periods. At other times they gesticulated wildly and talked in the unknown tongue. *La-Lu-Le*, they kept crying, with the accent first on one syllable and then on the other, and in times varying from love to despair. *La-Lu-Le!*

They had intervals of reason, but those grew fewer and shorter. After the first day they made no attempt to take food or drink, even in their rational moments, and they lost the power of their limbs and lay in long rows on the beds and couches. We worked unceasingly to minister to them. The supply of food grew short, and Phyllis and I went out and raided some of the shops that had been hurriedly left with the doors open, and we brought what we had found back in a baker's barrow, that the two of us had scarcely strength to push. I have no words to describe the awful silence of the deserted houses and streets.

The lights seemed to have more power to weaken us while we were separated from the doctor and Doris, and similarly they were more affected while we were absent. So we kept together in the evening. We were all too exhausted to say much. Phyllis and I sat hand-in-hand the others sat a little way apart, but they had ceased to quarrel.

"You have gained my great respect and admiration, Miss Fane," the doctor told her, and she bowed and wiped her eyes.

"I am glad that I shall die with a man," she said.

We had little sleep that night. Several of our patients died. Their stars grew larger and brighter and more substantial—they felt like a spot of mist if you touched them—and at the end they went off together.

The third day more died, and the rest were in a stupor. The air was fill of showers of lights that fell in a long rain of triangles. They were the outskirts of a dissolving world that was falling upon us, a shriveled old gentleman, who had escaped attack, declared. There was probably a more material core, he said, that would come soon. That would be the end of things. He was a scientist whom men had called great, he told us but his name did not matter. These things did not matter now. He went on slowly, leaning on his stick, towards Beckenham. Someone whom he loved had been buried there for thirty years, he told us, and the "love-lights" (he called them so) would be waiting for him on her grave, he hoped.

More of our patients died in the afternoon. Phyllis and I went always arm in arm when we were not attending to them. The doctor and Doris kept away from us as much as possible because their ghostly masters struggled with ours, and they wished to save us from annoyance during these last sad hours.

"You lucky people!" Doris said. "Don't look like that, doctor! You and I are luckier than some. Let us do our work together, dear friend, and hope for the best."

"God bless you, dear, brave girl," he said, and kissed her hand.

There were only twenty-two of our patients left at the close of the afternoon, and these did not understand anything that we said. Doris fainted from overwork, and Phyllis seemed in a sort of coma. The doctor and I had to feed them also. He and I were so weak that we could scarcely move, and, the four of us seemed bound closely together by the lights. He and Doris were unable to resist them any longer, and drew closer and closer together as they sat on the sofa, after she had revived from her faintness.

"It isn't my fault, Miss Fane," he apologized. "I am sorry if it causes you annoyance."

"No," she smiled up at him. "It doesn't. I think it is near the end, doctor. I am glad to be with you."

He drew her head down on his shoulder. "It is near the end," he said. "You will be more comfortable so."

We sat very still for half an hour. There was no sound except when the stars of those who had died fluttered by. We could hear them now. They seemed growing into substantial bodies, and we into unsubstantial spirits. Then gradually everything seemed to change. We found that we could move more freely, not that we were stronger, but because our bodies had less weight. The air seemed full of something that we could not see, only feel; and it grew swiftly dark, an hour before sunset.

"What is coming, Frank?" Phyllis asked, in an awed whisper.

"The end of all things, dear," I said. "I suppose it is the 'core' of the dead world coming upon us, as he said. We are together, dear. It has not been without its happiness, this sad time."

"No, dear. I have been with you."

The darkness grew suddenly darker, and looking out of the open window—

we were in the long room where most of our remaining patients were—we saw a shapeless mass overhead, shutting out the sight of the sky; a bluish, ashy grey, with portions bulging out like low mountains, and black gaps between, where seas might have been. The Blue Books say it was from ninety to a hundred miles away; but it seemed almost to touch us then. Why it did not touch us quite even the Royal Commissioners do not know.

The weight seemed now entirely gone from our limbs. I suppose because the attraction of the other world counterbalanced the attraction of gravity. There was no light, except the faint shine of the plague-lights on our breasts, and as we watched, holding our breath, these suddenly floated upward.

"They have left us!" Phyllis cried. "The love-lights! Don't love me any less."

"I shall always love you, Phyllis," I assured her, "if there is no light left in the world." But she fainted and did not hear me.

I think I must have fainted too, for it felt as if time had passed when next I remembered anything. Through the window I saw the dark world still hurrying by, escorted by battalions of tiny twinkling lights. I could not see if they were still in triangles of three. They were—thank God!—Too far. In the room it was inky dark. A few of the patients, come to their senses, were calling in feeble, frightened voices to ask what had happened, and where they were.

"The lights have gone," the doctor was telling them. "I do not know what the darkness may bring. But we are in the Hands of God, dear friends— the hands of God!"

IT WAS THE MORNING of the 19th of June when the sun shone again on the pale, enfeebled people who were left—humans, men and women as before. The Royal Commission has narrated in Appendices XXIV to XXXII how the work of the world was put together again, like a map that had been dissected for a puzzle. I only know the small happenings around me. We tottered about getting food and drink. Some who had met during the plague settled down where we were, and many who had parted went off to seek those they had lost. Children came down from their homes to find their parents, and parents went off to look for their children, and we smiled and wiped our eyes. Presently some went off to the churches and set the bells ringing, and all of us gathered there.

We shuddered still as we looked after the black mass passing away in the sky above, drawing after it a misty aurora of light; the plague-lights that had invaded our earth, struggled with us, and slain; and failed after all. Henceforth we were left our own little world, and the world of each is small. Mine is larger than some for I am Phyllis's and she is mine.

Indeed I am tempted to say that ours is a world of four since the doctor and Doris and we are almost as inseparable as if we were still bound by our stars; but they struggle no longer since the evil went.

It was in a pause from our work of helping those who were feebler than ourselves that we understood this. We were sitting down together to the crusts and water that we had collected for lunch, and the doctor placed Doris a chair touching his.

"You aren't bound to sit beside me now," he said, laughing cheerfully, and wiping his forehead with his handkerchief he had worked very hard among the sick. "You can order me to the opposite side of the table—or the world if you wish."

"But I can't wish." Doris said softly; and suddenly he put his hand under her chin and lifted up her face, and she looked up at him smilingly, and held gently to the sides of his coat. Phyllis and I took up our fragments of lunch, and went out in the garden and ate it under a tree. "God bless them," I said, "and all on earth that live and love."

"Amen!"

Phyllis put her arm through mine, and gazed where the dead world, with its trail of pale light, was growing dim afar.

"Perhaps He sent them—the love-lights—to teach us to love. Who knows if they were a blessing, after all!"

That is the lesson that we have learnt from the plague of lights. It is not included in the forty-three recommendations of the Royal Commission, and that is why I have written this story.

What the Rats Brought

Ernest Favenc

THIS STORY BRINGS TOGETHER two related period threads. One is world catastrophe, which we have already touched on. The other is the vampire. The fascination with the villain became popular in the late Victorian period almost certainly as a result of the Jack the Ripper murders in 1888. There were earlier popular villains, not least Dick Turpin, Spring-Heel'd Jack, Sweeney Todd and Robert Louis Stevenson's Mr Hyde (*The Strange Case of Dr. Jekyll and Mr. Hyde* was published in 1886, just before the Ripper murders). However the definitive villain-hero must surely be Count Dracula created by Bram Stoker in his 1897 novel *Dracula*.

Whilst the following story features vampires, they're not the dead-alive, but genuine vampire bats. Even so, the very mention of them as part of a world catastrophe has all the connotations of steampunk imagery.

Ernest Favenc (1845–1908) was born in England but emigrated to Australia in 1864 and for some years worked on various cattle stations. He also took part in gold prospecting and became skilled at living off the land in the remote Australian interior. His abilities led to him being appointed as leader of an expedition in 1878 that explored the territory between Brisbane and Port Darwin to survey for the possibility of a railway link. After the expedition he married and settled down to a life as a writer and journalist. Several of his books are of science fiction interest including *The Secret of the Australian Desert* (1895) and the collections *The Last of Six* (1893) and *Tales of the Austral Topics* (1894). An expanded version of the latter book, edited by Cheryl Taylor with extensive notes on Favenc was published in 1997. —**M.A.**

IT WAS DURING THE PROLONGED DROUGHT OF 1919, just about Christmas time, that the steamer *Niagara* fell in with an apparently abandoned barquentine about fifty miles from Sydney.

It was calm, fine weather; so, failing to get any response to their hail, the chief officer boarded her.

He returned with the report that she was perfectly seaworthy and in good order, but no one could be found on the ship, living or dead.

The captain went on board, and, being so close to port, he was thinking of putting some hands on her to bring her into Port Jackson, when a perusal of the barquentine's log-book in the captain's cabin made him hesitate.

From the entries it appeared that the crew had sickened and died of some kind of malignant fever, the only survivors being three men—a passenger, one sailor, and the cook.

The last entry, which was nearly three weeks old, stated that these three had provisioned a boat and intended leaving the vessel in order to make for Australia, as the only chance of saving their lives, as they felt sure that the vessel was infested with plague.

The value of the barquentine and cargo being considerable, and the weather settled, the captain determined to take her into port.

He put three volunteers on board to steer her, took her in tow, and brought her into Port Jackson, and anchored off the Quarantine Ground.

On reporting the matter to the medical officer, he was ordered to remain at anchor, until it was decided what course to take.

The season was very hot and unhealthy, and when the story spread it occasioned a slight scare amongst the citizens.

Both vessels were quarantined, and the barquentine thoroughly examined.

When it was found from the log that the deserted craft had sailed from an Indian port; where the plague that had so long devastated Southern Asia was then raging furiously, the consternation grew into a panic.

It was determined to take the vessel to sea and burn her, for nothing less would pacify the public.

The claim of the owners and the salvage claim for compensation were rated, and the *Niagara* towed the derelict out to sea, set fire to her, and then returned to undergo a term of quarantine.

Nothing further occurred, and in due course the *Niagara* was released, and the people forgot the fright they had entertained.

The drought reigned unbroken, and the heat continued to range higher than ever. Then, when the winter had passed, and the dry spring betokened the coming of another summer of drought and heat, a mortal sickness made its appearance in some of the low-lying suburbs of Sydney.

When it had grown to an alarming extent, grim stories got to be bruited about, and a tale that one of the sailors of the *Niagara* had told was repeated.

He was on watch the night before the vessel was to be destroyed, the two ships lying anchored pretty close together.

It was about two o'clock when his attention was drawn to a peculiar noise on board the plague ship.

He listened intently, and recognized the squealing of rats, and a low, pattering noise as though all the rats on the ship were gathering together.

And so they were.

By the light of the moon his quick eyes detected something moving on the cable. The rats were leaving the ship. Down the cable they went in what seemed to be an endless procession, into the water, and straight ashore they swam. They passed under the bow of the *Niagara*, and the sailor declared it seemed nearly half an hour before the last straggler swam past.

He lost sight of them in the shadow of the shore, but he heard the curious subdued murmur they made for some time.

The sailor little thought, as he watched this strange exodus from the doomed ship, that he had witnessed an invasion of Australia portending greater disaster than the entrance of a hostile fleet through the Heads.

The horror of the tale was augmented by the fact that the suburbs afflicted were now haunted by numberless rats.

People began to fly from the neighborhood, and soon some of the most populous districts were empty and deserted.

This spread the evil, and before long plague was universal in the city, and the authorities and their medical advisers at their wits' end to cope with and check the scourge.

The following account is from the diary of one who passed unscathed through the affliction. Strange to say, none of the crew of the *Niagara* was attacked, nor was the boat with the three survivors ever heard of.

THE WEATHER is still unchanged.

It seems as though a cloud would never appear in the sky again.

Day after day the thermometer rises during the afternoon to 115 degrees in the shade, with unvarying regularity.

No wind comes, save puffs of hot air, which penetrate everywhere.

The Harbor is lifeless, and the water seems stagnant and rotting.

And now, dead bodies are floating in what were once the clear sparkling waters of Port Jackson.

Most of these are the corpses of unfortunates, stricken with plague-madness, who, in their delirium, plunge into the water, which has a fatal fascination for them.

They float untouched, for it is reported, and I believe with truth, that the very sharks have deserted these tainted shores.

The sanitary cordon once drawn around the city has long since been abandoned, for the plague now rages throughout the whole continent

The very birds of the air seem to carry the infection far and wide.

All steamers have stopped running, for they dare not leave port, in case of being disabled at sea by their crews sickening and dying.

All the ports of the world are closed against Australian vessels.

Ghastly stories are told of ships floating around our coasts, drifting hither and thither, manned only by the dead.

Our sole communication with the outer world is by cable, and that even is uncertain, for some of the land operators have been found dead at the instruments.

THE DEAD ARE NOW BEGINNING TO LIE about the streets, for the fatigue-parties are overworked, and the cremation furnaces are not yet available.

Yesterday I was in George Street, and saw three bodies lying in the Post Office Colonnade. Dogs were sniffing at them; and the horrible rats that now infest every place ran baldly about.

There is no traffic but the death-carts, and the silence of the once noisy street is awful.

The only places open for business are the bars; for many hold that alcohol is a safeguard against the plague, and drink to excess, only to die of heat-apoplexy.

People who meet look curiously at each other to see if either bears the plague blotch on their face.

Religious mania is common.

The Salvation Army parades the streets praying and singing.

The other day I saw, when kneeling in a circle, that two of them never rose again. They remained kneeling, smitten to death by the plague.

The "captain" raised a cry of "Hallelujah! More souls for Jesus!" and then the whole crew, in their gaudy equipment, went marching down the echoing street, the big drum banging its loudest.

As the noise of their hysterical concert faded round a corner a death-cart rumbled up, and the two victims were unceremoniously pitched into it, one of the men remarking, "They're fresh 'uns this time, better luck!"

Such was the requiem passed on departed spirits by those whose occupation had long since made them callous to suffering and death.

All the medical profession stuck nobly to their posts, though death was busy amongst their ranks; and volunteers amongst the nurses, male and female, were never wanting as places had to be filled.

But what could medical science do against a disease that recognized no conventional rules, and raged in the open country as it did in the crowded towns?

Experts from Europe and America came over and sacrificed their lives, and still no check could be found.

All agreed that the only chance was in an atmospheric disturbance that would break up the drought and dispel the stagnant atmosphere that brooded like a funeral pall over the continent.

But the meteorologists could give no hope.

All they could say was that a cycle of rainless years had set in, and that at some former time Australia had passed through the same experience.

A strange comet, too, of unprecedented size, had made its appearance in the Southern Hemisphere, and astronomers were at a loss to account for the visitor.

So the fiery portent flamed in the midnight sky, further adding to the terrors of the superstitious.

It was during one night, walking late through the stricken city, I met with the following adventure.

My work at the hospitals had been hard, but I felt no fatigue. The despair brooding over everyone had shadowed me with its influence.

Think what it was to be shut up in a pest city without a chance of escape, either by sea or by land!

I wandered through the streets, Campbell's lines running in my head, "And ships were drifting with the dead to shores where all was dumb."

Suddenly a door opened, and a young woman staggered out, and reeling, almost fell against me.

I supported her, and she seemed to somewhat recover from the frightful horror that had apparently seized her.

She stared at me, and then said, "Oh! I can stand it no longer. The rats came first, and now hideous things have come through the window, and are watching his breath go out. Are you a doctor?"

"I am not a doctor," I answered; "but I'm one of those who attend to the dying. It is all we can do."

"Will you come with me? My husband is dying, and I dare not go back alone, and I dare not leave him to die alone. He has raved of fearful things."

The street lamps were unlighted, but by the glare of the threatening comet that lit up the heavens I could see her face, and the mortal terror in it.

I was just reassuring her when someone approaching stopped close to us.

"Ha, ha!" Laughed the stranger, who was frenzied with drink; "another soul going to be damned. Let me see him. I'll cheer him on his way," and he waved a bottle of whiskey.

I turned to remonstrate with the fellow, when I saw a change come over his face that transformed it from frenzy of intoxication into comparative sobriety.

"Your name, woman; your husband's name?" He gasped.

As if compelled to answer, she replied, "Sandover, Herbert Sandover?"

"Can I come too?" Said the man, addressing me in an altered tone. "I know Herbert, knew him of old; but his wife doesn't remember me."

"Keep quiet, and don't disturb the dying," I said; and giving my arm to the woman, went into the house.

On the bed lay a man, plague-stricken, and raving in delirium.

No wonder.

On the rail at the head of the bed and on the rail at the foot sat two huge bats.

Not the harmless Australian variety that lives in the twilight limestone caves; nor the fruit-eating flying-fox; but a larger kind still, the hideous flesh-feeding vampire of New Guinea and Borneo.

For since Australia became a pest-house the flying carnivora of the Archipelago had invaded the continent.

There sat these demon-like creatures, with their vulpine heads and huge leathery wings, with which they were slowly fanning the air.

And the dying man lay and raved at them.

Disturbed by our entrance, the obscene things flapped slowly out of the open window, and the sick man turned to us with a hideous laugh, which was echoed by the strange man who had joined us.

"Herbert Sandover," he said, "you know me, Bill Kempton, the man you robbed and ruined. I'm just in time to see you die. I came to Australia after you to twist your thievish neck, but the Plague has done it. Grin, man, grin, it's pleasant to meet an old friend."

I tried to stop him, but vainly; and from the look on the dying man's face I could see that it was a case of recognition in reality.

The woman had sunk upon her knees and buried her head in her hands.

Kempton still continued his mad taunting. Taking a tumbler from the table he poured some whiskey into it, and drank it.

"This is the stuff to keep the plague away," he shouted; "but you,

Sandover, never drank. Oh no! Too clever for that. Spoil your nerve for cheating. But I'll live, you cur, and see you tumbled into the death-cart."

So he raved at the dying man, and one of the great vampires came back and perched on the windowsill.

Raising himself in bed by a last effort, Sandover fixed his eyes on the thing, and screamed that it should not come for him before his time.

As if incensed by his gestures, the vampire suddenly sprang fiercely at him, uttering a whistling snarl of rage.

Fixing its talons in him and burying its teeth in his neck, it commenced worrying the poor wretch and buffeting him with its wings.

Calling to Kempton, I rushed forward to try and beat it off, but its mate suddenly appeared. Quite powerless to aid, I picked up the woman, who had fainted, and carried her out of the room.

Kempton, now quite mad, continued fighting the vampires, but at last, torn and bleeding, he followed us into the street.

I was endeavoring to restore the woman, and he only stopped to assure me that the devils were eating Sandover, and then reeled off.

When the woman came to her senses I left her by her own request, to wait till the Death-Cart came round.

I called there the next morning, but never saw her again.

Amidst such sights and scenes as these the summer passed on, burning and relentless. The cattle and sheep were dying in hundreds and thousands, and it looked as though Australia would soon be a lifeless waste, and ever to remain so.

ONE MORNING IT WAS PASTED up that news had come from Eucla that the barometer there gave notice of an atmospheric disturbance approaching from the southwest.

That was all, and no more could be elicited.

The line-men at the next station started to ascertain the cause of the silence; and after a few days they wired to say that they had found the men on the station all dead.

But the self-registering instruments had continued their work, and the storm was daily expected from Cape Leuwin.

The days preceding our deliverance from the pest were some of the worst experienced; as though the approaching storm drove before it all the foul-brooding vapors that had so long oppressed us, and they had assembled to make a last stand on the East coast.

One morning I felt a change, a cool change in the air.

Going into the street, I saw, to my surprise, many people there, gathered

together in groups, and gazing upwards at a strange sight.

The vampires were leaving the city. Ceaseless columns of them were flying eastward, and men watched them with relieved faces, as though a dream of maddening horror was passing away.

Then came a sound such as must have been have been heard in the quaint old city of legendary lore when the pied piper sounded his magic flute.

The pest rats were flying.

All that day it continued, and some reported that they plunged into the sea and disappeared.

At any rate, they vanished utterly, and with them other loathsome vermin that had been fattening on the dead and the living dead.

Everyone seemed to see new life ahead.

Men spoke cheerily to each other of adopting means of clearing and cleansing the city, but that work was taken out of their hands.

That night the cyclonic storm that had raged across the continent burst upon us. All the long-dormant forces of the air seemed to have met in conflict.

For three days its fury was appalling. The violent rain and constant thunder and lightning added to the tumult.

No one stirred out during those three days of tempest and destruction.

Nature in her own mighty way had set to work to purge the country of the plague.

It was while this storm was at its fiercest that the Post Office tower and the Town Hall tower were shattered and hurled in ruins to the ground. No one, so far as I know, witnessed the catastrophe.

The morning of the fourth day broke calm, clear, and beautiful.

At midnight the tempest had lulled; and when daylight came, the sun rose in a sky lightly flecked with roseate morning clouds.

Accompanied by a friend, I started out to see the ruined city, and those who were left alive in it.

The streets still ran with floodwater, but the higher levels had pretty well drained off; and once they were gained, our progress was easy.

Martin Place was choked with the ruins of the tower, and the many other buildings that had succumbed; while not a single verandah was left standing in any street. We went to the Harbor.

The tide was receding, carrying with it the turbid waters that rushed into it from all points; carrying with it, too, wreckage and human bodies.

A strong current was setting seaward through the Heads, and bore out to the Pacific all the decaying remnants of the past visitation.

The deserted ships in the Harbor had been torn from their moorings and either sunk or blown ashore.

Wreck and desolation were visible everywhere, but the air was pure, cool, and grateful; and our hearts rose in spite of the difficulties that lay before us, for the looming horror of the plague had been lifted.

OF WHAT FOLLOWED, your histories tell you.

How the overwhelming disaster knit the states together in a closer federation than legislators ever had forged.

How from that hour sprung forth a new, purged, and purified Australian race.

All this is record of the Australian nation; mine are but some reminiscences of a time of horror unparalleled, which no man anticipated would have visited the Southern Continent.

The Great Catastrophe

GEORGE DAVEY

THE FOLLOWING is another disaster story set in the future and which shows some of the growing pessimism about the over reliance on new technology, and especially on electricity. I can find out nothing about George Davey, although he was also a passable artist as he illustrated his own story when it appeared in *The English Illustrated Magazine* in 1910. —**M.A.**

I
THE EXPERIENCE OF A SURVIVOR

**EING ONE OF THE FEW HUMAN BEINGS** that escaped alive from the disaster of London, I have been asked to describe my experience. It is now almost four months ago since the tragedy occurred, and in America have appeared hundreds of disjointed accounts, fragmentary stories, biographs, and records, which have given the American public, at least, a general idea of the event; but, as I was an actual eyewitness to almost everything that took place, I am able to give several details which will, I think, be of some interest to our electrical officials.

In the first place, I am glad to learn that we and other nations are taking the lesson. In the city of New York already the council has disconnected several electrical conduits, and I hear that the German tribunal has ordered all district telegrams to be sent by the old-fashioned method of wires. I expect this will be inconvenient to German residents, but it is better so until further investigation into the cause of the London disaster can be made.

It is an undeniable fact that we have had many warnings at various times of the liability of electricity to get out of human control, and actually as far back as the year 1912 I find an account in a very rare copy of an old newspaper, printed in London at that time, and called the *Daily Record*, which, I think, is one of the first of the warnings which have occurred at intervals during the last two centuries. It is an account of an electrical train accident at Liverpool, which took place in a tunnel, and a few people were killed. Then there is the well-known Auckland affair; and the sensational episode at the capital of Japan; also the disaster which happened to one of the Pacific Trust's aeroplanes about seven years ago; and here in Chicago there are still a few residents who can recollect the curious incident of the green man, which again shows the unknowable paths electricity may take.

Now, to proceed with my story, it was on the evening of the 42nd-3rd (or, as they would have called it in the old romantic days, August the 7th) that I first witnessed what I know now to have been the preliminary sign of the subsequent events. The preceding night, I remember, a severe thunderstorm had occurred, which, it was reported by the news agencies, had somewhat disturbed the wires at many of the overhead airship stations, and I have an idea that this circumstance had a good deal to do with the catastrophe. I do not agree at all with Councillor Gruvier's theory that the first cause took place under the earth, in spite of the fact that he is our premier electrician. However, on the evening of the 42nd, I was returning from business, and left my auto-car at the office, preferring to walk, by way of a change; and I remember I was amused by a fussy old gentleman, who accosted me, and remarked that "he was glad to see I preferred the good, old-fashioned method of walking, friend. In his young days, friend, there wasn't so many of these confounded electric chair-cars about! Nowadays, every little whipper-snapper who owned a cent could rush about on his car, and they ought to be made to have a license, friend, a license!"

I had been traversing the Great Portsmouth Road, and even then there seemed to be a vague sense of impending disaster—an indefinable feeling of danger.

The Great Portsmouth Road (I believe it is now reopened) is very similar to most of our great American roads. The monotonous, low whirring of the thousands of auto-cars, the yelling of the traffic directors, and every now and then the heavy clanging of some airship bell overhead. I remember, also, on that night very few people were walking, and I had nearly the whole of the side footways, reserved for pedestrians, to myself. Soon I turned into Regent Street, one of the oldest streets in the city, and a principal side street of the Great Portsmouth Road, and here I paused to gaze awhile at the scene below me.

The numberless cars, vehicles, and public trains were all speeding as swiftly as ever to their destinations, bewildering the eye, when suddenly everything seemed to be forcibly stopped by some invisible power; in an instant the yelling and confusion were terrific; nearly every car crashed into another, people were thrown out and under wheels, and even as I looked showers of blue sparks darted along the great public conduits on each side of the way, and I felt a curious sensation, as of an electric shock.

By this time many people had joined me on the footway, and were excitedly exchanging opinions as to what was the matter.

The whole duration of the episode was hardly ten minutes. The road officials made investigations, and could discover nothing wrong; one or two cars began to move again, and very soon traffic was resumed in the ordinary manner. With the exception of one or two slight injuries no one was hurt. Although I was puzzled by the incident, I did not think it very serious; but, being a journalist, I had no doubt it would make "good copy," so rushing to the nearest telephone office, I speedily sent an account of the affair in to my newspaper.

After this I proceeded to my lodging, a couple of rooms in one of the Municipal Housing Company's buildings. I went to bed, still pondering over the strange occurrence I had witnessed, and at last I fell to sleep. It must have been about half-past three in the morning when I was awakened by the great public alarm bell, and a tremendous roaring and shouting outside; hastily dressing myself, I rushed out, and not troubling to wait for the lift, went down the circular stair-slide, crowds of people going down with me, asking each other in alarmed tones, "What was wrong? What has happened?"

I did not find out what was the matter, even when I got into the street, but thousands of frightened people were running along the footways, and numberless cars and vehicles were going full speed along *both sides* of the road, in one direction. "Run for your lives!" People were shouting, and the cry was taken up by a thousand voices echoing into the air. Out into the crowd I was carried along, buffeted and bewildered. Even in this panic, which was only the beginning, many people were thrown over the balustrades of the footways, to be crushed and mangled by the racing cars beneath. Many were the calls for "Ambulance! Ambulance!" But the ambulance officials had disappeared. Yet no cause for this great panic could I see; neither was it any use inquiring. Several people I asked, like myself, simply did not know. All the same they were as panic stricken as the others.

One man I asked, however, replied in an excited fashion:

"I tell you, friend, it's a punishment from God! I know it! I know it! And a green flame, a—" and then this extraordinary man was borne along out of my hearing.

Then, being (though I say it myself) somewhat of a logical disposition, I made up my mind to see the danger for myself before running away from it; so I commenced to push and fight my way in the opposite direction.

II

EVERYWHERE I WENT were thousands—nay, millions—of people, all panic-stricken; and as I progressed further towards the east, I began to hear more news. Some said the whole of London was on fire; some said it was a green fire; one man, brawny and half naked, tore along, screaming, "The lightning! The lightning!"

I must have been an hour, at least, fighting and pushing my way with no particular aim, only always against the crowd. Presently I heard a roaring and crashing, and the yelling of the people seemed to grow louder; the heat, also, began to grow more intense, and I judged I was nearer to the scene of the fire, for then I thought it nothing more important than a large block of buildings burning. Then, suddenly turning a corner, I came into full view of it at the end of a long street, and, sure enough, it was only a fire—but *what* a fire! The flames were of a brilliant green color; volumes of smoke rose, fortunately overhead, for it has since been discovered that the slightest breathing of this smoke meant death.

Out of the green flame lightning flashed continually in all directions, and huge balls of fire were hurled into the air.

One of these electric fireballs descended close to where I was standing. People near yelled and stampeded, several being knocked over, and trampled on; with a fierce hissing noise the fireball came down, killing and scorching every living thing within an area of several meters.

Electric sparks shot from the victims; but even as they struggled, the rushing people quickly passed over them, and they were literally obliterated. Then I began to catch the infection of terror myself. The green flame, spreading with frightful rapidity, had come within one hundred meters from where I was, and nothing could stand against it; the boasted fireproof buildings were worse than useless: the green flame melted them at the joints like lead, and the vast steel girders came down, crashing, killing, and maiming hundreds at a time.

My pen is powerless to depict the terror of the people. No car or vehicle could move in the dense mass of people, and many were being broken up in the crowd; men, women, and children were fighting, screaming, pushing, raving, and trampling each other under foot. Wherever I turned it was the same; lightning flashed, and fireballs descended frequently, and wherever they fell they always left a heap of burnt, blackened, and crushed human beings.

No one seemed to know in which direction lay the most danger, and I decided to try and get towards the river; so even I was compelled to fight and struggle for my life, as the others.

III

I WAS RATHER SURPRISED to find my progress towards West-minster fairly easy, but this was partly due to my cutting through the side streets, while the largest crowds were all going down the great main roads; and it was while in one of these side turnings that I witnessed a most terrible incident.

It had already been discovered that the airships would not fly owing to the atmospherical influence of this great electrical cataclysm; yet, on arriving at the Charing Cross Overhead Station, I saw that an attempt was being made to fly one of the Southern Counties Company's aeroplanes, and huge crowds of people were flocking up the staircases to it, and badly overcrowding it.

All this I could dimly perceive by gazing upwards as I hurried along.

In the main road directly under the station, and blocking the direction in which I wanted to go, the huge crowds roared and surged. Presently there was the clanging of a bell, and a shouting, as the anchors of the aeroplane were cast off. I was afraid, and something within me impelled me to draw back.

Fascinated, I watched the airship, as the propellers began to revolve; the vessel moved a few feet—and then *down* it fell, with its tremendous burden of human life, on to the struggling mass of people below, and with the screams of the dying in my ears I covered my eyes with my hands, to shut out the sight, and fled.

At last, I succeeded in getting to Westminster. My object in going there was to see if there was any possibility of escaping by water. The river Thames, as everyone knows, has been built over for some years, being simply a wide subterranean river, used by the British government as a dockyard for the submarine navy.

Erected across the river, at regular intervals of about two hundred yards, were wide traffic bridges composed entirely of steel, and along each embankment were situated the great artificial ice-storage houses, belonging to the British Food Trust.

The great steel-girdered bridges, and the approaches thereto, were one vast congested mass of struggling and frantic humanity. I was swept along in the crowd, and at last I was wedged into a jutting corner on one of the bridges, a prisoner with very little hope of escape.

I could see the river, into which hundreds were jumping or being thrown; under the water the submarine electric lamps still burned, making the stream transparent, and showing drowning people fighting each other underneath—a sickening sight, but I was used to horrors by now.

It was fortunate for me that I was in a great measure guarded by the jutting corner I have mentioned, for I was, at least, protected from serious injury. Out in the crowd people were being crushed to death, their bodies still maintained upright by the pressure of the others. One poor old man came near me, with tears of terror streaming down his face; his arm was fractured, and he was moaning with pain and despair. Another man was bawling. "Oh! Oh! My ribs are broken! Keep back! Keep back!" But he was borne down, overwhelmed, and trodden upon. Still another man, who saw my advantageous position, with fierce oaths tried to force me from it; but I fought with him desperately, and he did not succeed. And so the fearsome riot went on.

By this time the green fire, which had been working rapidly along the river from the east, had already begun to lick the balustrade of the next bridge; and here, again, I feel utterly powerless to describe the scene. At the near approach of the fire the great public electric lamps went out, and everything was lit up by that ghastly, unforgettable green flare; the deadly fireballs descended in showers upon the frenzied people on the bridge; lightning flashed everywhere; loud deafening explosions rang in my ears, heightened by the tremendous reverberating booming of the crashing and falling steel girders and buildings.

The river was choked with the dead and dying, and the fire spread swiftly over all, embracing everything in its clutches, until at last it approached the bridge which I was on, and, making desperate efforts, the people managed somehow to get moderately clear. My skin was scorched and blistered with the fearful heat; lumps of iron, stones, and flaming debris descended continually. On the ground in front of me were injured and helpless people, who were being electrocuted before my eyes, blue sparks flying from their bodies. Over these I jumped and stumbled in my dash for safety; and, as I passed, I could feel the tingling electricity passing through my veins.

And so I rushed blindly on until I was just off the bridge, and then I was struck on the head by a piece of falling debris. I became unconscious, and owe my salvation to the fact that I managed to fall under the shelter of a great doorway of one of the riverside houses.

When I became conscious again, I was in absolute darkness—an inky blackness—and, curiously enough, the first thought which came to my mind was, "Is this death?" But I was alive, sure enough; my skin still burned and smarted, and my head was heavy with pain.

However, stumbling to my feet, I groped around in the darkness, and speedily felt what I guessed to be a beam of steel. I moved, collided with something, and some bricks and stones came rattling down. Then I stumbled over a plank, and in falling (I shudder at the remembrance) I clutched something cold and fleshy—a dead man's hand. I tried to find the arm, but came into contact with more steel substance, and at last realized that this man was crushed to death and that I was *buried alive*? Perhaps it is to my credit that I did not go mad; probably it was because I felt too weak. I was famished with hunger and parched with thirst, but I sat down and felt almost resigned, though if I had had a revolver I should undoubtedly have shot myself there and then. By extraordinary fate I had been saved from one death, yet it seemed only to die in a worse fashion, and blank despair filled my heart as I sat in that maddening blackness. After some time I happened to look upwards, and was astonished to find something which seemed to be an irregular patch of blue in the roof of my prison. My reason told me what it was; it was the sky—the glorious sky! The beloved sky!—And the new day was approaching.

Scrambling and climbing over the debris I succeeded in reaching the roof-hole, and after a tight squeeze I was free!

But what an appalling sight met my gaze! This had been a calamity, indeed. As I scrambled into the sunshine there was still an uncomfortable sense of stifling heat in the air, the ground was hot under foot, and all the miles of charred and blackened ruins were still glimmering and smoking, although there was nothing left that could burn; but there was no sign of the terrible green flame. It had passed. But the bodies! Thousands and thousands, so far as the eye could reach, mangled, shapeless, unrecognizable.

I looked back to the heap of ruins that had become my prison. Mine had been a miraculous escape. The building that had collapsed over me was one of the great ice-storage houses; and the proximity of the ice and the river greatly nullified the heat of the flames, and to this I owe my life.

The rest of the story is well known to the civilized world; everyone knows how the indescribable and as yet unexplained something ran its course of destruction in twenty-four hours, and it was on the morning of the second day when I saw the ruins. On that day the noble Rescue Brigades had already commenced to arrive from the districts of Kingstown, Liverpool, Paris, Berlin, and other places, and I received food and help, and further description is needless.

Meanwhile, the peoples of the world are waiting. Our chief electricians must give us the solution. Many of our great living districts are masses of electricity.

The sword of ancient Damocles is hanging over our heads, and who shall be the next?

Within an Ace of
the End of the World

ROBERT BARR

THE OPTIMISM for the wonders that new technology might bring was sometimes matched in fiction by the concern over how it might be used, or misused. The idea that food production could be increased and made synthetically may seem to solve the problem of world-wide famine, but it has its parallels today in our own concerns over genetic engineering. In the following story it was the raw materials for this improved food production that would soon lead the world to global disaster.

Robert Barr (1850–1912) was an important writer and editor. Born in Scotland he had gone to Canada with his family when still a child and later became a school teacher. In 1876, following his marriage, he became a writer for the *Detroit Free Press* before returning to England in 1881 to establish a London-based edition of the paper. These early days as a journalist had shown his determination as he would at times place himself in danger in order to get a story. In 1892, along with Jerome K. Jerome, he started the magazine *The Idler.* Barr and Jerome often disagreed over how the magazine should be run but Barr remained proprietor until his death in 1912, when *The Idler* died with him. Barr was as at home writing historical fiction or detective fiction as he was producing science fiction. He is probably best remembered today for his detective stories in *The Triumphs of Eugene Valmont* (1906), but his science fiction should also be remembered. "The Doom of London" (*The Idler*, November 1892) depicts a London suffocated by smog whilst "The Revolt of the—" (*The Idler,* May 1894) portrays a future in which women are in charge. —**M.A.**

THE SCIENTIST'S SENSATION

THE BEGINNING OF THE END was probably the address delivered by Sir William Crookes to the British Association at Bristol, on September 7th, 1898, although Herbert Bonsel, the young American experimenter, alleged afterward that his investigations were well on the way to their final success at the time Sir William spoke. All records being lost in the series of terrible conflagrations that took place in 1904, it is now impossible to give any accurate statement regarding Sir William Crookes' remarkable paper; but it is known that his assertions attracted much attention at the time, and were the cause of editorial comment in almost every newspaper and scientific journal in the world. The sixteen survivors out of the many millions who were alive at the beginning of 1904 were so much occupied in the preservation of their own lives, a task of almost insurmountable difficulty, that they have handed down to us, their descendant, an account of the six years beginning with 1898, which is, to say the least, extremely unsatisfactory to an exact writer. Man, in that year, seems to have been a bread-eating animal, consuming, per head, something like six bushels of wheat each year. Sir William appears to have pointed out to his associates that the limit of the earth's production of wheat had been reached, and he predicted universal starvation, did not science step in to the aid of a famine-stricken world. Science, however, was prepared. What was needed to increase the wheat production of the world to something like double its then amount was nitrate of soda; but nitrate of soda did not exist in the quantity required— *viz.,* some 12,000,000 tons annually. However, a supposedly unlimited supply of nitrogen existed in the atmosphere surrounding the earth, and from this storehouse science proposed to draw, so that the multitude might be fed. Nitrogen in its free state in the air was useless as applied to wheat-growing, but it could be brought into solid masses for practical purposes by means of electricity generated by the waterfalls which are so abundant in many mountainous lands. The cost of nitrates made from the air by waterpower approached £5 a ton, as compared with £26 a ton when steam was used. Visionary people had often been accused of living in castles in the air, but now it was calmly proposed to feed future populations from granaries in the air. Naturally, as has been said, the project created much comment, although it can hardly be asserted that it was taken seriously.

It is impossible at this time, because of the absence of exact data, to pass judgment on the conflicting claims of Sir William Crookes and Mr. Herbert Bonsel; but it is perhaps not too much to say that the actual beginning of disaster was the dinner given by the Marquis of Surrey to a number of wealthy men belonging to the city of London, at which Mr. Bonsel was the guest of the evening.

THE DINNER AT THE HOTEL CECIL

EARLY IN APRIL 1899, a young man named Herbert Bonsel sailed for England from New York. He is said to have been a native of Coldwater, Michigan, and to have spent some sort of apprenticeship in the workshops of Edison, at Orange, New Jersey. It seems he did not prosper there to his satisfaction, and, after trying to interest people in New York in the furthering of his experiments, he left the metropolis in disgust and returned to Coldwater, where he worked for some time in a carriage building establishment. Bonsel's expertness with all kinds of machinery drew forth the commendation of his chief, and resulted in a friendship springing up between the elder and the younger man which ultimately led to the latter's divulging at least part of his secret to the former. The obstacle in the way of success was chiefly scarcity of money, for the experiments were costly in their nature. Bonsel's chief, whose name is not known, seems to have got together a small syndicate, which advanced a certain amount of capital, in order to allow the young man to try his fortune once more in New York, and, failing there, to come on to London. Again his efforts to enlist capital in New York were fruitless, the impending war with France at that period absorbing public attention to the exclusion of everything else. Therefore, in April, he sailed for England.

Bonsel's evil star being in the ascendant, he made the acquaintance of the wealthy Marquis of Surrey, who became much interested in the young man and his experiments. The Marquis bought out the Coldwater syndicate, returning the members tenfold what they had invested, and took Bonsel to his estate in the country, where, with ample means now at his disposal, the youthful scientist pushed his investigations to success with marvelous rapidity. Nothing is known of him until December of that year, when the Marquis of Surrey gave a dinner in his honor at the Hotel Cecil, to which were invited twenty of the richest men in England. This festival became known as "The Millionaires' Dinner"; and although there was some curiosity excited regarding its purport, and several paragraphs appeared in the papers alluding to it, no surmise concerning it came anywhere near the truth. The Marquis of Surrey presided, with Bonsel at his right and the Lord Mayor of London at his left. Even the magnates who sat at that table, accustomed as they were to these noted dinners in the City, agreed unanimously that they had never partaken of a better meal, when, to their amazement, the chairman asked them, at the close of the feast, how they had relished it.

A STRIKING AFTER-DINNER SPEECH

THE MARQUIS OF SURREY, before introducing the guest of the evening, said that, as they were all doubtless aware, this was not a social but a commercial dinner. It was the intention, before the company separated, to invite subscriptions to a corporation which would have a larger capitalization than any limited liability concern that had *ever* before been floated. The young American at his right would explain the discoveries he had made and the inventions he had patented, which this newly formed corporation would exploit. Thus introduced, Herbert Bonsel rose to his feet and said—

"Gentlemen, I was pleased to hear you admit that you liked the dinner which was spread before us tonight. I confess that I never tasted a better meal, but most of my life I have been poor, and therefore I am not so capable of passing an opinion on a banquet as any other here, having always been accustomed to plain fare. I have, therefore, to announce to you that all the viands you have tasted and all the liquors you have consumed were prepared by me in my laboratory. You have been dining simply on various forms of nitrogen, or on articles of which nitrogen is a constituent. The free nitrogen of the air has been changed to fixed nitrogen by means of electricity, and the other components of the food placed on the board have been extracted from various soils by the same means. The champagne and the burgundy are the product of the laboratory, and not of the wine-press, the soil used in their composition having been exported from the vine-bearing regions of France only just before the war that ended so disastrously for that country. More than a year ago Sir William Crookes announced what the nitrogen free in the air might do for the people of this world. At the time I read his remarks I was engaged in the experiments that have now been completed. I trembled, fearing I was about to be forestalled; but up to this moment, so far as I know, there has been made no effort to put his theories into practical use. Sir William seemed to think it would be sufficient to use the nitrates extracted from the atmosphere for the purpose of fertilizing the ground.

But this always appeared to me a most roundabout method. Why should we wait on slow-footed Nature? If science is capable of wringing one constituent of our food from the air, why should it shrink from extracting the others from earth or water? In other words, why leave a job half finished? I knew of no reason; and, luckily, I succeeded in convincing our noble host that all food products may be speedily compounded in the laboratory, without waiting the progress of the tardy seasons. It is proposed, therefore, that a company be formed with a capital so large that it can control practically all the waterpower available in the world. We will extract from earth, air, and water whatever we need, compound the products in our factories, and thus feed the whole world. The moment our plant is at work, the occupations of agriculturist, horticulturist, and stockbreeder are gone. There is little need to dwell on the profit that must accrue to such a company as the one now projected. All commercial enterprises that have hitherto existed, or even any combination of them, cannot be compared for wealth-producing to the scheme we have now in hand. There is no man so poor but he must be our customer if he is to live, and none so rich that he can do without us."

THE GREAT FOOD CORPORATION (LIMITED)

AFTER NUMEROUS QUESTIONS and answers the dinner party broke up, pledged to secrecy, and next day a special train took the twenty down to the Marquis of Surrey's country place, where they saw in operation the apparatus that transformed simple elements into palatable food. At the mansion of the Marquis was formed The Great Food Corporation (Limited), which was to have such an amazing effect up on the peoples of this earth. Although the company proved one of the most lucrative investments ever undertaken in England, still it did not succeed in maintaining the monopoly it had at first attempted. In many countries the patents did not hold, some governments refusing to sanction a monopoly on which life itself depended, others deciding that, although there were certain ingenious novelties in Bonsel's processes, still the general principles had been well known for years, and so the final patents were refused. Nevertheless, these decisions did not interfere as much as might have been expected with the prosperity of The Great Food Producing Corporation (Limited). It had been first in the field, and its tremendous capitalization enabled it to crush opposition somewhat ruthlessly, aided by the advantage of having secured most of the available waterpower of the world. For a time there was reckless speculation in food manufacturing companies, and much money was lost in consequence. Agriculture was indeed killed, as Bonsel had predicted, but the farmers of Western America, in spite of the decline of soil tilling, continued to furnish much of the world's food. They erected windmills with which electricity was generated, and, drawing on the soil and the air, they manufactured nourishment almost as cheaply as the great waterpower corporation itself. This went on in every part of the world where the Bonsel patents were held invalid. In a year or two everyone became accustomed to the chemically compounded food, and even though a few old fogies kept proclaiming that they would never forsake the ancient wheaten loaf for its modern equivalent, yet nobody paid any attention to these conservatives; and presently even they could not get the wheaten loaf of bygone days, as grain was no longer grown except as a curiosity in some botanist's garden.

REMARKABLE SCENE IN THE GUILDHALL

THE FIRST THREE YEARS of the twentieth century were notable—for the great increase of business confidence all over the world. A reign of universal prosperity seemed to have set in. Political questions appeared easier of solution. The anxieties that hitherto had oppressed the public mind, such as the ever-present poverty problem, provision for the old age of the laborers, and so forth, lifted like a rising cloud and disappeared. There were still the usual number of poor people; but, somehow, lack of wealth had lost its terror. It was true that the death rate increased enormously; but nobody seemed to mind that. The episode at the Guildhall dinner in 1903 should have been sufficient to awaken the people, had an awakening been possible in the circumstances; but that amazing lesson, like others equally ominous, passed unheeded. When the Prime Minister who had succeeded Lord Salisbury was called upon to speak, he said

"My Lord Mayor, Your Royal Highnesses, Your Excellencies, Your Graces, My Lords, and Gentlemen: It has been the custom of Prime Ministers from time immemorial to give at this annual banquet some indication of the trend of mind of the Government. I propose, with your kind permission, to deviate in slight measure from that ancient custom (cheers). I think that hitherto we have all taken the functions of Government rather more seriously than their merits demand, and a festive occasion like this should not be marred by the introduction of debatable subjects (renewed cheering). If, therefore, the band will be good enough to strike up that excellent tune, 'There will be a Hot Time in the Old Town Tonight,' I shall have the pleasure of exhibiting to you a quick-step I have invented to the rhythm of that lively composition (enthusiastic acclaim)."

The Prime Minister, with the aid of some of the waiters, cleared away the dishes in front of him, stepped from the floor to his chair, and from the chair to the table, where, accompanied by the energetic playing of the band, he indulged in a break-down that would have done credit to any music-hall stage. All the applauding diners rose to their feet in the wildest excitement. His Royal Highness the Crown Prince of Alluria placed his hands on the shoulders of the Lord Mayor, the German Ambassador placed his hands on the shoulders of the Crown Prince, and so on down the table, until the distinguished guests formed a connected ring around the board on which the Prime Minister was dancing. Then all, imitating the quickstep, and keeping time with the music, began circling round the table, one after the other, shouting and hurrahing at the top of their voices. There were loud calls for the American Ambassador, a celebrated man, universally popular; and the Prime Minister, reaching out a hand, helped him up on the table. Amidst vociferous cheering, he said that he took the selection of the tune as a special compliment to his countrymen, the American troops having recently entered Paris to its melodious strains. His Excellency hoped that, this hilarious evening would cement still further the union of the English speaking races, which fact it really did, though not in the manner the honorable gentleman anticipated at the time of speaking. The company, headed by the band and the Prime Minister, then made their way to the street, marched up Cheapside, past St. Paul's, and along Fleet Street and the Strand, until they came to Westminster. Everyone along the route joined the processional dance, and upward of 50,000 persons were assembled in the square next to the Abbey and in the adjoining streets. The Prime Minister, waving his hand towards the Houses of Parliament, cried, "Three cheers for the good old House of Commons!" These being given with a tiger appended, a working-man roared, "Three cheers for 'is Lordship and the old duffers what sits with him in the 'Ouse of Lords." This was also honored in a way that made the echoes reach the Mansion House.

The *Times* next morning, in a jocular leading article, congratulated the people of England on the fact that at last politics were viewed in the correct light. There had been, as the Prime Minister truly said, too much solidity in the discussion of public affairs; but, linked with song and dance, it was now possible for the ordinary man in the street to take some interest in them, etc., etc. Foreign comment, as cabled from various countries, was entirely sympathetic to the view taken of the occurrence by all the English newspapers, which was that we had entered a new era of jollity and good will.

A WARNING FROM OXFORD

I HAVE now to speak of my great-grandfather, John Rule, who, at the beginning of the twentieth century, was a science student at Balliol College, Oxford, aged twenty-four. It is from the notes written by him and the newspaper clippings that he preserved that I am enabled to compile this imperfect account of the disaster of 1904 and the events leading to it. I append, without alteration or comment, his letter to the *Times,* which appeared the day after that paper's flippant references to the conduct of the Prime Minister and his colleagues—

THE GUILDHALL INCIDENT
To The Editor Of The TIMES:
"Sir,—The levity of the Prime Minister's recent conduct; the levity of your own leading article thereon; the levity of foreign reference to the deplorable episode, indicate but too clearly the crisis which mankind is called upon to face, and to face, alas! under conditions which make the averting of the greatest calamity well-nigh impossible. To put it plainly, every man, woman, and child on this earth, with the exception of eight persons in the United States and eight in England, are drunk—not with wine, but with oxygen. The numerous factories all over the world that are working night and day, making fixed nitrates from the air, are rapidly depleting the atmosphere of its nitrogen. When this disastrous manufacture was begun, 100 parts of air, roughly speaking, contained 76.9 parts of nitrogen and 23.1 parts of oxygen. At the beginning of this year the atmosphere round Oxford was composed of nitrogen 53.218, oxygen 46.782. And here we have the explanation of the largely increased death-rate. Man is simply burning up. Today the normal proportions of the two gases in the air are nearly reversed, standing—nitrogen, 27.319, oxygen 72.681, a state of things simply appalling: due in a great measure to the insane folly of Russia, Germany, and France competing with each other in raising mountain ranges of food products as a reserve in case of war, just as the same fear of a conflict brought their armies to such enormous proportions a few years ago. The nitrogen factories must be destroyed instantly, if the people of this earth are to remain alive. If this is done, the atmosphere will gradually become nitrogenized

once more. I invite the editor of the Times to come to Oxford and live for a few days with us in our iron building, erected on Port Meadow, where a machine supplies us with nitrogen and keeps the atmosphere within the hut similar to that which once surrounded the earth. If he will direct the policy of the Times from this spot, he may bring an insane people to their senses. Oxford yesterday bestowed a degree of D.C.L. on a man who walked the whole length of the High on his hands; so it will be seen that it is time something was done. I am, sir, yours, etc."

JOHN RULE

"Balliol College, Oxford."

The *Times* in an editorial note said that the world had always been well provided with alarmists, and that their correspondent, Mr. Rule, was a good example of the class. That newspaper, it added, had been for some time edited in Printing House Square, and it would be continued to be conducted in that quarter of London, despite the attractions of the sheet-iron house near Oxford.

THE TWO NITROGEN COLONIES

THE COTERIE IN THE IRON HOUSE consisted of the Rev. Mr. Hepburn, who was a clergyman and tutor; two divinity students, two science students, and three other undergraduates, all of whom had withdrawn from their colleges, awaiting with anxiety the catastrophe they were powerless to avert. Some years before, when the proposal to admit women to the Oxford colleges was defeated, the Rev. Mr. Hepburn and John Rule visited the United States to study the working of co-education in that country. There Mr. Rule became acquainted with Miss Sadie Armour, of Vassar College, on the Hudson, and the acquaintance speedily ripened into friendship, with a promise of the closer relationship that was yet to come. John and Sadie kept up a regular correspondence after his return to Oxford, and naturally he wrote to her regarding his fears for the future of mankind, should the diminution of the nitrogen in the air continue. He told her of the precautions he and his seven comrades had taken, and implored her to inaugurate a similar colony near Vassar. For a long time the English Nitrogenists, as they were called, hoped to be able to awaken the world to the danger that threatened; and by the time they recognized that their efforts were futile, it was too late to attempt the journey to America which had long been in John Rule's mind. Parties of students were in the habit of coming to the iron house and jeering at the inmates. Apprehending violence one day, the Rev. Mr. Hepburn went outside to expostulate with them. He began seriously, then paused, a comical smile lighting up his usually sedate face, and finally broke out into roars of laughter, inviting those he had left to come out and enjoy themselves. A moment later he began to turn somersaults round the iron house, all the students outside hilariously following his example, and screaming that he was a jolly good fellow. John Rule and one of the most stalwart of the divinity students rushed outside, captured the clergyman, and dragged him into the house by main force, the whirling students being too much occupied with their evolutions to notice the abduction. One of the students proposed that the party should return to Carfax by hand-springs, and thus they all set off, progressing like jumping-jacks across the meadow, the last human beings other than themselves that those within the iron house were to see for many a day. Rule and his companions had followed the example set by Continental Countries, and had, while there was yet time, accumulated a small mountain of food products inside and outside of their dwelling. The last letter Rule received from America informed him that the girls of Vassar had done likewise.

THE GREAT CATASTROPHE

THE FIRST INTIMATION that the Nitrogenists had of impending doom was from the passage of a Great Western train running northward from Oxford. As they watched it, the engine suddenly burst into a brilliant flame, which was followed shortly by an explosion, and a moment later the wrecked train lay along the line blazing fiercely. As evening drew on they saw that Oxford was on fire, even the stonework of the college seeming to burn as if it had been blocks of wax. Communication with the outside world ceased, and an ominous silence held the earth. They did not know then that London, New York, Paris, and many other cities had been consumed by fire; but they surmised as much. Curiously enough, the carbon dioxide evolved by these numerous and widespread conflagrations made the outside air more breathable, notwithstanding the poisonous nature of this mitigant of oxygenic energy. For days they watched for any sign of human life outside their own dwelling, but no one approached. As a matter of fact, all the inhabitants of the world were dead except themselves and the little colony in America although it was long afterwards that those left alive became aware of the full extent of the calamity that had befallen their fellows. Day by day they tested the outside air, and were overjoyed to note that it was gradually resuming its former quality. This process, however, was so slow that the young men became impatient, and endeavoured to make their house movable, so that they might journey with it, like a snail, to Liverpool, for the one desire of each was to reach America and learn the fate of the Vassar girls. The moving of the house proved impracticable, and thus they were compelled to remain where they were until it became safe to venture into the outside air, which they did some time before it reached its normal condition.

It seems to have been fortunate that they did so, for the difficulties they had to face might have proved insurmountable had they not been exhilarated by the excess of oxygen in the atmosphere. The diary that John Rule wrote showed that within the iron house his state of depression was extreme when he remembered that all communication between the countries was cut off, and that the girl to whom he was betrothed was separated from him by 3,000 miles of ocean, whitened by no sail. After the eight set out, the whole tone of his notes changed, an optimism scarcely justified by the circumstances taking the place of his former dismay. It is not my purpose here to dwell on the appalling nature of the foot journey to Liverpool over a corpse-strewn land. They found, as they feared, that Liverpool also had been destroyed by fire, only a fringe of the riverfront escaping the general conflagration. So enthusiastic were the young men, according to my great-grandfather's notes, that on the journey to the seaport they had resolved to walk to America by way of Behring Straits, crossing the English Channel in a row-boat, should they find that the shipping at Liverpool was destroyed. This seems to indicate a state of oxygen intoxication hardly less intense than that which had caused the Prime Minister to dance on the table.

A VOYAGE TO RUINED NEW YORK

THEY FOUND THE IMMENSE STEAMSHIP *Teutonic* moored at the landing-stage, not apparently having had time to go to her dock when the universal catastrophe culminated. It is probable that the city was on fire when the steamer came in, and perhaps an attempt was made to board her, the ignorant people thinking to escape the fate that they felt overtaking them by putting out to sea. The landing-stage was packed with lifeless human beings, whole masses still standing up, so tightly were they wedged. Some stood transfixed, with upright arms above their heads, and death seemed to have come to many in a form like suffocation. The eight at first resolved to take the *Teutonic* across the Atlantic, but her coal bunkers proved nearly empty, and they had no way of filling them.

Not one of them knew anything of navigation beyond theoretical knowledge, and Rule alone was acquainted with the rudiments of steam engineering. They selected a small steam yacht, and loaded her with the coal that was left in the *Teutonic*'s bunkers. Thus they started for the West, the Rev. Mr. Hepburn acting as captain and John Rule as engineer. It was fourteen days before they sighted the coast of Maine, having kept much too far north. They went ashore at the ruins of Portland; but embarked again, resolved to trust rather to their yacht than undertake a long land journey through an unknown and desolated country. They skirted the silent shores of America until they came to New York, and steamed down the bay. My great-grandfather describes the scene as somber in the extreme. The Statue of Liberty seemed to be all of the handiwork of man that remained intact. Brooklyn Bridge was not entirely consumed, and the collapsed remains hung from two pillars of fused stone, the ragged ends of the structure that once formed the roadway dragging in the water. The city itself presented a remarkable appearance. It was one conglomerate mass of grey-toned, semi-opaque glass, giving some indication of the intense heat that had been evolved in its destruction. The outlines of its principal thoroughfares were still faintly indicated, although the melting buildings had flowed into the streets like lava, partly obliterating them. Here and there a dome of glass showed where an abnormally high structure once stood, and thus the contour of the city bore a weird resemblance to its former self—about such as the grim outlines of a corpse over which a sheet has been thrown bear to a living man. All along the shore lay the gaunt skeletons of half-fused steamships. The young men passed this dismal calcined graveyard in deep silence, keeping straight up the broad Hudson. No sign of life greeted them until they neared Poughkeepsie, when they saw, flying above a house situated on the top of a hill, that brilliant fluttering flag, the Stars and Stripes. Somehow its very motion in the wind gave promise that the vital spark had not been altogether extinguished in America. The great sadness that had oppressed the voyagers was lifted, and they burst forth into cheer after cheer. One of the young men rushed into the chart-room, and brought out the Union Jack, which was quickly hauled up to the mast-head, and the reverend captain pulled the cord that, for the first time during the voyage, let loose the roar of the steam whistle, rousing the echoes of the hills on either side of the noble stream. Instantly, on the verandah of the flag-covered house, was seen the glimmer of a white summer dress, then of another and another and another, until eight were counted.

AND FINALLY

THE EVENTS THAT FOLLOWED belong rather to the region of romance than to a staid, sober narrative of fact like the present; indeed, the theme has been a favorite one with poets and novelists, whose pens would have been more able than mine to do justice to this international idyll. America and England were indeed joined, as the American Ambassador had predicted at the Guildhall, though at the time his words were spoken he had little idea of the nature and complete accord of that union. While it cannot be denied that the unprecedented disaster that obliterated human life in 1904 seemed to be a calamity, yet it is possible to trace the design of a beneficent Providence in this wholesale destruction. The race that now inhabits the earth is one that includes no savages and no warlords. Armies are unknown and unthought of. There is no battleship on the face of the waters. It is doubtful if universal peace could have been brought to the world short of the annihilation of the jealous, cantankerous, quarrelsome peoples who inhabited it previous to 1904. Humanity was destroyed once, by flood, and again by fire; but whether the race, as it enlarges, will deteriorate after its second extinguishment, as it appears to have done after its first, must remain for the future to determine.

FRANK L. PACKARD

SO FAR, MOST OF THE STORIES have either been set in the contemporary Victorian/Edwardian period or in the near future, but now it's time to move far ahead in time, by over a thousand years to the fourth millennium. Although H. G. Wells took us into the far distant future in *The Time Machine*, he only took us a little over two centuries ahead in *When the Sleeper Wakes*, and it was rare for writers to go too far. Technological innovation was gathering pace but it was still all relatively new and it was difficult to see beyond the next horizon.

There were the occasional exceptions. Simon Newcomb, for instance, explored the last days of a future Earth in "The End of the World" (*McClure's Magazine*, May 1903), set at least 6000 years in the future. Camille Flammarion likewise saw the last days in *Omega* (1897) which follows events up to 200,000 years in the future. Both Newcomb and Flammarion were astronomers and thus used to thinking on a cosmic scale. It was unusual for stories to actually consider society and events in detail in the far future.

Of special interest in the following story is that it describes an already existing Terran Empire with other colonised planets. This is remarkable for 1906, although there were a few earlier stories, most notably *The Struggle for Empire* (1900) by Robert W. Cole, set in the year 2236, and which also sees all the planets of the solar system colonized and ruled from Earth (in fact from London!).

What may be surprising about the following story is that it's written by Frank L. Packard (1877–1942). Packard was a frequent contributor to the pulp magazines and was best known for his Raffles-like character Jimmie Dale: a socialite playboy by day but a safe-cracker and house-breaker by night. But the creation of Jimmie Dale was still eight years away when Packard wrote "An Interplanetary Rupture". The story may have been inspired by the Russo-Japanese War of 1904–5 for which President Theodore Roosevelt served as mediator at the peace conference which resulted in the Treaty of Portsmouth in September 1905.

—M.A.

**N THE ELEVENTH DAY OF AUGUST**, in the year of our Lord three thousand one hundred and two, the city of Washington, capital of the World, was the scene of unusual commotion. Rumors of the rupture with Mercury were current. It was true that Earth's minister to that planet had not been recalled, and that Mercury' ambassador was still in Washington; but this in no way disguised the fact that relations between the two planets were strained to their breaking point.

The enormous Edifice of Deliberations, erected at a cost of one billion of dollars, teemed with bustling humanity, and emanated a sense of tremendous activity.

The House of Delegates was in continuous session. Speeches of members from the States of Russia, Germany France, and South America were warlike in their tone, rising to a white heat of eloquence to lose some of their intensity against the milder and more prudent counsel of the honorable members from England, America, China, and Japan. Yet from all, even to the smaller States of Holland and Belgium, there was an undertone that plainly evidenced the fact that the Assembly of the World would brook no humiliation.

In the circular chamber that occupied the eastern wing of the building the Supreme Council of Earth were seated: twelve men, the clearest, shrewdest brains upon the Globe. The room was bare of decoration save that from the ceiling hung festooned the national banner, the flag of the World, blood red with a white dove in its center, adopted A.D. two thousand five hundred and thirty-two, at the confederation of Earth's divisions into one vast nation under one government and one Head.

The Head, Mr. Sasoa, was speaking with great calmness:

"Gentlemen." He said. "Interference with the astral Mizar is unquestionably a *casus belli*. Ceded to us by interplanetary treaty in two thousand nine hundred and seventy, Mercury's present action cannot be considered in any light but one of impertinent intrusion upon our sovereign rights."

The members of the cabinet bowed their heads in grave assent.

The Most Honorable Mr. Sasoa then continued: "It has never been Earth's desire to pursue a policy of colonization: to extend her lawful boundaries of empire beyond her own immediate sphere. You are all thoroughly conversant with the conditions that brought Mizar under our government and control. For over an hundred years this dependency has been wisely and prudentially governed, and today I believe we are justified in asserting that our rule has been efficacious, not only to our own commerce, but to the welfare of the universe at large.

"Mizar's value as a strategical base is incalculable, and realizing this, Mercury has stopped at nothing to possess himself of this astral. The trickery that has at last resulted in Mizar's petition to Mercury to be received as his dependency, and their coincident refutation of this government's authority is but the culmination of the despicable policy Mercury has pursued.

"Gentlemen, you are here assembled for the gravest duty that has ever fallen to the lot of an Earther. I hold in my hand an ultimatum from Mercury, received within the hour, demanding that our forces be withdrawn from Mizar *ex tempore*. It now becomes your solemn duty to pass upon this document. The House of Delegates is awaiting our decision, and I believe I may say without hesitation that they will ratify any determination we may arrive at."

The Most Honorable Mr. Sasoa resumed his seat in an unbroken silence.

During half an hour no word was spoken. The document passed from member to member, whose lips, as he handed it to his neighbor, set in a hardened line of grim determination. The examination completed and the paper again in the possession of the Head, all eyes were turned upon the Minister of War.

Acknowledging the unspoken request, General William K. Parsons rose from his seat. His face was drawn and haggard from a sleepless night, his voice, though stern, wavered a little from the stress of emotion that possessed him, as he said solemnly:

"Most Honorable Head, and Gentlemen, I vote for war."

He raised his hand to quell the outburst of enthusiasm his declaration had evoked.

"I vote for war, Gentlemen," he repeated; "but with perhaps a truer knowledge of exact conditions than is possessed by the majority of those present. Mercury has chosen his time well. At the first glance it would appear that in event of war it would he fought out around Mizarian space. That is not so. The battleground will be our own planet Earth and the space immediately surrounding us.

"Through pretext of extended maneuvers, Mercury has assembled within instant striking distance of Mizar four hundred of the heaviest ships in his aerial navy. Opposed to which are fifty of our vessels at present awaiting orders at Mizar's capital.

"Roughly speaking, Mercury's navy comprises 2,000 ships against our total available force of 1,000. He will not, however, dare to send against us more than 1,500, as the balance he will require for the protection of his

astral colonies and his own planet. With this superior force arrayed against us, we cannot hope to defend both Mizar and Earth.

"I said that he had chosen his time well. We must bear in mind the fact that this year Mercury makes his transit, during which he will pass not only between the sun, and ourselves but equally between Mizar and ourselves.

"While I am of course aware that Mercury is greatly inferior in size to ourselves; still we must remember that the large number of colonies belonging to him, coupled with his huge navy, make him a most formidable opponent In this respect I might liken him to your ancestors, Mr. Chamberlain," he said, bowing gracefully to the honorable member from the State of England, "when before the confederation England was a nation.

"I have but one more word to say. Should we declare for war our ships must be immediately withdrawn from Mizar until the transit shall be accomplished. Our fleets abroad at Saturn, Mars, Jupiter, Venus, Uranus and Neptune have already been aerographed rendezvous with all speed at Tokio, St. Petersburg, London, New York, and San Francisco for supplies."

As General Parsons ceased speaking, the honorable member on his left, and after him in rotation each member of the council, rose, and in solemn tones repeated the General's formula:

"I vote for war."

"The decision is unanimous," announced the Head. "It but remains to transmit the result of our deliberations to the House of Delegates."

With a mighty shout that body passed the vote. Members standing upon their desks in a frenzy of patriotism sang the national anthem. The die was cast—the Earth at war.

The Secretary of State, in his official aerocar and attended by his suite, landed upon the residential roof of the Mercurian ambassador to acquaint him with Earth's reply to his government's ultimatum. That astute diplomat suavely expressed "his unspeakable regret" at the unfortunate termination of the affair; turned the business of his embassy over to the Minister from Saturn, and left the Earth with all speed. Meanwhile the Earth's ambassador to Mercury had received his instructions to transmit to that government the World's emphatic refusal to comply with their demands; that duty accomplished to repair at once to Washington.

At the expiration of two days, the admiral commanding the Mizarian squadron had reported at the war office in Washington. Closely following him within a few hours were the fleets from Venus and Mars. That of Jupiter might be expected in eight days, while the few detached vessels doing duty in far Saturn, Uranus, and Neptune had their return orders countermanded as their combined strength would not be of material aid, and it was feared that they might fall into the hands of the enemy; besides, as their voyage would consume from three to six weeks, it was hoped that ere then the crisis would be passed.

On the morning of the 15th, reports had reached the war office from every officer commanding squadrons that his respective detachment was ready for duty. At 10 a.m. of that day orders were issued for immediate mobilization of all fleets at Washington. At 3:30 p.m. General Parsons entered the assembly hall in the House of Delegates, where the admirals were awaiting him. They rose respectfully as he took his place upon the dais.

"Gentlemen," he said abruptly, "you will be seated. I have called you together that you may understand the general plan of campaign. We have reason to believe that the enemy's attack will not be made before the 24th of the month, perhaps not until the 25th. In other words, at a time immediately preceding that period when his base is in closest proximity to Earth, thus placing him in a position to utilize every available unit of strength of which he is possessed. At his transit then, we must expect the crucial stroke. Should that fail him, he must be obliged to withdraw as his base recedes. This will leave us free to turn our attention to Mizar, as we in turn shall have the advantage in respect to distance with our stellar dependency, whose position relative to ourselves does not, as you are well aware, change.

"I desire to caution you on no account to risk unnecessarily a single unit that we can ill spare. You may rest assured that in any event you will have an opportunity of measuring strength with the enemy.

"You will at once take up position and governing yourselves by atmospheric conditions, maintain an altitude that will enable you to observe the enemy's planet to the best advantage. By cruising at the same rate of speed as the Earth's axial velocity, but in the opposite direction, you will, making such corrections as Mercury's movements demand, preserve a position which will of necessity intercept the enemy's attack. You will report at frequent intervals to the war office and final orders will be issued to you when the enemy's approach has been signaled from the observatories. To your stations, gentlemen, and may the Supreme Power guide you."

Within the hour 883 mighty engines of destruction rose like gigantic birds, and for an instant steeped the city in a dim twilight as they hung suspended over it; then forming in parallel columns they were swallowed up in space.

Immediately following the departure of the fleet, General Parsons made a rapid inspection of Earth's fortifications. Surrounding each city of the World at regular intervals of the sixth part of a circle were the batteries, stored with ammunition, capable of throwing their enormous missiles of deadly destructiveness with equally deadly precision a distance in the perpendicular equal to the space governed by the law of gravitation; within which range the enemy must of necessity approach to make their attack effective.

On the 20th, General Parsons reported to the council that every method of defense was in perfect condition and that the result was in the hands of a Higher Power.

On the 22nd, a tramp freighter badly battered, her two forward aeroplanes shot completely away and her hull riddled like a sieve, reported herself from Mizar after an almost miraculous escape. Her captain, in his statement to the authorities, said that the enemy had occupied the entire astral and were busily engaged in erecting new fortifications. Private authentic advices *via* Venus and Hecklon, on the next day confirmed the report and added that Mercury was massing his entire fleet together with an enormous number of transports, preparatory to an extended and decisive movement.

Daily the excitement had grown, tremendous in its intensity, until it reached its height; gradually giving way to a patient and calm state of fortitude to accept the future as it should unfold itself. The thought transmitters of the great journalistic syndicate, with precision and dispatch, kept every Earther informed of each minute detail leading up to the momentous crisis soon to be experienced.

So by this means the world learned that on the 23rd the observatories had reported the face of Mercury obscured for a time as if somebody had come between it and the Earth's line of vision. This could only be construed as signifying that the Mercurian fleet was in its way. Immediately following this announcement; the admiral commanding the World's fleet reported a decided and increasing attraction of his polarity needles towards Mercury, indicating an immense aggregation of metallic bodies in space rapidly approaching.

General Parsons received this dispatch with a grim smile. All that man could do he had done. Massed aboard 5,000 transports, distributed at the different World centers and capable of being mobilized at a few moments notice, was an army totaling ten million men. Should the enemy effect a landing they would at least experience a stubborn resistance. He

ran the various details rapidly over in his mind, then in a few sharp, clear sentences he dictated his final orders to his chief of staff for transmission to the admiral commanding.

At 3 a.m. on the morning of the 25th, reports began to pour into the war office. At 4 a.m. it was established beyond question that the invading host would make contact with the Earth's boundary of gravitation at a point directly over the city of New York. Obviously it was the enemy's intention to make that the point of attack.

For the first time in many weary, anxious hours General Parsons permitted a smile of satisfaction to light up his countenance. To attack New York would bring the Mercurian fleet within range of all batteries bounded by Boston, Providence, Philadelphia, and Baltimore. No more auspicious move could be made for the defenders of Earth.

Messages were instantly dispatched to the transport fleets to mobilize on the Jersey shore, and there General Parsons, accompanied by his staff, at once repaired to assume personal command.

At ten minutes before five, a dispatch from the admiral commanding stated that he was within striking distance of the enemy, whose fleet consisted of close to 1,400 men-of-war, convoying an enormous number of transports.

The first gray streaks of dawn were suddenly obliterated. The chief of staff swirled from the instruments.

"The enemy is within range, sir."

The next instant General Parsons pressed the key connecting with the district batteries. A moment later and the World trembled as if in the throes of a mighty earthquake. The batteries of twenty cities had opened fire, launching one hundred thousand tons of vast explosive full in the face of the advancing host. For two minutes Earth's miniature volcanoes belched forth their deadly hail.

"What is the effect of the fire?" Demanded the General.

"Observers report heavy damage, sir," replied the chief of staff, "a number of vessels sunk and many in apparent distress. The enemy is seeking refuge in a lower altitude and is already out of range of all batteries but New York's."

One by one the batteries had ceased firing as their range was exhausted, until only the guns from New York continued the bombardment. General Parsons from the deck of his dispatch boat swept the scene before him with his glasses. The enemy had changed their formation. Their battleships were now above to cover their transports as they landed beneath them.

Less than a mile and a half away Earth's merchant ships, swarming with men, were drawn up on the *qu vive* for action, while, in a huge circle around the enemy, Earth's men-of-war were sweeping with incredible speed, silently, grimly, waiting only the command that should launch them into a conflict of frightful carnage.

As the Mercurian transports touched the ground preparatory to disgorging their men, General Parsons swung sharply round:

"Order New York to stop firing and the fleet to attack from above," was his quick, decisive command.

Even as he spoke, in execution of his order, there was a lull as New York's batteries became silent, another instant, and a continuous and steadily increasing roar as the guns of ship after ship of Earth's navy came into action.

The Mercurian admiral, seeing the damage that his transports would of necessity sustain from the battle raging over their heads, and secure in the belief that they were well able to take care of themselves until he could dispose of Earth's navy, so heavily outnumbered by his own, fell into the trap that General Parsons had skillfully laid for him. And as if to remove any hesitancy from his mind, at that moment Earth's fleet broke and fled incontinently. The enemy pursued them in hot haste.

The moment General Parsons had been waiting for had arrived. If the enemy's navy outnumbered his own, their transports were numerically inferior to Earth's, an advantage he meant to utilize to the utmost.

From where they had lain hidden in the rear, one hundred of the heaviest battleships of Earth's navy rose like vultures, and swinging into line swept forward with irresistible ferocity upon the enemy's troopships. The effect of the maneuver was fearful in its result. The battleships plowed through and through the densely packed transports, their heavy armor plate crushing vessel after vessel, transforming them into hideous, misshapen sepulchers. Once, twice, and again, with pitiless fury, the battleships dashed into the midst of the enemy throwing them into disastrous confusion, leaving behind them a havoc indescribable: a vessel torn in twain; an unrecognizable conglomeration of wreckage, from whose depths emanated the heart-rending shrieks of the dying, shrill out-cries of pain and terror, anguish and horror from tortured souls, and in fearful contrast the awful stillness of the mangled dead

And now General Parsons had ordered a general-advance. The breaches made in the enemy's ship ranks were speedily filled by Earth's advancing transport line, so that before any considerable body of the Mercurian army had effected a landing, the Earthers were locked ship to ship with their adversaries, the crews and troops engaging in a hand-to-hand *melee*. In front and rear, on either flank, swarmed the remainder of Earth's transports, welding the whole into one compact mass of bloody carnage.

The strategy of the movement was apparent. In response to the urgent appeals for aid from the commander of the Mercurian army, the enemy's fleet, now hotly engaged by the admiral commanding the Earth's warships, made back to protect his transports. Finding it impossible to make any attack on his enemy without endangering his own army, the Mercurian admiral signaled his *confrere* to join him.

In response to this command the vessels not already disabled rose slowly, while Earth's ships clung to them like barnacles, fighting desperately for a mastery that spelled their very existence.

Above the battling transports as they rose was a scene beyond the power of man to pen. Fighting with unparalleled savagery, Earth's navy was pressing the attack with splendid brilliancy.

The huge engines of destruction rushed at each other with terrific speed, to recoil from the shock battered and stunned and helpless, to reel and turn and sink in hideous gyrations from the dizzy height, crushing themselves into unrecognizable shapes on the ground beneath.

And above the roaring and flashing of the guns, the wild, hard, pitiful cries of the dying, came the deeper toned note of nature's protest as peal on peal of thunder shook the air. Across a sky now turned to inky blackness, great forked tongues or lightning leaped and twisted and turned, lighting up in awful splendor a ghastly hell of unutterable chaos.

With the advent of the transports, the Mercurian line of battle was thrown into disorder. General Parsons, with the advantage his superiority of numbers gave him, had cleverly maneuvered to force them into the midst of the enemy's battleships.

The admiral commanding Earth's fleet, now joined by the detachment that had already done such gallant service with General Parsons, swept down upon the confusion. Above, below, on either side the Earthers swarmed, picking out their antagonists to pour a withering fire upon them. Desperately the Mercurian admiral struggled to withdraw his ships and reform his line of battle. The transports blocked every move. Most of the enemy's troopships were now in General Parsons' hands, and in their vast numbers and stubborn disregard for life were hemming in and separating the Mercurian men-of-war from each other. As these huge fighting machines in their fury turned upon their puny antagonists to sweep them from their path, another and ever after that another transport would take the place of its disabled mate; now rising in the air above to allow themselves to fall crashing full across a warship's deck, now ramming from below and now from either side, until here and there, succumbing to the attack, a mighty battleship, wounded, disabled, battered and stricken, heeled slowly over and pitching forward went hurling Earthwards; a testimony of the indomitable valor of General Parson's command.

Again and again, with bewildering rapidity, General Parsons would withdraw from the attack to allow Earth's fleet to dash into the fray. Again and again the same tactics were employed and with each onslaught the savage fury was redoubled, the slaughter multiplied a hundredfold.

All through that awful day and into the still more fearsome night the conflict waged with unabated vigor. In its trail across the American continent the storm-blown fleets scattered blood, tributes to the grim earnestness of war.

There in the drear recess of a mountain canon, or perchance upon a wide and desolate plain, a once proud ship had fallen. And as its poor frame quivered in the throes of death, so its imprisoned dead joined with it as sacrificial offerings upon the dear altar of patriotism.

Here full across a city street, or mayhap upon the roofs of houses, settling where they had plunged in headlong flight, lay queer ghostly shapes well befitting their new use as casements for the dead. Hideously twisted walls of pale phosphorescent metal that in the night-light shimmered balefully; things that once had vaunted proudly their planet's flag.

The people huddling together in little knots and crowds, exposed to the storm that beat them pitilessly, gazed upon the scene that passed above their heads with a fear that blanched men's faces to a ghastly white, while women sobbed and moaned in a delirium of fright. The children clinging at their knees sought comfort from the nameless dread that paralysed their very lips, and seeking comfort, found in their mothers' faces a cause for terror beyond any they had ever known.

And, as if in mockery of the mimic show of man, the battle of the elements grew apace until the watchers drew back with shuddering, soul-sick awe before the manifestation of Almighty Heaven's wrath, and turning from it, ran, hiding their eyes to shut out the terror that gripped their souls, and with trembling, bated breath prayed God to bring the dawn.

AT LAST THE MORNING BROKE, and with it came the beginning of the end. The enemy's last sullen stand was all but over, their resistance almost done. Suddenly, even as the Earthers' cheers acclaimed the hour of victory, a little dispatch boat rose high in the air, turned rapidly, and made with all speed for Washington. Upon her deck the surgeons were bending anxiously over the unconscious form of General Parsons.

Hours later the weary physicians sighed in relief. The General's eyes opened to glance questioningly at the faces around him.

"Tell me," he said.

They took his hands and pressed them. The surgeon-general stooping over him whispered the one word: "Victory!"

General Parsons' countenance lighted up for an instant with a gleam of joy. Then he turned his head away. The features that had been set in inexorable determination in the battle softened with infinite sadness; the eyes that had so sternly viewed the frightful slaughter, brimmed with tears.

"At what a cost," he murmured.

"Oh, God! At what a cost."

Three months later in the circular chamber that occupied the eastern wing of the Edifice of Deliberations, the Council of Earth were seated. Upon the table before them was spread an official document.

The Head, Mr. Sasoa, was speaking:

"Gentlemen," he said, "you are here assembled to pass upon the proposed treaty with Mercury as prepared by our commissioners. You are familiar with the contents. Those points insisted upon by our delegates have been ceded to us. Will you ratify this treaty? Will you vote for peace or war?"

General Parsons rose slowly to his feet.

"Most Honorable Head, and Gentlemen," he said, quietly, "I vote for peace."

The honorable member on his left, and after him in rotation each member of the council, rose, and in solemn tones repeated the general's formula:

"I vote for peace."

In the silence that followed, Mr. Sasoa drew the document toward him, then the scratching of his pen proclaimed the ratification of the "Second Treaty of Washington."

The Last Days
of Earth

GEORGE C. WALLIS

WHEN THE IDEA for this anthology arose this was the first story that came to mind. It struck me that it epitomised the steampunk imagery, for although the story is set 13 million (yes, million) years in the future, the couple—who happen to be the last two humans alive—are still staunchly Victorian. It is full of wonderful ideas about the future, but ideas clearly limited by the technology of the day. And yet it is a potent story and one that I feel packs as big a punch now as it did when it first appeared in 1901.

George C. Wallis (1871–1956) was a printer turned cinema manager who produced a fair quantity of boys' books and science fiction from at least 1896 to 1947, a career thus equalling that of H. G. Wells's in span if not in influence. He was, though, the only Victorian writer of science fiction who also contributed to both the American and British science fiction genre magazines of the twenties and thirties. His last book was a lost-race novel, *The Call of Peter Gaskell* (1947). —**M.A.**

**MAN AND A WOMAN** sat facing each other across a table in a large room. They were talking slowly, and eating—eating their last meal on earth. The end was near; the sun had ceased to warm, was but a red-hot cinder outwardly; and these two, to the best of their belief, were the last people left alive in a world-wilderness of ice and snow and unbearable cold.

The woman was beautiful—very fair and slight, but with the tinge of health upon her delicate skin and the fire of intellect in her eyes. The man was of medium height, broad-shouldered, with wide, bald head and resolute mien—a man of courage, dauntless purpose, strenuous life. Both were dressed in long robes of a thick, black material, held in at the waist by a girdle. As they talked, their fingers were busy with a row of small white knobs let into the surface of the table, and marked with various signs. At the pressure of each knob a flap in the middle of the table opened, and a small glass vessel, with a dark, semi-liquid compound steaming in it, was pushed up. As these came, in obedience to the tapping of their fingers, the two ate their contents with the aid of tiny spoons. There was no other dining apparatus or dinner furniture upon the table, which stood upon a single but massive pedestal of grey metal.

The meal over, the glasses and spoons replaced, the table surface clean and clear, a silence fell between them. The man rested his elbows upon his knees and his chin upon his upturned palms. He did not look at his fair companion, but beyond her, at a complicated structure projecting from the wall. This was the Time Indicator, and gave, on its various discs, the year, the month, the day, the hour and the instant, all corrected to mean astronomical time and to the exact latitude and longitude of the place. He read the well-known symbols with defiant eyes. He saw that it was just a quarter to thirteen in the afternoon of Thursday, July 18th, 13,000,085 A.D. He reflected that the long association of the place with time-recording had been labour spent in vain. The room was in a great building on the site of ancient Greenwich. In fact, the last name given to the locality by its now dead and cold inhabitants had been Grenijia.

From the time machine, the man's gaze went round the room. He noted, with apparently keen interest, all the things that were so familiar to him—the severely plain walls, transparent on one side, but without window-frame or visible door in their continuity; the chilling prospect of a faintly-lit expanse of snow outside; the big telescope that moved in an airtight slide across the ceiling, and the little motor that controlled its motions; the electric radiators that heated the place, forming an almost unbroken dado round the walls; the globe of pale brilliance that hung in the middle of the room and assisted the twilight glimmer of the day; the neat library of books and photo-phono cylinders, and the tier of speaking machines beneath it; the bed in the further corner, surrounded by yet more radiators; the two ventilating valves; the great dull disc of the Pictorial Telegraph: and the thermometer let into a vacant space of floor. On this last his glance rested for some time, and the woman's also. It registered the degrees from absolute zero; and stood at a figure equivalent to 42° Fahrenheit. From this tell-tale instrument the eyes of the two turned to each other, a common knowledge shining in each face. The man was the first to speak again.

"A whole degree, Celia, since yesterday. And the dynamos are giving out a current at a pressure of 6,000 volts. I can't run them at any higher efficiency. That means that any further fall of temperature will close the drama of this planet. Shall we go tonight?"

There was no quiver of fear nor hint of resentment in his voice, nor in the voice that answered him. Long ages of mental evolution had weeded all the petty vices and unreasoning passions out of the mind of man.

"I am ready any time, Alwyn. I do not like to go; I do not like the risk of going; but it is our last duty to the humanity behind us—and I must be with you to the end."

There was another silence between them; a silence in which the humming of the dynamos in the room below seemed to pervade the whole place, thrilling through everything with annoying audibility. Suddenly the man leaned forward, regarding his companion with a puzzled expression.

"Your eyelashes are damp, Celia. You are not crying? That is too archaic."

"I must plead guilty," she said, banishing the sad look with an effort. "We are not yet so thoroughly adjusted to our surroundings as to be able to crush down every weak impulse. Wasn't it the day before yesterday that you said the sun had begun to cool about five million years too soon for man? But I will not give way again. Shall we start at once?"

"That is better; that sounds like Celia. Yes, if you wish, at once; but I had thought of taking a last look round the world—at least, as far as the telegraph system is in order. We have three hours' daylight yet."

For answer, Celia came and sat beside him on the couch facing the disc of the Pictorial Telegraph. His left hand clasped her right; both were cold. With his right hand he pulled over and held down a small lever under the disc—one of many, each bearing a distinctive name and numeral.

The side wall became opaque; the globe ceased to be luminous. A moving scene grew out of the dullness of the disc, and a low, moaning

sound stole into the room. They looked upon a telegraphically-transmitted view of a place near which had once been Santiago, Chili. There were the ruins of an immense white city there now, high on the left of the picture. Down on the right, far below the well-defined marks of six successive beach-lines, a cold sea moaned over an icy bar, and dashed in semi-frozen spray under the bluff of an overhanging glacier's edge.

Out to sea great bergs drifted slowly, and the distant horizon was pale with the ice-blink from vast floes. The view had scarcely lasted a moment, when a great crack appeared on the top of the ice-front, and a huge fragment fell forward into the sea. It overturned on the bar, churning up a chaos of foam, and began to drift away. At the same instant came the deafening report of the breakage. There was no sign of life, neither of man nor beast, nor bird nor fish, in that cold scene. Polar bears and Arctic foxes, blubber-eating savages and hardy seals, had all long since passed away, even from the tropic zone.

Another lever pressed down, and the Rock of Gibraltar appeared on the disc. It rose vast and grim from the ice-arched waters of a shallow strait, with a vista of plain and mountain and glacier stretching behind it to the hazy distance—a vista of such an intolerable whiteness that the two watchers put on green spectacles to look at it. On the flat top of the Rock—which ages ago had been levelled to make it an alighting station for the Continental aerial machines—rose gaunt and frost-encrusted, the huge skeleton framework of one of the last flying conveyances used by man.

Another lever, and Colombo, Ceylon, glared lifeless on the disc. Another, and Nagasaki, Japan, the terminal front of a vast glacier, frowned out over a black, ice-fining sea. Yet more levers, and yet more scenes; and everywhere ice and snow, and shallow, slowly-freezing seas; or countries here black and plantless, and there covered with glaciers from the crumbling hills, No sign of life, save the vestiges of man's now-ended reign, and of his long fight with the relentless cold—here ruins, on the ice-free levels, of his Cities of Heat; here gigantic moats, excavated to retard the glaciers; here canals, to connect the warmer seas; here the skeletons of huge metallic floating palaces jettisoned on some ice-bound coast; and everywhere that the ice had not overcome, the tall masts of the Pictorial Telegraph, sending to the watchers at Greenwich, by reflec-ted Marconi waves, a presentment of each sight and sound impinging on the speculums and drums at their summits. And in every daylight scene, the pale ghost of a dim, red sun hung in a clear sky.

In the more northern and southern views the magnetic lights were as brilliant as ever, but there were no views of the extreme Polar Regions.

These were more inaccessible than in the remote past, for there lakes and patches of liquid and semi-solid air were slowly settling and spreading on land and sea.

Yet more levers, and yet more; and the two turned away from the disc; and the room grew light again.

"It appears just as we have seen it these last two years," said the man, "yet to-day the tragedy of it appals me as it has never done before. I did not think, after all the years of expectation and mental schooling, that it would seem like this at the last. I feel tempted to do as our parents did—to seek the safety of the Ultimate Silence."

"Not that, Alwyn—not that. From generation to generation this day has been foreseen and prepared for, and we promised, after we were chosen to remain, that we would not die until all the devices of our science failed. Let us go down and get ready to leave at once."

Celia's face had a glow upon it, a glow that Alwyn's caught.

"I only said 'tempted,' Celia. Were I alone, I do not think I should break my word. And I am also curious. And the old, strange desire for life has come to me. And you are here. Let me kiss you, Celia. That . . . . at least, is not archaic."

They walked hand-in-hand to a square space marked out on the floor in a corner of the room, and one of them pressed a button on the wall. The square sank with them, lowering them into a dimmer room, where the ceaseless humming of the dynamos became a throbbing roar. They saw, with eyes long used to faint light, the four great alternators spinning round the armatures; felt the fanning of the rapid revolutions upon their faces. By the side of each machine they saw the large, queer-shaped chemical engines that drove them, that were fed from dripping vats, and from many actions and re-actions supplied the power that stood between their owners and the cold that meant the end. Coal had long been exhausted, along with peat and wood and all inflammable oils and gases; no turbines could be worked from frozen streams and seas; no air wheels would revolve in an atmosphere but slightly stirred by a faded sun. The power in chemical actions and re-actions, in transmutations and compoundings of the elements, was the last great source of power left to man in the latter days.

After a brief glance round the room, they pressed another button, and the lift went down to a still lower floor. Here a small glow-lamp was turned on, and they stood before a sphere of bright red metal that filled the greater part of the room. They had not seen this many times in their lives. Its meaning was too forcible a reminder of a prevision for the time that had at last arrived.

The Red Sphere was made of a manufactured element, unknown except within the last million years, and so costly and troublesome to produce that only two Red Spheres had ever been built. It had been made 500 years before Alwyn and Celia were born. It was made for the purpose of affording the chosen survivors of humanity a means of escaping from the earth when the chemical power proved incapable of resisting the increasing cold. In the Red Sphere Alwyn and Celia intended to leave the earth, to plunge into space—not to seek warmth and light on any other member of the Solar System, for that would be useless—but to gain the neighbourhood of some yet young and fiery star. It was a terrible undertaking—as much more terrible than mere interplanetary voyages as the attempt of a savage to cross the Atlantic in his dugout after having learned to navigate his own narrow creek. It had been left undared until the last, when, however slight the chance of life in it, the earth could only offer instead the choice of soon and certain death.

"It appears just as it did the day I first saw it and was told its purpose," said Celia, with a shudder she could not repress. "Are you sure, Alwyn, that it will carry us safely?—That you can follow out the Instructions?"

For generations the Red Sphere and all appertaining to it had been mentioned with a certain degree of awe.

"Don't trouble yourself on that point. The instructions are simple. The necessary apparatus, and the ten years' supply of imperishable nutriment, are already inside and fixed. We have only to subject the Red Metal to our 6,000 volt current for an hour, get inside, screw up the inlet, and cut ourselves adrift. The Red Metal, thus electrified, becomes, as you know, repulsive to gravitation, and will so continue for a year and a half. By that time, as we shall travel, according to calculation, at twice the speed of light, we should be more than half-way to one of the nearer stars, and so become subject to its gravitation. With the earth in its present position, if we start in a couple of hours, we should make F. 188, mag. 2, of the third order of spectra. Our sun, according to the records, belonged to the same order. And we know that it has at least two planets."

"But if we fall right into F. 188, instead of just missing it, as we hope? Or if we miss, but so closely as to be fused by its heat? Or if we miss it too widely and are thrown back into space on a parabolic or hyperbolic orbit? Or if we should manage the happy medium and find there be no life, nor any chance of life, upon the planets of that system? Or if there be life, but it be hostile to us?"

"Those are the inevitable dangers of our plunge, Celia. The balance of probabilities is in favour of either the first or second of those things befalling us. But that is not the same as absolute certainty, and the improbable may happen."

"Quite so, Alwyn; but—do you recollect if the Instructions make any reference to these possibilities?"

"To—? Yes. There is enough fulminate of sterarium packed in the Sphere to shiver it and us to fine dust in the thousandth part of a second—if we wish. We shall always have that resource. Now I'll attach the dynamo leads to the Sphere. Get your little items of personal property together, and we shall be ready."

Celia went up the lift again, and Alwyn, after fixing the connections to several small switches on the surface of the Sphere, followed her. They sat together in the darkening twilight of the dim room above, waiting for the first hour to pass. They spoke at intervals, and in fragmentary phrases.

"It will be cold while the Sphere is being prepared," said Alwyn.

"Yes, but we shall be together, dear, as we have been so long now. I remember how miserable I felt when I first knew my destiny; but when I learned that you were chosen to share it with me, I was glad. But you were not, Alwyn—you loved Amy?"

"Yes."

"And you love her still, but you love me, too? Do you know why she was not chosen?"

"Yes; I love you, Celia, though not so much as I loved Amy. They chose you instead of her, they said, because you had a stronger will and greater physical vigour. The slight curve we shall describe on rising will bring us over the Heat-house she and her other lover retired to after the Decision, and we shall perhaps see whether they are really dead, as we believe. Amy, I remember, had an heretical turn of mind."

"If they are not dead, it is strange that they should not have answered our Marconi and telepathic messages after the first year—unless, of course, as you have so often suggested, they have retired to the interior of the other Red Sphere. How strange that it should have been left there! If they have only enough food, they may live in it till old age intervenes, secure from all the rigours that approach, but what a tame end—what a prisonment!"

"Terrible. I could not endure the Red Sphere except as we shall endure it—travelling."

So the hour passed. They switched the electric current into the framework of the vehicle that was to bear them into space. All the radiators ceased to glow and all the lights went out, leaving them, in that lower room, in absolute darkness and intense cold. They sat huddled together against the wall, where they could feel the thrill of the humming dynamos, embracing each other, silent and resolute; waiting for the end of the cold hour. They could find few words to speak now, but their thoughts were the busier.

They thought of the glorious, yet now futile past, with all its promises shattered, its ideals valueless, its hopes unfulfilled; and seemed to feel in themselves the concentration and culmination of the woes and fears of the ages. They saw, as in one long vista, the history of the millions of vanished years—"from earth's nebulous origin to its final ruin;" from its days of four hours to its days of twenty-six and a half; from its germinating specks of primal protoplasm to its last and greatest, and yet most evil creature, Man. They saw, in mental perspective, the uneven periods of human progress; the long stages of advance and retrogression, of failure and success. They saw the whole long struggle between the tendencies of Egoism and Altruism, and knew how these had merged at last into an automatic equilibration of Duty and Desire. They saw the climax of this equilibration, the Millennium of Man—and they knew how the inevitable decay had followed.

They saw how the knowledge of the sureness and nature of life's end had come to Man; slowly at first, and not influencing him much, but gaining ever more and more power as the time grew nearer and sympathy and intellect more far-sighted and acute; how, when the cold itself began, and the temperate zone grew frigid, and the tropic temperate, and Man was compelled to migrate, and his sources of heat and power failed one after the other, the knowledge of the end reacted on all forms of mental activity, throwing all thought and invention into one groove. They saw the whole course of the long fight; the ebb and flow of the struggle against the cold, in which, after each long period, it was seen that Man was the loser; how men, armed with powers that to their ancestors would have made them seem as gods, had migrated to the other planets of the system, only to find that there, even on Mercury himself, the dying sun had made all life a fore-known lost battle; how many men, whole nations, had sought a premature refuge from the Fear in the Ultimate Silence called Death. They saw how all the old beliefs, down to the tiniest shreds of mysticism, had fallen from Man as a worn-out garment, leaving him spiritually naked to face the terrors of a relentless Cosmos: how, in the slow dissolving of the ideal Future, man's duties and thoughts were once more moulded with awe and reverence to the wishes of the Past.

They saw the closing centuries of the struggle; the discovery of the Red Metal; the building of the Spheres that none dare venture to use, but which each succeeding and lessening generation handed down to the next as a sacred heritage only to be put to test in the last resort; they

remembered, in their own childhood the Conference of the Decision, when they two had been chosen, as the only pair of sufficient vigour and health and animal courage to accept the dread legacy and dare the dread adventure of seeking a fresh home in the outer vastness, so that haply the days of Man might not be ended; and they remembered, only too well, how the rest of humanity, retiring to their last few houses, had one and all pledged each other to seek the Silence and trouble the chilly earth no more. They knew how well that pledge had been kept, and in the darkness and silence of the room clutched each other closer and closer.

And at last they heard the Time Indicator in the uppermost room ring the peal of the completed hour, and knew that in their own lives they must act the final scene in the long life-tragedy of the earth.

Alwyn's hand reached out and touched the switch, and the glow-lamp sprang into radiance again. In silence he handed Celia into the Sphere—which shone a deeper red now and coruscated strangely in the light—and then followed her, drawing the screw section in after him and making it secure. Within, the Sphere was spacious and comfortable, and, save where thickly padded, transparent, even to the weak incandescence of the lamp. It was also pleasantly warm, for the Red Metal was impervious to heat. The man's hand went to the lever that worked through the shell, and pushed aside the strong jaws of the spring clamp that held the Sphere down; and as it went, he looked into the woman's eyes. He hesitated. There was a light in her eyes and his, a feeling in her heart and his, that neither had seen nor experienced before.

"It's madness, Celia," he said, slowly. "It's not too late yet. The moment I pull this lever over the Sphere will tear its way up through the building like an air-bubble through water, but until then it is not too late."

This was not a question in phrase, but it was in fact. Celia did not answer.

"Isn't it a miserable folly—this deference to the past? Don't we know perfectly well that death is as certain out there as here?" The man went on.

Then Celia answered: "Yes, Alwyn; Man, life, everything, is a most miserable folly. But we have nothing to do with that: we can't help it. We don't know, until we try, what fortune may yet meet us. We should be untrue to our ancestors, cowards and recreants to ourselves, if we drew back now. Even in face of the unconscious enmity of the whole Universe of Matter, let us remember that we are living and conscious yet."

As so often in the past, the woman was the man's strengthener in the time of need. Alwyn pulled over the lever, and cried, with antique impulsiveness:

"Forgive me, Celia! We will not give in, not even against a hostile universe! She moves!—We go!"

There was a sudden shock that threw them staggering against each other for a moment; a rending, tearing, rolling crash of masonry and metal, and the Red Sphere rose through the falling ruins of the house and soared up into the night, slanting slightly to the west as it rose. One brief glimpse they had of the dials of the Time Indicator falling across a gap of the ruin; and then their eyes were busy with the white face of earth beneath and the clear brilliance of the starry dome above.

They were still clinging to each other, when both caught sight of a small dark object approaching them from beneath. It came, apparently, from a black spot on the chill whiteness of the landscape to the west of their abandoned home, and it was travelling faster than themselves.

They gazed down at it with sudden interest, that, as they gazed, turned into acute apprehension, and then to a numb horror.

"The other Sphere!"

"Amy and her lover!"

While they spoke it grew definitely larger, and they saw that a collision was unavoidable. By what caprice of fate it had so fallen out that the helpless paths of the two Red Spheres should thus come to coincide in point of space and time, they could not imagine. The idea of leaving the earth might, by magnetic sympathy, have occurred to both couples at about the same time, but the rest of the unlucky coincidence was inexplicable. They turned from looking at the second Sphere and sought each other's eyes and hands, saying much by look and pressure that words could not convey.

"They did not mean to keep the pledge of the Decision," said Alwyn. "The desire for life must have come to them as it came to me to-day, and Amy must have remembered the Instructions. I can understand them coming up faster than us, because their Sphere was in a sheet-metal shed in the open, and so would start with less opposition and greater initial velocity. But it is strange that their path should be so nearly ours. It can only be a matter of minutes, at the rate they are gaining, before the end comes for all of us. It will be before we get through the atmosphere and gather our full speed. And it will be the end of Humanity's troubled dream . . . . . And Amy is in that. . . . ."

The thought of possible malice, impulsive or premeditated, on the part of the occupants of the second Red Sphere, never entered into the minds of those of the first.

"The responsibility of action rests upon us," said Celia. "They evidently cannot see us, against the background of the black sky. They are coming up swiftly, dear."

"It will have to be that: there is no other way. Better one than both," said the man.

"Be what, Alwyn?"

"The fulminate of sterarium."

"It will not injure them?"

"No; not if we fire the fuse within—about—three minutes. It must seem hard to you, Celia, to know that my hand will send you to the Silence so that Amy may have the last desperate chance of life. Somehow, these last few hours, I have felt the ancient emotions surging back."

The hand that clasped his gave a gentle pressure.

"And I, too, Alwyn; but their reign will be brief. I would rather die with you now than live without you. I am ready. Do not be too late with the fulminate, Alwyn."

They swayed together; their arms were about each other; their lips met in the last kiss. While their faces were yet very near, Alwyn's disengaged right hand touched a tiny white button that was embedded in the padding of the interior.

There was an instantaneous flash of light and roar of sound, and the man and woman in the second sphere were startled by the sudden glare and concussion of it, as their metal shell drove upwards through the cloud of elemental dust that was all that remained of the first Red Sphere and its occupants.

The silence and clear darkness that had been round them a moment before, had returned when they recovered their balance; and in that silence and clear darkness, the man and woman who had not been chosen passed out into the abyss of the Beyond, ignorant of the cause and meaning of that strange explosion in the air, and knew that they were alone in Space, bound they knew not whither.

The Plunge

GEORGE ALLAN ENGLAND

ALTHOUGH THE LAST STORY saw the end of the world, I chose to finish with this story, partly because it has all the standard images of steampunk, but also because it has an almost "into-the-sunset" ending.

Its author, George Allan England (1877–1936), was one of the pioneers of science fiction in the pulps, a contemporary of Edgar Rice Burroughs who also sold fiction to Hugo Gernsback, the publisher of the first science fiction magazine, *Amazing Stories*. He is best remembered for his trilogy which takes its name from the first book, *Darkness and Dawn* (1912), set a thousand years hence when civilisation has been all but wiped from the face of the Earth following some uncertain catastrophe. The two main protagonists have survived into the future through suspended animation but now they awaken to discover a world struggling to recover. Other novels of note include *The Empire in the Air* (1914), in which Earth is threatened by beings from another dimension and *The Golden Blight* (1912), in which a scientist holds the world to ransom in the hope of ending war.

Compared to the above the following is a rather more simple story of airships, near disaster and heroics. —**M.A.**

I

**ITH A SIGH**, the girl let both hands fall into her lap. The book she had been listlessly reading escaped from her gloved fingers—fur-gloved, even as she herself was wrapped in furs. Though the month was June, and the stupendous aero-liner *Imperatrice* had only half an hour before demagnetized its electromagnetic disks and cleared from the Pacific Transport towers at Honolulu, the thin, cold atmosphere of more than two miles aloft nipped keenly.

The girl leaned back in her deck-chair, with the glow of the auroral induction lamp above her, and gazed a trifle wistfully across the aft concourse, out beyond the rail through the clear blackness of the night. Far, very far astern a dull reddish gleam on the horizon—a gleam that faded even as she watched it—bespoke the fires of Mauna Loa smoldering against the sky.

Hungrily dark, below silvery cloud-masses on which the vivid whiteness of the full moon dazzled a mile beneath the liner as she roared on her appointed way, the Pacific rolled in terrible immensity. Across the deck, rhythmically swinging as the ship swayed and dipped along the Trades, sharply black shadows of the rail and of the stanchions supporting the upper deck cut the aluminum plates. The sky, a jetty void, sparkled with myriads of white spatters of flame. Lights and shadows contrasted with cold hardness on the passengers walking the decks or grouped along the rail. Through the perfect silence of the upper air, the gleaming *Imperatrice*, with suction-turbines shrilly whining, with hurricane-shields whistling in the empty dark, hurled herself at three hundred miles an hour toward Nagasaki, still nine hours' run to nor'-west by west.

Tired and melancholy, the girl looked with indifferent eyes at the voyagers muffled in their furs, some strolling idly about, some leaning on the rail, some with night-glasses searching out the abyss or aimed at the splendor of the moon. The thought of Japan roused a slight, momentary interest in her world-wearied heart. Yes, the loom of the blue-pearly haze that marked its coasts at dawn, or the vertical shafts of radiance, by night, shooting to mid-heaven from the Nippon Republic's aero-lighthouses, to guide the pilots peering from the hooded bull's-eyes of the conning tower—these still possessed a certain lure for her. Yet only a little, for after so many trips afar what real novelty could anywhere remain?

"Dear, dear, what a tedious old world this has become!" She yawned behind her glove. "I ought to have been born in the days when things really happened—the old days of real life—the days when people didn't have to content themselves with merely reading of adventure!"

She settled back still farther in her chair, listened to the zooning of the wind amid the wires and taut cables, and let her gaze wander over the many rows of life-preservers hanging under the deck roof, each a combination antigravity turbine and vacuum-belt. The glow, above, now more clearly lighted up her face. One could see that the girl was just a trifle pale, with wondering and contemplative gray eyes rather far apart; with tawny hair parted at one side and drawn away from broad brows; with full yet delicate lips, passionately red.

For a moment she lay there, lulled by the threnody of the gale, the shuddering vibration of the tremendous hull driven by its ion-motors, the sibilant hissing of the air-intakes as the vacuum chambers adjusted their lift to the needs of the ship.

"A tedious old world, indeed!" She repeated, closing her eyes with resignation; while the vast fabric of the liner, paced by the racing moon that fled before, roared westward, ever westward, swift and terrible upon the wings of night.

II

THE SCRAPING OF A CHAIR at her side aroused her. She turned her head and looked. A line of annoyance drew between her brows. To be interrupted by the intrusion of a stranger, just when she had been feeling most comfortably pessimistic, was annoying.

She was about to resume her meditation when something in the newcomer's face arrested her attention. Though it was shaded by a cap of silver fox-skin, she seemed to have recognized him. He looked undeniably familiar.

She studied him a moment. He seemed a man no longer young, nor yet old—a man "between two ages," as the French say; forty perhaps. The wrinkles at the corner of his eyes bespoke observation, world-wisdom, sagacity, tempered by a saving sense of humor. His mouth, holding a pipe, showed strong lips; his chin was molded on lines that might perhaps, be just a little hard.

The girl appraised him with spurred interest. Indubitably a large man, well above the six feet that the human male now averaged, not even his heavy furs could conceal a certain lithe strength distinctive in an age of physical ease. Her eyes fell on his right hand, which was bare; a big hand, white, powerful, yet with fingers that bespoke the artist.

He wore a single ring of dull gold; an unsymmetrical pattern—an eagle, one wing furled, one spread, with marvelously carven feathers. The eagle's eye was fashioned of a diamond; its claw grasped another. A strange ring, thought the girl. A ring that somehow singularly befitted that white, virile hand.

She leaned back again, piqued at herself for the interest she had felt. The book in her lap slid off; it slapped the deck sharply. Stooping, the man removed the pipe from his mouth. He picked up the book and glanced at it. With an odd smile, he looked at her—and then she knew him.

"Norford Hale!" She exclaimed involuntarily, angry at the quickening of her heart, the burning of her cheek.

"Why, you're my Romney girl!" Said he. "How did you know me?"

"Oh, I've known you for years and years," she answered, seemingly without knowing just what she was saying. "Everybody does, I fancy. You are Norford Hale, aren't you?"

He nodded, smiling still; and now she noted his sun-tanned face and steady eyes.

"I can't deny it—Romney," said he.

"Why do you call me that?" She demanded. "How on earth can you know my nickname, the name my friends all call me?"

"Who could help it? I've had more than a few pictures of you, cut from magazines, these last few years. Who doesn't know Romney's portrait of Lady Hamilton? You must be a reincarnation of her, or something of that sort. At any rate, I've long been calling you my Romney girl. You don't know it, but you were the heroine of my 'Nights on Parnassus.' Romney reminds one of gypsies and all that, too; I've always fancied you a wanderer, an unconventional, outdoor, woodsy kind of girl—are you?"

"Please don't let's get personal, on two minutes' acquaintance," she remarked, rather severely.

"I beg you a thousand pardons!" He returned, with just a tinge of mockery that by no means escaped her. He held out the book. "Allow me to give back my latest—and worst piece of modern materialism."

"It is bad," she agreed, taking the book. "It's nearly put me to sleep several times. I call it my soporific."

He laughed heartily, showing fine teeth.

"Romney," said he, "you're the first frank and truthful human being I've met in years. My next book shall certainly be built about you."

"Not if it's going to be like this one!" She protested. "Jamais! Why do you write this way, when you can write so very differently if you want to? Why do you do it?"

"Why? Because I must," he explained. "The public demands it. Publishers are slaves of the public, and I am a slave of the publishers. That makes me a slave raised to the nth power. This kind of thing is only a symptom of a world gone into fatty degeneration as a result of a gross surfeit of creature comforts. Shall I knock out my pipe?"

"No, you needn't. Father smokes from morning till night, and doesn't even use cartridges. Still sticks to the untidy old habits of his grandfather and insists that loose tobacco is the only thing in the world, for him. I'm used to it. The only way you can really please me will be to stop your terrific materialism. Why not give us another pure romance of the old days—the days when there was adventure in the world, and romance? The period, say, of 1900 to 1925? Another book, for instance, like *The Quarry* or *Llewellyn?*"

He shook his head and for a moment kept silence, then drew at his pipe. It was dead. He slipped a fresh cartridge into it, pressed the knurl that set the rim glowing, and puffed the tobacco to ignition.

"Another book like those?" He queried. "Impossible! All that's dead now, and has been these twenty years past. The modern world isn't a romantic world, that's all. Fifty-odd years ago, at the time of the final war, or even thirty, when the United Republics were still fledglings, some romance still survived. But since then—"

Eloquently he blew a lance of smoke into the sheltered air of the 'tween-decks.

"You see," he added, "now that there's no war, no poverty, no crime, no misery, no peril, no accident, no struggle any more, to try men's souls, all the exciting elements of romance have disappeared. When there hasn't been a fatal accident of any moment either on land or sea or in the air, for a decade or two, you can imagine the state of dull complacency into which the world has relapsed. It's magnificent of course, but it's fatal to the state of mind that my particular brand of labor needs as a culture-medium."

He made a gesture of impatience, frowning with displeasure.

"Literature has grown as dull as life itself!" He exclaimed. "The world of other times used to look forward to the actuality of to-day as to a wonderful ideal, never realizing that it was just the uncertainty and danger and cruelty of life that gave birth to powerful situations and real literature. Men were real men in those days; women were real women. Today we're all a flock of tame, colorless, self-satisfied nonentities. All the zest of life, all the big, powerful, primitive emotions are dead and gone, forever—and exit all excitement, all tension, all romance!"

The girl, leaning forward, looked at him with sudden enthusiasm.

"My own thought, to a T!" She agreed. "Only, I've never formulated it before, or tried to express it. I'm awfully glad you see things as I do, and understand. If I'd found you conventional, self-satisfied, smug, you don't know how you'd have disillusioned me, or how sadly you'd have destroyed an ideal—"

"An ideal?"

"I mean," she parried hastily, "I'd have been terribly disappointed. You and I both view the world from the same angle, that's evident. A world surrounded by every safeguard and choked with material comfort—why, it's a dead world! What could be more stagnating than perfection? What more deadly than secure monotony? I've wished all my life—oh, how I've wished!—That I might have lived in the old days when life meant struggle and achievement, when there were obstacles to overcome and sufferings to conquer, when at least a little of the primitive was left in men and women, and when romance meant more than a vague memory!"

Silence, a moment, between them, while the man smoked and seemed to weigh her words. Suddenly she spoke.

"Why write at all?" She demanded. "In your capacity as a surgeon you're of inestimable value to the world. The whole world knows you that way. Why not abandon your other work, which you've no heart in any more? Why drift with the tide and follow the dull, modern current of materialism?"

He cast a strange glance at her. For a minute the woman and the man looked into each other's eyes. Then suddenly:

"You're really Jeanne Hargreaves'?" He demanded.

"Yes. Why?"

"How strange that I should meet you thus!" He commented, ignoring her question. "So you're Linwood Hargreaves' daughter, eh?"

"Yes. I'm on my way to meet him now, in Osaka."

The man kept silent. He pushed back his cap a little, and ran his fingers through his hair, still more black than gray.

"Let's walk a bit," he suggested. "The night's too fine for us to miss it, sitting back here in a corner."

She agreed. Together, in silence under the soft glow of the lights, they paced the deck, a turn or two; a deck reminding one more of a city street, so numerous the throng was, than of anything ever seen in the old days of surface navigation. A confused murmur of speech blurred the air, fused with the throbbing of powerful electrocons. Here and there the glower of burning tobacco and its grateful odor told of one habit, at least, which not even half a century of the New Order had been able to eliminate.

They paused, presently, by the rail just abaft the kinetogram office, and looked out over the world of cloud and sea, which under the moonlight seemed to hollow upward like a vast cup, its rim fading into inchoate vagueness. Far overhead, the black bulge of the vacuum-chambers blotted out the vivid pinpricks of the stars. The creak and strain of struts and braces vaguely recalled sea-vessels of former times, Beyond the gale-breaks the outlines of whose vast out-riggers loomed against the sky, a 300-mile-an-hour hurricane was raging terrible beyond all words—a hurricane lashed into being by the hurtling trajectory of the ship herself, as she cleft the night—but on deck only a mild breeze was loitering.

A faint cloud-wrack immensely high, now and then slightly tarnished the moon. A mile or more below, as Jeanne and the novelist bent over the rail, they saw the shadow of the *Imperatrice* that skimmed at terrifying speed across the shining fields of vapor—fields that, gapped here and there, showed the black abysses of the ocean spinning backward, ever backward, toward the east.

Very far away to northward, a fine, slim spear of white light stabbed upward through the night. On the horizon, quiverings of radiance reached out, felt into the void, leaped and died—tenuous arms of illumination shot upward from the great aerial centre at Port Howard, on Lisiansky Island. The woman and the man kept a moment's silence, peering into the stupendous gulf of emptiness that rushed away beneath them:

Hale spoke first.

"In the old days," said he, blowing a trail of smoke, "even this common-place scene, in itself, would have been considered romantic and exciting. Writers would have reveled in it and artists would have portrayed it. What an easy time they had, in those days, when there were still really new things in the world to describe! It seems hard to realize, doesn't it, that an aerial trip around the world was once something to talk about and make 'copy' out of?"

"Just imagine!" Jeanne commented.

"And now—"

"Of course. Now that China and India and Thibet are weekend excursions, on tourist schedules, what can be left to wonder at or be romantic about?" He stifled a yawn, with difficulty. "Not one uncivilized or semi-civilized place in the whole world—even the very Esquimaux and Patagonians sophisticated and selling postcards—bah! In these days of motive power drawn from the sun or from polar currents streaming to it, these days of synthetic foods, etheric energies, and all-embracing mechanism, what part is left for the personal equation?"

"Civilization? Ugh! I detest it! I'd give a year of my life—five years—for

a touch of the real, the raw, the primitive! Life has become as dull as men and women themselves. Are there any real women in the world to-day? "I've never met one. That's why I've never married—"

He gestured outward with his hand, despairingly. She smiled with certain bitterness.

"Real women?" The girl exclaimed. "Show me a real man first! Extinct! I've always thought so; but until tonight I've always been too polite to say so. Somehow, with you, politeness and subterfuge seem as stupidly unreal as all the rest of this super-civilization. I wonder, now—"

A sudden flare of light, far outshining the moon, interrupted her speech. The brilliance flooded the whole sky, dazzled upon the spinning clouds below, and for a second glared with noonday radiance. Every minutest detail of the ship stood out in startling relief.

A wailing, screeching note cleft the high air, grew swiftly louder as the light brightened, then ended in a thunderous crash that shook the liner from lookout to extremest rudder-plane.

Then, instantly, the light glared below. The novelist, leaning over the rail as the staggered liner heeled sickeningly far to port, saw a swift streak of bluish flame—flame that roared, that coruscated—plunge like a rocket into the enveloping fleeciness of the clouds, and vanish.

III

A DULL CONCUSSION shuddered through the *Imperatrice*, then two more in quick succession. Flames gushed, aft. Confused cries, shouts, and tumult rose on the right. Everywhere echoed that most terrible of all sounds; the shrieking of women. Came the trampling of feet running along the decks, which already—as the stupendous aerocraft slowed, drunkenly swaying—had begun to slant at a perilous angle.

Flung against him by a jostling of terrified passengers, the girl caught Norford Hale's arm. She sensed how hard and rigid that arm was, as he stiffened himself to shield her and braced himself against the bending, creaking rail to meet the shock.

Still another detonation, aft, shivered through the mangled liner, now yawing off in a wide, descending spiral. All at once the lights died. The frozen moonlight stared in on a panic-maddened mob driving along the promenade past them, as the two clung to their sheltering corner behind the kinetogram house.

Groaning, suddenly splintering, a whole long section of the rail ripped outward. With a gasp, Jeanne buried her face on Norford's breast to shut away the horrifying sight of more than a hundred human beings hurled in fantastic gyrations into black space. That sight she did not witness; but not even her gloved hands, pressed tight against her ears, could shut away the screams of the lost wretches—screams almost instantly muted, far below, to silence.

"A meteor!" Cried the man, staring aghast. "Everything provided for—foreseen—but this!"

Scrambling away from the horrible void; clutching with mad hands, tearing at one another, grappling anything that promised any slightest hold, the stampeded horde of men and women—with all too many children—God knows—fought away from the blank vacancy where the rail had vanished.

On hands and knees they scrambled up the steeply-slanted deck, in the moonlight, utterly brutalized by sickening panic. No traditions of self-restraint and heroism controlled them, such as had prevailed in the old sea-days. All pretenses of organization and authority were instantly swept away. Discipline there was none, in that lax-fibred multitude. In one moment of time, decades of calm, sleek, full-fed civilization, civilization perfectly balanced and urbane, civilization poised, confident, and self-satisfied, had all been starkly swept away.

The primitive in man had instantly surged hot, brutal, raw, to the surface.

Unheeded now were the perfectly futile commands of such few officers as still strove to restore order. The shouts of the stewards—themselves paralyzed with terror—made no slightest impression as they tried to direct the donning of the life-preservers, crying that there was no danger—a palpable lie, since already the *Imperatrice* was staggering to her death.

Hale shuddered with a profound horror as he sheltered the half-fainting girl in his arms. He hears her crying out some unintelligible thing.

"There, there, Romney! Don't look." He mechanically tried to soothe her, himself transfixed with fear, but still he stood his ground. He remained there, steadfastly, shielding her from the surge and thrust of the mob. By the hard moonlight and the waxing glare of the flames now licking the after decks, he watched the panic-stricken wretches tear at one another, crawl swarming over one another, push and crowd and fling one another back to death. A certain wondering pain filled his analytic soul that such things could be. He, all his life a physician, used to the follies and weaknesses of human beings, had never yet witnessed such anguished selfishness. For many years a writer and an imaginer of things, he never once had imagined anything like this reality.

The man was afraid, horribly and agonizingly afraid, yet he retained his self-command. He knew, even, it was not death he feared. He had lived richly and fully. Death, as such, could not terrify him. Yet he too sensed the clutch of panic. Men can face the slavering sea that rolls to engulf them, and with some composure yield themselves to its embrace; but to feel an aircraft—a speeding aircraft that bears one through the emptiness of space—suddenly stricken helpless, to sense its reeling fall, to see the hungering abysses of the sky yawn black and void beneath—this thing no man can experience without physical nausea and a profound and agonizing torture of the soul.

Yet the man fought it back. He struggled to clear his brain and senses. Pale to the lips, with the sweat of anguish on him and with staring eyes, he still sheltered the hysterical girl. He still kept from wildness and mad, futile deeds; still forced himself to reason and to think. Swiftly he tried to plan what he must do to save Jeanne Hargreaves.

For the moment their peril was not deadly—barring, of course, any general explosion that would hurl the wreck into the sea, a mile and a half below. The *Imperatrice*, though punctured, might still survive a while. The swarming stampede, now rapidly thinning as some climbed up through doors and windows, and as dozens and scores of screeching maniacs slid and dropped away from the almost vertical decks, could not reach them in their vantage-corner. This constant lightening of the ship, too, might delay its plunge. The horrible jettison of human lives might help to save their own.

The *Imperatrice* had now heeled over almost directly on what, in the old days, would have been called its beam-ends. Lying on its side, the shattered hull staggered in drunken spirals vast and slow. Nearly all the passengers on its lower side had already been slid into the sea. Those on the upper side were still safe from this peril; but the flames now licking upward and along that higher side of the ship explained the agonizing screams that drifted from those decks out into the stillness of mid-heaven.

Quivering with horror, Norford tightened his grasp on the girl. As the ship had rolled over, he had adjusted his position, so as to remain upright, with Jeanne.

"Come, come!" He adjured her sharply. "Look alive, now! No time for hysterics here! Your foot, there, beside mine—so—now, then, lean back against the deck!"

Their feet now rested on a stanchion connecting the deck with the one that had been above it. The deck itself, now vertical, gave them support against which to brace themselves. Their position, fairly secure, was none the less terrifying.

Far below them now appeared nothing but the dazzling shine of the moonlit clouds—clouds ever drawing nearer—on which the ink-black shadow of the ship drifted idly before the wind. And through gaps in the cloud-floor, ever they beheld the waiting blackness of the sea.

IV

"**LIFE-PRESERVERS!** We'll jump!"

The idea, oddly enough, now first occurred to Hale. None of the preservers seemed to have been used, on his deck. So swift had been the catastrophe and so sudden the heeling-over of the ship that few of the passengers there had even so much as tried to strap on one of the devices.

Decades of complete aerial safety had rendered even the idea of peril absolutely remote. For many years these gyroscopic devices, actuated by a leap from aloft, had been carried only as a matter of routine. Now in the moment of disaster they were not used, they could not be.

Hale determined to make at least a try for the girl's life and his own. Action followed hard on that decision.

"Stand right here," he commanded. "Don't move. So long as you keep your feet braced on this metal beam, with your shoulders to the deck, you're all right. I'm going to leave you for a minute."

"Leave me? What for?" She stammered, aroused by his words.

"Life-preservers. See there?" He pointed where they hung, dangling ten feet away, alongside the now vertical wall that had formed the deck-roof.

"How—can you?" She gasped, staring at the life-belts, dimly visible in the heavy shadows now shrouding all the under portion of the ship.

"How? Along this stanchion, of course."

"You—you can't!"

For an answer he merely commanded: "Stay where you are. Don't move." Carefully gauging the distance, he threw off his furs and dropped them into the gulf, then boldly walked forward along the aluminum girder.

This girder had a breadth of no more than four inches. It lay horizontal, or almost so. Beneath it, nothing but the sheer vacancy of a mile and a half drop to the Pacific. On either hand, nothing to grasp. The distance to the belts was only a few feet, but those few feet held appalling possibilities.

Hale did not hesitate. Steadily; he advanced along the beam, step by step; both arms: extended sideways, swaying as he balanced. He reached the life-preservers—each a combination of anti-gravity apparatus and vacuum-belt, with water-distiller, signal light, and, concentrated food—unhooked two with considerable difficulty, and, turning, faced the girl.

She, shivering and blanched to a dull waxen pallor, stared at him as though hardly comprehending. Far above, from the upper side of the doomed liner; confused cries and screams still drifted down to them; but these had now grown fewer and fainter. The burst of flames along that upper side had swiftly thinned the multitude of trapped wretches.

Now all at once a greenish glare began to flame around the stem of the vast fabric. Its widely-spreading brilliance cast leaping lights and shadows all along the up-tilted deck, swept bare of life.

Back toward the girl started Norford. Burdened now by the cumbersome apparatus; he found the return harder by far. But step by step he still advanced, now hesitating as he swung with the drunken yaw of the ship, now again creeping forward. And still in muted horror the girl watched him as he came that perilous way above the gulf. Her face showed ghastly as his own, in the weird virescence of the blazing aero-liner.

A thunderous explosion, aft, echoed the hissing rush of a tremendous, searing geyser of flame.

Hale, nearly overbalanced by the shock, leaped and caught the agonized hand she reached to him. Shaking and mute; they clung to each other.

"Off with your furs—and into one of these—quick!" He panted.

She struggled out of her coat, and dropped it, grotesquely flapping as it spun away through the clouds. Then she tried to adjust the life-preserver, but in vain. Numbed with terror, her hands quivering violently and her whole body shaking, she could neither put on the belt nor adjust the straps. Gasping, she tried to speak. Dry tongue and quivering lips refused their office. Her teeth began to chatter violently with the cold.

"Here; your arm through this—now, so—now the—other!" Hale directed, in a shaking voice. He clung there, precariously, to his footing; he helped her at imminent risk of being himself precipitated into the depths.

The liner meanwhile, her whole stern now roaring into white-hot, gaseous flame, had become a monstrous torch against the sky, spiraling down ever down toward the clouds, with accelerating speed. Her huge prow rose, swaying helplessly and drunkenly toward the impassive moon. In the black of the night-sky she whipped her streaming hair of fire weirdly and terribly aloft.

She had now assumed almost a vertical position. The flames, licking up along her from the stern and also bursting from the bow, had driven most of the survivors; fighting, clawing, screaming, to the forward observation-deck. Out from topsy-turvy saloons and staterooms—places of horrible, mocking luxury—they scrambled. Insanely battling for refuge, they crawled up, up the sickening angles of the aerocraft's mad inversion.

Some few, cooler than the rest, managed to put on their life-belts and launch away; but only a part of these made the correct adjustments. Most of them fell like lead, the gyroscopic neutralizers failing to work after the initial plunge. Probably not over two-score, in all, reached the surface of the Pacific still alive.

Scorched from the liner by the anguish of shriveling heat or numbed by poisonous gases, the others dropped off. Some, actually on fire, leaped into the abyss and swirled away, torches of living flame. As ripe fruit falls, clustered, from the bough they fell. Men, women, children, singly and in groups, seared by the roaring gusts of incandescence, flung themselves into moonlit vacancy. Horribly whirling, they vanished.

Merciful oblivion received all these before their bodies broke against the midnight blackness of the sea; its surface—struck at such speed—hard as a plate of burnished steel.

Clinging to their perilous niche below the flaming, drifting hulk, Hale and Jeanne tugged with bleeding fingers at the adjustments of their belts.

"Quick!" He commanded. "She's going fast—we've got only a minute, now!"

He drew the last buckle tight about her, while the glare of the on-sweeping conflagration flooded them with a ghastly, yellow-greenish glare. Puffs of hot smoke and strangling gases swirled about them. Within the wreck, dull concussions vibrated. The last sustaining vacuum-chambers were collapsing.

"All right?" Demanded Hale, strapping his own belt fast. "Now, then, off with you! Jump!"

The girl, shaking terribly, sank almost fainting against him.

"Oh—I can't, I can't!" She gasped. "We're still a mile high—and the sea—"

"It's that or burn to a crisp here!" He shouted with sudden passion, above the roaring of the gas-flames.

Still she could not muster courage for the leap.

Brutally he seized her, with overmastering rage. They grappled a second. Reeling, they swayed together on the narrow beam. Then he dominated her; he broke her desperate clutch and hurled her bodily—her scream piercing his ears—into the void.

A second he watched her drop like a plummet, in the moonlight, as he crouched pale and sick upon the dizzy perch.

"Thank God!" He breathed, thinking to see her swift trajectory checked just before she plunged through the cloud-curtain still a thousand feet below.

Delaying no longer, he stood up again. He leaped boldly outward from the flaming wreck; he plumbed after her into the horrifying nothingness of the abyss.

V

RETURNING CONSCIOUSNESS—for the sheer drop before his own apparatus had functioned had robbed him of his senses—brought him a confused realization of cold, of motion, of dim light. For a moment he understood nothing. Then his mind cleared, and he knew that he was swinging on the surface of a troubled sea, heaving on league-long rollers, with moonlit clouds slow-drifting far and far above him.

Buoyed by his vacuum-belt he rose, fell, and heaved up again on the crumbling surges. Here, there, he made out a few twinkling sparkles of light, like stars moving on the breast of the mighty waters; signal-flashes from such of the survivors as had lighted them. He vaguely distinguished dim forms, hardly distinguishable against the blackness of the sea-men and women who, like himself, had reached the sea with life-pelts. Living? Dead? He could not tell. But one or two nearer things, wallowing limply, in the supreme abandon of death, told him of those who had leaped with no supporting apparatus.

Vague thoughts drifted through his brain. Had any kinetogram been sent from the *Imperatrice*, for rescue, he wondered dully. And sharks—were they plentiful in this latitude? How long could one survive, under these conditions?

Then the thought of Jeanne stabbed him full-awake. A great clarity of mind returned to him, with renewed vigor of body. He detached the now useless gyroscope from the belt, and let it drift away, in company with the welter of deck-chairs and wreckage that littered the sea. After this, he turned the knob of his signal-lamp, which flashed away bravely over the dark and gleaming swells.

"Romney!... Ohe-e-e-e!... Romney!" He shouted through cupped hands, as he flung aloft on marching crests of brine.

No answer. A few faint cries, but none from her.

All at once he noted a greenish flare in the heavens, almost directly overhead. Now he could distinguish a vibrant roar, louder than the swishing hiss of the combers. Spiraling downward, the *Imperatrice* had just sunk through the clouds, which were illumined for a long distance by its streaming banners of incandescence.

A moment he closed his eyes. The flaming aero-liner, now less than a mile aloft, threatened to precipitate its blazing, glowing wreck upon him.

The anguish of death wrought strong in Hale; but through it all he felt a kind of wild, barbaric exultation.

"This, this," he thought subconsciously, "is an end such as in these days any man might envy!" His only regret was that he might not live to write a stirring tale of the adventure; his only sorrow crystallized about the death of Jeanne, for even though the girl was living still, death was inevitable unless quick rescue could be made.

He shouted again and again, vainly. Then he fell a-wondering where she might be; how many from the ship might still survive; how death might come to him; what the sensation of dying really might be like.

The brightening glare of the liner once more drew his gaze. Down, ever downward, staggered the flaming craft, on which not a single being now remained alive. Slowly she wheeled about and about. Dark objects and a rain of dripping fire fell from her constantly. Out of her uprearing bow, flames were streaming full-volumed toward the zenith—a splendid, horrifying spectacle, affronting the calm moon.

Once more the man hailed:

"Romney! Romney!"

A gust of incandescent gases puffed from the liner's bow. The gigantic craft seemed to empty herself in a second. She staggered, rolled slowly over, and gathered momentum downward. In a vast and rushing spiral she plunged; roaring into white heat; shot swiftly off to the left, and—violently exploding—leaped into twisted wreckage.

A stupendous concussion rolled its echoes over the sea as the shattered, glowing skeleton of metal surged into the waves.

Up leaped a Vesuvius of steam, writhing in snowy belchings under the moonlight. Hissings of tortured waters drowned the seethes of the waves and the death-cries of the struggling wretches annihilated by the hulk.

Then, for a moment, silence, while Norford—cradled upward on the breasts of the sea—dimly perceived a boiling, spuming writhe of brine that marked the liner's grave.

A column of gaseous blue flame belched from the waves, writhed aloft and vanished.

Impassive, the sea covered all. The *Imperatrice* was dead.

VI

OVERBORNE WITH HORROR, Norford Hale lapsed from knowledge of all things. Then—after how long a time he knew not—he once more found his senses.

"Where is Romney?"

The thought stabbed him. He rallied his forces, shouting to the vacancy of night and moonlight-sparkling sea.

A voice answered him, on the third call—her voice, off somewhere to windward.

"Romney! Oh, Romney! Where are you!"

Lifted on a crest, he peered across the moving plain of waters vast and slow. Now the tiny dots of signal-lights had grown fewer, scattered wide and vanishing upon the bosom of the primal mystery of old ocean. Not all man's towering achievement, not all his sublime skill and science, had yet dethroned the sea from its supremacy. Terribly unconquered, it still rolled indomitable as when first the naked savage faced it, awed and wondering.

Again and again Hale shouted, till his throat went raw.

A signal-light rose as though answering, two or three hundred yards away farther, perhaps—he could not tell. Hale thought he heard a cry drifting down-wind.

Drawing the aluminum paddle from its sheath alongside the vacuum-belt, he drove himself toward that reply.

"Romney!"

"Here! Oh, here, here!"

"Safe?"

"Yes!" She shouted, as he neared her.

"Are you?"

"Yes—thank God!"

He labored hard, and made his way to her. Each searched the other's face, wan and haggard under the moonlight and the flare of the signals.

"Oh, Norford!" she gasped, her teeth still chattering violently, for even in those latitudes the sea was chill.

"Romney!" He exclaimed, reaching out to her. Their hands clasped and held. And silence fell between them.

So few now, and so far, had become the scattered signal-lights still remaining that the two seemed all alone there together in a universe of deep, impassive sky and restless sea that loomed away, away to nothingness. Above, the clouds had now cleared a little, showing patches of the heavens, infinite abysses of space where shone diadems of mild-glowing stars, softened by the tropic moonlight.

A sibilant hissing all at once drew Hale's attention.

"What's that?" He asked, listening keenly. At first he did not understand; but as the sound continued, with an ominous gurgitation of water, he suddenly knew. The greater depth to which he was now sinking—the rapid disappearance of his buoyancy—these alone would have told him the truth.

For a moment numb dread possessed him, but he mastered it. He forced himself to speak with an approach to calm.

"Romney," asked he, "If—if you should be left all alone here, would you be very much afraid? Would you hold your nerve and—try to wait for rescue?"

"Alone?" She cried. "How—why?"

"You may as well know," he answered plainly. "You'll have to, anyhow, in a minute or two. My vacuum–belt has sprung a leak. Hear that sound? Air and water are entering it. In a very short time—well—"

"You mean—?"

"Yes, Romney. It's a case of goodbye. Your belt, alone, can't possibly sustain us both. Here, girl! Give me your hand again. I'll just say goodbye, and God keep you! Then I'll paddle away. Of course you understand you mustn't see—"

Aghast, she stared at him. Then sudden fire leaped into her wide eyes. "Take mine, and let me go!"

"What?"

"I'm of no use in the world! It will never miss me. You, with all your splendid achievements and powers—"

"Nonsense, Romney! You're mad!"

"I'm going to do it, I tell you!" she cried passionately. "You've been my ideal for years—it doesn't matter now if I tell you. You shan't die; you mustn't! I showed myself a coward when you saved me from the ship. Now let me show myself a woman! I've lived empty and idle. Let me die to serve the world—and you!"

Already she was laboring at the buckles, to loosen them. He seized her hands and held them fast.

"No, no, no!" He forbade her. Already he was sinking far lower. "You mustn't, Romney—mine—you can't now it's too late!"

She struggled to free herself for her stern purpose. He, seizing his paddle, struck out away from her.

"Norford! Come back, come back!" She gasped.

"Good-bye—God keep you, Romney!" He answered, now sunk far into the heaving hills of brine. A great calm and a supreme gratitude enfolded him. The girl, he felt, was safe. And he, unable to loosen the metallic belt, must in a minute or two be drawn into the depths of rest eternal.

"I've lived a man's life"—the thought soothed him. "I shall die a man's death. For that, thank God!"

He ceased his paddling, now that he had attained a fitting distance, and for a moment lay inert, hearkening the ever more rapid gurgle of the incoming air and water. More and more heavily now he wallowed, his buoyancy all gone. He reached a weary hand and extinguished his light. Romney should not, at least, see that disappear beneath the sea-floor, when the final moment came.

An echo of a long forgotten sonnet rose to him:

Drained is the cup that holds both Heaven and Hell; Peace deep as peace of those divinely drowned

In leagues of moonlit waters, wraps me round. And it is well with—me— yea! It is well!

Again he heard Romney's call. He glimpsed her light, away to leeward. Vaguely he smiled, murmured a goodbye and with supreme abandon yielded himself to the engulfing sea.

VII

THE SHOCK OF A HARD BODY in collision with his shoulder jarred him awake from this mood of euthanasia. Instinct flung out his arms. His clutching hands caught something, slipped, held, and once more wrenched loose; then finally got their grip and clung there.

He sensed he was no longer sinking, was not dead, might still survive. The ripe moonlight on that southern sea showed his reopening eyes that he was grappling the netted side of a monoplane life-raft—a raft that must have fallen from the *Imperatrice* rather than have been launched, for in that swift, all-mastering panic not a single one had been set free.

Life and the instinct to live gushed up in Norford Hale. Many long years still stood between him and his natural term of being; the blood still rushed hot and keen through his arteries. And "Life!" Cried every atom of him, in clamant choruses. He found that the struggle he had thought ended had only just begun.

With freshened energy he toiled up out of the welter and the foam, out upon the swaying safety of that float. One by one he undid the hampering buckles of the now water-logged life-belt, and saving only the paddle and the food-cartridges slid the useless apparatus back into the sea. Still sucking air and brine, it sank, eddying in the moonshine down and away to black deeps.

As it disappeared, hopes welled up in Norford Hale, and burning thoughts, and eager yearnings after supreme possibilities that set his pulses hammering. He stood up then, filled his domed chest with splendidly reviving breath, and through hollowed palms belled into a long cry to Jeanne, across the night.

He listened, in suspense, searching the gloom for her light, but seeing none. A sick fear crept upon him as he called and called again.

Her answer! He heard it, all at once, drifting down-wind to him. All at once her light showed once more, a star upon the vast waters.

Joy so poignant as his was almost pain, as he knelt, plunged the paddle overside, and with splendid energy began driving the raft toward Jeanne.

AFTER A CERTAIN WHILE, two figures sat together on the raft that cradled easily over the vast Pacific rollers. Millions of moving sparkles flashed from the sea, struck out by the moon—the moon now disked in solid silver, now "stooping through a fleecy cloud" and shining there with softened glory.

Night wore on; and now the moon, dimming as the east began to glow, hid drooped almost to the vague mists that pearled the horizon. The stars blanched and died; but, watching them, the man saw one star moving on the edge of the sea—a star that waxed, that mounted on the sky—a star that spoke of life.

"Look!" cried Norford, pointing. "A kinetogram was sent, after all! See there—rescue!"

The girl, all disheveled, wet and shivering, raised her eyes to the swift-approaching searchlight of the aerocraft. For a moment she peered at it in silence; then she smiled.

"Can this be A.D. 2016?" She asked wonderingly. "Things like this happen only in books—books of the old days—"

"Books of life!" Said Norford, with his arm about her. "Don't you see— this plunge has been a plunge back into life, real life, for us? Romney mine, a story like this can have only one ending! And was it you, Romney, was it you, who told me that Romance was dead?"

She bowed her head, yearning against his breast. His arms made home for her.

"I told you that," she faltered, "before I knew what a man could be— before either of us had drunk the wine of primitive emotion—before I owed you the life that's yours now, if you want it!"

He slid the eagle ring from his finger.

"Give me your left hand, Romney," he bade. "The air has made us one; the symbol of these wings shall always bind us!"

Her answer was to kiss the ring that he had put upon her finger. Kisses and tears, together, sanctified it.

"You would have died that I might live!" He whispered. "You are my woman, Romney girl!" He put her head back from his heart, turned up her face, and crushed her mouth to his. "Mine, mine!" Said he. "You are my woman now!"

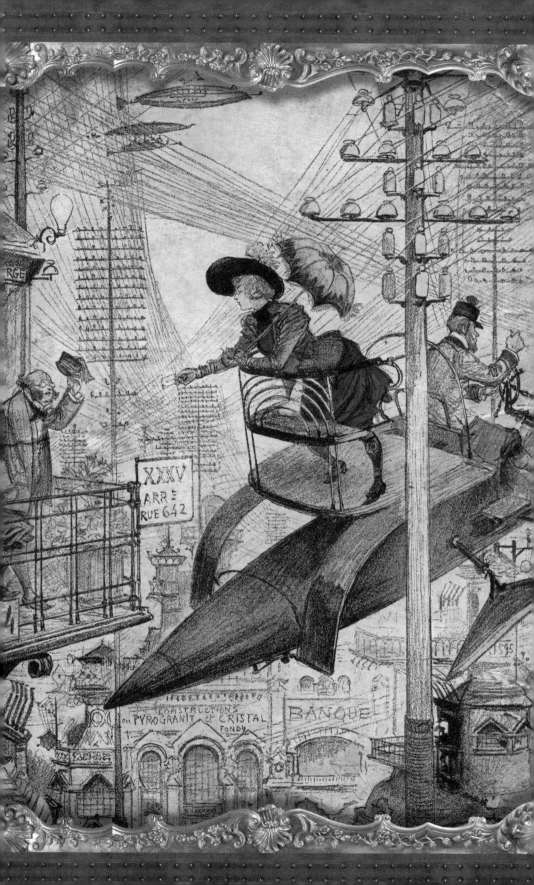

CREDITS

MIKE ASHLEY is the author and editor of over 90 books in the fields of science fiction, crime fiction and the supernatural. His books range from *Algernon Blackwood: An Extraordinary Life* to *The Time Machines*, the first in a series about the science-fiction magazines. He won an Edgar Award for *The Mammoth Encyclopaedia of Crime Fiction*, a Stoker Award for *The Supernatural Index,* and received the Pilgrim Award for lifetime contribution to science fiction research.

PAUL DI FILIPPO has over twenty-five published books to his credit. He lives in Providence, RI, USA, with his mate of three decades, Deborah Newton, his chocolate-colored cocker spaniel Brownie, and a calico cat named Penny Century.

LUIS ORTIZ lives and works in New York City as a creative director and advertising artist. He is the editor, along with Earl Kemp, of *Cult Magazines: From A to Z*, and author of *Emshwiller: Infinity X Two,* which was nominated for both the Hugo and Locus awards.

ILLUSTRATIONS

Library of Congress: frame on pages i, 13, 20–21, 50–51, 69, 76, 89, 92, 95, 109, 131, 134, 158, 189, 201, 205, 214–215, 219, 238, 242, 252, 258, 266–267, 272–273, and 288; 233 (swings)

Private Collection: 29 (photo)

All other images, graphics and design elements sourced from Depositphotos, Dreamstime, Fotolia, iStockphoto.com, the Scott Russo Archive, and Shutterstock.com

SOURCES

"Mr. Broadbent's Information" by Henry A. Hering, first published in Pearson's Magazine, March 1909.

"The Automaton" by Reginald Bacchus and C. Ranger Gull, first published in The Ludgate, January 1900.

"The Abduction of Alexandra Seine" by Fred C. Smale, first published in The Harmsworth Magazine, November 1900.

"The Gibraltar Tunnel" by Jean Jaubert, first published as "Le Tunne de Gibraltar" in Je Sais Tout, 15 March 1914. This translation by Ethel Christian first published in the American edition of The Strand Magazine, September 1914.

"From Pole to Pole" by George Griffith, first published in The Windsor Magazine, October 1904.

"In the Deep of Time" by George Parsons Lathrop, first published in The English Illustrated Magazine, March and April 1897.

"The Brotherhood of the Seven Kings: The Star-Shaped Marks" by L. T. Meade and Robert Eustace, first published in The Strand Magazine, June 1898.

"The Plague of Lights" by Owen Oliver, first published in The London Magazine, October 1904.

"What the Rats Brought" by Ernest Favenc, first published in Phil May's Illustrated Winter Annual, 1903–4.

"The Great Catastrophe" by George Davey, first published in The English Illustrated Magazine, February 1910.

"Within an Ace of the End of the World" by Robert Barr, first published in McClure's Magazine, April 1900 and in The Windsor Magazine, December 1900.

"An Interplanetary Rupture" by Frank L. Packard, first published in The Monthly Story Blue Book Magazine, December 1906.

"The Last Days of Earth" by George C. Wallis, first published in The Harmsworth Magazine, July 1901.

"The Plunge" by George Allan England, first published in Snappy Stories, April 4, 1916.